CHASING SERENITY

A RIVER RAIN NOVEL

KRISTEN ASHLEY

Chasing Serenity

A River Rain Novel Book 2

By Kristen Ashley

Copyright 2021 Kristen Ashley

ISBN: 978-1-952457-56-2

Published by Blue Box Press, an imprint of Evil Eye Concepts, Incorporated

BOOK DESCRIPTION

Chasing Serenity
A River Rain Novel, Book 2
By Kristen Ashley

New York Times and *USA Today* bestselling author Kristen Ashley brings a new novel in her River Rain series...

From a very young age, Chloe Pierce was trained to look after the ones she loved.

And she was trained by the best.

But when the man who looked after her was no longer there, Chloe is cast adrift—just as the very foundation of her life crumbled to pieces.

Then she runs into tall, lanky, unpretentious Judge Oakley, her exact opposite. She shops. He hikes. She drinks pink ladies. He drinks beer. She's a city girl. He's a mountain guy.

Obviously, this means they have a blowout fight upon meeting. Their second encounter doesn't go a lot better.

Judge is loving the challenge. Chloe is everything he doesn't want in a woman, but he can't stop finding ways to spend time with her. He knows she's dealing with loss and change.

He just doesn't know how deep that goes. Or how ingrained it is for Chloe to care for those who have a place in her heart, how hard it will be to trust anyone to look after her…

And how much harder it is when it's his turn.

ABOUT KRISTEN ASHLEY

Kristen Ashley is the *New York Times* bestselling author of over eighty romance novels including the *Rock Chick, Colorado Mountain, Dream Man, Chaos, Unfinished Heroes, The 'Burg, Magdalene, Fantasyland, The Three, Ghost and Reincarnation, The Rising, Dream Team* and *Honey* series along with several standalone novels. She's a hybrid author, publishing titles both independently and traditionally, her books have been translated in fourteen languages and she's sold over five million books.

Kristen's novel, *Law Man*, won the *RT Book Reviews* Reviewer's Choice Award for best Romantic Suspense, her independently published title *Hold On* was nominated for *RT Book Reviews* best Independent Contemporary Romance and her traditionally published title *Breathe* was nominated for best Contemporary Romance. Kristen's titles *Motorcycle Man, The Will*, and *Ride Steady* (which won the Reader's Choice award from *Romance Reviews*) all made the final rounds for Goodreads Choice Awards in the Romance category.

Kristen, born in Gary and raised in Brownsburg, Indiana, was a fourth-generation graduate of Purdue University. Since, she has lived in Denver, the West Country of England, and she now resides in Phoenix. She worked as a charity executive for eighteen years prior to beginning her independent publishing career. She now writes full-time.

Although romance is her genre, the prevailing themes running through all of Kristen's novels are friendship, family and a strong sisterhood. To this end, and as a way to thank her readers for their support, Kristen has created the Rock Chick Nation, a series of programs that are designed to give back to her readers and promote a strong female community.

The mission of the Rock Chick Nation is to live your best life, be true to your true self, recognize your beauty, and last but definitely not least, take your sister's back whether they're at your side as friends and family or if they're thousands of miles away and you don't know who they are.

The programs of the RC Nation include Rock Chick Rendezvous, weekends Kristen organizes full of parties and get-togethers to bring the sisterhood together, Rock Chick Recharges, evenings Kristen arranges for women who have been nominated to receive a special night, and Rock Chick Rewards, an ongoing program that raises funds for nonprofit women's organizations Kristen's readers nominate. Kristen's Rock Chick Rewards have donated hundreds of thousands of dollars to charity and this number continues to rise.

You can read more about Kristen, her titles and the Rock Chick Nation at KristenAshley.net.

ALSO BY KRISTEN ASHLEY

Rock Chick Series:

Rock Chick

Rock Chick Rescue

Rock Chick Redemption

Rock Chick Renegade

Rock Chick Revenge

Rock Chick Reckoning

Rock Chick Regret

Rock Chick Revolution

Rock Chick Reawakening

Rock Chick Reborn

The 'Burg Series:

For You

At Peace

Golden Trail

Games of the Heart

The Promise

Hold On

The Chaos Series:

Own the Wind

Fire Inside

Ride Steady

Walk Through Fire

A Christmas to Remember

Rough Ride

Wild Like the Wind

Free

Wild Fire

Wild Wind

The Colorado Mountain Series:

The Gamble

Sweet Dreams

Lady Luck

Breathe

Jagged

Kaleidoscope

Bounty

Dream Man Series:

Mystery Man

Wild Man

Law Man

Motorcycle Man

Quiet Man

Dream Team Series:

Dream Maker

Dream Chaser

Dream Bites Cookbook

Dream Spinner

Dream Keeper

The Fantasyland Series:

Wildest Dreams

The Golden Dynasty

Fantastical

Broken Dove

Midnight Soul

Gossamer in the Darkness

Ghosts and Reincarnation Series:

Sommersgate House

Lacybourne Manor

Penmort Castle

Fairytale Come Alive

Lucky Stars

The Honey Series:

The Deep End

The Farthest Edge

The Greatest Risk

The Magdalene Series:

The Will

Soaring

The Time in Between

Mathilda, SuperWitch:

Mathilda's Book of Shadows

Mathilda The Rise of the Dark Lord

Misted Pines Series

The Girl in the Mist

Moonlight and Motor Oil Series:

The Hookup

The Slow Burn

The Rising Series:

The Beginning of Everything

The Plan Commences

The Dawn of the End

The Rising

The River Rain Series:

After the Climb

After the Climb Special Edition

Chasing Serenity

Taking the Leap

The Three Series:

Until the Sun Falls from the Sky

With Everything I Am

Wild and Free

The Unfinished Hero Series:

Knight

Creed

Raid

Deacon

Sebring

Wild West MC Series:

Still Standing

Other Titles by Kristen Ashley:

Heaven and Hell

Play It Safe

Three Wishes

Complicated

Loose Ends

Fast Lane

ACKNOWLEDGMENTS FROM THE AUTHOR

The idea for the River Rain series was swimming in my head in February 2020, right before a year that would go on to shake the globe with illness, death, social unrest and a (hopeful) reawakening.

When we were all told to stay home in order to stay safe and no one knew yet how bad it was going to get, or how long it would last, but the fears ran deep and were real, some friends (you know who you are, Kristin and Kathy) encouraged me to do what I used to be able to do before I made my living writing.

When I had an idea for a book I was obsessed with, drop every-thing...and write it.

This used to be my most favorite thing in the world to do.

But now, although getting these ideas still happens all the time, I have to abandon them because I have writing schedules to keep, a business to run and a life to live.

As lockdowns blanketed the world, I came up with the brilliant (I *will* say so myself) idea of doing this with my Chicklets (if you don't know who that is, it's what I call my readers) by gathering input, ideas and casting polls on Facebook.

Through this process, it came to be that, in an uncertain time, and for me, being on the cusp of what would become months and months of alone time (with my cat), I was not alone. Even doing something that, for me, is a very private, solitary undertaking.

Writing.

It was a beautiful experience, having that togetherness in a time so rife.

What came of it is *After the Climb*, the prequel to the River Rain series.

And I so enjoyed connecting on something that is really very intimate for me (writing a book) with my readers, that I decided that every book in this series, I would write the same.

As such, this was something I did for this book, Chloe and Judge's story, *Chasing Serenity*.

It was a no less beautiful experience the second time around, I look forward to continuing and I hope my Chicklets do too.

For *Chasing Serenity*, I want to thank all my readers who contributed ideas, shared their thoughts or cast their votes in the polls.

However, it's important for me to single out Marsha Elder and Amanda Young.

When we were deciding what animals Judge and Chloe would have, Marsha and Amanda offered up tributes to their lost fur babies, Zeke and Montana. The love in their suggestions for these two pups shone bright for me, and therefore I've memorialized both Zeke and Montana in this book.

Marsha and Amanda, I hope I served your puppers well. Thank you so very much for trusting me with them.

I would also like to give a shout out to Marine Paturel. She shared some wisdom about French names that sparked a discussion about a variety of things that, as a writer, are vital.

You cannot know everything, have lived or traveled everywhere, nor do you always have the time or resources to do deep dives into every nuance of a book.

But it's no fun as a reader to read something you know is off, or as a writer to get something wrong that's going to take your readers out of the story.

Marine saved me from that by giving her time and input that set off a conversation that I found incredibly illuminating and useful.

So, thank you, *chérie*.

I also need to shout out to Kat Mazzeo, who came up with the idea for the name Camp Trail Blazer. Upon vetting that name, I found it's an initiative in Brooklyn that's been around for a while (so if you have kids and live in NYC, check that out). But it's also perfect for what will become a fictional camp for this series.

Last, I want to thank the brains and heart and soul behind Blue Box Press. Their enthusiasm and support, creativity and drive. I have never in my life had so much fun discussing marketing and cover options.

As ever, it's good to be in business with you, Liz Berry, Jillian Stein and MJ Rose. It's good because it feels safe, because I know you care, and because you give me the space to put out the best book I can.

You know I love you for many reasons, those are just a few of them.

Now, as ever…read on and…

Rock on.

For Jillian Stein

In the time I've known you, I could have dedicated a dozen books to you.
I was waiting for something that was perfect for you.
But you are who you are: the coolest, hippest, chicest, most loving and
supportive chick ever.
So the wait for what was just right for someone as awesome as you would be
forever.
And since this book is ours, sister...
In essence spawned in a cabin a couple of years ago...
Stretching its wings now...
This will do.

Love you.

PROLOGUE

THE LECTURE

Corey

 *ifteen years ago...*

GENNY WAS DOING SOMETHING IN THE KITCHEN WITH A SUMMER SALAD. Tom was off with Matt at their club, playing tennis, destined, from a recent call from Tom, to be home soon in order to eat the dinner Genny was preparing. Sasha was doing cartwheels on the beach.

And Chloe was on the terrace, arms crossed on her chest, ostensibly keeping an eye on her little sister, but mostly glaring at the sun glinting off the sea.

To Corey's mind, when it came to Tom and Genny's children, he thought Matt was okay. Too much like his father, a man who Corey put up with, but Corey had no patience for anyone, especially men, who got everything easy in life, like Tom Pierce had.

Life was not easy.

You suffered for what you earned.

Worked for it.

Cheated for it.

Stole for it.

Whatever you had to do to *get it*.

Tom, his looks, his talent on the tennis courts, his easygoing manner, sly smile, and inability to put up with any shit, it all fell in his lap.

Including Genny.

Sweet, beautiful, talented Genny. One, if not *the* most beloved actress in America.

Sasha, Genny's youngest, Corey simply did not understand. Although she had some of Genny's features, including her sunshiny blonde hair, she was not like either her mother or her father.

Or anyone Corey knew.

But Chloe, the eldest...

If she didn't so look like Tom, she could be Corey's child.

Smart as fuck.

Shrewd as hell.

Chloe Pierce calculated any situation she was in within seconds, deciphering what outcome would serve her purposes the best, and then she set about doing that.

And she was ten.

Corey adored her.

So now, seeing her seething about something, he went out to the terrace, and he did this not only because, as Genny's nearly life-long friend, Corey was there, as he often was, for dinner with the family, and Genny was busy with cooking, so he was bored.

He did it because he was interested in whatever was occupying Chloe Pierce's mind.

As he approached, Chloe sent him a ten-year-old's version of a look that said *fuck off*.

And he adored her more.

There were fair few people on that earth who had the courage to send him looks like that, considering he'd amassed the wealth, and thus the power, to buy and sell practically anyone.

Corey ignored the look and moved to the lounge chair next to where she sat at the end of hers, close to the sheet of clear glass set into the railing of a terrace of a house that rested above the cliffs of Malibu.

He sat on his chair's end too.

"Spill," he ordered.

"I don't wanna talk, Uncle Corey."

"*Want to,*" he corrected, and heard her instantly suck her teeth in annoyance at the criticism.

Corey fought smiling.

"I'll repeat, spill," Corey pressed.

She didn't.

Corey waited.

She still didn't.

Corey continued to wait.

Chloe was no fool. In fact, there wasn't any vestige of that trait in any cell of her body.

She knew her Uncle Corey would have what he wanted.

So she didn't push it any further.

"There's…"

She trailed off, and Corey gave her more time.

She picked it up again. "Kids are bullying Matt at school."

This took Corey by surprise.

Matthew Pierce was the vision of his father.

At nine years old, already tall, dark, with boyishly handsome features. He was gifted in athleticism. He was clever.

Though what he also was, was introverted.

He was not a leader, like Chloe (and Tom).

He was not outgoing, like Sasha (and Genny).

He was perfectly happy doing his own thing.

To the point, even at his age, living in a house full of people, he was reclusive.

Like Corey.

The perfect target for jealousy.

The perfect target for bullies.

"And this is your issue because…?" Corey asked.

Her head whipped around to him, and now she was giving him a ten-year-old's look that said she thought he was stupid.

"He's my brother," she snapped.

"He can fight his own battles."

"Well, he isn't," she retorted.

Corey found this interesting, but not startling.

In all probability, Matt couldn't care less about the bullying.

Even at nine years old, his intellect was such (and his parents' lessons were as well) that he was not unaware that the fates had seen fit to grant him more of almost everything than most people received.

The boy had happily married, exceptionally successful, wealthy, loving parents.

Good looks.

Brains.

Not to mention, if Tom kept honing it, what would be Matt's version of physical excellence.

Matt Pierce didn't need anyone, and not only because he already had it all.

That was just him.

He just didn't.

"Has it occurred to you that your brother doesn't care?" Corey inquired. "I'm sure it hasn't escaped your notice that he's perfectly fine in his own company."

"It hasn't, Uncle Corey, but bullies shouldn't get away with being bullies. *One*," Chloe returned.

One.

She had a list.

Corey fought a smile.

"*Two*," she continued, "he's my brother, and no one messes with my brother."

He nodded and said nothing because he knew there was a three.

"And *three*," she went on, "he's a Pierce. And *no one* pulls crap with *a Pierce*."

"You're right," he agreed. "So what are you going to do about it?"

That took her aback.

"What?"

"What are you going to do about it?" Corey repeated.

"They aren't bullying me," she pointed out.

Corey held her gaze in a manner that she did not look away.

Not that she would.

Another thing about the girl he liked.

Then he stated, "Do not ever, Chloe, *ever* let anyone harm someone you love."

A feeling welled up in his chest, instantly threatening to overwhelm him.

Used to this sensation, having experienced it for years, with little effort, Corey shoved it back down and kept speaking.

"It doesn't matter what you have to do, if you think it's bad, but it stops that harm, you do it. If you think it's naughty, and it stops that harm, you do it. Even if you think it's wrong, though it will stop that harm, *you do it*. No hesitation, no messing about. *Just do it*."

Chloe stared at him.

"The same with you," he carried on. "Do not let anyone walk all over you, Chloe Marilyn Pierce. Don't you *ever* allow that to happen."

She gave it a moment, and then she asked, "So you think I should...*do something*?"

"I think you've already waited too long."

Corey watched as Chloe considered this.

And he was unsurprised when, after she spent hardly any time in this contemplation, slowly, she smiled.

Chloe

Nine years later...

"Are you *mad*?" Pierre asked me.

I stared at him, for the first time wondering why I'd spent a single minute with him.

Was he cute?

Yes.

Did he have a good body?

Yes.

Did he give me my very first, not-given-to-myself orgasm?

Yes.

Was he an asshole?

Apparently…yes.

My voice was ice-cold, and I was pretty pleased with myself at the sound of it, when I noted in return, "You told me you'd never sell it."

"I'm an artist!" he cried.

The drama.

Boring.

In that moment, I made a pact with myself that I vowed to keep.

Only *I* would bring the drama to a relationship.

I modulated my voice and did not cut the tie between our gazes.

"You said it meant everything to you. You said you'd cease being you without it in your possession. You said you'd be ninety, and you would die in a room where, on the wall, that portrait you painted of me hung."

"I *do* need to feed myself, Chloe," he sniped.

No one, not a soul, disregarded money the way he did (unless not doing it served his purpose, like now), who did not have it in the first place.

Didn't grow up having it.

I was that person too.

But Mom did a lot of charity work, so did Dad, they made certain we understood that we were very lucky and many, in fact most others, were not.

Pierre and I had never discussed money (because, how gauche), and he didn't live in a fabulous apartment in a posh part of the city, though it wasn't rundown or seedy or anything like that.

Still…

I knew Pierre was like me.

So this whole thing was a big sham.

All of it.

Including his promises to me.

As I looked at his dark, loose, long locks, the perfection of his nose, the breadth of his shoulders, his gangly frame, for the first time I saw through him.

He was a sham.

A fake.

A pretender.

Maybe even worse.

A wannabe.

And I had to admit to more than a little concern that my affections for him shifted so quickly.

But they did.

I could walk away…

No.

I *was going to* walk away.

And what worried me was…

I didn't care.

I decided to think about this later and moved to begin packing, at the same time my mind swung to considering my next step.

Hotel for a few days while I found a flat to rent (and did the work it took to convince my parents I needed to rent a flat in Paris, and they needed to allow me the use of my trust fund to do that, or better, not allow me and instead, simply give the money to their darling daughter in order that she get the most out of her discovering-herself time in Europe).

One thing I knew, I wasn't leaving France.

Not on my life.

When I dragged out a piece of my luggage (there were three), Pierre was there.

"What are you doing?" he asked.

"Packing," I said in a bored tone, one that I didn't affect.

I was, indeed, bored.

Done.

Over this.

On to the next adventure.

"Packing? Just like that?"

I turned from unzipping and opening my suitcase to him.

"You need to get that painting back," I told him. "And you need to destroy the other one. You also need to give me all the pictures you took of me and erase any digital copies you have."

His mouth dropped open.

He then used it to say, "That is not happening."

"You don't have my permission to use my image, Pierre. It's illegal for you to sell those paintings or use those images for monetary purposes without my permission."

I was no Hollywood starlet rushing into the latest hip club, ripe for any paparazzo's lens, needing it at the same time feeling it wholly an invasion of my privacy.

I had posed for Pierre for the thrill of it. I'd done it because I had feelings for him. I'd done it because I loved his work and wanted to be a part of it. I'd done it because it was fun, and I thought it was cool. I'd also done it because I thought he wasn't going to sell them.

But bottom line, I'd acted as his model.

And first, he needed to pay me if he was going to make money off me.

Second, he needed my permission.

"That's rubbish," he bit out.

"Do you know who I am?"

It wasn't arrogant posturing.

But for God's sake, he knew I was Imogen Swan and Tom Pierce's daughter. America's sweetheart and one of the best tennis players ever to walk on a court.

They were two of the most famous people on the planet.

Of course I knew what I'd just said was far from rubbish.

And he knew it too.

"They are *my* paintings," he asserted.

"It's *my* body. *My* face," I fired back. "I own them, and you cannot use them unless I *grant you permission*. And I'll remind you, I posed for you because you said you were *never* going to sell the paintings you painted of me. 'Never' for you lasted less than three months. But the true meaning of never is *never*, Pierre. Which means you lied to me about your intentions when you took those pictures and did that work. Now, if you don't want to turn over or destroy all you have, you can give me a million euros. I think that's fair compensation."

His eyes grew huge.

And the French rolled off his tongue.

I was learning the language, but I didn't catch even half of it.

"English," I demanded.

"I am not giving you a million euros, Chloe. I am not getting that painting back. I am not destroying the rest. And you are not leaving."

"Oh, I'm leaving," I confirmed. "And I advise you rethink your course of action."

This time, his eyes narrowed. "Are you threatening me and leaving me at the same time?"

"Well, it's not exactly a threat, but for the most part, yes."

Now, as he took in my tone, actions, and demeanor, it hit him.

I was, in fact, leaving.

Suddenly, he appeared wounded.

Suddenly and genuinely.

This did not make me pause.

Truth told, I didn't care that he had pictures of me nude, or sold them. I had a great body, I was proud of it, and his work was *amazing*.

This was about something else.

Something far bigger.

It was the promise broken.

The betrayal.

Uncle Corey a lot of the time could be creepy (these times when he was around Mom).

But the man was a multi-billionaire tech czar.

Which meant he was no idiot.

So he gave great advice.

Every time he gave it, I stored those little gems so I could take them out and polish them when the time was nigh.

Obviously, with one of those gems, the time was nigh.

"Get that painting back and destroy the rest, or pay me, Pierre, those are your choices," I summed up. "Now, it'd be easier to do this," I motioned to the suitcase, "if you went off and got a coffee."

He stared at me, thrown, angry, hurt.

What he didn't do was go and get a coffee.

I sighed and then got down to business, taking my time and making perfectly sure I got everything because I wasn't coming back.

At the door, I decided it might be uncool just to sweep out, even if it would be dramatic and what I wanted to do.

Thus, I halted, turned to him and said softly, "It's been fun."

He stopped sulking (what he'd been doing the entire time I packed), and the hurt dug deep in his hazel eyes.

"Fun?" he whispered. "It's been *fun*? Chloe, *mon cœur*, you're the love of my life."

I studied him quizzically because that truly perplexed me.

"How can that be?" I asked, genuinely wanting to know.

"How can that...how can it... How can it be?" he asked in return. "Have you not been here," he tossed his arm out to indicate the flat, "with me for the last six months?"

"You lied to me," I stated flatly. "And you don't lie to someone you love."

His head snapped like I'd slapped him.

"Good-bye, Pierre," I said.

And with that, not looking back, not knowing that I'd never see him again, but even if I did, I knew I wouldn't care, I left.

And checked into The Ritz.

Judge

Five years later...

. . .

"You have no direction."

Judge sat opposite his girlfriend of the last year and a half, Megan, and said nothing.

She did.

"I need a man with ambition. Drive. Who knows what he wants and goes after it, works for it, *fights* for it."

Judge remained silent.

"Judge, are you listening to me?" she asked, though she didn't wait for him to answer, probably because he was staring right at her, and he was doing it hard, so she had to know he was listening. She carried on, "I mean, I'm sorry. This is rough. But you always say we need to be honest with each other. And this is me being honest."

That got him talking.

"Right then, let's be honest, Meg. *Really* honest. What you're saying is, I'm not going in the direction *you* want me going. My life goals aren't what *you* want them to be. I know what I want, you know I do. I know who I am, you know that too. It's just that those things aren't what *you* want. Am I right?"

Her face twisted. "No man wants to hike for a living."

Okay.

Now he was getting pissed off.

"After all this time together, is that what you think I do?"

She shifted on her barstool.

She knew what he did, and she knew that was bullshit.

And...

Yeah.

Barstool.

They both lived in Arizona. But he lived in Prescott, she lived in Phoenix, a two-hour drive from each other, so it wasn't like they were living together or even saw each other every day.

Though, they were exclusive and had been for over a year. He went out of his way to make time for her, get to Phoenix to see her.

Meg?

Not so much, but to be fair, her job didn't allow her to.

Still, not so much.

She was a reporter for a local station. She was aiming to sit behind the desk as an anchor, and after she achieved that, she wanted to move on to bigger and better things.

Or, he should say, stand on the set and talk at a camera, something he did not get why it was the thing. Judge thought when newscasters did that they looked like the awkward folks at a party, standing around not knowing who to talk to. It was his opinion, when you listened to the news, you needed to trust that the person giving it to you was taking it seriously, not gabbing while waiting for a tray of hors d'oeuvres to be passed around.

Needless to say, Meg did not share this opinion.

Judge ran an outreach program for a massive outdoor store that had over seventy locations in the US. A program aimed to get urban kids out into nature.

He hiked with the kids...a lot.

He also hiked by himself and did other things outside...a lot.

But most of his job was about raising money, ditto awareness of the issue, and the profile of the program, as well as managing the logistics that included hundreds of volunteers in dozens of cities doing hundreds of hikes a year.

He wasn't paid enough to afford a BMW. But even if he was, he wouldn't buy one.

He also wasn't homeless.

But they were here, at a bar, and Meg was ending things with him, when they'd committed to each other over a year ago. They regularly, if not all the time, slept at each other's sides. They'd gone on vacations together. And they'd met each other's families.

Or, she'd had dinner with his dad.

His mom?

Absolutely not.

"Though, a lot of men and women would want to hike for a living," he went on. "Around fifty million people in the US alone regularly hike."

"Judge—"

He wasn't done.

"You're not an outdoors person. That's cool. I don't care because you're smart as hell and goal oriented. You're interesting. You're funny. You're sweet. And you're beautiful. I want you to have what you want. I want to support you in your goals. I want you to be happy. What I *don't* want is for you to mold me into who you think I'm supposed to be to fit into your life."

Right.

The *real* honesty?

This had been an issue.

It being one right then, he wasn't blindsided by it.

She'd said some things. There had been more than a few looks when he'd been with her and shared with others what he did. She'd done some suggesting, urging and downright pushing.

He just thought she'd get over it when he didn't bend and definitely didn't break.

Her expression had softened when he'd told her all the things he found attractive in her, because Meg liked compliments. She told him her love language was words.

So he gave her words, because that was what she needed and she was upfront about it, even if he wasn't a flowery speeches kind of guy.

She also thought what he said opened a door for her, and even if it didn't, she tried to stroll through.

"You can get involved down here. In Phoenix," she said. "There are a lot of charities you can work for. On the whole, there are just tons more opportunities down here. And truly, Judge, you're wasted up there. You're whip smart, and when you talk, people listen to you. You're a natural leader. You *should* be with a bigger program. You *should* be seeking new challenges. You *should* be reaching for something higher."

"Organizations that pay more, have advancement opportunities and don't require me to travel," he filled in what she left unsaid.

She opened her mouth.

But this shit from Megan wasn't the only pressure Judge had about this same subject.

And if he didn't put up with it from the other source, he was not going to put up with it from his girlfriend.

"Meg, no," he cut her off before she could use it. "I love my job. I love what I do. *I love it.* I've told you that. More than once. Does that mean nothing to you?"

"Do *I* mean nothing to you?" she retorted.

Uh.

No.

"I could ask you the same thing," he returned. "And your answer would be rougher, babe, because it isn't me breaking it off with you because you're not what I want, and you won't adjust your life to make yourself into that. So the only answer you could give me is, not much. I don't mean much to you. You're seeing the wrong man. And now, it's over because you've either figured that out, or you're cutting your losses before you invest any more time with me."

She appeared insulted. "Judge, I love you."

Okay.

That *totally* pissed him off.

"And you're ending things not because I'm a dick to you. Not because I lie or cheat or steal. Not because I flirt with other women in front of you. Not because we fight. Not because we have differing opinions we believe in strongly and we can't get around those differences. But instead, because *you* think I have no direction or ambition when I do have direction *and* ambition."

He saw her start to intercede.

But he was far from done.

"I want, and I'll add that I work very hard, to get kids moving their bodies. To show them how extraordinary nature is. Introduce them to vistas that don't include concrete and asphalt. Where the air is fresher, and the stars shine brighter. I want to explain to them how important it is we guard these things, keep them safe and pure, and what it'll mean when we don't. Because they're going to be in the positions soon where they have no choice but to do something about it, and they need to start thinking about that now."

She again tried to say something.

But he hadn't even gotten to the most important part of it.

So he didn't shut up.

"And above all, just to let them know they aren't forgotten. There are people who give a shit about them and what they experience and want to broaden those experiences, their minds, and bottom line think they're worth spending time with. And I don't know, Meg, if that isn't good enough for you, then you're right. Though I wouldn't take you to a bar to dump you after we spent over a year of our lives together. But that makes no difference. You're right. We're wrong. And it's time to end it."

With that, and her staring at him, he slid off his barstool, pulled out his wallet, opened it and tossed enough money on the table to pay for their drinks and the food that had not yet been delivered.

"I gotta get home," he said. "Text me when I can come to your place to get my shit. I'll pack yours up and bring it when I do that."

He started to leave, but she caught his forearm.

"Are you really just walking away from me?" she demanded.

He stopped and looked down at her. "Sorry, did I steal your exit?"

She took her hand from his arm. "There's no need to be a dick."

Unh-unh.

No.

"Hang on a second, you told me five minutes ago, *in all honesty*, that you thought I had no direction, no drive and that I didn't know what I wanted *or* how to go after it in a preamble to dump my ass. And I've given you what you want. We're through, and I'm walking away because I'm not real hip on sitting here after you've kicked me to the curb and watching you pick through a plate of tater tot nachos because eating two expends your allotment of calories for the day. And I'm being a dick?"

Right.

That was definitely dick-ish.

His sister (or that would be stepsister, but she'd been around so long, he didn't really think of the "step" part of that) said often that he looked like the Zen master. Mr. Outdoorsman. Mr. Easygoing. One with nature, one with humanity. But piss him off and all that was out the window.

And she did not lie.

"Maybe, when I said fight for something, I meant me," she suggested with not a small amount of hurt.

His stomach clutched.

It was not a good feeling.

"And how would I do that, Meg?" he asked quietly.

"Well, you could *not* live a hundred and thirty miles away."

Judge closed his eyes and dropped his head.

Because that meant *quit your job and move to Phoenix*.

"Judge," she called.

He opened his eyes and looked at her, what was happening fully registering.

This was it.

They were over.

And he wasn't okay with that.

Because he was in love with her.

"I want more of you, would you quit your job and move to Prescott?" he asked.

A hard shell slammed down over her eyes as she replied, "I know what you're doing, but there are far more opportunities *for both of us* in Phoenix."

"And then you get a job in LA, and I follow you there. And then New York, and I follow you there. Right?"

"There are programs for kids, in nature, for the environment, everywhere, Judge. You can't get away from any of them."

He'd been bending, because he'd been considering what she was saying and what was happening between them, because she was right, and he didn't want to lose her.

However, the last part of what she said struck him.

You can't get away from any of them.

Who exactly was "them"?

"Do you want kids, Meg?" he asked.

Her head twitched.

One of her tells.

"Of course," she lied.

Holy fuck.

She'd lied.

About wanting *kids*.

If he had it right, because this was so important to him, they'd had this conversation on their third date.

If it wasn't their third, it was their fourth.

And that wasn't the last time they'd talked about it.

"Do you want kids, Meg?" he repeated.

"We've talked about this, Judge," she snapped.

Another tell. She quickly got belligerent when she was called on something she couldn't defend.

"Yes, and you told me you did. Now, I'm not sure you were being truthful."

"Are you saying I lied?"

"I'm saying your hair shakes when you're hedging. And your hair just shook."

She knew not to challenge him on things like that. You didn't deal with children on a regular basis, not to mention donors, and not be hyper-attentive.

"I think I'm realizing I'm one of those later-in-life-for-a-family women," she admitted, like it was nothing.

But it was not nothing.

It was big shit.

And she knew it.

"You'd mentioned that, and I told you I wasn't real big on being in my fifties, and living the life with my family that I want, rather than being in my thirties or forties. And you agreed, saying you wanted the same thing."

"You'll be fit until you die, Judge," she scoffed. "You'll be hiking and biking and camping when you're eighty."

"Sure, but time doesn't discriminate. There's no arguing I'll be fitter in my thirties and forties. And when my kids are young, I want them to enjoy me when I'm also young."

"Judge—"

"This is a big shift, Meg, anything behind it?"

"Judge."

He didn't cut her off that time. She just didn't continue.

"Earlier, did you intend to end us or change us?" he asked.

It was slight, but she lifted her chin.

She had a dimple in it.

He'd thought it was cute.

He still did.

"I need a man who will fight for me," she declared.

"I get that, because I need a woman who will do the same for me."

It was impossible for him to put more meaning into those words.

And she knew precisely why.

She flinched.

Shit.

That said it all.

He remained standing, she sat there, and they stared at each other.

And suddenly, he got it.

He understood.

He understood where he was at.

And he understood where she was too.

This meant he got closer to the table, to her, because they both needed him to share it.

"Honest to Christ, this isn't meant to hurt you, Meg, but I'm in love with you."

Her expression warmed.

"But I don't love you," he finished.

Her face went blank.

"And if you're honest with yourself," Judge continued, "you'll see you feel the same way about me. We're great together. We're great in bed. We've had great times. But there's a reason neither of us is willing to give in order to have more of the other. We don't fit. We don't share the same goals. We don't find the same things important. There's nothing wrong with what you want or what you think is important. There isn't anything wrong with where I'm at with all that. They just don't go together, and I think we both knew it, you just got us on the road where we'd get it."

Her eyes were crazy, and as such, concerning as they moved over his face and she said, "I don't think I knew it. I think I just blew it."

"Give it some time, honey," he said gently.

"Judge—"

He cut her off then by leaning in and pressing a hard kiss on her mouth.

When he pulled away, he didn't go far when he said, "Bottom line, it's been fun, you're fantastic, and I'll never forget it, Meg."

Her mouth opened.

But so they could both get on with things, Judge walked away.

And he didn't look back.

CHAPTER 1

THE TWO WORDS

Judge

*N*ow...

CONSIDERING THE FACT HE'D BROUGHT IN A COFFEE FOR HIS BUDDY, RIX, who managed the store, Judge was down on the floor where Rix's office was, not on the top floor where his was, so he saw her when she walked into the shoe section.

He'd dated Meg.

And before Meg, there was Jess.

And before Jess, there was Kimberly.

They all had different color hair, Meg and Jess were tall, Kim was not.

But even so, Judge had a type.

He knew it.

And that woman who'd strolled up to the shoe displays?

She was his type.

Multiplied by a thousand.

Christ, she was beautiful.

And bad news.

He could tell that last by the outfit, including her ridiculous, high-heeled booties.

He'd worked at River Rain Outdoor stores for nine years—starting as a sales associate when he was still going to college and advancing to director of the Kids and Trails program.

In all that time, he didn't think he'd ever seen a woman walk into any of their stores wearing shoes like hers.

And when he came down again a half an hour later to hit Rix's office to make some copies because the copier in the corporate offices at the top level was busted, he noticed she was still there.

He also noticed he had further evidence she was bad news.

That evidence?

The sheer number of boxes of boots that she was trying on scattered around her.

She looked like she'd not set foot on a hiking trail in her life.

And she looked like she was there because she'd already trolled through all the boutiques around the square, but this hadn't assuaged her shopping fix, because nothing really did.

Therefore, there was a possibility, after making a member of staff bring her fifteen pairs of shoes, she'd walk out not buying anything.

She'd do this not thinking a thing of it.

However, he noted some of the boots she was trying on were riding boots, and Judge could see that round ass of hers in the saddle on top of a horse.

Wearing a riding habit.

Even if she was trouble, and he had not the slightest interest (or he was telling himself that), he couldn't keep his eyes off her.

Because he was a moron.

That said, she caught his gaze every time.

So he was looking.

But so was she.

His instincts proved true when he came down for the third time with more to copy, and he again walked through the shoe section to get to the office in the back. Doing this close to where she was seated, still trying on boots, because, yes, in the fifteen minutes between then and now, he had not stopped being a moron.

And again, she caught his gaze.

He had no clue why, but as her gorgeous hickory brown eyes hit his, he muttered, "Nice booties."

Her back shot straight, and she demanded, "What did you just say?"

Yup.

Moron.

He shook his head in an effort to shake some sense into it, then dipped his chin to her and kept walking.

"Excuse me," she snapped, and Judge continued on his way, but looked over his shoulder at her. "What did you just say to me?" she repeated when she caught his eyes.

"Nothing, miss, have a nice day," he replied.

"Do you work here?" she asked.

He drew breath into his nose, stopped and turned to face her.

She'd been sitting.

She was now standing.

Fucking fuck.

Straight on and standing close to her?

She wasn't beautiful.

She was stunning.

Facing her, not for the first time, Judge wished Prescott was a good two hours further from Scottsdale. Being an easy drive away, it was one of the weekend playgrounds for people like her.

Now, it was September, when temperatures around Phoenix were gearing down, so things would peter off with folks from down south coming up to get away from the heat.

Coming up to play weekend warrior, do stupid shit at campsites, bring up their guns and shoot things when they had no clue how, or any intention of field dressing a deer, not to mention eating its meat.

Tossing their water bottles during a hike, and not doing that in trash receptacles.

Having disposable water bottles at all.

Looking down on the townies.

But there she was.

Tall. Shiny, chocolate brown hair. Slender but curvy.

But for Judge (outside the hair, and those long-ass legs), it was her neck.

Her neck was long and graceful, which made her seem almost...

Vulnerable.

When he knew she was probably not.

And her hands.

Those hands were insanely beautiful.

Because of the man he was and the life he liked to live, even though it made him stupid, and this was part of the reason he was a moron (and all the other parts surrounded his taste in women as well), he got off on the way she dressed.

Judge had always liked a woman who looked after herself in that way (and others, and those others didn't revolve around her hiking or climbing or doing something to keep fit, but instead things like giving herself facials and having polished nails—like he hadn't learned the hard way, repeatedly, that opposites did not attract).

Her way of dressing was overtly expensive. Smart. Lowkey dramatic (and yeah, she made those opposing concepts work together). And she had a definite personal style she was completely confident in.

She also had a significant attitude, if the flash in those eyes was anything to go by.

"Is there something I can help you with?" he asked.

"So you do work here," she stated.

"I do, ma'am, I—"

He said no more when she griped, "Oh my God, do *not* call me 'ma'am.'"

Judge nearly laughed.

Instead of doing that, he started, "I'm sorry, I—"

He again got no more out.

"You *should* be sorry," she declared. "Do you often walk through the store that employs you, making personal comments to the customers?"

He'd done that.

He'd said two words, but the words he said were not what he meant, and she hadn't missed it.

It was uncool.

But he knew why he did it.

Because he didn't even know this woman's name, and she was under his skin, so he'd done it angling for what was happening right then.

The particulars of that, however…

They weren't something he was going to think about.

And now he needed to move on from what he'd instigated and get far away from her…and fast.

"You're right, I should have kept my mouth shut," he admitted. "You have my apologies." He patted his chest with a flat palm. "Sincerely. I was out of line."

She watched his hand on his chest, and for some reason, she got even more ticked when she did.

She then raised her eyes to his.

And he felt a variety of things in a variety of places (and regrettably, one of those places was his dick), when he saw she was not going to let this go.

She was going to dig in.

Deep.

"And I asked, do you do that often?" she demanded.

"I apologized, and—"

"An apology must be accepted," she sniffed.

"And it should be," he shot back, "if it's genuine. Which it was."

She raised a perfectly arched, perfectly waxed, dark brow.

"Was it?" she asked, making clear she knew the answer and it wasn't what was about to come out of his mouth.

"Of course it—"

"Please," she drawled. "Don't assume I'm stupid."

"I'm not assuming you're stupid," he returned. "In fact, if I made an assumption about you, that wouldn't be it."

What the fuck are you doing, man? Don't goad the woman. Walk away.

Her head cocked, which wasn't a surprise. What was in it undoubtedly was her weapon of choice.

"And what would that assumption be?" she inquired.

"How about you get on with your day, and I do the same thing?" he suggested.

"No, I'd really like to know what that assumption would be," she pushed.

And Judge let her push him.

He knew why he did.

He also wished he didn't.

He looked her down and up, then down again, making sure to take in the boxes of riding boots, hiking boots, rain boots, and for shit's sake, a pair of mountaineering boots, and finally, the delicate, expensive, spike heeled booties she'd walked in on, then back to her.

"You're very aware the cost of your shoes could feed dozens of children for a week, and you still used that money to buy them. I'll leave it at that," he shared.

She blinked, rapidly, several times, because what he said was out of line.

And he saw it happening.

Before, she was miffed.

Before, she was in a mood.

Now...

She was *pissed*.

Precisely his intention.

Because she was fantastic.

And he was an idiot.

"So do you verbally attack all the women that you make erroneous judgements about who come into this store?" she asked. "Or," she drifted one of her beautiful hands in a spiral through the air, "wherever you might be."

"Only ones that have fifteen pairs of boots they've made one of our associates go fetch for them when, let's be honest, you don't even know what mountaineering is."

She made an irritated noise clicking her tongue before she retorted, "I'm sure when I get back to Duncan's and ask, he can explain it to me."

That was when Judge blinked.

Not rapidly. The opposite.

And only once.

Duncan?

She wouldn't have mentioned "Duncan" unless she meant Duncan Holloway.

His boss.

In fact, everyone's boss. He was founder and CEO of River Rain stores.

Judge couldn't believe this. Duncan was strong, fit, a good-looking guy, but he was also old enough to be her father and wasn't that type of dude.

"Duncan Holloway?" he asked.

"One and the same," she confirmed.

"You're seeing Duncan?"

She shook her head. "He's a friend of the family."

Well, that made more sense, even if Duncan was one of the most down-to-earth people Judge knew, and this woman appeared to be...*not*.

"And you're dropping his name because...?" he prompted.

"I'm dropping his name because I don't think he'd be very happy one of his employees is wandering around his store, throwing shade."

This was absolutely true. Duncan would not like that.

That said...

"I wasn't wandering around throwing shade," he asserted.

No, when he'd thrown his shade, he'd pinpointed it at her.

Another hitch of her perfect brow.

"But I'll remind you," Judge continued, "not five minutes ago, I tried to avoid this discussion and not three minutes ago, I apologized, *genuinely*, for saying something I shouldn't. I then tried to *end* this discussion. It was *you* who wouldn't let it go."

"And are you in the habit of confronting and arguing with customers?"

"I think at this juncture, doll, you might want to ask yourself why you're so curious about what I'm in the habit of doing. So curious about it, you're detaining me with this conversation and won't let me get on with my workday."

Definitely, she'd been pissed.

Now she was furious.

"Are you inferring…?"

She was too angry to finish that.

He still answered it.

"Not sure I need to infer anything. I had somewhere to go, and I was intent to get there. Now," he swept a hand to indicate the floor between them, "I'm standing here having a ludicrous conversation with you."

"What's your name?" she snapped.

"Judge," he informed her easily.

She planted both hands on her hips, fingers wrapping around her more than likely three-hundred-dollar jeans.

Long, slender fingers with perfectly rounded nails tipped in a rich wine color which was probably what her mouth tasted like.

Shit.

He was enjoying this.

Which was why he really needed to walk away.

He didn't walk away.

"Well, isn't your name apropos?" she asked acidly.

Judge did a one-shoulder shrug.

Her eyes caught fire.

And her voice was rising. "Are you serious?"

"Calm down," he said softly.

"You're telling me to calm down when you just accused me of being some frivolous female who'd rather walk on diamonds than fund school lunches?"

Her voice definitely had risen now, as had her drama, the latter significantly.

And okay…

She was *something*.

He needed to walk away.

He still did not walk away.

Instead, he smirked.

He then watched, and enjoyed the show, as she took in his smirk, and behind those beautiful eyes, her head exploded.

"That isn't even close to what I said," he pointed out.

"Are you now *correcting* me?" she yelled.

And that was when Judge got concerned.

Because she was beautiful, even more when she was riled, but it was hitting him that, from the beginning, her reaction seemed extreme.

Was she just some privileged chick having a hissy fit?

Or was there something else going on?

Like, *why* was a family friend staying with Duncan?

Was his ex-wife up to her shit again?

"Seriously," he said quietly. "Calm down."

Bending at the waist, she leaned his way. "You *must* be old enough to know *never* to say that to an aggravated woman." She leaned back. "Or a non-aggravated one for that matter."

Why would he say that to a non-aggravated one?

He didn't ask that question.

He got closer to her, realizing something else. They were gathering an audience.

He kept speaking quietly when he said, "You're not aggravated, honey. You're ticked. You okay?"

"Don't ask me if I'm okay after you behaved like an absolute ass to me."

"Yes, I did, and I apologized, and you're drawing this out for some reason and I just want to know if you're all right."

"I *was* fine until *you* messed up my day."

"Well, you're not fine now."

"And you made me that way."

"By saying 'nice booties'?"

"It wasn't the words, it was the tone, and you know it."

"I do, and I apologized for it."

"It shouldn't have been said in the first place."

"I know that, hence the apology."

"I hope those two words were worth it, since it might mean your job," she snapped.

He stood still and stared down at her.

She was tall, even in stocking feet, which was what she was in right now.

Though, if she was wearing her fancy booties, he'd still be taller than her.

But he wasn't thinking of something he'd normally be thinking of as he noted her height standing that close to a woman like her.

How the drop would be the perfect distance for kissing her.

He was thinking she was going to tell Duncan about their ridiculous conversation and get him in shit.

He loved his job, lived for it.

So that couldn't happen.

"I said two words," he growled.

This time, she got closer to him.

A lot closer.

"You were being an asshole intent on making some point about how I live my life, and it is not okay."

An asshole?

Saying two words?

"Listen, sweetheart, if you've got some issue with how you live your life, don't work that out with me."

"I have utterly no qualms with the way I live my life," she returned.

"If that was the case, the *two words* I said wouldn't have triggered you into an overblown reaction," he retorted.

Her chin shot back into her neck. "Overblown?"

"We're standing here still discussing your reaction to *two words*."

"Just because you have one doesn't mean you get to wander around *being* one to hapless females," she shot back.

He one hundred percent caught her drift.

"Now you've called me an asshole *and* a dick over *two words*," he rumbled.

"I didn't call you a dick."

He used what she'd said earlier against her. "You inferred it."

With that, she tossed her hair.

The woman *tossed her hair.*

And her doing that only made him want to sink his fingers into that thick, glossy mane.

For fuck's sake.

"I call them as I see them," she sniped.

"Nice," he bit off.

She got even closer, so close, he could smell her perfume.

Bright and flowery, but also spicy.

Like jasmine and pepper and orange.

Gorgeous.

Expensive.

Shit.

"You wouldn't know nice if it walked up and rubbed itself all over you," she declared.

"From that, I'm beginning to get why you intend to draw this conversation out until we reach a new millennium."

Her eyelashes fluttered irately. "If you're suggesting I *want* your attention, you are sadly mistaken."

"Who's in whose space, doll?"

"I'm not a doll," she clipped.

But didn't get out of his space.

"Just to point out the obvious, I'm not interested," he lied.

And did not get out of her space.

"Like I would even," she scoffed.

He'd put money down that she would.

She really would.

And she'd love every minute of it.

He'd see to that.

Which meant he had to end this.

"You tell Duncan what went down, don't put your drama queen spin on it."

She was now openly insulted.

"Drama queen?"

"I said nothing about diamonds or school lunches," he pointed out.

"I can read between the lines."

"I'm sure. You can also blur them or bold them if it suits your purposes to overexaggerate them."

"How much more do you think you know about me just because of my *fabulous* booties?"

He dipped his face so close to hers, he could swear he could feel the tip of her nose.

And then he whispered the god's honest truth.

"Everything."

Her eyelashes fluttered again.

Not irate.

Not flirting.

She seemed rattled.

Smelling her.

Having her gorgeous eyes that close.

Her mouth that close.

Her that close.

He finally got smart, turned and got the fuck away from her.

And fast.

If Duncan heard about that incident, he'd be pissed as shit, Judge knew it.

Duncan also knew Judge, and whatever spin she put on, he wouldn't believe it (not if she embellished it), even if what instigated that incident had been all on him.

As he walked away, Judge ignored their audience and went to Rix's office. He then ignored Rix rolling his wheelchair into his own office and grinning up at Judge, visibly struggling to keep his mouth shut because, no doubt, he'd been part of that audience.

Judge ignored Rix too, *and* his grin, finished with his copies and skirted the shoe section when he returned to his desk on the top floor.

Even though what he was doing meant he was going to need the copier a lot that day, and his Volunteer Coordinator Alex was down in Phoenix leading a training session, so he couldn't ask her to do it, he also made certain he didn't leave his desk until she had to be long gone.

He did not spend the rest of the morning or the afternoon (and, fuck him, the evening) worrying about her talking to his boss.

Nope.

He did not.

And because he did not, he knew he was screwed.

Because whenever his mind went to that scene—and it did that a lot, too much—it focused on only one thing, and it wasn't the thing he should be focusing on.

It was on the fact that he wished he'd asked her name.

CHAPTER 2

THE WORLD

Judge

*T*he next afternoon, Judge approached the line in Wild Iris Coffeehouse to get an afternoon jolt of joe.

He also did this to get away from the office because the entire morning he'd been taking shit from everyone about his confrontation with the hot chick in the shoe section.

And that everyone included his buddy, Rix.

It also included River Rain's COO, Harvey Evans.

In fact, Judge had started the day walking into his office and seeing a pair of woman's mountaineering boots on his desk with a note propped on them that said, She forgot these. Next time you see her...

And yeah, that note was in Harvey's handwriting because Harvey was River Rain's second in command.

He was also a jokester.

So he was often also a pain in the ass.

In other words, Judge needed a break.

What he did not need was that break to include the gorgeous

brunette whose gorgeousness and attitude got his shit in a sling in the first place.

In other words, he *really* didn't need her to be standing two people ahead of him in line.

Which she was.

He further didn't need for her to be wearing a tailored blazer and another pair of jeans. This pair of jeans had the hems cuffed once, and that cuff was thick, so they not only showed her pretty ankles but also the sky-high, spike-heeled nude pumps she wore.

Not to mention, he didn't need her hair piled on top of her head, long tendrils drifting down, that baby hair that grew under the back hairline acting like neon pointing at the vulnerable beauty of the nape of her neck.

No, he did not need any of that.

But there it was.

Right in front of him.

Fuck.

Him.

She hadn't even turned around and he knew it was her.

He'd know that hair anywhere.

That neck.

Those legs.

That ass.

Shit.

Disaster struck before he could retreat, find somewhere to kill ten minutes and come back when the coast was clear.

She seemed to sense him (or at least sense his eyes lingering on her neck) and peeked over her shoulder.

When she did, he saw that she was still wearing her mirrored aviators, because, standing in a line inside a coffeehouse, why would she take them off when she killed it by wearing them?

That was, she killed it until she took them off, something she did when she caught sight of him.

Slowly, she lifted one of those amazing hands and removed them from her face only to shove them in her gleaming mound of hair.

Christ, he was jealous of a pair of shades.

Her made-up eyes—including false eyelashes, in the middle of the day, at a coffeehouse in Prescott, Arizona—traveled the length of him, and he was pretty sure when she started, she was going for disdain.

If that was what she was going for, she failed spectacularly.

Because every inch of him her eyes moved along, which was all of him, felt like it was getting a physical touch.

Or a taste.

One she savored.

Judge savored it too.

Big time.

She seemed to jolt herself out of it, and when she began to turn as if to dismiss him, Judge had to intervene.

Obviously.

"Yo," he called.

She stopped turning and glared at his face.

"How's it going, babe?" he asked like they were friends. "Today a better day for you?"

Her mouth, which was artfully coated with a slick raspberry color, dropped open.

"You get those boots you needed?" he pressed.

"You're a jackass," she returned.

The two people between them looked at her, at him, and then their bodies shifted a little out of the way.

Though it was Wild Iris. They didn't shift so much that it would shift them out of the line.

He smiled at her.

Her eyes narrowed on his smile.

"And yes," she stated haughtily, that cute nose of hers lifting a hint further up in the air. "I got exactly what I needed for myself *and* my mother. So that associate you were so worried about my overworking made his commission. Splendidly."

Splendidly.

Did any warm-blooded American girl under the age of eighty say the word "splendidly?"

He didn't ask after that.

"Staff don't get paid commissions," he shared. "They're paid a living wage. Commissions breed competition and pushy salesmanship, which makes customers uncomfortable."

He knew she wanted to, but she didn't hide the fact she was interested in that tidbit.

"Though, thanks. Any little bit helps," he went on.

As he knew it would, this comment completely offended her.

"I bought two pairs of Frye riding boots. It was hardly 'any little bit,'" she huffed.

"You wanna go back there and, like...talk to him?" the woman behind her suggested, and it made Judge chuckle, because she didn't offer for Judge to come forward and be in line with the brunette.

No one wanted to wait longer for their coffee, not ever, but especially not at Wild Iris.

And he kept chuckling when this suggestion put the brunette on the spot because it was rude to talk through people. However, it would also appear rude to turn her back on Judge in the middle of a conversation.

She struggled with this a beat, shuffling forward in line while she did. They all followed. Then she inclined her head to the patron and moved to Judge.

Judge was not unaware that this decision made him really fucking happy.

Too happy for his peace of mind.

Yeah, he had that conflicting thought.

Because the happiness involved *her*.

She stopped at his side.

Same perfume.

Awesome graphic tee that had lines on the material that made up the back of a seated tiger.

A tee he'd seen somewhere before.

His eyes moved from her shirt to her face.

"You into wildlife conservation?" he murmured.

"No, I'm into very long fur coats, preferably made of baby seals, and bunnies used for cosmetic testing."

She was totally lying, and not only because Judge knew you got that tee for a donation to the WWF.

So either she was into doing something, or someone she knew was, and she got the spoils.

It might be door number two.

But he hoped it wasn't.

"Mm-hmm," he hummed.

The line moved again, she turned to face forward, and they shuffled with it.

"What's your name?" he asked something at that point he pretty much needed to know.

She looked up at him. "Judy Jetson."

Of course he wouldn't get a straight answer.

Christ, this woman was the shit.

He chuckled again. "That's not it."

"Pebbles Flintstone?" she asked, like he could confirm.

He shook his head.

She kept at it. "Ginger Grant."

"I think we're getting closer."

She rolled her eyes and again faced forward.

"What's your name, doll?" he pushed.

She tilted just her eyes up to him.

Mm-hmm.

He was getting the middle-of-the-afternoon fake eyelashes.

They absolutely worked.

"Chloe," she told him.

Chloe.

Perfect.

She was totally a Chloe.

"Chloe?" he said. "That's all I get?"

"We're not doing this, you know," she declared.

"Doing what?" he asked.

She waved a hand between them. "This. You're going to work for

Duncan and I'm going to be Duncan's friend and never the twain shall meet."

"I didn't ask you to marry me," he pointed out.

The mess of hair on top of her head swayed with her reaction to his words and she suddenly became very focused on the line in front of them.

"Christ, sorry, are you...*into me?*" he asked.

But he knew.

She was.

Like she knew he was into her.

She turned to face him fully and snapped, "Of course not. You're very..." another round of looking him up and down, "*you.*"

The guy in front of them coughed.

"You're also very...*you*," he replied.

"I am very, *very* me," she drawled.

Fucking shit, it was insane, he barely knew her, didn't even know her last name.

But he had a new need when it came to her.

He needed to kiss her.

Hard.

"Yeah, you are," he murmured.

Her eyes rounded, but her mouth got soft, and again she turned and became fascinated with the line.

"I'm getting a coffee on my way back to Phoenix," she told the line. "Where I'm off to do my job and live my life because that's where I do both."

"Good choice, not hitting a drive-through and instead going out of your way for Wild Iris."

She made a noise of assent.

She then said, "I know what you do for River Rain. Duncan told me."

"Yeah?"

"So, you know, wandering the store, willy-nilly, preying on customers you think are overworking the staff is not your job. In fact, Bowie gave the impression that he didn't have anyone with that job description."

"Bowie" was Duncan Holloway, his boss. People close to him called him that. Judge had no idea why, but Chloe using that name gave new meaning to who she was to Duncan.

And Duncan might have given that impression, but he didn't say dick to Judge about it. And Harvey gave Judge shit about their altercation, he didn't sit him down and take a stripe out of him.

So clearly, Duncan knew her well because he didn't make a big deal out of something that wasn't a big deal.

"Breaks can get boring, and somebody's gotta look after them," he joked.

"Huh," she said.

Yeah.

She said "huh."

"Did you just say 'huh'?" he asked.

They advanced in the line, and her gaze tilted up to him again.

"You can't *say* 'huh,'" she informed him. "It's a noise, not a word."

"Did 'huh' just come out of your mouth?" he amended.

She gave him her full face, and when he got it, he realized he would have paid her for it.

"What of it?" she asked.

"How old are you?" he asked back.

"Old enough," she dodged.

"Eight-year-olds say 'huh,'" he told her.

"Excellent," she returned. "The age to which I aspire acting until I die."

He busted out laughing.

When he got it under control, she was glaring at him.

"I don't think I've ever met anyone like you," he admitted.

"Soak it in," she advised. "Because my hope is, you won't have another chance to do that."

She was so totally lying.

Because she was so totally enjoying this as much as he was.

He grinned at her.

They made the front of the line.

She ordered immediately.

"Turmeric dirty chai, macadamia milk, iced."

Of course she knew exactly what she wanted.

And it was complicated.

The woman behind the counter looked to Judge.

"It's just me on this order," Chloe said to her.

"No, it isn't," Judge contradicted. "I'm buying for both of us." And he was about to order, but Chloe spoke again.

"I don't let men who are a, not my friends or b, not my lovers buy things for me."

He shut his mouth and gave her a long look.

Pink hit her cheeks.

Which meant he gave her a huge smile at the same time wondering what else might make her blush.

She looked back to the cashier. "Just the dirty chai."

"And a Mexican latte," Judge added.

Chloe turned to him again. "I'm not paying for yours."

"No, you're not," he agreed. "As I said, I'm paying for both, and we're also not arguing about this because," he tipped his head to the line that had formed behind them, "there's eight people who want coffee, and they don't need to listen to us bicker for fifteen minutes before they can put their order in."

"Yeah, as entertaining as you two are, we don't need that," someone behind them said.

Judge was in danger of laughing again, but he didn't because those brown eyes flashed, and that was so spectacular, he was glad he didn't miss it.

She looked to the cashier. "I have a much fuller understanding of the meaning of 'crush the patriarchy…'" and with perfect timing she finished, "right now," and with that, she and her pumps swanned to the side.

Judge gave his name and paid for their drinks.

When he moved to the area where people were loitering, waiting for their coffees, he came to a stop right at her side.

And she didn't delay querying, "You know what irks me?"

"I know that question should probably have a modifier like 'at this moment,' or 'right now,' considering I'd guess a lot of things irk you."

She stared daggers at him for two long beats before she noted, "What irks me *in this current moment* is you being a gargantuan smartass."

In order not to miss anything, he grinned instead of laughing.

And he asked, "What irked you before I was a *gargantuan* smartass?"

"Why did you emphasize 'gargantuan?'" she asked in return.

"I don't think I've met a single soul who's used that word in an everyday sentence."

"It's a word you understand," she noted.

"Yup," he agreed.

"And you were, indeed, being a *gargantuan* smartass," she went on.

"I'll cop to smartass. Gargantuan?" He shook his head.

She rolled her eyes to the ceiling.

Yeah, he needed to kiss her.

"So what irked you before I was a smartass?" he pressed.

"Shall we say *continued* being a smartass?" she suggested.

"Chloe, give it up," he ordered.

She did that.

"She didn't ask my name at the counter. Therefore, it irks me that the name 'Judge' is going to be written on my cup."

It was his turn to stare, though he didn't do it with daggers. He did it with surprise.

Because...*what?*

"That irks you?" he inquired.

"You're annoying," she sniffed.

"You're just now headed to Phoenix to do your job and live your life. What's it matter my name is on the side of your coffee cup? You're eventually gonna throw it away."

"Did you miss me sharing you're annoying?"

"I hope your eyes are going to be on the road, and not reading your coffee cup."

"You know, don't think I don't know this is all kinds of fun for you."

She was absolutely right.

He just didn't know why she said that.

"I'm just—" he started.

"Flirting with the woman who you, being all you are," another eye-sweep of him, top to toe, "think is an easy get, but you also think she's just a throwaway," she finished.

Hang on a second.

Before he could speak, she kept going.

"A bit of fun. Someone you can make a shitty comment to one day. And because you're tall and hot and lanky and rustic and unpretentious and nature-loving and you have a noble job and a fabulous dimple, you also think the next day, you can see that woman and chat her up and maybe get a date that'll lead to you getting laid."

He knew better than to date her.

Still, he was one hundred percent angling for a date.

But not just to get laid.

He was fascinated by her, and even though he knew it would end up being no good for either of them, he wanted more.

"Then," she carried on, "you can tell your friends you hit that chick with the nice ass and the silly shoes. And in so doing, you don't think even for a second that maybe that chick's life has been turned on its head. That everything she knew is now gone. Everything she was certain of, everything that meant anything, everything that *mattered* has vanished. And she doesn't know quite how to live in a world without those foundations steady under her magnificently shod feet. That maybe she's looking for something to hold on to, something stable, not mercurial, like the whole world has suddenly become. Even if what she manages to hold on to is some new sense of self. But first, she has to find that. Which means, what she's *not* looking for is some flirt who treats her like fair game, no matter how incredibly attractive he is."

Judge heard all the compliments.

You bet he did.

It was all the rest that was souring his gut.

"So no, Judge," she continued. "I'm a bit of fun for you, a girl from the city who'll go back to the city, and you won't have any strings tied to you. But I don't want your name on my coffee cup. I want to go home and do my job and figure out how to live my life when up is down and a very serious wrong leads to a right that is very right, but it nevertheless breaks my heart, and anything that's meaningful in the world is absolutely not how I know that world to be."

"Chloe," he whispered, because he had no fucking clue what else to say.

"So you should have let me pay, *like I asked*," she stated. "Because now, I'm leaving. However, as you bought it, feel free to give my drink to someone else. I hope they enjoy the benefits of the turmeric. I've read more testing needs to be done, but I've found it's fabulous for inflammation and mood. Now, if you'll excuse me, I'm headed to a drive-through."

After she delivered that, she pulled her shades from her hair, perched them on her nose, and with steady, strong raps of her heels on the floor, she walked right out of the coffeehouse.

And with no other choice, Judge watched her do it.

————

It wouldn't be until the next day when he'd find out what was behind Chloe gutting him with that speech.

And the person with this information would not be the person Judge would put money down on having said information.

It started with a call.

Not a text.

Which was already a stunner.

He'd known Rix years, and he didn't know if the man had ever called him.

Texted him at five in the morning with, *Get your ass out of bed, it's trail time* approximately a thousand times.

But not a call.

Rix also didn't bother with preliminaries, like "Hey."

He just said, "Did you see it?"

"See what?"

"That whole thing with Imogen Swan, Corey Szabo, and Duncan?"

It was evening, and Judge had just finished a bison burger topped with homemade pimento cheese, some roasted fingerling potatoes, sautéed green beans and was now on his deck with a podcast, the sunset, his dog Zeke, and beer number two.

"What whole thing with Imogen Swan, Corey Szabo, and Duncan?" he asked.

Though the fact Duncan was mentioned in that mix was mildly interesting, it also wasn't because Judge wasn't a big gossip guy.

He'd seen some of Imogen Swan's movies, and practically every girlfriend he'd had had been superfans of hers. So he'd also seen most of the episodes of *Rita's Way*, her big TV show from a few decades back that made her a household name.

And everyone knew who Corey Szabo was, because everyone loved to hate him due to the fact he was richer than 99.999 percent of the population, and from all accounts, was also a huge dick.

Further, Szabo was famously a friend of Swan's and Swan's husband, Tom Pierce, the only one of that crew Judge knew well because he was a big tennis fan, and he could make a case that Pierce was one of the best to ever play the game.

And Judge, like nearly most sentient beings on the planet, knew that not long ago, shocking everyone, sitting alone in his twenty-million-dollar home outside LA, Corey Szabo had eaten a bullet.

That had reverberated around the globe.

The man who had everything took his own life.

That didn't only put the tech world, Wall Street, the gossip mill, and every computer engineer alive into a tailspin.

It put Imogen Swan fans in one too.

Because, not long before Szabo's suicide, the impossible had happened.

America's favorite couple, the solid-as-a-rock pair, proved they weren't that at all when Imogen Swan and Tom Pierce got a divorce.

So even Judge couldn't miss not only what Szabo had done, but also that everyone was on about how bad a year America's Darling, Imogen Swan, was having.

And having to publicly go through a divorce and sustain a blow like losing a close friend to suicide, even Judge, who barely watched TV and might occasionally see a movie, felt bad for the woman.

Rix interrupted his thoughts by laying it out.

"Szabo's ex got on some gossip show and spilled about how Duncan and Imogen were a big thing back in the day. She even used the words 'star-crossed lovers,'" Rix told him. "Totally into each other. Totally meant for each other. But Szabo, who was both their best friend, they'd all grown up together, broke them up. Lied about sleeping with her so Duncan would break things off so Szabo could have her. It's all over the store. It's all over *everywhere*."

This was a surprise, mostly because Judge had never met anyone famous (well, at least, not after he was old enough to form coherent thoughts, and he didn't count his father or grandfather as famous, because they were, but they were just family to Judge), much less knew someone who was best friends with two people who were two of the most famous people in the world.

Of course, everyone knew Duncan Holloway, but Judge didn't think of him as famous. He was just rich, and he was vocal about issues he held close to his heart. And in order to make a difference, he had to make the news, and he did.

But he was nowhere near Imogen Swan's and Corey Szabo's league.

"And some folks at the store did some googling, brother, and your girl in the shoe department..." Rix went on.

At that, Judge took his feet from the railing as he sat up.

"Yeah?" he prompted when Rix didn't finish.

"Her name is Chloe Pierce. She's Imogen Swan's oldest daughter."

Anything that's meaningful in the world is absolutely not how I know that world to be.

Well...

Fuck.

CHAPTER 3

THE ROSES

Corey

 hree years ago...

COREY SAT IN THE SECTION BESIDE THEM, FRONT ROW, WHERE IMOGEN told him to sit.

It was not his preferred location.

It wasn't because he couldn't watch her without being noticed doing it from his seat.

He also wasn't close to her. Couldn't touch her knee or take her hand.

She didn't need him, though, and the truth was, Corey would never have the seat he preferred.

This was because Genny had Tom, who as ever was right by her side.

Her son Matt was on her other side, her two men, looking after her.

On Matt's opposite side, Sasha was practically draped on her brother. Boneless with grief.

And everyone said Chloe was the dramatic one.

Corey felt when they did, they didn't pay enough attention to Sasha.

Though, Corey assuaged his irritation at this seating arrangement by settling into the fact Imogen had been firm about him sitting right at the front. A place of honor.

A member of the family.

Making this more so, before finding her own seat, she'd leaned in and murmured, "Take care of Chloe."

Which brought to mind...

He looked to his right and saw Chloe sitting beside him.

Pure Chloe, she'd worn a dramatic black hat. A mournful number angled perfectly on her head with a wide brim that sloped theatrically down in a wide bell shape that covered her eyes. Though the black of the hat had an expensive sheen, the brim, also black, was transparent, making it reminiscent of a mourning veil.

There were two people in this world that could pull off that hat.

Chloe.

And Marilyn.

This thought took Corey's attention to the front of the room, where there was a magnificent funeral spray of ivy, other greenery, blush-colored roses that were so pale, they were nearly cream, and more blush roses tipped with the most vibrant of pinks. All of this was interspersed with blooms that were a bold green peppered with small, fluffy white blooms along the stems. And in the midst of the spray, a massive pale pink satin bow with curling, trailing ends.

Beside it was a large picture of Marilyn Swan.

Imogen's mother.

Chloe's grandmother.

Corey's godsend.

Genny had selected a photo of her mom of which Marilyn would approve.

Not a shot from weeks or months or even a few years ago, when, due to the magic wielded by a stylist, she still had her lustrous dark hair, but regardless of how hard she fought against it, she showed her age.

No.

Genny had picked a picture of when Marilyn was young and beautiful. Smiling candidly, sitting outside in the sun at a table with a coupe glass filled with pink liquid held in her hand. Her lips were her signature perfect red, her lush, seductive eyes that came from her Italian heritage slightly narrowed with laughter. A devil-may-care aura around her that was so strong, it was captured on film.

That was the Marilyn he remembered.

That was the Marilyn who would idle in her car at the curb an hour to midnight on his birthdays while Genny and Duncan would creep up his lawn and free him of the hell that was his home. That was the Marilyn who had a birthday cake waiting for him at her house. Where they sang the song to him and he blew out the candles. And even when the years had passed and it was Duncan who was driving, because he'd gotten old enough to do it, Gen as always at his side, they'd come get him, but it was Marilyn who made sure there was cake.

Candles.

Ice cream.

And presents.

That was just one of the many things she did in the decades Corey had known her that made Marilyn more precious to him than his own mother.

Because his own mother had done none of that.

Not on his birthdays.

Not ever.

Indeed, he had an enormous cache of memories of the woman in that picture. A woman who got more out of life in a small town in Illinois than practically anyone he'd met in all his dealings and travels, outside her daughter, her son-in-law and her grandchildren.

Because she'd taught Imogen right.

Life was meant to be lived.

And along the way, you took care of the people that mattered.

Imogen, like her mother, was a master at both.

He stared at that portrait and then he looked left.

Tom was in the end seat of their row, by the aisle, but Genny had leaned forward to dab her eye with a handkerchief.

Tom didn't miss it and he turned to his wife, his broad back blocking Corey's view of Gen but exposing Matt and Sasha on Genny's other side.

The rest of that row was empty.

A familiar feeling rushed up his throat, filling it, temporarily causing him to experience blind panic that it would suffocate him as he returned his attention to Marilyn's portrait.

They were one down.

One down.

Someone should be there, and he was not.

He should be there.

Marilyn adored him.

She'd want him there.

Genny needed him there.

Corey needed him there.

But Duncan was not there.

Because of Corey.

The feeling in his throat cleared when he felt a touch on his hand.

He turned to his right to see Chloe gazing at him from under her hat-veil.

"She liked you," she said, and it was not lost on him what she meant.

She wasn't being cruel.

As was her way, she was being honest.

In his entire world, only four people had truly liked him.

Genny.

Marilyn Swan.

Robert Swan.

And Duncan Holloway.

Until he made that last person walk away.

And stay away.

"She loved you," he replied.

It was the wrong thing to say.

If a single look could share the world had just ended, Chloe's did right then.

He'd forgotten.

He'd forgotten how close those two were.

"I'm sorry," he murmured, "of course, you already knew that."

"It's all right," she whispered, having turned her gaze to the spray of flowers.

"Did you pick those?" he asked.

"I said red. Blood red. Like her signature lipstick. Mom picked those," she told him. And then, "Of course, Mom was right. Gram would love that arrangement. Particularly the fact there are about a hundred more roses than are needed and Mom asked for it to be broken down when this is all done and the bouquets made from it sent around to the local nursing homes."

He was not surprised at all that Genny requested this.

At this juncture, it seemed the low drone of voices in the packed space (save the front row, it was just Genny's immediate family...and Corey in the front row) was dying away, so Cory looked over his shoulder to see the pastor making his way down the aisle.

The service was about to begin.

The man stopped at Genny and Tom, bent and took Genny's hand, held it, speaking to her at the same time nodding, like he was agreeing with his own self.

Corey wanted to tackle him, demand he not touch her, just get his ass up front, say his words and get this done so Gen was not sitting in front of a room full of people. Some of them family. Some of them friends. Marilyn was social and popular.

But a lot of them, he knew, were craning their necks to get a good look at Imogen Swan, Tom Pierce...

And Corey Szabo.

"This, she'd hate," Chloe said, and Corey returned his attention to her.

"She would," he agreed, moving his gaze back to the pastor.

"She was religious and everything, but she told me she just wanted us to cremate her, have a big party, no tears, no ceremony, lots of booze and fattening food, and when we got back home, throw her ashes in the ocean."

The ocean.

Corey actually had to close his eyes for a moment as that memory assailed him.

Though, only a moment.

"It's good I have a driver," he noted as they both watched the pastor leave Gen and Tom and start to move to the front of the room where the lectern was next to the spray and the picture.

"Why?" Chloe asked.

"Because, if your mom and dad don't already have said plan, you and I are going out to get shitfaced drunk."

Chloe snorted, and startled, because Corey did not often (as in hardly ever) make anyone laugh, he slid his gaze to her.

Her lips were trembling with the effort it took for her to stop smiling.

"Are you in?" he asked.

"Can we drink pink ladies?" she returned.

Marilyn's preferred drink.

In fact, the portrait before them shared that.

"You can, I will not," he refused.

He caused no offense. Quite the contrary, her lips were trembling again.

"I will also buy you two dozen of them, if that's what it takes," he offered.

"If you're buying, you're on."

"Excellent," he muttered just as the pastor cleared his throat.

The man started speaking, and the good news was, he knew Marilyn and he liked her. Therefore, even as he began, his tone was warm, and it was clear he was feeling his own grief.

Excellent.

That would soothe Genny.

Chloe leaned into Corey so far her arm was pressed to his.

"Uncle Corey?"

He turned his head and tipped his chin down to catch her gaze.

"Thank you," she said.

He stared into her pretty brown eyes, wondering what another girl who had a different father but the same mother might look like.

He then shut that thought away, grabbed Chloe's hand and faced front.

He would feel it minutes later, and in doing so, it would make him again turn his head left.

To see Gen angled a bit forward, her eyes aimed at Corey holding her daughter's hand.

She caught his attention on her, lifted her gaze to his and gave him a small, grateful smile that did nothing to alleviate the anguish on her face.

That smile made Corey feel good.

Even so, he was shocked that, with Chloe's fingers curved around his, that made him feel better.

Genny returned her focus to the pastor, and Corey gazed at Marilyn's picture.

If it were him, there would be a million roses crammed into that room, and he would not give that first fuck what anyone thought of the gesture, the largess, or the excess.

Because, growing up, there was one woman on this earth who made Corey feel loved.

And now...

She was dead.

IN THE END, SITTING WITH CHLOE AT A LOCAL BAR, HE DRANK PINK ladies.

Because it made Chloe laugh.

And it would have made Marilyn smile.

CHAPTER 4

THE PARTY

Chloe

𝒩 *ow...*

"HOLY CRAP," SULLY SAID, EYES ON ME AS HE WALKED INTO MY ROOM AT Bowie's house.

Well…

If I must.

Sasha and my room, since, like now, when we were both there at the same time, we shared it.

However, even if Sasha was up from Phoenix visiting Mom and Bowie more often than I was, I liked to think of this lovely little mountain-chic suite as mine, since I'd claimed it first.

Though, Sasha being up here all the time concerned me, and not because it meant she was stuffing the room with plants and had added a hideous piece of macramé to the décor (though, mark me, that also was a concern—please, Lord, take me back to when she was preppy and sporty, I could work with that—there were very few style trends I could not spin, and therefore could not embrace, Sasha's boho was one of them).

No, what concerned me about Sasha being up in Prescott all the time was that she wasn't up here doing a job, or looking for employment, or volunteering at a youth center or taking pottery classes or anything even remotely worth her time.

In fact, except hanging with Mom and Bowie, and playing poker with Bowie and his buds, she didn't do much of anything at all.

So *obviously*, that was concerning.

"Totally already told her, Judge is gonna be on his knees begging, he sees her in that getup," Gage replied to Sully's opener.

"She says she doesn't care." Sasha entered the conversation, bouncing onto her knees on the bed next to where Gage was lounged across the foot of it, drinking a glass of champagne.

My youngest new "brother," Bowie's second son, had wholeheartedly embraced his newfound quality of life (that being the soon-to-be-official stepson of a ridiculously famous, insanely wealthy movie star), something I wholeheartedly *adored*.

I turned my attention to Sully, who was older and most assuredly already his own man.

I had time to mold Gage.

Sullivan was…

Sully.

To that end, my second youngest new "brother" had a bottle of beer in his hand.

Sullivan and Gage were Bowie's sons. And since Mom and Bowie (what I called Duncan, because he gave me the famous "Bowie Story," and he told me to call him that) were getting married (they'd become engaged a week ago, on Christmas, but we'd learned not too long ago that it was a long time coming (*decades*)), we were all going to be family.

Sasha, Matt and I had just gotten a running start at creating that with Bowie and his boys.

Sully and Gage fell in with our plans, and even though it hadn't been long, we were already thick as thieves.

This made Mom and Bowie happy.

And that made me happy.

Even if, in a part of me I'd never share with anyone, it killed me.

But now, I focused on the three who currently shared the same space as me.

Sasha was in a glittery, slouchy, champagne sequined dress that was pinched in at the drop waist. It fell in an uneven hem around her mid and upper thighs as well as falling very far off her shoulder. It sported wide, flowing sleeves.

An unsurprising choice for Sasha, seeing as every edge, except her neckline, was trimmed in a short line of bone-colored fringe.

I could have done without the fringe, but the dress as a whole was celebratory and sparkly, and she had a stunning collarbone and shoulders, so it would do, and as ever, she looked gorgeous.

Sully was in monochrome: smart, dark wash jeans and a navy button-up. Gage was in light gray trousers and a midnight blue button-up.

The boys were casual-*ish* (as far as I could tell, this was dressed up for the both of them), but they were ludicrously handsome and had such good bodies they could be in ratty jeans and tees, and it would still work for a New Year's Eve party.

As for me, I was in white satin.

High-waisted, flat front, wide-legged pants with a hidden button waistline and matching sleeveless top that was cropped on a curve—it just touched my back waistband, but in the front it went up enough to show a hint of the midriff.

One could, if one was not me, describe it as a classy tube top.

But I was me, so I did *not*.

"I haven't seen Judge in months," I reminded them. "I'm grateful for that. And the only part about Bowie's yearly company New Year's Eve bash in this palatial mountain manor that I'm not looking forward to is the fact that Judge RSVPed yes."

"She's totally lying," Sasha stage-whispered to Gage. "One of the first things out of her mouth when she showed two hours ago was to ask Bowie if Judge was coming."

Gage grinned as he sucked back three quarters of his glass of champagne.

I watched him do this and made a mental note to share with Gage at a later date that one did not *chug* champagne.

"I don't know, Coco," Sully said, using my nickname, which I had granted permission for them both to do, regardless of the fact that they would have done it anyway. He wandered in and threw himself on the bed with the other bodies already on it. "If you don't care Judge is gonna be here, you tricked yourself out for nothing. This is not a fancy deal."

"Anything is what you make of it," I retorted.

"Well, what you're gonna make of Judge in that getup is a mess. You're my big sister and *I* half have the hots for you," Gage declared.

I arched a brow. "Only half?"

He grinned at me. "Okay, five eighths."

I allowed him a small curve of my lips as I shook my head and looked back in the mirror to try to decide if I should settle in with just the one delicate but dramatic gold, full-ear cuff that peeked out of the hair I'd left to hang loose (though I'd added curl) or if I should add more jewelry.

I was still doing this when there was a quick rap of knuckles on the door and then Bowie, keeping hold of the handle, swung his upper body in.

His eyes did a scan of me and widened before he muttered, "Shit."

Well, that was a reaction.

"Judge is screwed," he went on.

I blew out an exasperated breath.

I mean, as far as they knew, I'd had *one singular* confrontation with the man four months ago at Bowie's store (no one knew about the coffeehouse scenario, because I told no one, not even Sasha, who I told almost everything, or Matt, who I told absolutely everything).

I was hardly pining for him (because I was *so* not interested, he was a cad).

And I knew men like Judge Oakley (Bowie had filled in his last name).

He didn't go without for long.

He was probably coming with a date.

And *no*.

My heart did not just prick at that thought.

Absolutely not.

Really, it didn't.

(Drat it, it did.)

Bowie's lips twitched then he took in the rest of the occupants in the room.

"People are showing," he announced.

"Cool, Dad," Gage said, but didn't move.

"Harvey and Beth showed ten minutes ago," Bowie continued.

"Right, forgot to tell you guys when I got up here," Sully shared, he then needlessly rectified that. "Harv and Beth are here."

Bowie let out a beleaguered sigh before he concluded, "And right now, they're down there, facing the onslaught, when no one used to show on time, but now everyone is showing on time. And they're doing it pissed at me because I banned phones and they all wanted to ask Genny for a selfie that they could put on Instagram. Now, does anyone in here want to help me, Matt, Harvey and Beth run interference with the seventy people that are right now strolling through the front door making a beeline to Genny? Or do you all wanna party up here and leave her to the wolves?"

"On it!" Gage decreed, rolling off the bed.

Sully pushed off immediately too.

And of course they did.

They were good guys.

Like Bowie.

The best.

Also, in a swish of sequins, a noise that I found one of the top five sounds of all time, not to mention with the grace of an athlete, Sasha dropped to a hip and swung her legs over the side of the bed, putting her feet decked in ropy gold high-heeled sandals on the floor.

I was wearing a pair of sleek, pointed-toe, death-defying-heeled, white leather mules.

It'd taken me three hours of combing through seventeen websites to find them.

But as was my wont when I had something I desired, I put the time needed into the endeavor, and I got it.

My shoes were, obviously...*everything.*

"Coming?" Sasha asked as she moved by me.

"Be right down," I replied, reaching for my peachy-pink lip stain which was almost a neutral, but not quite because...understated with jewelry and makeup, the outfit packed an even bigger punch.

"Cannot wait to see this Judge guy," she said as she and the boys moved to the door to follow Bowie out. "I've been to the store like...*a bazillion times* to try to catch a glimpse. He's elusive."

"I saw him a couple of days ago having breakfast at Zeke's," Sul said.

"*Ohmigod*, why didn't you say?" Sasha cried.

Their voices were fading down the hall, and I was putting an unnecessary layer of stain on my lips, since I'd already applied the first one and it was called stain for a reason.

I was doing this allowing myself a moment to feel the fact that the truth of it was...

I did not want to go down there.

No matter what I said, I did *not* want to see Judge.

Why?

Especially when I was looking this fabulous?

Because I'd let him in.

I'd shared things with him I wasn't even admitting to myself.

In fact, when I'd shared these things, I couldn't believe what was coming out of my mouth, because I hadn't allowed myself to consciously think of them.

The double why...

As in, why did I do this?

I did it because he was handsome, and he was funny, and he was flirty, and he didn't take any of my shit.

I did it also because he had warm brown eyes I could stare into for days and an easy smile that made me feel that ease, down deep, a place he shouldn't be when I barely knew him.

But the last thing I needed was some hookup with one of Bowie's employees that was never going to last, making future nights like tonight awkward for everybody.

Specifically, Mom and Bowie.

They needed no awkwardness.

They needed no troubles.

They needed smooth sailing.

Because after the downright rotten, heinous, traitorous shit Uncle Corey put them through, they'd earned it.

And they deserved it.

So far, it seemed, so good.

We all got along, even Matt dug Bowie, and Matt was a loner. Sometimes you just never knew with him. But he openly liked Bowie.

Also, Dad and Bowie got on with each other. They weren't best buds, but they could share space amicably. Which was useful, since Mom and Dad were still the best of friends and none of us wanted one of those ugly situations where they had to share us between them so we never got to have both of them together.

All of us together.

Dad hadn't come up for tonight, which would just be weird, but he'd been around the entirety of Christmas and it'd all been good.

Last, Mom and Bowie were just...happy.

Pretty much all my life I'd seen Mom that way (and I didn't think too long about that).

But I got the impression from the boys and Bowie (not to mention Harvey, Bowie's best friend) that wasn't *de rigueur* with Duncan "Bowie" Holloway.

He was a great guy. Outside of my dad, *the best*.

I was glad he finally had that happiness.

At the same time, it haunted me.

So no, I didn't need any entanglements with the resident player at River Rain Outdoor Stores Corporate Headquarters. Even if he did something cute, like run a program for kids to get them out into nature.

But Duncan had these parties every year, and he liked throwing them. I could tell by the way Mom shared how he'd been prepping for it, refreshing the evergreen boughs of their Christmas decorations, cooking with Bettina, their housekeeper, lugging in trays and boxes of catering and decorating stuff.

Hell, I'd done a walkthrough before I'd come up to start getting ready and the place was decked out.

The motif was pinecones, cream candles, copious strings of miniature LED lights threaded through winter greenery, and juniper-colored cloth napkins (Bowie was a famous environmentalist, even the glasses for beer were real glass, definitely not a paper napkin or a piece of plastic in sight).

Still, it was Bowie's brand of festive, and it said a lot about him that he'd have the seventy employees he employed in his Arizona stores into his own home for a big bash on New Year's, doing this every New Year's Eve.

It was very Bowie.

And I couldn't hide in my (and Sasha's) bedroom because a handsome man who'd probably brought a fresh-faced, bubbly mountain girl as a date was downstairs.

I had to get down there.

My stain had dried, and I looked amazing, so I had no further excuses not to *be* down there.

So I slicked on the gloss over the stain, dropped the tube in my evening bag embossed with swoops of pearls (and I *did* have my phone, I went nowhere without it), and I threw one more glance at myself in the mirror.

Divine.

I headed out.

In a fairy tale, he would have been at the foot of the stairs, catching my eye the moment I appeared at the top of them and staring at me while I drifted down as if he was having difficulties not falling at my feet the minute I cleared the last step.

Up until a couple of years ago, I could convincingly make the argument my entire life was a fairy tale.

But I'd learned.

No life was a fairy tale.

I descended the stairs and cleared the growing crowd in Bowie's massive entryway with its crowning mezzanine and hit the great room.

I then wasted no time going to one of the two bars Bowie had set up that had a bartender who could make mixed drinks and pour chilled glasses of champagne and craft beer from a tap (there were hammered copper tubs stationed around the space filled with bottles of beer, if you preferred, as well as small blue bottles of a local company's sparkling water, so if you liked, you could also help yourself).

I got my flute of champagne and floated away from the bar, took a sip, and above the rim of my glass, surveyed the candlelit, festive-LED-lit, lights-on-dim, soft-rock-coming-from-the-Sonos space.

And I saw it was a party in the mountains given by a mountain man.

But it sure was pretty.

I also saw that, apparently, Judge wasn't keen on meeting the famous Imogen Swan, because he wasn't one of the first to arrive.

"Green Acres is apparently the place to be."

This was uttered directly into my ear from behind.

I turned, looked up and saw my handsome brother standing there.

The blood one.

Matthew.

"It's good you, Mom and Sash are all in to cover the whole satin and sequins front so the locals didn't have to concern themselves with that," he continued to tease.

I gave my brother an eye roll and searched for Mom.

I found her standing in the curve of Bowie's arm at the entryway to the great room. She was smiling at some guests and wearing a striking red satin dress that left one shoulder bare, had a billowing balloon sleeve on the other, and came down to an angle hem that ended above the knee at one side and kissed her ankle on the other.

It was the perfect dress for her.

(Said me, who selected it.)

Although we were far from the only ones who put in an effort—some of the men were wearing sports jackets, one I saw in a suit (though, no tie), and the women had definitely gussied up—the Hollywood faction was not hard to spot.

"She is who she is, I am who I am, and Sasha did the best she could do," I returned. "At least we can count our lucky stars our baby sister doesn't have flowers in her hair."

Matt smirked and lifted his scotch and soda to his lips, doing his own scan of the crowd as he did so.

Once he'd swallowed his sip, he said, "I like her new style. I think it suits her."

I gave the only response I could give.

I harumphed.

He chuckled and looked at me. "She's finding her way, Coco. And I think it's a good thing she's out from under his shadow."

I felt my spine straighten at this.

Because when he said "his," he meant Dad's.

It was true, growing up, Sash and Dad were two peas in a pod, both the most active, athletic, competitive ones (Matt slid in at number three of that bunch, though Mom and I didn't compete), and for Sasha, all of that was gone.

As mentioned, it concerned me, including Sasha losing the entirety of her drive, which was something she rode, if memory served, since kindergarten.

But even if they weren't my favorite things back in the day, I missed the sweaters and tailored skirts and chino shorts and blue oxford button-downs she used to wear.

Mostly, though, I missed Sasha having focus.

Aim.

Goals.

And even more than that (*far* more than that), I missed Matt and Dad getting along, respecting each other and openly loving each other.

Something, since even before the divorce, when we came to know that things were going wrong with Mom and Dad's marriage, they did not.

Or at least Matt didn't.

"Matt—" I started.

He cut me off, his face going hard as he did. "We are absolutely, one hundred percent not talking about that."

I turned to face him fully. "Can you absolutely, one hundred percent give me a time when we *will* talk about this? Considering the fact I've brought it up repeatedly for over a year and you keep putting me off."

He tried to dismiss it by saying, "It is what it is."

"It is, indeed, that." I couldn't keep the snap out of my voice. That said, I didn't really try. "Going back to the fact that what happened between Mom and Dad happened."

"Chloe—"

"And Mom has moved on from it."

"Chlo—"

"But regardless, it is *hardly* your place to make *her* keep paying for Dad hurting her the way he did. Furthermore, it's hardly your place to keep *him* paying for it when he's already lost everything."

"He hasn't lost you or Sash, or as you said, Mom," Matt bit out.

"If you think he isn't in agony that she's rekindled her first love and is happy beyond measure, then you are not nearly as intelligent as I thought," I bit back. "He is. He's writhing with it. He doesn't need this ongoing, and ludicrous, and unnecessary, and just plain hurtful estrangement with his son carrying on and on *and on*."

"He cheated on her," he growled.

My heart pitched.

"I'm aware of that." I gritted between my teeth. "He made a huge mistake. He's human."

Matt shook his head. "It's my thing with Dad, and it has nothing to do with you."

"You're wrong about that too," I clipped.

"Well, way to go," he drawled. "You've shown your face at Duncan's party for five minutes, and you've ruined it for me."

I felt utterly no guilt.

"You need to get over yourself," I advised.

"And you need to go fuck yourself," he retorted.

I blinked, because Matt could be stubborn, and remote, and brutally honest.

But he was never a jerk.

He prowled away, and I immediately turned my attention in the direction of Mom, who I hoped did not witness the tenseness of that exchange, only to see she was engaged with talking to someone.

But Bowie was watching me closely.

I pasted a jaunty smile on my face and lifted my flute.

He returned my smile, but I could tell he didn't buy my jauntiness.

Damn.

"I like my ass, as fat as it is, and God granted me a good head of hair, but you in that outfit makes me grieve the loss of my perky tits."

Heddy, a longtime friend of Mom's who serendipitously lived in Prescott, had sidled up beside me.

She used to be in the acting biz.

Now, she worked in a title office, had two boyfriends she refused to commit to (and they were all down with that, having their freedom but also having company when they felt like it), and three dogs.

She had a smart mouth and the ability to tease relentlessly.

So obviously, I adored her.

"If I hear you call your ass fat again, I'll stop speaking to you for a year," I sniffed.

"Couldn't have that," she replied, grinning up at me.

"And it's not fat, it's curvaceous," I noted.

"I stand corrected," she said.

"You certainly do," I retorted, lifting my glass to take a sip, intending to restart our conversation by saying hello and telling her she looked cute when I felt something tickle along the side of my neck, a sensation that made my gaze wander the room.

When it did, I saw Judge was there, across the space, standing next to the other bar set up in the corner by the fireplace (which was now burning merrily away).

He had a sturdy glass filled with beer in his hand and a smile on his face as he listened to an extortionately handsome, built man who was standing with him.

As if it had a physical touch, the minute my gaze hit him, Judge Oakley's eyes swung to me.

And fixed on me.

And he stared.

And *stared*.

And drat it all, I felt my skin heat, because the look on his face said he saw white satin for about five seconds before his imagination chucked my outfit, and now he saw something entirely different.

Thank God my strapless bra was padded.

"It's my understanding this party is PG rated. Some drinking. The likelihood of a buffoon or two over-imbibing, because there's always the likelihood of a buffoon over-imbibing. If we're lucky, perhaps they'll make a lowkey scene that we can enjoy, but they'll regret in the office in a couple of days. However, you two keep staring at each other like that..." Heddy began. "We'll just say we've already hit NC-17."

I tore my gaze from Judge, pulled myself together and turned to Heddy so he had a side view and hopefully the sense that I'd dismissed him.

"Let me guess, that's Judge," she deduced.

The instant she said his name, my mind conjured the image I'd recently relished of him in deep indigo jeans and a black crewneck, a pair of cognac oxfords on his feet. His longish-on-the-top, light brown hair was swept back, but the fact it had a tendency to curl in big waves was not controlled.

And his stubble that was just perhaps a week or two from being defined as a beard was sublime.

I'd forgotten (purposefully, and with no small amount of effort) how attractive he was.

I now very much remembered.

God.

I took a sip of my champagne to cool the burn.

Heddy cut into my (I had to admit) fevered reverie.

"Remind me again what's wrong with him?" she asked, but she didn't wait for me to answer. "Because, not to be surface-oriented, but he looks close to pretty damned perfect from here."

"He's a rake," I stated.

Her brows rose even as her eyes twinkled. "That bad? A *rake*?"

"Well," I mumbled, "I don't know if he's a rake. I'm just using my rather substantial understanding of the opposite sex to make that determination."

"Do tell, my lovely," Heddy encouraged. "What makes a rake?"

"He's an audacious flirt," I supplied.

Although she was still very amused (*very*), she also now looked confused.

"Flirt?" she asked. "I thought you two got in a huge fight."

Damn it.

He hadn't flirted our first meeting, *exactly*.

He had flirted our second meeting, definitely.

The one no one knew about.

"You can flirt and fight at the same time," I decreed, then started making things up. "It's part of what makes a rake."

"I see," she muttered, visibly fighting a smile.

"Whatever, is he coming over here?" I asked.

She glanced to the side, then she said, "No."

No?

"Well then…" Hmm. "Good," I stated.

"Mm-hmm, good. As women have known for nigh on a couple of centuries, they gotta steer clear of those rakes," she declared. "Then again, for nigh on eternity, they've been running to those rakes in droves. Which, I don't know, I'm not up on the fine points of rakish-ness, but I think that's how they *become* rakes."

Due to the fact I found anyone who was cleverer than me to be maddening, I glared at her.

She just grinned at me.

"Oh...my...*God*," Sasha whispered, coming up to us and crowding in. "The guys told me Judge is here. They pointed him out. And...*wow*."

I do not care my sister finds him attractive, I told myself. *I do not care that she's stunningly beautiful, lively, and sweet, and that he will not miss any of that. I do not care that I made myself clear the last time I saw him, and he obviously absorbed what I said so he will keep to himself and allow me to do the same. I do not care that this opens things up to him possibly flirting with Sasha. I do not care that he was standing alone with his friend, without a woman near him. I do not care about any of this.*

I do not.

(I did.)

"Fortunately, he has manners and is steering clear," I declared.

"Yes, fortunately," Heddy agreed, making no attempt to hide she didn't mean either word.

"I don't think it's fortunate, he's *gorgeous*," Sasha said.

"I need more champagne, do either of you need a drink?" I asked.

"I'm good," Heddy answered.

"You need—" Sasha started, staring at my half-full glass and looking confused.

"Toodles for now," I interrupted her, giving an index-finger wave, then headed back to the bar, gulping down the champagne I had left along the way.

So, apparently, earlier, I was wrong.

There *were* times when chugging champagne was appropriate.

And now was one of them.

CHAPTER 5

THE DANCE

Chloe

For most of the time that my family had been living in Phoenix after they moved from LA, I'd been in France.

Even though I'd been in Arizona awhile, for a relative newbie, it sneaks up on you. As such, I had not had the experience I needed to understand that, in the summer, Arizona was sweltering hot. In the late fall and early spring, Arizona was sheer perfection. In the winter, during the day, it was heaven.

But at night, it was damned cold.

Go up to Prescott, it was colder.

Up here in the mountains where Bowie lived, *freezing.*

And as such, mountains plus freezing meant there could be snow.

And there was.

A beautiful blanket of pristine, white, holiday snow covering the earth and tufting the pines.

It was gorgeous by day, breathtaking by moonlight, but I had not taken this into account when I'd packed.

Of course, I had a poofy parka that I kept up here for times when I needed it.

But I'd consider boiling oil poured over my skin before I put it over this outfit.

This made it fortunate I'd brought my alabaster pashmina, which was wide and long and warm.

Even so, it was doing very little to keep the chill at bay as I stood outside on Duncan's back veranda, standing at the railing, staring at the moonlight gilding the lake and casting ornamental shadows of the crested pines across a bed of blue-white.

I was there because I needed to escape.

This wasn't because Judge had so far (for hours) completely avoided me.

I'd noted (because, regrettably, I'd looked) that he'd talked to Sully (several times). To Gage (also several times.) To Duncan and Mom (once, for what seemed like an excruciatingly long time). I even saw Sully introducing him to Matt and Sasha.

He didn't get anywhere near me.

I did not care.

(I cared.)

No, what drove me out into the biting air was something else.

I kept my body facing the railing as I slightly turned my head and slid my eyes into the room.

And saw Mom laughing with Beth and Heddy, and I hated it about me, but I breathed a little sigh of relief that she was thus, one of the few times Bowie wasn't at her side.

Bowie.

At her side.

I closed my eyes tight and heard my sister's hissed words of not ten minutes before, another reason I was out in the cold, literally and figuratively.

"It's none of your business, Chloe. I mean, seriously, do you think for a second that Mom is fired up about *you* getting in his face? She doesn't need Dad and Matt not talking and *you* and Matt not talking *either*. Stop being so damned nosy and even more freaking *bossy*. Leave him *alone*."

Needless to say, Matt had a conversation with our sister.

Also needless to say, she was taking his side.

Further something I personally thought was needless to say, I could opine about her doing this because, if someone took Matt to task for carrying his resentment about Dad on for far too long, they might also take her to task for being adrift.

Wisely, I decided not to bring up that last point when Sasha told me off.

I could try, but as I'd done it countless times before, I knew I'd fail in any effort to brush aside one of my siblings being mad at me. A sheer impossibility when both of them were.

We might bicker, even have words, but we didn't fight much.

However, when we did, it upset me.

Greatly.

Therefore, definitely in a cold war with Matt, and tensions escalating with Sasha, I was standing, freezing my satin-covered ass off, facing a new year that was going to be upon me in under ten minutes, and thinking this was becoming typical.

Out with the shitty old.

And in with the shitty new.

On this thought, my eyes flew open, and I emitted a surprised peep when a weight landed on my shoulders.

I whirled, and when I did, the heavy camel hair overcoat I was suddenly wearing whirled with me.

And there stood Judge, and he did it close, with a thick burgundy scarf wrapped around his neck and his hands lifted.

To me.

He used them to pull the lapels so tightly closed at my chest, my upper body swayed at the same time it contracted with the snug fit.

He kept his hands there as he lifted his eyes from them to mine and said in his deep, and now seemingly irritated voice, "You're a lunatic."

"Well, hello," I replied. "So very lovely to see you again."

He scowled at me, and it was then I smelled his cologne.

He hadn't worn cologne the other times I'd been in his presence.

For my peace of mind, I wished he hadn't worn it now either.

My nose picked up the herby head note of basil, definite heart note of plum with the base note of cedar.

If I had built the scent myself, I would have picked the same things for him, though I probably would have gone for bergamot or mint as a head note.

"You're barely clothed, are you trying to freeze yourself to death?" he demanded, breaking into my fervent mental scent concocting.

"Allow us both, upon our much-dreaded reunion, not to exaggerate," I replied. "I'm hardly *barely clothed.*"

"Every guy in there has been staring at your tits, or your ass, all night long," he shot back.

I stared up at him.

"If Sully, Gage, Duncan, Harv, your brother, Rix *and* me hadn't been liberally disbursing death glares, I could have easily punched fifteen men in the throat tonight."

My gaze skittered to the windows, vaguely wondering who Rix was, not so vaguely wondering if this was true.

"Chloe, look at me," he growled.

Yes.

A growl.

I looked to him even as my entire body got warmer, and it wasn't all due to the coat.

I also started to feel peeved.

These contradictory emotions weren't alarming.

For me, this happened a lot.

He tightened his fists in what I hoped was his own coat (I hoped this not only because it would be bad that he stole someone else's for this interlude, but also it was a fabulous coat and said many good things about his level of taste—good things, I hastened to remind myself, I did not care about).

"Now, see, I came tonight expecting you to be here," he stated. "And I came tonight expecting to have a conversation with you. And so I came here ready to apologize. But now, after hours of your horseshit, I'm wondering what I should be apologizing for."

My...

Horseshit?

"You came here to—?"

I didn't finish that question.

"I came here for Duncan's yearly gig, and yeah, I came here hoping to talk to you."

"Well, I've been here all night," I pointed out.

"I have too," he returned.

Did he mean…?

"Are you saying you expected *me* to come to *you*?" I asked, my words dripping with my feelings on the absolute absurdity of that idea.

"Fuck yeah, I expected you to come to me. How else was it gonna go?"

Apparently, I was going to need to state the obvious.

This, I did.

"You could have come to me."

"Really? Was it me who verbally handed you your ass months ago?"

Hmm.

"And let's talk about that," he continued, taking his hands out of his coat but doing it moving into me so I had no choice but to move back. As I didn't have far to go, it didn't take much before I hit railing, but he kept coming, so he was *this close* to his body touching mine. He then leaned into a hand on the railing so he was even closer, and mostly fencing me in. "That was uncool."

His last three words were difficult for me to process, because I had a nose full of deliciously plummy cedar and an eye full of a very pissed-off Judge Oakley.

Since, due to his silence, it seemed something was required of me, I parroted, "Uncool?"

"You making those assumptions of me."

My brain scrambled through a fog of cedarwood and glittering brown eyes in an effort to try to remember what assumptions I'd made of him.

I didn't have enough time to succeed in this effort before Judge carried on speaking.

"For months, I felt like a dick. For months, I worried about you. For months, I kicked my own ass because you made me think I'd kicked you when you were down. Then, for the last four hours, watching the ice queen hold court nowhere near me, I wondered how I became guilty of being the player out for nothing but to tap your ass when all I did was be very obvious about the fact I'm interested in you."

I was catching up, and as such, I reminded him, "You seem to forget our first encounter, *you* made assumptions about *me*."

"Give it up, Chloe," he returned instantly. "I apologized for that and you're a big girl. I was pulling your pigtail and you know it. You also didn't tell me to fuck off. You jumped right in. Both times. And now we're playing," he twisted at the waist (though did it and still managed not to move an inch out of my space) and flung an arm behind him to indicate the party inside, "these games?"

"I'm not playing any games," I returned.

His eyes dropped to his coat then came back to mine.

"Your mom's a movie star and still, I spent time getting to know her tonight, finding out she's one of the most down-to-earth ladies I've ever met. Even in red satin. What's your excuse?"

"I hardly wore this for you," I scoffed.

"Who'd you wear it for? Shasta?" he retorted.

Shasta was Bowie's husky dog, one of three dogs and two cats (and a rabbit) in his (and now Mom's) menagerie.

But oh no.

He did *not*.

He did not get to think *anything* I did was for him.

I straightened, which meant his coat that I happened to be wearing brushed his chest.

"I don't dress for men," I hissed.

"Coulda fooled me," he fired back.

"You have a high opinion of yourself."

"Not really. Though I didn't think he was, turns out tonight my buddy Rix was my wingman. 'Cause he tells me, when I wasn't looking at you, you were looking right at me."

Rix.

This indubitably was his rough-hewn, handsome friend.

Damn it all.

When I was on my game, I could sniff out a wingman from twenty paces.

But even not on my game...

What was I thinking?

He read my face, I knew he did when he grunted, "Yeah."

"I'll have you know, Judge Oakley—"

"Know my last name, do you?" he inquired drily. "You pretend you weren't into me to someone, even though you asked about that?"

Oh my God!

He wasn't to be believed!

"Yeah, babe, I get this shit," he declared. "Been here, done this kinda crap too many times."

"You could have kept far away," *as you have all night,* I did not finish.

His brows rammed down. "When you floated out here wearing material that has zero insulation properties? I know an invitation when I see one."

Oh...my...*God!*

He wasn't to be believed!

"I didn't come out here as an invitation to you, Judge," I snapped.

"You also didn't refuse my coat, or my company," he returned. Then punctuated that with the highly effective, *"Again."*

I lifted my hands toward the coat to do the first in order to move on to the last.

"Don't even *fucking* think about it," he warned low.

I stopped moving because no one had ever spoken to me like that.

No one.

And I detested it.

Just about as much as it turned me on.

God damn it.

"Seriously, you're gonna freeze to goddamn death," he snarled.

"It isn't your concern."

"Chloe—"

I shook my head. "No, Judge. Whatever you think this is—"

"I know what it is."

All right.

I was getting angry.

"You know *nothing*," I bit.

"I know you laid me out at Wild Iris, but if you hadn't done that, and instead gave me some time, we could've shared our coffees that day. Stopped the bullshit and got to know each other. And maybe made plans to do that some more. And probably made more plans. Until you shared what was behind your big speech and I could have been there for you in whatever way you might've needed me. That didn't happen. You assumed I was an asshole. You assumed I had no intentions other than to get me some. You assumed I treat women like trash. And then you left me with nothing but worry for you. And tonight, when we could clear things up, you made a bullshit play."

The worst part about that?

I had.

I'd assumed, even so far as *accused* him of being all those things.

I said them right to his face.

"Instead," he went on, "I found out from some gossip bitch on freaking YouTube, for fuck's sake, about all the heavy you've been dealing with, your family's been dealing with…"

My mind froze and so did my body as I stared up at him.

But he didn't seem to notice.

Ten!

"…and I spent the time between then and now concerned for you because that heavy is really fucking heavy. I get here tonight, hoping to clear the air and see where you're at, but I find you've got no intention to be real. I suspect you've got a quota of how often you're real, *really* real, and you hit that when you spouted all that shit to me at the coffeehouse."

Six!

"Now who's making assumptions?" I asked.

Five!

"Correction," he gritted. "Educated guesses that come not only from your behavior, but experience."

Four!

"Well, it seems you should steer clear of a woman like me."

Three!

"Seems that way."

We glowered at each other.

Two!

"It also seems like it's going to be another banner year," I remarked sarcastically.

One!

Happy New Year!

The shouts and squeals and hoots came from inside, so happy and loud they were barely muted by the double-paned glass.

And Judge's hand came out of nowhere, curling around the side of my neck, his thumb under my jaw pushing up, tilting my face to his.

Then his mouth was on mine, warm and firm.

Now, I would spend a great deal of time on a great number of occasions from that moment onward wondering why I did what I did next (it was weak (and inaccurate), but I blamed New Year's).

However, I did it.

I opened my mouth.

And his tongue slipped inside.

Tasting his warmth, tasting Judge, I arched into him.

His fingers dug into my scalp.

Our tongues tangled.

I liked to dance, all kinds of dance.

But especially slow dances.

And this one was the best.

The best of my life.

Judge broke it and stepped back.

He then whispered, "Happy New Year."

I breathed.

Heavily.

And this rendered me unable to speak.

It didn't render me unable to see, and what I saw was what I'd seen in the shoe department at River Rain, in Wild Iris, in Bowie's living room,

The most beautiful eyes in the most handsome face I'd ever encountered in my life.

"Give the coat to Duncan," he ordered. "He'll bring it into the office."

I blinked.

Repeatedly.

And quickly.

But with not another word, Judge turned and walked away from me, into the house, through it, and as I had a view to it, even if it was obstructed by bodies, I nevertheless saw the front door open and close behind him.

CHAPTER 6

THE CALL

Chloe

ne week later...

IN WHATEVER WAY YOU MIGHT'VE NEEDED ME.

"Chloe? Are you alive in there?"

I came out of my head and into my office, focusing on Mi-Young.

"Where were you?" she asked. "Because I kinda wanna go there, and it also scares me."

Where was I?

I was back, a week ago, on Bowie's veranda, going over, yet again, some of the things that Judge had said to me.

Things I had missed at the time.

Like, *wearing material that has zero insulation properties.*

Of course, what he'd said after that was utterly ungentlemanly.

But the bottom line was, he'd worried about me being out in the cold.

There was also, *all I did was be very obvious about the fact I'm inter-ested in you.*

Which were, of course, words a girl might obsess on.

Though, I was above that.

(I so was *not*.)

As well as, *I spent the time between then and now concerned for you because that heavy is really fucking heavy.*

He was so right.

It was fucking heavy.

And it was so sweet that he'd get that.

Not to mention the things he said that concerned *me*.

Such as, *been here, done this kinda crap too many times.*

And, *educated guesses that come not only from your behavior, but experience.*

I really did not want to know what that meant.

(But the time I spent thinking about it, I totally did.)

All of that said, outside ruminating on my temporary insanity of participating in that amazing kiss, the thing that took the most of my attention was, *in whatever way you might've needed me.*

How would that go, having the man in my life be there in whatever way I might need him?

And then, how would it go, when he eventually did something awful, and he was gone, but I still needed him?

"Okay, now you're freaking me out," Mi said, and I again had to force myself to focus on her.

"I just…have a lot on my mind," I replied. "It's application time, and that's always stressful."

"I hear that," she muttered, staring down at our "conference table" (which was in quotes because it was small, round, barely seated four people, was tucked into a corner of my equally small office that I had perhaps budgeted a *tad* too much into making spectacular, so I wasn't sure what kind of conferences it could host, considering it barely fit me and Mi and only me and Mi ever sat at it—when we had full staff meetings, I took us all out to a nice restaurant).

"We can try adding on a few more," I suggested. "Say, go from doing a candidate a quarter to one every other month."

She looked at me, fear in her eyes.

I understood her fear.

It was fear for the amount of work that would be and money it would cost that we had to raise for the program we ran that we were currently discussing.

"Okay, maybe not," I mumbled.

"We need more publicity for this program," she said, not for the first time.

My neck instantly started itching.

"Mi—"

"Hear me out," she requested.

"Is it something I haven't heard you say before?" I asked.

Her expression grew determined. "Maybe not, but I really want you to listen to me this time."

I sighed and then rolled a hand, even if, in it, I was holding my Marilyn Monroe inspired Mont Blanc pen with its ivory barrel, rose gold accents and pearl at the base of the clip.

"You are Imogen Swan's and Tom Pierce's daughter," she stated.

"I know—"

She held up one of her pretty, petite hands, which was Mi. She was pretty, exceptionally so, and petite. I looked like an Amazon next to her.

I loved our dichotomy, it *so* worked when we were out on the prowl (though Mi didn't prowl anymore, she was now very taken).

I further loved that she was one of the few people I knew who understood and loved herself in a way everyone should aspire to.

It was perhaps unprofessional (though I didn't care), but the truth of the matter was, I just loved her.

Outside of Sasha, Mi-Young was my best friend, which made work even more fun than it normally was (and I never did anything I didn't think was fun, especially not for a living).

In other words, at receiving The Hand, I stopped speaking.

"You can't get away from that, Chloe. And if more people knew you ran this program—"

"We'd get more applicants," I pointed out.

"We'd get more *clothes* to give to more applicants. We'd get more *volunteers* to help more applicants. Department stores and designers would be falling all over themselves to support what we're doing."

Left unsaid, *If Imogen Swan endorsed it.*

Further left unsaid, *By becoming the face of it.*

"We're far from the only ones who offer makeover services to women who don't have the means to put their best foot forward, clothing-wise, while trying to get a leg up in life," I told her something she knew.

"We're the only ones with an extensive interview process and internship opportunities, so we can write them meaningful recommendations letters. And we are absolutely the only ones that don't only offer them an interview outfit and a new hairstyle but give them the full lineup of cosmetics and facial care they need and a solid starter wardrobe so they don't have to spend the money to invest in one when they get the job. That's a head start for any woman. Corporate or office jobs have a wardrobe they expect in such a way they should pay for it because it's essentially a uniform. Because it is, it isn't an expenditure they'd normally make. And if you're spending money on clothes, you aren't spending it on other things you need to do to achieve what all our ladies want to do when they come to us. Getting ahead in life."

She didn't have to explain my own program to me.

She did it to drive home her point, so I didn't call her on it.

I drawled, "I'm not sure we're the *only* ones who do that."

"One of the few," she retorted. "Coco, this program has the potential to be a true non-profit. We could get 501(c)(3) status. Be tax-exempt. We could apply for grants. Fundraise. *Hire staff.*"

She jerked a thumb over her shoulder to indicate the door to my office, which led to a tiny hall, which led through our stock rooms and eventually fed into my boutique.

Which was fabulous.

This boutique was where she and I worked. Mi-Young as my store manager, me as owner and buyer. We had four other staff, a full-time and two part-time sales associates, a website/newsletter/social media person, and interns worked with me and the rest of the staff to get skills and experience to pump up their resumes.

But here, at this tiny conference table, was where she and I ran my true love.

A small, tidy program that I seeded with some of my trust fund money and kept funded by allocating five percent of my profits to it. Along with requesting customers to round up their purchases, all that extra going into the program. Last, receiving additional funds (though they weren't much, they were still steady) through a donation option on website sales.

We referred to it as Triple F.

Fabulous Foot Forward, a program where we did just what Mi said. We accepted applications from women who wanted to move on, and move up, but life circumstances made it difficult for them to afford the trappings of what would make HR managers across the country sit up and take notice.

We didn't only offer makeovers, clothes, cosmetics and experience working with us at the store doing everything from sales to online customer service and website design to marketing, inventory and buying.

We had a group of volunteers who helped our candidates write their resumes and taught them interview tactics and follow-up.

Triple F was my brainchild.

My baby.

My pride and joy.

Mine.

And as such, even if Mi was very right, we'd be able to do so much more if I used my familial connections to do it.

I just couldn't.

Because our previous applicants might have eventually found out I was Imogen and Tom's daughter, but in one part of my life, this most important one, I wanted to be just me.

Chloe Pierce.

Fashion-forward small business owner and feminist who put time, effort and money into helping her sisters build a better life for themselves.

After jerking her thumb to the door, she said, "Everyone out there is with you on this, we all love it, we want it to grow. But already, it's a lot."

We had the means to pick a single applicant every quarter. Four women a year. I did the wardrobe stylist stuff. We had hair stylists who did free hair and makeup artists who gave free makeup tutorials. And I had ins with people so we could get some products and clothes for free or at cost.

But just going through the applications every quarter took us days. And it wasn't easy, because everyone was worthy. It took an emotional toll to turn people down or ask them to re-apply the next cycle. A toll that wasn't completely wiped clean with the good work we were able to do for a couple of fabulous ladies.

"You could make a call and be on a morning news program," Mi went on, paused, held my gaze, and finished, "Your mom could make a call and probably get on the *Today* program."

"That's not happening," I said flatly.

"Coco—"

"Let it be mine." I now spoke softly, and she shut her mouth. "For a few more cycles. Let me see if I can figure out how to raise a bit more cash. If I can make some more inroads with some suppliers to get more donations. Maybe, if we can raise the funds to hire someone part-time, it'll make the difference and we can add a candidate or two to each cycle without it becoming a burden that'll burn us all out."

She nodded, and I knew it wasn't that she had any hope of me hiring someone part-time.

It was my soft voice.

It was knowing how much this meant to me.

"I shouldn't have pushed," she said.

I rolled my eyes. "Please, shut up."

"I—"

Mi didn't finish what she was saying because there was a knock on the door.

I called, "Come in!"

Madison, one of our part-timers, a student at ASU, opened the door and came in, saying, "Mail arrived." She looked to us at the table then across the space to my desk. "Here or there?"

"Desk, please," I requested.

She moved that way, and I watched as she did, because there seemed to be a big manila envelope in the pile of mail.

Had I ordered a sample I forgot?

Or, almost better, a catalog.

"We're done and I gotta get back on the floor," Mi-Young said, rising from her chair.

"You come back to the floor, maybe I can pop down the street and get us some coffees?" Madison asked.

"Dirty chai," I ordered immediately.

"That means yes to coffee," Mi-Young said on a smile as they both exited my office. But Mi-Young stopped at the door and looked to me. "Open? Or closed?"

"Open, *ma chérie*," I murmured as I got up from my own seat, my mind already ticking to the next thing to do.

I headed to my desk, and it must be said, I was never too busy to appreciate my office décor.

I did this during the short journey.

Simple white desk, no drawers. White credenza behind it, precisely the same width as the desk. Two gold lamps on the credenza framing a piece of art on the wall that looked like a golden branch with golden leaves growing from the top of that bureau. White glass accoutrements. Acrylic trays. Compact forever floral arrangement of pink and yellow flowers. And a stack of old *Vogue* magazines on either side of the credenza, piled high, on top of which were framed designer sketches (left, Givenchy, right, Valentino).

My rolling office chair was upholstered in gold velvet, the seat in front of my desk was a square bench covered in green velvet and trimmed in gold. I had a built-in wall of cupboards to one side that included filing cabinets and a hidden printer so I didn't have to see anything messy or techy (I used a laptop, which was closed and set in the credenza whenever it wasn't needed, it also matched the décor, being a Mac Air in gold).

The walls were a buttery cream.

And then there was the round conference table.

It was overkill for my position as only a very recent entry into the retail world, not to mention this small room.

It was perfect.

I had an upscale shop in the Melrose District on 7th Avenue in Phoenix, a large-ish space sandwiched between vintage shops, other boutiques, galleries, restaurants and bars. A district that proudly called itself a "gayborhood."

I would move far more stock in Scottsdale.

I didn't want to be in Scottsdale.

Nothing against it, I spent a goodly amount of time there, but I wanted people to find us in the midst of life and vibrancy. For passers-by and window shoppers, I wanted us to be a surprise. I wanted mature women to come in and feel young. I wanted young women to come in and learn that there was no expiration date on fabulous.

Scottsdale was Scottsdalian, and it was awesome in its way.

Everyone felt safe and welcome in the Melrose District.

So that's where I wanted to be.

In the thick of things.

I stopped behind my desk and reached directly for the big manila envelope, because samples were samples, but I preferred to think of them as surprise gifts.

And everyone loved a gift.

Me especially.

I could feel immediately it wasn't a sample, it was paper.

So perhaps a catalog of possible *future* samples.

I grabbed the Meissen Ming dragon letter opener Dad gave me as a store opening present, slit the envelope open and slid out the contents, seeing it was not a catalog.

It seemed to be a pile of photos and paper.

A thick, embossed, cream notecard was attached to the top with a gold paperclip, and the card said in bold black, SAVE YOUR MONEY.

And chillingly, this wasn't all it said.

It ended with, YOUR UNCLE WILL ALWAYS LOOK OUT FOR YOU.

It ended with a distinctive -R.

This was chilling because Mom was an only child and Dad had one sibling.

A sister.

And her husband's name was William.

Even with that mysterious initial, my uncle could only be...

"Corey," I whispered, pulling the card away and seeing a black and white 8 x 10 of a very attractive, mature—what seemed from the gray shading in the photo—blonde lady.

I didn't understand.

I shuffled through the papers.

More pictures and a report.

This report read like a detective's report.

A detective's report—I flipped forward to see—at its end was signed again simply "-R."

A detective's report on a woman named Susan Shepherd.

The woman my father was unfaithful to my mother with.

Mom officially engaged to, and happily ensconced with Duncan, in the days after Christmas, I had hired a PI to find out who she was.

I had not done this out of malice or spite or misguided curiosity, because I might occasionally dabble in the first two, my curiosity was *never* misguided.

I'd done it because I knew my father. And knowing him, I knew he would never, *not ever*, cheat on my mother with just anybody.

Whoever she was, she'd meant something to him.

Whoever she was, they'd connected, and not just physically.

And Mom was now ecstatically happy with Bowie.

I needed...

And I could not emphasize this enough...

I *needed* Dad to be happy too.

However, even though I paid my PI far too much money, he'd been coming up with zilch.

It was, apparently, the secret of the ages.

Until whoever this R was who sent this.

Whoever that was being someone who did the bidding of a dead man.

And whoever that was was very good at what he did. Because I didn't hire a hack.

And this mystery detective had found her.

Not only found her…

I sifted through the pile…

I had everything on her.

Name. Address. Email. Cell. Education. Social.

She was wealthy (I had bank records).

She'd moved to Phoenix from Indiana a few years ago.

And she was infamous, but not of her own doing.

She'd been, some years ago, kidnapped by a serial killer.

She'd barely survived his final rampage.

I'd heard of this guy, in the peripherals of living life, like you learn of people like this.

Everyone had.

Dennis Lowe.

My God.

My God.

My phone rang.

Staring at all that was now strewn across my pristine desk, I reached for my cell, not even looking at it, and I took the call.

I put it to my ear.

"Hello?"

"Are you gonna hold my coat hostage, or what?"

I shook my head a little, still staring down at the emotional carnage on my desk. "Sorry?"

"Chloe?"

Susan Shepherd.

She wasn't as beautiful as Mom, but she was very pretty.

Very pretty.

And she'd been kidnapped by a *serial killer.*

God, Dad.

Such a sweet sucker for the damsel in distress.

"Chloe."

"Yes?" I whispered.

Nothing on the phone until, "Babe, you okay?"

I laughed. Laughed and laughed.

But nothing was funny.

"*Chloe.*" That was sharp.

"Sure," I stated fake-breezily, but I couldn't quite wring out the depths of sarcasm infused in that one word. "I'm fine. *Parfait.*"

Perfect.

I'd had that once.

A perfect life.

"What?"

"Perfect," I whispered, concentrating.

Concentrating very hard at not coming apart at the seams.

"Where are you?"

"Sorry?"

"Where...*are*...you?"

"In my office."

"In Phoenix?"

"Of course."

"*Fuck,*" he clipped.

His intense frustration brought me fully into the conversation.

A conversation I was having *with Judge Oakley.*

"Why are you being rude?" I snapped.

"Because you're two hours away, and not at Duncan's, which I can get to in fifteen minutes."

Why was he saying this?

"If you want your coat so bad, Judge, I'll see to it that you get it."

Though, he'd have to wait because I'd brought it home with me, and I would not admit to anyone but myself that was far from an oversight when I'd packed to come back to Phoenix on New Year's.

What could I say?

It smelled like him.

"I don't give a fuck about my coat, Chloe."

"Is that not why you called?" I asked.

"It was, until you sounded a second away from bursting into tears."

Oh no.

He already knew far too much.

"Now, we're talking about something else," he concluded.

"I'm fine," I declared.

"You are *now*. A second ago, you were losing it."

God damn it.

"I was fine then too," I lied.

Poorly.

Even I could hear how hollow that sounded.

Usually, I was a virtuoso with a little white lie. I'd been honing my craft since before I could form coherent sentences.

Case in point, I remembered stealing a donut when Dad wasn't looking. I was two. When he turned around and asked who did it, regardless of the fact I held the purloined donut in my toddler fingers, I pointed at Matt, who I wasn't sure had teeth yet.

Or perhaps that wasn't a memory and just that Dad *and* Mom told that story to *everybody*.

Judge seemed to leach me of this genius, which was tremendously annoying.

"I see," he said disbelievingly. "So what you mean is that you had time to pull your act together, and I use the word 'act' purposefully."

"I can't even *begin* to imagine who gave *you* my telephone number so you could delight me with your insights into my character when you *barely know me*."

"Harvey."

I harumphed, and I didn't care that my doing so made him emit an appealing, surprised chuckle.

I carried on talking.

"Well, he's off my Christmas list and I've known him mere months.

However, in those months, Christmas occurred, so he will feel that sting, I assure you."

"You're that good with giving presents?"

"I am a master at accessorizing," I bragged without the least bit of humility because the subject didn't deserve it. I *was* a master at these things. "I am a master at wine pairings. I am a master at space-economizing packing. And I am a master at gift giving."

I decided not to include my talent with lying in that list since, so far, I had yet to demonstrate it to him.

Not to mention other reasons.

"Space-economizing packing?"

"When on holiday, each day requires three outfits, Judge," I retorted like he was dimwitted. "*You* go to Paris for a week and try to fit everything you'll need in the two measly seventy-pound bags you're limited to without mastering the art of space economy. Specifically, when you'll be shopping whilst there, so you'll need extra space for your return."

He burst out laughing.

I should have hung up.

I didn't.

I listened.

Because it was deep and rich and full of humor and life.

I had learned Judge Oakley did not hold back when he laughed.

It was a remarkably satisfying sound.

Though, I did listen while drumming my fingers on my desk, due to, I told myself, impatience when it was actually (I refused to admit) that I hated I was listening to it over the phone rather than in person.

"Three outfits?" he asked through his residual chuckles.

"Yes. With shoe changes." Pause, then, so he could understand fully, "And handbag changes."

"No airline gives you two seventy-pound bags," he informed me.

"They do in first class."

"'Course they do," he murmured, humor tingeing his tone.

"Lest you forgot, I'm filthy rich," I told him, not knowing if I did it trying to repulse him or test him (and this was an actual successful lie, because my parents were, but regardless of my healthy trust fund (which I didn't count because I didn't earn it), I was not).

"You'd think a rich chick wouldn't steal a guy's coat," he teased.

If it was a test, which I decided it wasn't (though it was), he would have passed.

Time to end this.

"Judge—"

"*Parfait* means perfect in..." He let that trail for me to fill in the blank.

"French."

"Right. You speak it?"

"I lived there for three years."

"Right. Seems a natural fit. I'm surprised you came back."

"My beloved grandmother died, then my parents' long, loving marriage disintegrated," I stated coldly.

And then my uncle blew his brains all over a priceless painting.

His tone was vastly different, just as mine had been.

But his was as warm as his laugh, though without the humor.

"Chloe—"

"I'll get the coat to Bowie."

"You'll *get* it to him? Can't he just bring it to the store from the house?"

Damn, *damn.*

Shit.

"I mistakenly packed it," I sniffed.

"You can't *mistakenly* pack an overcoat."

He was *so* right.

God.

"Especially you," he continued, "being a master at space-economizing packing and all."

I walked right into that one.

What had become of me?

"Are you quite finished haranguing me about your coat?" I demanded.

"Sure. I can be finished *haranguing* you about my coat if you'll talk to me about why you sounded like your world was ending when you picked up the phone."

"I've said repeatedly I'm fine."

"*Parfait*, which I don't know French, I still think it also might mean *bullshit*."

"You might not be done," I stated acidly. "But I am."

"Don't hang up on me, Chloe, please," he said quickly.

I hesitated.

And then his voice became soft, gentle.

God.

Beautiful.

"Talk to me."

So beautiful.

So dangerous.

"I'll get the coat to you, Judge."

"Chloe—"

"As soon as I can."

"Give it to me yourself."

Seeing him again, in his tall, rustic, brown-eyed, broad-shouldered wonder?

Not on my life.

"Goodbye, Judge."

"Chloe—"

I hung up.

I then turned the sound off my phone, set it face down on my desk, and I did not see the contents of the file on my father's lover scattered across my desk.

I heard Judge saying, *Because you're two hours away, and not at Duncan's, which I can get to in fifteen minutes.*

He didn't care about his coat.

He heard in my voice that something was wrong, and he was going to come to me.

He was annoyed that getting to me would take too long.

And he barely knew me.

But he was going to come to me.

My phone lit from underneath, someone was calling.

Or calling back.

I plopped in my chair with not even a nuance of my carefully cultivated elegance and stared at a picture of the very attractive Susan Shepherd on my desk, not thinking that this woman had played a part in turning my life upside down.

I did it thinking, *He was going to come to me.*

And then I shoved that thought aside and wrote myself a note to fire my private investigator.

Tout de suite.

CHAPTER 7

THE TEXTS

Chloe

*T*wo days later, I had somewhere to be, and I needed to get into my red Evoque and get there, but instead I was sitting at my desk at the store, torturing myself by scrolling through a variety of text strings.

Text string one, Matt.

Me, five days ago: *We need to speak.*

Also me, four days ago: *I think you know by now, you can't avoid me forever.*

And he did. He knew I'd fly to Indiana, if I had to, just to get in his face and put an end to this grudge he was holding.

Another me, yesterday: *At least tell me how things are going at Purdue. Sully says you're neck deep in studies. But your sister would like to hear from you directly. Are you all right?*

Point of note, Sully was in his final year at Purdue, and before we even knew Sully, Matt had been accepted in veterinarian school there, ditching his final year of med school in LA to switch medicines. He'd started his first semester there just days ago. Boon for him, he knew someone there. Bummer for him, I'd checked (daily) and the weather there was so far from what it was in LA, it wasn't funny.

It was a ballsy move (these not unknown for Matt to pull) that fortunately didn't make either Mom or Dad angry at him.

They wanted him to be happy.

I did too.

I also wanted him to talk to me.

Another point of note, all those texts from me, even if there were days in between, they were back-to-back.

Matt hadn't responded.

Still.

Text string two, Sasha.

Me, five days ago: *You know you can't hold a grudge.*

Nothing from Sasha for two whole days.

I was rather proud of myself for having patience through those days before I tried again.

Me: *I have Free People samples.*

Sash: *Really?*

Important to note at this juncture that this was evidence of the advantages of a little white lie.

Me: *No. But we need to go to lunch or have coffee or go eat cupcakes, do something SatC or we'll lose our sister cards.*

Sash: *I'm up in Prescott. Next week?*

Like it was harder for her to schedule me in her nothing than it was for me to schedule her into my whirlwind life in the Valley of the Sun.

Me: *Tuesday. Breakfast Club at the Biltmore. Ten o'clock.*

Sash: *Yippee!*

Me: [gif of Marie from the *Aristocats* rolling her eyes]

Sash: [gif of humongous teddy bear blowing a kiss]

Although I was upset (and let's face it, aggravated, he *really* needed to get over himself) at my estrangement with Matt, I was happy Sasha was moving on.

However, the person I'd want to talk to about the file I got from the mysterious R would be Matt. That said, I would never in a million years (at this juncture) talk to him about it, what was in it, how I got it, and how it seemed Uncle Corey was still up to his bullshit machinations beyond the grave and how creepy that was even if it might also be a boon.

It also came with more emotions about Uncle Corey, ones I battened the hatches down on tightly because I was not going to go there.

But I needed to talk to someone about it, and not Mi-Young because…well, it was family stuff.

I trusted her implicitly.

Even so, it didn't need to be said this ran deeper.

In other words, I was weighing the options of talking about it to Sasha.

However, she seemed…*fragile* somehow. Her usual breezy, cheery self that was her even when she wasn't all boho but instead preppy and overachieving was still in place. She was the quintessential sunny California girl, no matter what clothes she wore.

It just seemed like a façade now.

She knew I had designs on helping Dad find some happiness (okay, plotting toward that).

But that file was something else.

The last text string was, you guessed it, with Judge.

He'd started it.

Judge, not long after our conversation: *Hanging up. Uncool.*

I'd ignored that.

The next morning, from Judge: *Ghosting. Even more uncool.*

Point of note, I prided myself on my iron will. To my recollection, of my nearly quarter of a century on this planet, I'd worked tirelessly to fortify it, starting in kindergarten, when my bestest, best, bestie Brittany was being bullied by that little fucker, Andrew. He'd push her over. She'd cry. The teacher would be all touchy, feely, let's-discuss-our-actions, on *both* parts, even Britt's, when she did nothing but be cute and shy and an easy target, and our teacher wanted this discussion when we were *five*.

As I saw it, the actions were, he pushed her because he was a spoiled little shit, she fell down, and it made her cry.

Even though I knew my parents would lose their minds, when I'd had enough, I did what I had to do.

Consequences be damned, the next time he'd pushed her, I'd gone right up to him and punched him in the sternum as hard as my little girl arm could do it.

He'd howled like I'd cut him with a blade.

And then it had been *Andrew* who'd been causing havoc for weeks, but *I* got in serious shit with the teacher and principal discussing with my parents my "alarming" tendency toward violence.

Mom and Dad were pissed and worried (incidentally, I distinctly remember Uncle Corey winking at me when he'd been at the house and Mom told him this story).

I found even at five I cared about the worried, but not the pissed.

I also learned from that incident.

Don't do something, for yourself or someone else, that'll get your ass in a sling.

Be smarter.

From then, to now, I made it my mission to do just that.

Go forth.

Do what I had to do for myself or someone I loved.

Damn the consequences.

But when I did it, be smart about it.

And I very much wanted to guard my heart which meant, in all that was happening in my life and the lives of the ones I loved, guard my peace of mind when it came to Judge.

But for some reason I could not fathom, I found it impossible to allow him to think I was ghosting him.

Though, I did make him wait precisely one and a half hours before I responded to his ghosting accusation.

Me: *You don't know this about me, because you don't know me, but I'm a busy girl.*

Judge, playing no games (Lord help me with this man), this coming immediately: *You OK?*

Me, timing it for sixteen minutes later: *I was okay yesterday.*

Judge, again immediately: *You were lying yesterday.*

Me, giving it nearly twenty-seven minutes that time: *You're delusional.*

Judge, after only maybe five minutes passed: *Whatever. Are you timing your responses so I won't think you're into me?*

Annoying!

Me: *Cad.*

Judge: *I've gone from asshole and dick to player to cad. I have to look up cad, but I think that's progress.*

Me: *Is there some reason you're bothering me? I ask this because, you might have missed it with your selective male ears, but I DID mention previously I was a busy girl.*

Judge: *Just wanna check in on my coat. It was a gift. I wanna make sure you're taking real good care of it.*

I knew he was teasing, flirting, but I found this snippet of information about Judge interesting.

And it was then it occurred to me that I'd given a lot away in our few meetings, but he'd given nothing away.

I knew he was beautiful.

I knew I loved his laugh.

I knew preliminary research showed he was an exceptionally skilled kisser.

I knew he worked for Duncan.

I knew the work he did for Duncan provided evidence that he might genuinely be a good guy (when he wasn't acting like a cad, of course).

And I now knew someone gave him that fabulous coat.

That was all I knew.

It did nothing for my peace of mind, it clanged mightily against my iron will.

But still, I did it.

I asked.

Me: *A gift?*

Judge: *From my dad.*

Me: *He has good taste.*

Judge: *In everything but women.*

Then another one from Judge on the heels of that: *Though he's proved he can learn.*

Uh-oh, uh-oh, *uh-oh.*

Clang! Clang! Clang!

My mental alarm went Defcon One as the assault to my shields went in overdrive.

Because this did not intrigue me.

I *needed* to know what that meant.

Needed it.

I knew he was trouble.

I didn't know the letters in the name "Judge" spelled *d-i-s-a-s-t-e-r.*

So, of course, this was when I ghosted him.

I'd heard from him twice right after that: *You there?* and *You get busy?*

And I'd heard from him this morning: *Get too real for you?*

Then...nothing.

Nothing from me in return.

Therefore, now I had Matt still angry with me. Sasha being too... whatever she was, to deal with the file our dead Uncle Corey had some mastermind private dick procure for me. When he started getting real, I'd blown off Judge precisely as he said I had. Making that worse, he was doing it sharing about himself.

And I needed to get my ass in my car so I could go over to Dad's house because Bowie and Mom were down from Prescott, we were having dinner together (at Dad's!) because they had something to talk to me about.

All Dad would say about it was, "A project we want you to get involved in."

I did not want to have dinner with my beloved father, my beloved mother, and my mother's beloved fiancé, who I also was falling in love with, but who was not my dad.

I further did not want to get involved in a project with the three of them.

A project I knew, without them telling me, was their way to make sure the PR around Mom and Bowie being together, and Mom and Dad not, and all of us being family anyway, stayed positive. This, no matter that Uncle Corey's bitchface ex, Samantha, had told the world on a YouTube gossip show that Dad cheated on Mom.

(Don't worry, at the time, we'd lied and said she lied. Still, that fix was far too easy in the midst of the brouhaha when stuff like that could go underground only to surface at a later date, strike, and then you're dying of venom poisoning before you knew the snake was even there. And one thing I hated most in this world was snakes.)

So, no.

I did not want any of this.

Even so, I turned off my phone, shut down my laptop and put it away, cleared my desk, grabbed my bag and headed out to my car.

CHAPTER 8

THE GREENWAY

Chloe

I wanted to hate it.

But it was impossible.

Dad's flying-solo house was *everything*.

Situated in a posh, quiet, golf course community with a club that had tennis courts he could use, large lots for the houses and a strict HOA policy that decreed you could not park on the street, it was located in an up, up, upper scale area between Scottsdale proper and North Scottsdale.

My favorite parts of the house were the wall of windows that faced Dad's black-mosaic tiled pool with adjacent hot tub and a minimalistic water feature that ran in a soothingly slow river in a raised section down one side of the pool to peacefully fall into it at the far end. This as well as Dad's enormous kitchen that had solid ash, smooth-front cabinetry topped with white quartz that was three inches thick.

His firepits (both of them) didn't suck either.

I had, in the many mental ramblings I'd been assailed with since their marriage disintegrated, wondered if the move to the high-rise

Mom kept when they split was one of the blows their marriage had suffered.

Dad was a house man. He never quite fit in Mom's condo. And I thought of it more as *her* condo even when Dad lived in it with her, also even before she gutted it after he left and made it all glamor. It had been beautiful and roomy when Dad was there, and the views were insane, but he'd always seemed like a fish out of water.

Nevertheless, Dad had been all-in to move from LA to Phoenix. Tennis. Golf. Cycling. Hiking. Wide open spaces that weren't an hour and a half's drive away, and some of them were right in town. It was an active person's haven, regardless of the sweltering summer heat.

In fact, thinking on this as I pulled into his drive, he never fit in LA either.

We were there, thus *he* was there because Mom's work, for the most part (unless she was on location), was there.

If it had been his choice, we probably would have grown up in Phoenix, or somewhere in Florida. Not Cali at all with its traffic, mudslides, wildfires and earthquakes. Definitely not LA.

Tom Pierce was private. He hated the traffic. He detested the smog. And even if he had politically liberal tendencies, he leaned toward a conservative lifestyle.

I parked with these new thoughts uncomfortably tumbling in my head, because I wanted to be one of those women who were one and done with cheaters.

But my dad was not that man.

And it forced me to face the fact that there were reasons behind anything, including betrayal.

Which brought me to now, considering how much he gave of himself so Mom could have what she needed in ways none of us realized.

Including Mom.

Also, maybe, Dad.

I was so stuck on these thoughts, until that moment when I'd angled out of my car, I hadn't noticed that not only was Bowie's Tesla

SUV parked in Dad's drive, a velvet-red Jeep Cherokee was parked there too.

Apparently, someone else was coming to dinner, or at least they were at the house, because I had looked at Cherokees when Dad helped me buy my car (thus knew the term "velvet-red," which I thought was lush, the name and the color). And though Dad had helped, and he'd favored the Cherokee, he didn't own a Jeep.

The garage door was open, so I went through the space, hitting the interior door, which I went through too.

I entered a tidy mudroom that had Dad's running shoes lined up with his golf shoes, plus his clubs, as well as a large, bespoke bag I knew contained no less than five tennis rackets.

Just Dad's collection of sports stuff seemed to belie high-rise living, which didn't afford mud rooms and tons of storage space.

I passed the door to the utility room on my way into the kitchen, calling, "*Je suis ici!*"

I hit Dad's kitchen and the first person I saw standing there was...

Judge.

What the hell?

"Are you stalking me?" I demanded.

He grinned.

"Word was, you two knew each other," Dad said, and I dragged my gaze from Judge to watch Dad approaching me wearing faded jeans and a lightweight, dove gray sweater.

Tall, lean but broad along the shoulders, incredibly handsome, threads of silver in his dark hair, he'd given me that (mine without the silver...yet, though, mine could have also come from my grandmother, either way worked for me) and his eyes.

Until Judge, I'd thought no other man was more beautiful than my dad.

No.

Wait.

I didn't just think *until Judge*.

(But I did.)

"Hello, beautiful," Dad murmured before he leaned in and kissed my cheek.

"Father," I greeted curtly.

He pulled back with brows drawn at my tone as he looked at me.

"Hello, darling," Mom greeted, swanning in wearing white jeans, a tan belt, and a soft denim shirt, cute tan booties on her feet.

An outfit of which I approved, mostly because I'd purchased each piece for her, and then I'd spent two hours with her in her closet explaining the variety of outfits she was allowed to create with the different pieces.

That outfit being one.

I met her halfway, and we did a continental kiss, brushing our lips on each cheek.

"Hey there," Bowie rumbled his greeting next, and it was accompanied by a warm hug.

When he let me go, I looked pointedly at him, at Mom, then to Judge.

Bowie did not miss my meaning.

"We're here to talk about Tom and me doing some PR stuff for the Kids and Trails program," he explained.

This made absolute sense.

And none whatsoever.

Perfect for PR not only for the program, but for our family.

Havoc on my brain.

"I see this is an excellent idea, however, I'm uncertain what part I play in it," I noted.

"We want you and Judge to produce the project, which should be video, digital and print," Mom said, and she did this looking all over my face, except in my eyes.

They'd seen me and Judge on Bowie's veranda. They'd maybe even seen us kissing.

And thus, now, they were matchmaking.

In so doing, they were throwing me and Judge together with an offer I couldn't refuse.

Oh. My. God!

How infuriating!

I mean, even though he ran the program, so he knew it far better than me.

And even though I knew all the players and had an innate talent for branding and marketing (if I did say so myself, which I did), not to mention, ran my own mutual aid program that might not be flourishing, but it worked.

So, this made sense.

And even though I had utterly no qualms with interfering in the lives of people I loved, case in point, me conniving to get Mom and Bowie together, and there Mom and Bowie were...together.

Still!

"We thought we'd talk about it over dinner," Dad entered the conversation. "Nail some things down. Get it started."

His *get it started* really meant *get it done* so he didn't have to hang out with Bowie for too long.

Mom and Bowie had reunited in September. It was now January.

But I knew that was nowhere near long enough for anyone to get used to the fact the love of their life had moved on.

Suddenly, I was getting ticked.

At Mom.

And not for her intervening with me and Judge.

But for her being entirely clueless about what she was doing to Dad.

Naturally, this meant I turned right to Judge and bit off, "We need to talk. Outside."

I then tossed my bag on Dad's kitchen table and flounced out the glass door that was one of several in the house that led to the back yard. And believe me, I was a girl who could *flounce*, and I didn't hesitate to put all my flouncing abilities into that one.

I also did not stop in the firepit seating area that was close to the house.

I did not head to the hot tub area that was also close to the house.

I headed beyond the pool, out to the remote seating area that sat on the edge of Dad's lot that butted, over a fence, a large strip of greenway that provided a wide, gorgeous, desert-landscaped buffer (however this "desert" had lush, green grass and numerous tall, shady trees). This was situated between the houses on Dad's side and the houses on the other side.

It had walking trails and some practice putting greens, not to mention attractive exercise areas.

Totally Dad.

The pads on the built-in semicircle bench that surrounded another firepit were black with white piping.

His furnishings around the pool area and throughout the house were divine, partially because I micromanaged his interior designer until (I was pretty sure) she was *this close* to quitting.

We got the job done, though.

When I whirled on Judge, I wanted to be surprised that he was right behind me—no lag, he was with me all the way—but I wasn't.

I also wanted this not to feel awesome.

But it did.

"Right," I launched in, "we need to handle this."

He shoved his hands in his jeans pockets.

Jeans and a black Henley.

A tightfitting one.

I'd already sensed he had a magnificent chest, this item of apparel just proved it and I hadn't even seen him with his shirt off.

Lord, this man.

"Handle what?" he asked.

I didn't begin to open my mouth in answer before he went on.

"By the way, it's super fucking cool what you do to assist women in getting better gigs."

It was good my mouth was still closed; I could grit my teeth immediately.

He grinned at me again.

He then said, "Ice queen, my ass."

My jig was up.

"I'm going kill my mother," I stated casually, like I considered this activity every day.

Another grin.

Then, from him, "Do you ever wear anything other than heels?"

I was in mustard houndstooth slacks with a drop, double swoop, gold chainlink belt at the front, a slim, cream turtleneck and a pair of fire-engine red pumps.

"I came here direct from work, but…yes," I answered.

"Baby, those shoes," he murmured, low and hot. "My favorites so far."

"*Stop flirting*," I hissed.

He took his hands out of his pockets to cross his arms on his chest, which made his pecs bulge against the thermal fabric.

God damn it.

"Right. You're being serious. What are we handling?" he asked.

I felt a finger of happiness trail down my spine at the word "we" in that final sentence.

I ignored it.

"We need to get this done, no muss, no fuss, no delays. Preferably, having a working concept by Friday, have the project complete next week."

Slowly, his eyebrows rose.

"Say again?" he demanded.

"Completion date next week."

"Friday is tomorrow," he told me something I knew.

"It is," I confirmed I knew it.

"Chloe, I know you're pretending you're not into me—"

"Oh, for God's sake," I grumbled.

"But there is no way in fuck we can get this done properly in a week."

I lifted my nose.

Just a smidge.

"Well, I don't want my father dragged through this any longer than necessary, so what do you think? Two weeks? Most, three? And we handle them through technology. Until we produce the video, Dad isn't involved physically at all. And if we can manage it, his stuff will be shot separate."

Judge looked confused.

And then he did not.

"Chloe," he said gently.

Yes, he figured it out.

I said nothing.

He took a step closer, and his voice was quieter when he said, "Okay, honey, I get you, but they both sound really into this idea. Tom and Duncan came up with it, and they seem willing to work together on it."

"My father would run through a hail of gunfire to make my mother happy."

Oh no.

Oh *shit*.

Was I going to cry?

I turned my head a tad and got myself together.

When I faced him again, his expression told me he didn't miss anything.

Not a thing.

And just that expression was going to make me lose it.

"Don't be nice to me, Judge," I whispered.

"Okay, baby, I'll start being a dick again."

"Okay, good," I said shakily.

He didn't start being a dick.

He just looked at me like he wanted to be Superman so he could scoop me into his arms and fly away.

"You're being nice!" I accused.

"Right, right." He nodded. "Uh…"

He said no more.

I narrowed my eyes at him. "Can you *not* be a dick?"

He shrugged. "I want that for you, but I'm coming up with nothing."

"You didn't have a problem with it when we first met," I reminded him.

"I wanted your attention when we first met. I've got it now."

"Argh!" I griped then stomped to the chest-high fence that separated Dad's space from the communal space.

I glared at the deep, perfectly clipped flowering hedge that stood in the way of the fence and the thick strip of green grass before the walking trail started.

Privacy without privacy.

An unobstructed view with obstructions.

Ingenious.

I folded my arms on top of the fence and looked out at the view without seeing it.

I felt Judge come up beside me and lean into his side, facing me.

"Probably a waste of my breath, but still gonna ask you to talk to me," he said.

God help me, I didn't deny him.

I went for it.

"Mom's happy. Deliriously so. She and Bowie were really...they were...they were really..." I cleared my throat, "in love. Back in the day."

"Yeah, I heard," he said softly.

"And, um...*now.*"

"I noticed."

"So, she's all in with that and she doesn't get..."

I trailed off.

Judge picked it up.

"That your dad's still in love with her."

I looked up at him. "She gets it, she's just..."

I again couldn't finish.

Judge again did it for me.

"In her bubble."

I turned away, muttering irritably, "Something like that."

"It's more?"

"It's clueless," I told the greenway.

"Pardon?"

I tipped my head to him. "Clueless. And actually, thoughtless. I mean, the reasons why...the whole thing behind...the split...wasn't...

good." I was talking haltingly because I had to talk, get it out, but I couldn't do it and give anything away. I found it easy to talk to him (as much as that peeved me), but he was nowhere near being a member of my very tight Circle of Trust. "But her doing this, her being okay with this, being a part of it, championing it is almost...cruel."

"Cut her some slack, honey," he suggested gently. "She's allowed her happiness."

"At the expense of someone else?"

"Yes."

My head jerked.

"Happiness is worth anything," he declared.

Oh my.

He kept going.

"Your dad is going to be okay. He's a mature adult who knows better than you where he's at. If he couldn't handle this, he'd have said no."

"I'm not sure about that."

"He still didn't say no, and if he can't handle it, and he agreed to it, how is that on her?"

I'd been looking at him.

Now I was glaring at him.

As it seemed with me (not that I was hiding it), Judge didn't miss anything.

Which had to be why he asked, "Why are you suddenly pissed at me?"

"Because you're making sense and you being logical doesn't fit with my mini-tantrum."

A pop of his dimple and, "Ah."

"I still want this done quickly."

"For your dad?"

I turned to face him. "You're right about all you said. But the fact remains, he's in hell and he might be willing to do a good thing for your program because it's something that's close to his heart. He's always given time to anything that gets kids into sports or interested in stepping away from their TVs and PlayStations, getting outside and being active. This will still kill. And I want him to do what he feels he needs to do for Mom and Bowie, our family and the people who could benefit from the program. But I don't want it to last forever."

"You got plans this weekend?"

Of course I did.

"Why?" I asked.

"It's Thursday and we can't get started on it unless we get started on it. What are you doing this weekend?"

"Saturday during the day, I work. In the late afternoon/evening, Cooking Club with Mi-Young and her boyfriend, Jacob. We will consume that then go to a speakeasy and consume beverages. Brunch on Sunday with my friend Tiffany."

"I like to cook."

I stared at him.

Then I inquired, "Are you inviting yourself to Cooking Club?"

"Sure."

"We can't get program work done while we're frying chicken thighs," I noted.

"Back up, what *is* Cooking Club?"

"Once a month, me, Mi-Young and Jacob get together and cook a three-course meal, from scratch, from start to finish."

He loved this idea. I could tell.

"Who's Mi-Young?"

"My best friend and business associate."

"She work with you on your Fabulous Foot Forward program?"

Dear Lord, he even knew the name of my baby.

Totally going to kill my mother.

"Yes," I clipped.

"So she might have some good ideas and she knows your family dynamic, including the recent addition of Duncan."

Damn it.

"Yes, but—"

"So we can cook and brainstorm."

"You live two hours away and we're not done until late, and that's even before the speakeasy."

"I got buds down here I can crash on their couch."

"Do you also have an answer to everything?" I asked fake-sweetly.

"When it comes to you, no. But I'm learning."

Time to get over my emotion, get over how easy it was to talk to him, open up to him, and get us back on track...

That being both of us on different ones.

"Judge, I think—"

"You got a full-time job, I got a full-time job, and we live two hours away from each other. So, Chloe, we can either fit this in when and where, or we can make room for it. What's it going to be?"

"I don't like being backed in a corner," I noted crossly.

"I hate to point this out, but you put yourself there, babe. I got time. None of those folks inside have asked for a rush job. It's you who wants us to get this done quick. If you wanna take care of your dad, call your friends and tell them to buy a couple more chicken thighs."

"The. Club. Is. At. Mine. This. Time," I said through clenched teeth.

This delighted him.

Openly.

"Perfect," he decreed. "Text me your address."

He was so very wrong.

It was not *perfect*.

But someone had to look after my dad.

And with Matt across the country (and not talking to me) and Sasha...whatever she was, that was down to me.

Like it was always down to me with everything, one way or another.

So it was the only avenue available.

And thus, I had no choice but to take it.

Therefore, on a nod which received a blinding smile from Judge, I did.

CHAPTER 9

THE IVY

Corey

 wo years ago...

AS HE FOLDED OUT OF THE BACK OF HIS CHAUFFEUR-DRIVEN CAR, COREY saw her out on the patio of The Ivy, a rare flower amidst a riot of blooms, and he was not surprised at the sunglasses on her nose that were so enormous, Jackie O would be envious.

He knew she wore them not only because they were uber chic and she looked good in them, but they were perfect for her to hide behind.

There were a few things Chloe needed to hide from these days, he suspected.

Big things.

He walked up the narrow path to the front door of the restaurant through its close mass of people on the patio, ignoring the looks he was getting.

Corey was wearing his own Tom Ford sunglasses, but even so, he was a man that was very rarely missed.

Because of this, his bodyguards, both of them, were not joining them, but they weren't far away in watching his progress to Chloe's table.

Corey dipped his chin to the maître d' as he passed, and the man didn't bother offering him a mimosa or glass of champagne, which was standard practice upon arrival for brunch at The Ivy.

Corey had been there before, more than once, and it was known he did not drink during the day.

Ever.

He didn't because it made him groggy and lethargic, and until he fell into bed every night at midnight or one o'clock, he did not allow himself to be groggy or lethargic.

Ever.

When he arrived at the table, she had her face tipped up to him— that striking heart-shaped face that was the same shape as her mother's.

He stooped and kissed her cheek, already knowing someone, somewhere would take a picture. And that someone, somewhere, would likely sell it. And the photos of their brunch would be captioned by some human parasite who made a living from other people's successes and failures.

And Corey knew that Chloe Pierce, as the daughter of his best friends—one of those friends more famous even than he—would not be mistaken as Corey's latest arm candy.

They'd been seen together many times before, all the way back to when she was a baby.

Family brunch with tech tycoon Corey Szabo and Chloe Pierce, eldest product of the power couple, Imogen Swan and Tom Pierce, Szabo's closest friends, was a possibility.

Though, Chloe's name might not be mentioned at all.

But Imogen's would, certainly. Tom's was a good probability.

Corey wondered how Chloe felt about being the "eldest product" or "daughter of" and never really being Chloe.

He suspected she wouldn't voice her opinion out loud.

Nevertheless, she undoubtedly hated it.

He took his seat with his back to the patio, she was against the brick wall, framed in The Ivy's famed patio foliage, and a server was there immediately.

"Sparkling water and coffee," he ordered.

The server nodded and looked to Chloe.

All she said was, "Yes."

The man moved away.

Corey dipped his eyes and saw she had a mostly-consumed glass of champagne in front of her.

No fruit juice to get in the way of her alcohol.

A testimony to the times.

He'd noted that normally, Chloe was like Corey. She might find times to allow herself some freedom to be less than strictly in control of every breath of her life.

But those times were rare, and most likely when she was alone.

However, now, things were different.

"How are you?" he asked.

"Awful," she replied candidly. "How are you?"

"I'm well," he murmured. "Happy to see you."

"Really?" she queried. "That's a surprise since I haven't seen you since Gram's funeral."

This was catty.

They'd both been busy, he always was, and she was starting her store, and they lived in separate states, for fuck's sake.

A man would have to be mad or plain stupid not to know this cat had claws.

Corey just refused to be the target when she was aiming at someone else.

"Chloe," he said warningly.

She huffed out a breath and looked away from him.

"You're in LA on a buying trip?" he prompted when she seemed happy to study the cars parked on the street for the next hour.

She turned her attention to Corey.

"I'm here to escape."

He opened his mouth to offer another warning.

"He's moved out," she declared before he could. "Trial separation. But the way things are going, not that they share much, though we can tell, there's not going to be anything *trial* about it."

Corey leaned forward quickly and whispered a harsh, "*Quiet.*"

Her head jerked and her mouth slammed shut.

He did not move away, and he kept his voice as low as possible with her still being able to hear him when he ordered, "You do not speak of such things unless you know *precisely* who can hear them and you trust them *implicitly.*"

She didn't move, not a twitch, and she kept her sunglasses trained on him.

"And I hope you know that there are solely five people in that Circle of Trust and none of those people, save me, are sitting mere inches from you on this patio," he continued.

She drew a delicate breath into her nose that stated eloquently, in pure Chloe fashion, that she was irritated to be reminded, as well as remonstrated, about something she knew very well...but in her emotion, she forgot.

Then, because he needed to know, in his bones and soul he needed this knowledge, he broke his own rule and demanded, "Right, just tell me, are you looking after her?"

He meant Genny, to whom the impossible had happened.

Tom had cheated on her.

He'd admitted it.

They were attempting counseling.

This was failing.

And now, apparently, Tom had moved out.

After more than two decades, *finally*, this had opened the door to Corey. One he'd attempted to open years ago by tearing Genny and Duncan apart.

Those years ago, she had not stepped through.

And Corey knew, regrettably he knew this down to his bones and soul, she wouldn't eventually step through this time either.

Gen adored her husband, this betrayal had wrecked her.

And she had worshipped Duncan, and his loss had nearly destroyed her.

Corey had been in her life since she was eight. If she was going to grow those types of feelings for him, it would have happened already.

But now the door was opening.

A new door.

And it was opening.

Because he knew Duncan had, several years ago, undergone a divorce.

"Of course I am," she snapped, albeit quietly. "And him too."

Corey did not want to give that first shit about Tom.

However, Tom was the kind of man, just good through and through (which made this recent happenstance all the more shocking), where it was impossible to spend years knowing him, sharing time with him, being considered a part of his family, and not caring about him.

Corey had tried to do this.

It was a rare occurrence, but in this circumstance, he had failed.

So Corey allowed himself a vague sense of satisfaction that Chloe was seeing to things (though he'd never doubted it), not only taking care of Gen, but Tom as well.

"Matt and Sasha?" he demanded.

"Them too," she murmured, reaching for her champagne.

She turned her gaze away again as she sipped it.

He sat back and modulated his tone. "They're all right?"

He meant her brother and sister.

"Coping. As I said, I'm keeping an eye on things. We talk. We *all* talk, but Matt and Sash and I have our times to get things out. Just us."

"Good," he muttered and then moved as the server brought his coffee and water.

After the man had laid them down, he noticed both of them were ignoring the menus resting on their place settings.

"I'll return," he said, and drifted away.

Corey focused on Chloe, who, even if he couldn't see her eyes, he knew they were pointedly fixed on him.

"Yes?" he prompted when she said nothing.

"I'm looking after them," she stated.

He ignored the sugar and cream and lifted his coffee cup to take a sip of the black brew.

When he was finished and returning it to its saucer, he said, "I had no doubt. And I didn't mean to offend you, Chloe. But I'm sure you understand, considering the circumstances, why I had to ask."

"I'm looking after them," she repeated.

Corey's gaze intensified on her.

But he said nothing.

"So I'm looking after them," she said once again. "They're *all* looked after. Which begs the question, who's going to look after me?"

Corey relaxed.

He smiled.

And then he replied.

"Why, me. Who else?"

It took her a moment.

And then Corey was surprised at how honored he felt...

When Chloe relaxed too.

CHAPTER 10

THE OVERFLOW

Chloe

N̸ow...

MY DOORBELL WAS RINGING.

This wouldn't do.

I was a mess.

I was never a mess.

But I was a mess.

I'd changed my outfit three times, and in the end, decided to go for super casual.

A pair of distressed jeans and a gray T-shirt that said SURELY NOT EVERYONE WAS KUNG FU FIGHTING.

I paired these with bare feet, minimalist makeup (though, with a dewy highlight), my hair in a messy bun with just that perfect amount of trailing tendrils (that took me half an hour to achieve).

Accompanying this *ensemble* were the two-carat, princess-cut diamond earrings Mom and Dad bought me for my sixteenth birthday.

That was it for accessories.

I told myself this would make it easy, later, to throw on my patent-leather yellow Jimmy Choo pumps or my bow-tie detailed, robin's egg blue Prada, kitten heel slingbacks, tie a dashing scarf around my neck, shrug on a black blazer, and I'd be speakeasy ready.

What it was *not*, was an effort to show outdoorsy, down-to-earth Judge I could be down-to-earth too.

I further told myself I wasn't showing my playful side and that I could let my hair down, I was simply being comfortable in my own living space.

And I told myself Judge was just coming over to be in my home, with my friends, *and me*, to get the ball rolling on a project I wasn't looking forward to doing, but in the end, it'd do good for a lot of people.

I also told myself not to be concerned with the fact I'd sent an emergency text to Mom's housekeeper, Julietta, begging her to come over and make my townhome sparkly clean and tidy while I was covering at the store, something she'd not only agreed to do, she'd accomplished.

And I told myself I didn't do this in order to impress anyone who may soon be coming over with my stellar ability to juggle work, family and social lives, right alongside home, all of this swimmingly.

I told myself that I wasn't even yet twenty-five years old.

Therefore, this small two-bedroom, two-and-a-half bath, two-story townhome rental in the middle of the vibey bustle of downtown Phoenix was perfectly fine, rather than something bigger, grander, hipper, with a mortgage on it.

My kitchen with its white subway tile rising to the ceiling over white cabinets with black marble countertops, even if not large, was charming, with my plants in steel buckets and accoutrements in white, cream and crystal.

And my living room, with its streamlined, comfy beige twill couch and accompanying shocking-orange, fly-wing chairs atop a muted colored rug over black-and-gray, swirl glazed concrete floors and plant-based décor was both mod and chic as well as welcoming and comfortable.

All of this, I told myself, even if I had not yet been able to fully stamp the place with my personality, because I couldn't quite afford it. Not on my own dime. Not without dipping into my trust fund, which I'd already copiously dipped into.

And after having fun in France, and setting up the store, I now had this thing where, what I had, I would have because I'd earned it.

Thus, at this point, what I had wasn't a lot.

I told myself all this as I headed to the hall that contained the powder room that not only gave me an entry area but created an alcove in the kitchen were my stainless-steel kitchen sink was tucked away.

I also told myself I had time to get a handle on things.

Mi-Young was notoriously late.

Jacob was notoriously early.

It was 3:30 on the dot, when the festivities were set to begin, and I knew this doorbell would be them, splitting the difference.

I could pull myself together with them around. Not a problem.

Furthermore, surely Judge would be at least five, maybe ten minutes late not only due to his long drive, but also so he wouldn't perpetrate the rudeness of actually being on time.

However, I knew this hope was destined to be crushed as I traversed my short hall and saw through the glazed glass door, there was not the double-body of Mi-Young and Jacob.

It was the long body of Judge.

Right on time.

Drat the man.

I fought the need to duck into the powder room to check my hair, and instead arranged my face to mild disapproval and opened the door.

"I should have known," I said by way of greeting. "Right on time."

He looked me up and down but snagged on his down to read my tee.

He then burst out laughing.

God, that delicious, deep, no-holds-barred *laugh*.

It was like he was *trying* to irritate me.

I glared.

He caught my gaze and stated baldly, "Jesus, fuck, I really need to kiss you right now."

"You cannot," I denied. "We're simply acquaintances who were thrown together to do something worthy, but nonetheless the doing of it will be annoying."

"A hug?" he teased, that damned adorable and attractive dimple popping.

I rolled my eyes, stepped to the side, lifted a hand and gave it a flick to indicate he should come in, but I wasn't all that thrilled about the invitation.

His lips were twitching as he didn't hesitate to accept my invitation.

He stopped in the living room and looked around.

He then walked to the back door, which was not glazed glass, but clear as day, and peeked into my miniscule, fenced backyard.

He then turned to me.

"Your friends not here yet?"

I shook my head.

He nodded, looked up my stairs, then back to me before he asked, "No pets?"

"No," I forced out.

"You don't like them?"

"I have shared, I think more than once, that I'm a busy woman," I reminded him.

"Yeah, and I'm a busy guy, but I got an animal."

"Would you like something to drink?" I offered.

"This place not take animals?" he pushed.

"Yes, they do."

"But not cats, just dogs, and dogs need company, something you can't give, you being busy and all," he deduced.

"They accept cats."

He stared at me.

I stared back.

When this went on a perplexing amount of time, I queried, "Why are we discussing this?"

"Coming from the bathroom at Duncan's, I saw you down a hall, holding and cooing to a cat like it was your child."

I had indeed done that because my precious Tuck needed some loving care, what with all those nasty people around, traipsing through his domain.

"That was Tuck. He's Duncan's. Even so, he owns me. And as Tuck's minion, it's my responsibility to be available when he desires to lodge a complaint, something he was in need of doing, considering he's not a party type of feline," I shared.

Judge's lips turned up.

And then he remarked, "Considering your dedication to this servitude, I would doubly expect you to have your own."

"This seems a leap to make," I replied.

"Not really. You care way too deeply about the people in your life, not to mention the cat at Duncan's house, not to have something in that life that soaks up the overflow."

I sucked in a sharp breath.

He came to stand at the back of the couch and leaned a thigh against it, crossing his arms on that wide chest of his.

"So?" he demanded.

This was not his to have.

This was not getting-to-know-you time.

This was get-an-unwanted-task-started time.

My mind knew this (of a sort).

Apparently, my mouth didn't.

"I'm not allowed to have one," I admitted.

He appeared deeply shocked.

"Not allowed?"

"Again, do you want something to drink? I've decided on a signature cocktail for the evening. Homemade whisky sour."

"Are you allergic?"

God!

"Oh for goodness sakes," I snapped.

I then threw up my hands and gave in.

"When I rented this place, I went to the shelter and suffered temporary insanity, selected three cats and a dog for adoption and put in my application. Before I could pick them up, I told my mother I'd made these selections, and she lost her mind. Regardless, the shelter considered my living arrangements, and they would only allow me a single pet. They encouraged, due to my lack of outdoor space, a cat. I picked the worst off of my choices, Oscar, my darling, who had recently battled an untreated-for-too-long severe respiratory infection which caused his little kitty lungs some damage, making him prone to another one. We were careful, but alas, he contracted one. We fought it, his struggle was valiant, but he didn't make it for very long."

I took a deep breath so I could get through the last part, which was the hard part.

Then to be done with this, I gave it to him.

"I had him six months, which I hope were glorious for him. I'm still in mourning. Yes, I only had him six months, but he was a great cat. Truth is, I'm not ready. However, when I am, according to Mom, I'll either need to buy a farm or something akin to that, or I'm not allowed to go back to a shelter again on my own. There you go. Now, can we move on from this?"

"Totally knew you needed an overflow," he said quietly with an expression on his face as he gazed at me that I never wanted to see again.

Yes, it was *that* beautiful.

And therefore, *that* dangerous.

Ugh.

"Do you want a whisky sour, Judge?" I bit off.

"There's a lot of things I want right now," he replied.

Oh God.

I felt that in a variety of parts of me, and not all of them were physical.

I planted my hands on my hips and waited for him to get over it.

"But I'll take some water and we'll wait to make the sours when your friends get here," he allowed.

"Fine," I snapped, turned on my bare foot, and marched into the kitchen.

Judge followed me.

I opened my fridge door and asked, "Topo Chico with lime, Perrier or still spring?"

When he didn't answer, I looked over my shoulder at him standing at the butcher-block top, steel-based kitchen island I'd purchased to offer additional counterspace, a seating area and a delineation between cooking and living areas and saw him smirking at me.

"What now?" I asked.

"You sure you don't have five other varieties to offer me?"

Right.

That did it.

I closed the fridge door and turned to face him.

"Ground rules," I declared.

"This should be good," he muttered.

"*That*," I snapped, jabbing my finger at him. "That right there. None of that."

His brows went up. "None of what?"

"No teasing."

"Well, shit," he said through a grin.

A *flirtatious* grin.

Therefore, I added, "No flirting either."

"Hmm," he hummed but spoke no words.

"Also, no being super nice and thoughtful," I went on, determined, especially with this, to be thorough.

He leaned into a hand on my island and crossed his ankles like he had all night to talk about this and he was settling in.

Not to mention, looking forward to it.

"Okay, so what level of nice are we talking?" he inquired. "Like, low to medium nice or medium to high nice? Or should I just try to be a dick, so when I leave, your friends won't get in your shit about the fact you should date me seeing as we got great chemistry and I'm pretty sure we look perfect together."

I completely ignored that he was already breaking rule one, and possibly rule two, and I couldn't even begin to let his final words penetrate.

So I didn't.

"Solid medium nice is acceptable," I allowed, like I was taking him seriously. "Though, a few dickish remarks will be expected."

"We've already established I can't be a dick on command. I can only do it when I'm flirting with you. And you told me that's out, unless I can dickishly flirt with you?" He ended that on a suggestion.

But not a real one.

"Judge, I'm being serious," I warned him in a tone that was, I thought, quite serious.

"No, you're being hilarious, and cute, which, don't freak out. I'm sure no guy ever called you that because they've probably been too damned terrified of you. Oh...and you're also making me want to kiss you again."

"Judge—"

"Though I hadn't really stopped."

"Judge!"

"And you should know, the urge was nearly overwhelming when you told the Oscar story."

"Oh my God," I cried. "Every time I think you couldn't be more exasperating, you get more exasperating."

His face got serious.

"Sorry you lost him, baby," he said softly.

We could not possibly talk more about Oscar or I'd lose it.

"Stop it," I bit out. "That is *well* above medium nice."

He started moving.

Toward me.

And he did it talking about things I did *not* want to hear.

"I think I've replayed that kiss at Duncan's party a hundred times."

Only a hundred?

Goodness me, I had him beat by a mile.

I pivoted from a position with my back to the fridge and retreated.

Though I picked my direction poorly as I headed into the kitchen, which was another dead end. I had an out on the opposite side of the island. However, Judge noted that and shifted swiftly, cutting off that path of escape.

Alcove it was, damn it.

"Just to warn you," he started, "all I can do is be me. So as much as I'd be keen to give you everything you want if it's in my power to give, being mildly nice with dickish tendencies to your friends is not in my power to give."

During this speech, I'd been forced to stop due to me running into the kitchen sink.

Judge stopped due to him being in my space, and then he got more into it when he leaned in and put his hands on the counter on either side of me.

"You're almost short without your heels," he murmured, attention on my lips.

"I'm well above average height, I only seem short because you're well above average too."

His gaze lifted to mine.

And Lord help me, the look in that chocolate brown?

Damn.

"I'm only six four."

"That's tall."

"You gonna shut up so I can kiss you?"

Oh God!

"No."

He leaned closer.

I arched back over the sink.

He stopped leaning and started talking again.

"Okay, see, only fair I tell you how this is gonna go," he declared.

Then without hesitation, if you can believe, the man launched into telling me how this was going to go.

"Now, we got a project to iron out. Also, you and me, we got a heart-to-heart to have so I'll get why you've dedicated yourself to holding back when I know you want to give us a go."

Give us a go.

Us a go.

Yes.

Damn.

"I want nothing of the sort," I fibbed.

His face dipped to mine. "You opening your mouth, baby, the second I kissed you, tells a different story."

I used the lame excuse I was personally clinging to.

"It was New Year's."

"Bullshit."

"Judge," I whispered.

"Chloe," he replied, and dear Lord.

My name sounded amazing coming out of his mouth.

His eyes changed.

Turned-on, sexy hotness gone, they darkened with what, I didn't know.

I'd find out immediately.

It was fierceness.

And steely determination.

"I know you're going through some shit and I'm on record right now telling you I do not just want to get in your pants, Chloe. Make no mistake, that is one hundred percent something I want eventually, but I want more to be a person who's there for you, and while I'm doing it, get to know you. I've never met a woman like you. I thought I had, but you are unlike any woman I've ever encountered. Hell, any person. You're smart as fuck, funny as hell, uppity in a way I feel in my dick, you're full of love and compassion, you clearly don't give a shit what anyone thinks about you, and I fucking love the way you dress. So, I'm meeting your friends and we're gonna cook, then go out and drink, and generally have a good time tonight. You let me, I'll take horning in on your brunch tomorrow too. But after that, tomorrow afternoon, before I gotta get back to my house and my dog, we're ironing things out. Because the next time we're together, and that's gonna be soon, honey, it's gonna officially be a date. During that date you're gonna share about you, and whatever comes after that will be whatever it is."

"You have a dog?" I asked.

He closed his eyes.

I did not understand that reaction.

When he opened his eyes, my breath was stolen at the new look in them.

"Yeah, doll, I have a dog," he confirmed.

I didn't want to ask.

But I asked.

"Why do you look...the way you look?"

"Because in all that, you pulled out my dog. You didn't preen about the compliments or make excuses about why we can't go there or give me shit for laying my heart out..."

He'd laid out his heart?

Oh God.

He kinda did (in the sense that he *really* did).

"...you asked about me, my dog. And I'm looking forward to you getting to know me too."

I said nothing.

"You in with this plan?" he prompted.

I pressed my lips together.

His hitched.

"Chloe, I know you turn yourself out in spectacular ways, probably on an everyday basis. But no woman has her friends over to cook in her kitchen and does her hair in a way that a man is gonna obsess the entire time he's around her about how bad he wants to dig his hands in there and make it all come tumbling down."

I disregarded how that pronouncement affected my nipples, squinted my eyes and lied, "I did not do my hair like this for you, Judge. I just threw it up. It's a messy bun. It takes no time at all."

"I'm twenty-nine and have had three long-term girlfriends, starting my sophomore year in college." His eyes slid up to my hair and then down to mine. "So please, don't try to hand me that shit. I know exactly how long it took you to do your hair like that and I know why you did it."

"You're taking a great number of things for granted," I huffed.

He stared at me.

And then...

Well then...

He muttered, "Fuck it," both his hands rose to cup my head just above the base of my neck, his head came down, and he was kissing me.

I held out longer this time.

At least three whole seconds.

I would later clutch tight to that to salvage my pride.

But after those three seconds, the lure of what we'd experienced before, and the possibility of having it again were too much to bear.

I opened my mouth, Judge slid his tongue inside, and, sadly, there were no other words for it.

Without a cold night and a recent fight and a roomful of people to hold us back, we went at each other.

Desperately.

It would have been humiliating if it wasn't so damned *hot*.

The doorbell rang.

Judge tore his mouth from mine and growled, "Jesus Christ."

I was plastered to him, an arm curled tight around his neck, the fingers of my other hand sifted into his soft hair.

He had a hand fisted in the upswept hair above my nape, his other arm wrapped around me, holding me close even though he didn't have to because I was arched into him.

And we were both breathing like we'd run a sprint.

"You wanna try to convince me you're not into me after that?" he demanded.

I feared this was beyond even my profuse abilities to lie.

I pressed my lips together again, feeling the phantom of his still there, along with tingles and swelling, and mutely shook my head.

The doorbell rang again as Judge said, "Good. You at one with my plan?"

I kept my lips as they were, widened my eyes, and nodded my head.

"Good," he grunted. "You want me to get the door while you fix your hair?"

I felt my bun had come loose.

Thus, another nod from me.

"Christ, you're so fucking cute, being around you is goddamn torture," he grumbled.

"You could—" I started.

He took his hand from my hair and wagged a long, attractive finger in my face.

"Don't finish that," he warned.

I pressed my lips together again.

He watched, grunted unintelligibly this time, bent and touched his lips to my forehead and then let me go.

"We'll start the cocktails if it takes you another half an hour to get back to a style that's gonna fuck with my head all night," he threw over his shoulder as he rounded the wall on his way to the hall.

I glared at said wall after he disappeared.

But he had long legs. It would take him no time at all to get to the front door.

So I darted out of the kitchen and up the stairs to my vanity to fix my hair.

And it took an extra five minutes, but I absolutely did the needed repairs so it would fuck with Judge's head.

All night.

CHAPTER 11

THE RIDE

Judge

The next morning, at ten-thirty, not long after Judge pressed her doorbell, Chloe opened her front door.

He nearly howled with laughter.

Regardless of the copious beverages she'd consumed the night before, she was completely tricked out.

Cream jeans. Slouchy white button-up that was not buttoned very far up, a tangle of gold chains and pendants in her cleavage. Hair down and blown straight. Leopard print pumps.

And massive sunglasses on her nose.

Yes, wearing them inside.

But they did not hide the shitty look she wore on the rest of her face.

It was the look that did it.

He couldn't hold it any longer.

He burst out laughing, walked in, hooked her with an arm, kicked the door shut with his foot, and bent to her, pressing his lips to hers.

She made a noise of irritation before she did something surprising.

He'd just been going for a hard, closed-mouth kiss. Considering she had to be hungover AF, he didn't suspect she could take more.

But she melted into the kiss and opened her mouth to allow him entry.

That warm, sweet mouth?

Judge didn't decline this invitation.

However, he also didn't make her go without breath for long. It was a deep, wet one, but not a long one, and then he lifted his head.

"Mornin', gorgeous," he muttered, still smiling at her.

"I believe we should catalog this as evidence we don't suit," she groused.

"Why?" he asked, not giving a shit what she was going to say, because they totally "suited," and as far as he was concerned, that kiss wasn't evidence.

It was proof.

However, he asked because he knew whatever she came up with would be hilarious.

"You're a morning person."

He raised his brows, suddenly entirely interested in what she had to share, because that wasn't hilarious, it was surprising.

"You're not?"

"I. Am. *Not.*"

Part of him felt this shouldn't be a shocker.

That said, he'd never met anyone who was successful who wasn't a morning person.

And he'd clicked through her shop's impressive website, read every word about her Fabulous Foot Forward project, had numerous examples of how well she dressed, her pad was the shit and he'd found out last night that she wasn't yet twenty-five.

She was definitely successful.

"It might have gone better if you hadn't mixed whisky sours with wine then downed three boilermakers at the speakeasy," he noted.

She didn't quite bite back her audible groan.

Obviously this meant he had to keep at her.

"The boilermakers were a revelation. I'd never peg you as a beer girl."

"Blech," she mumbled.

"But I'm impressed," he went on, letting his eyes move down to her body, a mistake since he got an eyeful of gold and cleavage. He lifted them again to her shades. "It didn't affect your ability to trick yourself out this morning. Though, is the inside-sunglasses-wearing a thing with you? Or did your hangover give you vampiric tendencies?"

"I'm not hungover."

He chuckled at her lie.

"I'm not," she asserted. "Sasha has a smoothie she taught me to make that works wonders. Thus, I added it to my ritual."

It was an understatement that he felt super fucking good that he'd broken through with her the night before, or maybe it was when they were at her dad's place.

And he knew he did because he didn't have to push her for more.

She just offered it up.

"Before bed on a night of imbibing, I drink a tumbler of water. Upon awakening the next day, I take my vitamins, two migraine tabs, eat an egg on toast while I drink two more glasses of water, and I chase all that with Sash's smoothie. After that, *voilà*, hangover managed."

He couldn't see most of her face, but what he could see, she wasn't bullshitting him.

And it had to be said, he fucking loved she used words like "suited," "upon" and "*voilà*" without a shred of irony, not to mention said that last with a hint of a genuine French accent which was classy as hell.

"So what's with the glasses?" he asked.

Those glasses slid away from his face.

He gave her a gentle shake.

She pushed out a harassed sigh, turned again to him and shared, "My hangover regime is flawless. But even ten minutes with my chilled gel eye patches hasn't done much for my puffiness."

"I don't care about puffiness," he returned, and added, "I'm sure you're still gorgeous even with it."

She lifted her chin. "Thank you, but this is something you'll never know due to the fact these glasses will not be coming off until the puffiness has vanished."

He grinned down at her.

She studied him a moment then asked, "Are we going to stand together in my entry with our arms around each other for an hour?"

"Is that an option?"

"No."

He smiled. "Bummer. So I guess, no. Though, we're going to do it long enough for me to tell you how much I like your friends, how cute you are with them—"

"I'm not *cute*," she cut him off to say. "Neither are they. We're all almost *painfully* erudite and urbane, to the point people in close proximity become more sophisticated just being in our presence."

The best part about that, he had no idea if she was kidding or serious.

"Is that so?" he asked through another smile.

"Of course," she sniffed.

"I have to admit, I learned a lot when you and Mi got in that three-hour discussion, dissecting all of Moira Rose's outfits on *Schitt's Creek*. Me and Jacob were gripped with interest, especially considering the visual aids you forced on us as you looked them all up on your phones. I hope you two didn't mistake him falling face first into his mule. He wasn't falling asleep, he was in deep contemplation about the pros and cons of 'aggressive accessorizing,'" he teased.

"We didn't discuss it for three hours," she huffed.

"It felt that way," he muttered.

Her chin tipped just enough, he knew behind her glasses she was rolling her eyes.

"To finish what I was saying," he continued. "My favorite part of the night was making out on your front step for half an hour when I brought you home."

Her nose scrunched but her body pressed closer to his.

Yeah, that was her favorite part too.

"And I'll repeat my gratitude for your invitation to stay the night," he kept on.

It had killed him, and he'd questioned it a dozen times since he'd declined.

But they weren't there yet, she was drunk, and the bottom line was, it wasn't cool.

"A gentleman would not remind a lady of her inebriated indiscretion," she rebuked.

"Wait. Sorry, you should know, I'm not a gentleman."

She clicked her tongue, but she did it with one side of her lips hitching up.

"Do we need to head out to meet your friend?" he asked.

"Yes."

He liked it that word sounded disappointed.

"I'm driving," he decreed.

Her head tipped to the side. "Why?"

"I know you've been hydrating, but you drank so much, you still might have alcohol in your system."

"You can stop giving me shit now," she warned.

He gave her a crooked grin instead and murmured, "Okay, baby" before he dipped and touched his mouth to hers.

She pressed back.

He then let her go.

She clicked on her pumps into the house, and he followed her just enough to see her grab a small bag from the kitchen island.

"Ready?" he asked.

She nodded.

Judge led the way out, stopping after she closed her front door to lean in and test it to make sure it was locked.

He felt her eyes on him while he did this, and he felt her hand jerk slightly when he took it and held it as he guided them to the Cherokee.

It had jerked because she was surprised at the hand holding.

But she didn't pull away.

Since he needed to work on his gentleman skills, he opened the door for her, and he felt her gaze on him again as he closed it after she hiked her ass into his SUV.

He rounded the Jeep, climbed into his side, dropped his visor to let them fall, put on his own shades, started up, and they took off.

"Fashion Square, yeah?" he asked.

"Prep and Pastry is just outside. I'll show you where to park when we get there." She had her phone out and was looking at it. "Tiff is already there."

"Shit, are we late?"

"It's usually at least a half hour wait, Sundays, it can be longer. She got there early to put our names in." She dropped her phone in her bag. "Apparently, Tiffany is hungry."

He was too.

That was surprising, considering their meal last night was unexpectedly (for two chicks who clearly looked after their bodies) filling. Homemade bacon jam and brie puff pastry tartlets. Fried chicken thighs and the best waffles he'd ever eaten, made with heavy cream. Followed by a light pavlova covered in mascarpone cream, pomegranate seeds and raspberries.

He'd noted Jacob was mostly along for the ride (and the food), and it was Mi and Chloe who were the engines of the Club.

And it couldn't be missed it was organized to within an inch of its life.

It had a scheduled timeline, they all had stations, and as such, Judge spent most of his time hanging out at a counter and watching, talking sports and shit with Jacob, and spelling him at the fryer when that time came.

But the food was great, Chloe could really cook, and her friends were awesome.

City folk for certain, but that was a small part of how he grew up, so even if he didn't pick that for his life, he was comfortable in it.

"You have, as you predicted, Mi and Jacob's enthusiastic approval," she noted as he headed to the 10.

"Enthusiastic, eh?"

"Don't fish, Judge. You're likeable and you know it," she returned.

"How likeable?"

"We can just say, *chéri*, that I wasn't *that* drunk last night."

Well…

Shit.

"Baby, we're not there yet," he said low and gentle.

She had no response, so he glanced at her.

"Christ, did I hurt your feelings?" he asked.

"No one…"

She delicately cleared her throat but didn't say any more.

"Did I hurt your feelings by not spending the night last night, Chloe?" he prompted, quiet and careful.

He heard her take a sharp breath into her nostrils and then she said in a rush, "I'm the oldest. I'm expected…certain things are expected of me. It's natural, I'm sure, but it sometimes isn't the greatest that no one thinks to take care of me." Pause then, "You took care of me."

Jesus.

He got it now.

"Honey," he murmured.

"It's fine. It's life. Upon some reflection, I realized that was why I spent so much time in France. *J'adore* France."

And she pronounced "France" as "Frahnce" and didn't sound like a poser when she did.

Total class.

"But I needed a break," she concluded. "And it's just nice that you considered us. Me. That's all I'm saying."

"Of course," he replied. Feeling it didn't need a big deal made of it, and there was something more pressing to discuss, he asked, "No one?"

She didn't answer.

"You seem tight with your mom and dad. Duncan too," he noted.

"There's parental taking care of your children, no matter the age they are. And they've always done that. *Always.* I love them both, like crazy, and as far as I can tell, though there might be some prejudice, they're the best parents ever. But there are other things."

She said no more.

But he knew.

Heavy things.

Like your parents divorcing.

And your mom's best friend committing suicide.

And that was a huge-ass burden.

"I'm assuming we're talking about you helping your brother and sister to deal," he remarked.

"*Failing* in helping them," she corrected.

Another load to bear.

Suddenly, Judge was getting pissed.

"Your parents were in the thick of shit, especially your mom. But your brother and sister should know you've got your own baggage to unpack," he stated, his words edged and curt.

"Why especially my mom?" she asked, her words suspicious and guarded.

"Because she got divorced and lost her friend, both publicly, and how Corey Szabo went, I can't even imagine," he explained.

"Mm," she hummed.

There was more there.

He didn't push that.

He said, "It gets to be a lot, being the only one looking after yourself."

"Well, you see, the thing is, I did have someone looking out for me. I didn't realize it until it was too late, but he did it my whole life. And then he blew his brains out in the Pacific Palisades."

"Fuck," he bit.

"So, you know, he promised," she said. "He promised he'd look after me. And there are other things. Things he said to me. Things he taught me. Things that I found out with what he'd done, and things he'd done earlier, they were all great advice, but coming from him, they were a pack of lies."

Judge lifted his hand her way, palm up and said, "Hey."

She left him hanging for a couple of seconds before she slid her hand in his.

He gave it a squeeze then rested their hands on the console between them.

Only then did he say, "I'm here to listen, even if I'm up north and you have to call me. Okay?"

"I think we should probably get into this now, Judge," she stated.

He didn't understand why she'd want to do that, when they weren't far away from the restaurant and this was a lot.

But if that was what she needed.

"Okay, then I'm here now, so let's do it."

"No, I don't mean that. I mean you need to know there are some things you're not going to know about me, my life, the people in it. Not at first, I mean. Not until we've established...*something*. It upsets some, and it's caused issues in the past, but I hope you understand, unless I know I can trust you, there are parts of my life...my family's life..."

He got it.

Christ, yeah.

He got it.

Because in some ways, though nowhere near what she had to deal with, he had that himself.

Unlike him, however, she had a decent size family.

Lots of love.

But this meant she was still isolated.

"I get it," he told her.

"Does it upset you?" she asked.

He glanced at her to see she was looking at him.

His eyes were back on the road when he said, "I really do get it. I didn't put it together, but Duncan asked me to sign an NDA before I went to Tom's house. I just thought it was standard for people like Tom, your mom. That said, that doc was pretty thorough. I thought it was more about your mom. But I see now it's all of you."

"It's all of us, it's everything," she replied. "Don't believe a single thing you see out there, Judge. It's all carefully curated for your consumption or stolen and then twisted so someone can make money off it."

"Yeah," he muttered.

And yeah, he knew that part *real* well.

"But it comes down to the fact we are not normal people. I hear celebrities saying that and I think, 'Where's your mortgage? Do you struggle to pay for childcare so you can go to work? Do you hesitate to see a doctor because you can't afford the co-pay on your insurance? Or you have no insurance at all?' Of course, Mom and Dad eat and breathe and sleep, but their lives, and by extension *our* lives, are not normal."

"Yeah," he repeated, though that one short word came nowhere near to explaining how deep he felt it that she understood these things about herself, her family and the extent of their privilege in the world.

"And from the start, you have to get that."

"I get it, and I promise you, it doesn't scare me away."

She fell silent.

When he glanced at her again, he saw she was looking out the side window.

"It doesn't," he asserted.

"We'll see," she whispered.

Yeah, they would.

But now he knew, she'd been burned before.

Maybe badly.

Something else for later.

Time to move on from that.

"Sorry you lost Szabo, honey," he said softly.

"I'm not, he put my mother through hell."

And you, Judge didn't say.

He felt her shift and smoothly take her hand from his.

"Let's stop talking about me," she suggested. "We've been all about me all the time. Right now, go. The top five things I need to know about Judge Oakley."

He laughed. "No pressure."

"Do you not know yourself?" she challenged.

Right then.

"Got my dog while I was out running," he began. "Was on a trail, early, no one around, except him. He followed me home. No collar. No tags. Think it'd been a while since he'd eaten. Probably a miracle he didn't become the target of some coyotes. I put up signs, gave notice to the city and shelters. No one claimed him. But he claimed me. That's number one."

"Good number one," she said softly.

His mouth tipped up.

"Best friend is Rix, John Hendrix. Former firefighter. Used to be on the Hotshot crew. Wind turned, he got caught in a jam, tree fell on him. He lost both his legs from below the knee, but it was a straight-up miracle he even survived. He manages the Prescott store now."

"Rix? The man…that was…at Duncan's…?" she asked haltingly.

"Yup."

"But—"

"He has fancy legs he uses sometimes. His sitch is relatively new. My guess is, he's getting used to them. Mostly, though, he's in a wheelchair."

"Okay," she murmured.

"That's number one part two," he told her.

She laughed low.

He grinned at the road.

Then he got into the tough stuff.

"So skipping to number three. I love my job. Found my calling. Love Prescott. Love the mission and ethics of River Rain. Love the kids. Got great staff and volunteers. What we do is important. There'll come a time when the program will benefit from new blood and I'll need to move on, but I thank God that time is not now."

She said nothing for a spell before she prompted, "Okay."

He was taking their exit off the highway as he pointed out what she obviously missed, "My job is in Prescott, Chloe."

"Is that number four?" she asked. "Because that's one of the few things I know already."

"What I mean is, that's been a thing for other women in my life. Ones that have lived in Phoenix."

"Prescott is not the moon," was her only response.

Even so.

Message received.

He grinned at the road again.

Then he said, "Number four is, if I have a choice, I will take the road I've never traveled."

"Adventurous," she said under her breath.

"Yeah. There are things I like to do that I do a lot. But given the chance, I'll take it to try something new."

She touched his thigh.

He took her hint and gave her back his hand.

Her fingers curled around tight.

"And the last thing?" she asked.

"I grew up part-time in New York City. My dad operates a hedge fund. He made his first billion when he was in his early forties. It wasn't his last. His name isn't that close to Szabo's on a particular list, but it's not far away."

Her hand was now squeezing his tight.

"Your dad is Jameson Oakley?"

Of course she knew who he was.

"Yup."

"*Mais non*," she whispered.

"I think I know what that means, but…yeah."

"No wonder your coat is fabulous," she remarked.

He started chuckling. "Yeah, and I'll be taking that back with me."

"Of course," she said in that way women say it and mean, "not gonna happen."

Before he could ask why she seemed to have stolen his overcoat, she kept talking.

"Do *I* need to sign an NDA?" she asked, sounding half joking, but with her experience, also probably half serious.

"Dad would say absolutely. I say no. But you and me will have a deal."

"What deal?"

"You give me what you feel you can give, and along the way, I'll earn your trust. And vice versa. You are far from normal, and that's what interests me about you. But in that, what we share, we'll act like normal people. You get what you earn. Cool?"

"Cool," she agreed with a squeeze of his hand. "And *chéri*, it's best to come at it from the Indian School side."

That took them out of the deep, and eventually she guided him into underground parking at Fashion Square.

They walked up to the restaurant on the corner, and Judge met Tiffany, a full-figured, six foot two, heavily made-up female who was not biologically female.

She was either in transition, or today she just felt like being a she.

She looked him up and down as they approached, and after the introductions, turned right to Chloe. "Mi told me he was scrumptious." She turned to Judge. "And that's Mi's term, not mine," then back to Chloe, "but she didn't tell me he was *so tall*."

"Tiff finds it even more difficult than I do to nail down a tall guy," Chloe explained.

"No pressure," Tiffany purred.

"There's plenty of me to go around," he pointed out. "But just saying, after it goes around, I'm paying."

Tiffany shifted her attention back to Chloe. "Oo, I like him."

Chloe's shades were aimed his way when she replied.

"I do too."

And there it was.

Morning made.

JUDGE CAME UP FOR AIR AND SAID THE LAST THING HE WANTED TO SAY.

"I gotta get on the road, baby."

She pouted.

She was on her back on her couch.

He was on her.

They'd been making out.

He took some second base liberties, but mostly it was getting-to-know-you groping.

It was phenomenal.

Having her soft body under his was spectacular.

Smelling her, tasting her in his mouth.

Finally getting his fingers in her hair.

His lips on the length of that neck.

But he did have to go.

"I gotta get back to my pup," he told her. "Rix's got him, and he likes him, and he might not give him back if I don't go claim him."

She did an eye roll and grumbled, "I suppose that's fine."

"I will point out, we got zero work done on Duncan and Tom's promo."

She became interested in looking anywhere but his face.

She'd been there, but he still ran it down.

"There was the 'quick trip' to Nordstrom shoe department that you and Tiffany *had to make* that lasted an hour."

"Tiffany has an upcoming event."

"Tiffany didn't try on a single shoe. She only ordered the guy to get you fifteen pairs and you bought three of them."

She emitted an irritated grunt which was also affirmation because that happened.

"Then we *had to* stop for coffee at that scary coffee place."

"Cartel isn't scary."

"We walked in, and it was so silent, just us opening the door, I feared for my life the two dudes closest to it were going to beat us with their laptops."

"You get your coffee there if you're in Old Town," she informed him haughtily. "And *only* there."

He made no comment to that.

Instead, he noted, "Then we had to go by Sprouts."

"I have to do my grocery shopping on the weekend. If I don't, it won't get done, and I won't have fresh fruit or my weekly meat won't get salted."

"Which brings us to you ripping open all the meat when we got home and salting it."

"You clearly don't know how to cook," she sniffed.

"Not as good as you, but even if you're great at it, after the salting meat thing, you made me take you to The Gladly for one of their chopped salads."

"I had a craving."

"Which meant we had precious little time left and I made the executive decision to use it to make out."

"You surely did not miss that I concurred with this decision."

He grinned. "Yeah, I didn't miss that. But I'm gonna go to the office tomorrow, and Duncan's gonna ask where we're at, and it's really none of his business that you're really sensitive behind your ears and when you don't want to lose my mouth, you grab my lip with your teeth, and that's as far as we got."

"Please, don't share that with Duncan," she drawled.

Christ, she was something.

"Bottom line, are you coming up or am I coming back? And when that happens, what day is it gonna happen? And do not mention Saturday. That's our official First Date Night. And you're coming up to Prescott for that."

"I can't come up during the week, Judge, and I work the store on Saturdays."

"Since you do, do you have a day off during the week?"

She shook her head against her toss pillow. "Not really. We do good turnover in sales at the store. But the shop is young. We're still establishing clientele. I don't have the resources to invest in a ton of associates. I need to fill in."

"Right, then I'll load up my dog, take some time out of my workday since it's work we're doing, and come up. Wednesday?"

Her eyes lit with excitement.

But her mouth uttered a chill, "Sure."

"Are you more excited about me, or meeting my dog?"

"You, of course," she said, making it sound like a lie, when with the way she kissed, and held on when she did, he knew it was not.

"And that's a no on Saturday?" he went on.

"Can you come down?"

"I can't get you drunk at the Meadery if you don't come up."

Her nose wrinkled. "Mead?"

"Trust me."

"Is this casual?"

Obviously, she was an adventure girl too.

"Are you catatonic when you visit Prescott?"

She narrowed her eyes.

Then she said, "If it's casual, I'll be able to refresh my outfit easily. I can head up around four. Will that do?"

"Absolutely."

He was smiling again when he bent to touch his lips to hers.

He had to be quick about it when he lifted his head because she followed.

"And no distractions on Wednesday," he warned. "Work. Find a couple angles. Some messages. A hook. Something to present to them so we can start storyboarding and scripting."

Her hand was making its way from his shoulder blade to his ass as she murmured, "Yes, we can do that."

"Fuck it, I'll just come down and we'll make out all night," he muttered, and bent his head to take her mouth again.

It got heated, his dick was stirring, so he ended it.

Chloe made a displeased noise.

Then her pretty eyes moved all over his face before looking into his.

"I need to stop it and take care of Dad."

She probably did.

And a few days ago?

He thought it was incredibly sweet, her looking out for her father's peace of mind.

But after their convo in the car, he was wondering why the fuck Duncan and Tom made this deal, and then Imogen and Duncan roped Chloe in.

Yes, Tom Pierce championing the program would raise the roof on awareness, likely get a ton more kids enrolled, and that always went hand in hand with donations. He was a huge score for the program.

But Judge could have handled it by himself.

Imogen was matchmaking, maybe Duncan too, and possibly they'd pulled Tom in on it.

He just wished they'd thought it through.

"I could ask them if I can do it alone," he offered.

Her brows dipped. "I *can* concentrate, Judge."

"That's not what I mean."

What he meant dawned on her and she nodded.

But she said, "They trust me to look after Dad."

"He's a grown man. He can look after himself."

"What I mean is the entire family, as well as Dad. Look out for the whole. We don't...The Pierce-Swans don't do anything without someone at their back."

"Do you mean without Chloe at their back?"

"Sometimes," she hedged.

He shook his body on hers, which meant shaking hers.

"Okay, a lot of the time," she allowed. "Still, Mom's out, or she's not quite, but she still is. So it's me."

"I'll do the grunt work."

She shot him an arch look. "You were going to do that before."

He chuckled then gave her a quick kiss before he elaborated. "What I mean is, I'll shield you as best as I can."

At that, her mouth actually dropped open.

And at *that*, Judge officially got pissed.

"You mean to tell me, no one has ever shielded you?"

She clamped her mouth shut then used it to lie, "Of course they have."

"Only Szabo?"

She had to think about that one.

To put a fine point on it, she had to think about the lie she'd tell to get him not to be ticked about the fact that some dude who wasn't even blood, lived in another state and had jetted around the globe for most of his adult life, but was now very dead, was the only one who was at her back.

"Don't even try to lie about it," he growled.

She defended them. "Everybody has a lot on their plate."

"And you don't?"

She shut up.

"Doesn't matter," he bit off, knifing up from her and pulling her with him. When they were toe to toe beside the couch, he said, "I'm taking lead. *Not*," he said his last sharply, also lifting a finger to touch it to her lips when she opened them to speak, "taking over. We're in this together. But I'm lead. I'm buffer between Duncan and Tom. I'll do the grunt work and the comms, which I'll split between the two of them. They won't be in a meeting together. It's my program anyway. You make sure the Pierce-Swans are covered, give your dad moral support when needed, but the heavy lifting will be on me."

"You double up on meetings, that's twice as much work for you."

"If I need to talk to your dad, I have to come to Phoenix. Is that an issue for you?"

She got a smug look on her face. *"Bien sûr que non."*

"And that means no?"

She nodded.

"You like me," he teased.

"*You* like me," she returned.

"Yeah," he whispered. "I do."

Her face got soft.

He kissed her again.

With regret, he ended it and ordered, "Now, go up and get my coat."

"Hmm," was her weird reply. It was followed by a lie. "I took it to the dry cleaners."

Judge started laughing. "What is it with you and that coat?"

She gave a slight shrug. "It smells like you."

He stopped laughing.

And then he leaned so far into her, when he kissed her again, they were back on the couch.

In the end, he had to text Rix to say he'd be an hour later than he expected.

Rix said not to bother, Zeke was now his.

He went over to his buddy's house to get *his* dog anyway.

Incidentally, he left Chloe's place without his coat.

CHAPTER 12

THE BEQUEATHAL

Chloe

*T*he next morning, once I'd parked behind my store, I could barely wait to pull my phone out of my bag because a string of texts had come in while I was driving.

And I knew they were from Judge.

Like a little girl ripping into her presents Christmas morning, I yanked my phone out and saw Santa gave me what I wanted.

They were from Judge.

They included:

Wednesday, regardless of all that salted meat, don't plan to cook.

And then, *We'll order pizza.*

And then, *Best weekend this year so far, honey.*

The first made me laugh because of his reference to the meat.

The second made me crave the prosciutto and date pizza from Federal. It also made me wonder if Judge would like that, because I could have it waiting for him when he got to my house on Wednesday (or whatever pizza he wanted…from Federal).

The last made me laugh, because we were only two weekends into the year.

Still, his point was made.

Because I agreed.

Last weekend was the best I'd had in a long time.

These texts all came after last night's, *Home. And performed the miracle of convincing Rix to hand over my dog.*

To which I'd been in such a Judge Haze, I'd not hesitated to reply, *Good. Give him pets for me and tell him Auntie Coco looks forward to meeting him.*

This got, *Auntie Coco?*

To which, of course, I returned, *Shut up.*

And received, *At your command. Thanks for a fantastic time, doll. Sleep well.*

And yes, the Haze still influencing me, I'd returned, *I agree. And I will. You too.*

Not even getting out of my car, my thumbs went immediately to return something droll and meant to make him laugh that gorgeous laugh of his, or even just smile his warm, sweet smile, but I stopped myself, lifted the phone and tapped it against my forehead.

"What are you doing, Coco? What are you doing? *What are you doing?*"

Judge was not my type at all.

I went for artists and assholes (almost always one and the same, though assholes, in my experience, came in many varieties).

Judge was neither.

This wouldn't seem, to some, an issue.

It was an issue to me.

I could control my emotions with an asshole. I could hold back parts of me.

I could walk away from them.

I was okay with it if they walked away from me.

However, as big of an issue as this was, it wasn't the main one.

That top spot was occupied with Judge playing havoc on my peace of mind.

Because when I was with him, that was what I had.

Peace of mind.

When he was around, I was totally at one with the world, because that world centered around Judge, and I was totally at one with being with him.

Once I'd let my guard down, he was just…easy.

It was the first time I'd experienced this sense of calm since Mom and Dad sat us down and shared they were having problems, and those problems were serious.

An event that rocked my world. Matt's. Sasha's.

It was inconceivable.

And then it got worse.

It made no sense that Judge making me feel on solid ground again would, at the same time, unbalance me.

But it did.

And it did much more than that.

It terrified me.

We had spent one night and one day exploring what an us might be.

And still…

I needed to cool us off. Pull back. Reinforce my shields.

No.

Completely put a stop to it.

This just didn't seem to be something I was capable of when he was around.

Or even when he wasn't.

Or when he was just texting.

Doing this the moment he got home after he left me after we'd spent a day and a half together, and every moment of it was marvelous.

Then doing it more the next morning.

No playing games.

Connecting.

Making it clear he was looking forward to spending more time with me.

Making it clear I knew he'd enjoyed the time we had.

And when he was with me, making no bones about demonstrating he found me interesting, he found me amusing, he liked talking to me, he liked looking at me, he enjoyed touching me, even not intimately. Just affectionately.

I didn't know if a man had ever held my hand, but if he had, I hadn't remembered.

Maybe it had happened, and I didn't remember because it didn't matter.

And Judge mattered.

I sensed I would remember always the first time Judge took my hand.

Even when Judge wasn't around (like last night after he left, and all morning that morning), I'd fall into thinking about him, remembering things he'd said or looks he'd given me or that kiss in my kitchen.

Our activities on the couch.

I was borderline obsessed with him.

(Okay, maybe not borderline.)

And that wouldn't do.

It relinquished power.

And doing that made you vulnerable.

I couldn't have either.

Instead of returning Judge's texts, I opened another text string.

The one to Matt, who had yet to reply.

And since I was in a mood, but regardless, it was time, I didn't pussyfoot around.

As you seem to be on a mission to alienate yourself from your family, allow me to congratulate you. When it comes to your elder sister, mission accomplished.

After I sent that, I sent:

I said some things because I love you and worry about you, and I love our father and worry about him. And you're intent to make me suffer for that.

Suffer for love and worry.

I let that loose, then I lowered the hammer.

Well, fuck you too, Matt.

Don't bother with replying to this either. Even if you finally realize you're acting like an ass, I don't want to hear from you, because you'll need to give me some time to get over being pissed at you.

I sent that last, shoved my phone in my purse, pulled myself out of the car, and headed into the shop, not feeling like a woman who spent the weekend with a great guy. A great guy who she knew could mean great things to her, because he'd already become that.

Feeling like a woman who could start screaming, but she didn't because she wouldn't stop.

Or start crying, but she didn't do that either.

Because she was terrified she *couldn't* stop.

The good news was, I could be in a bitchy mood all by myself.

Mi-Young had Mondays off. On Mondays, I opened and took care of the store until one of the part-timers came in in the afternoon. Weekdays were never a rush, especially during the day. One to two staffers were okay even if I had a relatively large store space.

Fortunately, it had become all hands on deck on the weekends, but I tried to take Sundays off. It gave Mi-Young time with the staff without my presence there. And it gave me a day to relax.

But I didn't open for another thirty minutes.

I always arrived early enough to make sure the store was stocked, tidied, and as it should be. I could bring my laptop to the checkout desk to go through email and do other admin things after I'd opened.

I'd secured my purse in my office and was walking with phone in hand into the store when it rang.

I looked down and saw it was not a call from Judge to tease me about making him wait for a response (and I didn't know whether to be relieved or in despair about that).

It was Mom.

I took the call, saying, "*Motherrrrr*, calling is *so* nineties."

"I see it was unnecessary," she curiously said in reply.

"Sorry?" I asked.

"You're being you," she did not quite answer.

"Please elucidate," I demanded, wandering through the store with an eagle eye.

Though I knew I didn't need to bother, Mi never left it in anything other than pristine condition.

"You felt...*off* during dinner at your dad's," Mom said.

I stopped wandering and focused on the conversation.

"And then you didn't call...or text...to tell me off for ambushing you with Judge like that," she finished.

Whereas being with Judge brought peace of mind and being obsessed with Judge when he wasn't around played havoc at the same time reminded me that he gave me that was a tangle of confusing emotions.

This from Mom was flat-out not good.

Because I could let her off the hook in regards to her (deserved) guilt by telling her that Judge and I had gotten together that weekend and had a great time. Or to cover my ass in a variety of ways, I could lie that we did it to talk about the program, when we didn't.

Or I could avoid it entirely.

That said, Judge worked directly with Duncan in the same suite of offices. There was definitely mutual respect there, but they didn't strike me as chummy, so I doubted Judge would wander into Duncan's office with a coffee and a rundown of our time together this weekend. But, in passing, he could let it slip.

And if Judge told Duncan, Duncan would tell Mom.

Which put me in a pickle because my usual go-to was lying, that was what I was leaning toward now, and lying didn't work when it wasn't believed, or it could easily be refuted by another source.

A serious bother.

And this did not better my mood.

I evaded with, "We're meeting on Wednesday to nail down a message."

"Are you angry at me?" she asked.

Yes, I'm angry at you.

Yes, yes, I'm angry at you.

I'm SO FUCKING ANGRY AT YOU.

But that was not about Judge.

That was about something she couldn't change, something she

couldn't help, something that had happened to her, not that she made happen.

Something that was not her fault.

I was pissed all the same.

"Chloe?" she prompted.

I continued with my inspection of the store, stating drily, "I *can* manage my own love life, Mother."

"You calling me 'mother' is not giving me good vibes," she mumbled.

"Then perhaps butt out of my romantic liaisons."

"Are you saying Judge is a romantic liaison?"

God damn it.

When I didn't answer immediately, and it was not due to the fact a folded sweater was askew and I had to tuck my phone between ear and shoulder to right it, she continued.

"That kiss seemed to lean that way."

Of course she saw the New Year's kiss.

As I'd been the one being kissed, I knew there was no way in hell it could lean another way, even to an observer.

I decided to be blunt, which sadly made me repetitive.

"Mom, butt out."

"I like him, what I know of him. But Duncan likes him very much—"

"Is this butting out?" I snapped.

"I just want you to be happy."

"We're both after the same goal," I retorted. "But since it's my life, how about you let me bear the brunt of that, yes?"

There was a moment's hesitation and then, "I was wrong earlier, you don't seem yourself."

"I'm doing the walk-through before opening. I'm on until one by myself. I have things on my mind. No shade, Mom, but everything isn't about you."

Another hesitation before a quiet, "Ouch."

She felt the pain, but I flinched.

Even if I knew that was harsh, I couldn't find it in myself to take it back, smooth it over.

Are you looking after her?

Fuck you, Uncle Corey.

When I didn't rush into the breach I'd caused, Mom entered it.

"Are you coming up to Prescott soon?"

Yes, next Saturday.

"I don't know," I told her.

"Even though you're in the middle of something, I'd like to put a niggle in your ear to find some time to sit down with me to talk about your sister."

So she was noticing something was up with Sasha too.

And that was going to be on me to help out with…

Too.

"We'll plan that," I replied.

"Starting next month, I'll be in LA for three weeks of script run-throughs, wardrobe, that kind of stuff," she reminded me for some reason since I already knew this. "I'm trying to spend as much time with Duncan as possible before I go. He's going to spend the first week with me there, but he has to get back after that."

With nothing better to say about information I already knew, I said, "All right."

"I also have a wedding to plan, and I'd like my girls to be involved in that."

Instantaneously, I wanted to vomit.

"I'd never speak to you if you didn't," I forced out one of those rare lies that hurt to tell.

"Chloe, are you okay?"

I was for a day and a half, I'm not now.

"I'm fine, *Maman*," I said, my tone much warmer than it had been, and not only because the walk-through was complete, and outside that sweater, Mi-Young had left things just as they should be.

"All right, darling. I'll leave you alone now."

I never wanted my mother to feel like she was bothering me.

But I needed her to leave me alone now.

"Okay, speak soon," I replied.

"Yes, soon. Love you."

"Love you more."

"Impossible," she whispered.

God, I was *such* a *bitch*.

I made a kiss kiss noise and quickly hung up.

I then took a second to pull my shit together.

After that, I walked back to my office, grabbed my laptop from where it was locked in my credenza, the float from the safe, headed back out and set up the checkout desk.

I turned on our sound system, selecting a classy jazz duo playlist (piano and guitar) that I thought went great with the décor (I also allowed piano jazz, meditation classical, Yo-Yo Ma, Nina Simone, Diana Krall, Etta James, Billie Holliday, Harry Connick, Jr., Michael Bublé…and Lizzo).

Before I officially opened, I made certain the back door had caught, was bolted, and the alarm for that door was on, and then I headed up front to unlock that door.

I pulled the string on the neon sign by the window that was white against a gold background and said in a loping script OPEN. It was next to one of my window displays, these redone every two months. A display that I knew was stunning (they all were, and I did say so myself). I knew this because people often stopped and stared (then came in).

In fact, my front displays were getting to be a thing, with regulars and locals coming just to check them out (the former because I sent the news there was a fresh one in our newsletter).

I then turned to my store, which, after much consideration, and from the aesthetic, to the branding, to the décor, it worked perfectly, so I'd called it Velvet, and all at once, it washed over me.

I'd gone full-on art deco.

The focal point was a quartet of peach velvet, tulip swivel chairs on brass bases in the middle of the space flanking a low glass and brass coffee table.

The back wall was upholstered in tufted squares of the same peach velvet. The other walls were white.

There were round mirrors of varying sizes everywhere and geometric brass and white ceramic *accoutrements*. Even the brass-framed glass shelves were geometric, with the shelves being straight-sided ovals.

There was plenty of space to mill about. Not a single rack on the floor. All clothing rails and shelves were against the walls.

However, there were some glass-topped round tables with folded sweaters, tees or scarves, display stands containing jewelry, or glossy, milky ceramic counters topped with scented candles, lotions or bath treatments dotting the space. Though not a one of them was tall enough to in any way obstruct the eyeline from that upholstered wall.

All of this gave a feeling of lightness, openness. There was plenty of room to move around. Not a single nook existed where you would have to awkwardly squeeze past anyone.

And there was utterly no clutter.

I had a good deal of stock from numerous up and coming designers, a few established ones, some exceptional basics, and some pieces from artists.

But Velvet did not overwhelm you upon entry or at any moment when you were in it.

It might intimidate you because it was just that stylish.

But the bright, somewhat romantic, somewhat fun interior beckoned.

And hopefully eventually enveloped in warmth and inclusivity.

I made my way to the checkout desk and had just opened my Mac to pull up email and check if any online orders had come through that needed to be dealt with when the slight beep that sounded when the door was opened brought my attention to the front of the shop.

And my head immediately ticked to the side with who I saw stroll in.

He was not what I would expect of my first customer on a Monday.

Or ever.

Tall, maybe not as tall as Judge, but still, very tall.

Broad, definitely broader than Judge.

And ignoring the fact that he was openly alpha, perhaps even toxically so (the hero of that film *365 Days* came instantly to mind), he was this wearing an almost criminally well-cut suit.

And he was the most beautiful man I'd ever seen in my life.

He did not glance at a single item in the store.

He came direct to me.

And the way he did it staring at me, I reached a hand out to my phone sitting on the checkout counter, a tickle of fear trailing down my spine.

This man wasn't toxic (though he probably also was).

He was dangerous.

His dark eyes tracked my slight movement to the phone, giving indication he didn't miss a thing.

That didn't make me feel better.

"May I help you?" I asked when he was a couple of feet from the desk.

"Chloe Pierce," he stated, his voice accented in a way I couldn't call it from just his saying my name.

And it wasn't a question.

It was a statement.

He knew who I was.

Oh God, oh God, oh God.

"Yes," I said carefully.

"Did you get the packet I sent to you?"

What?

"I'm sorry?" I asked.

"The packet," he reiterated, and it hit me his accent was British. I wasn't exactly sure, but I thought it might be Welsh. "That included the detailed report that I sent to you."

I went perfectly still.

He read my stillness and thus didn't wait for an answer to that question.

He asked another one.

"Do you need assistance with that?"

Assistance?

With finding some angle to matchmake my father with the lover he'd taken that had destroyed his marriage?

And maybe my life?

I pulled myself together and inquired, "Did Uncle Corey send you?"

He lifted a veined, long-fingered hand, reached into his inside pocket of his blue suit jacket, and pulled something out.

I saw it was a ribbed, sterling card carrying case. On the spot, I tagged it as vintage.

And Cartier.

He flicked it open with his manicured thumbnail, pulled out a card and set it on the desk in front of me.

"If you ever need me," he said.

And that was that.

He spoke no more, asked no more, expected no more.

He turned around, and with a predator's grace, sauntered out.

The door closed and I realized I wasn't breathing.

I started doing that but could not tear my eyes off the door.

If you ever need me.

Uncle Corey.

I looked down at the card, reached out, picked up the thick, crisp cream stock and read the words in bold, modern, serif small capitals on the front.

It was just a name and a phone number.

The phone number was local.

Phoenix.

And the name was Rhys Vaughan.

R.

He was Uncle Corey's.

And he'd been left to me.

CHAPTER 13

THE DECISION

Chloe

𝒶fter the mysterious Rhys left, my morning didn't get better.

It started with a text from Sasha.

Brunch is off and just to say, it's all off between you and me until you stop being mean to Matt.

Receiving this, I was gripped with fury.

Utter *fury*.

Because my brother and sister were acting six years old.

Every quarter, I went through dozens of applications from women who had either been born to circumstances it was practically impossible to crawl out of or had been shit on repeatedly since their first coherent thought.

My brother and sister grew up in a beach house in Malibu. We'd all been given cars for our sixteenth birthdays. New ones. High performance ones. Not gently used ones with a hundred thousand miles on them. We went to private schools and our college was paid (or Matt's was, Sasha, as yet, had elected not to partake, and I didn't have any patience for the callowness of high school, I couldn't fathom continuing that journey to college and being confronted with what I considered the dregs of the earth: frat boys). And beyond that, we'd been given trust funds that were enough to set us up in business (case in point, I was standing in mine), hearth and home with a nest egg besides.

And on that dreaded day *far, far* in the future when we lost Mom and/or Dad, we'd be filthy rich.

Of late, I had thought we'd been fortunate in our lives to have had to deal with very little adversity.

I was changing my mind about this thought.

Those two could have used some adversity.

Now they were behaving like spoiled brats.

Though I shouldn't be surprised Matt called Sash to complain about me. Those two had been thick as thieves since children.

As Dad used to crow, "My son took one look at his baby sister with that peach fuzz and those big blues eyes, and it was all over."

It was.

I did my own thing all my life, for certain.

But I did it with an eye to them.

I was always the big sister. Looking after them. Close to each in our special ways.

But still left out.

And at times, ganged up on.

Honestly, I'd never really cared.

(Truly, it was what it was.)

But now it hurt.

Especially Matt.

He was protective of Sasha (as was I), and they were very close, but that didn't mean we weren't all tight. We were a close family. A loving family. We all had our place, and we all had our relationships as a whole and with each other.

My way with Matt was that he'd always been my confidant. I knew, especially as he grew older, that I could take things to him, and he'd listen, and he was wise for his age (or he had been).

I missed that.

I missed it because I missed it, but I missed it more because now, I *needed* it.

So, naturally, I texted back, *Excellent. I have no interest in dining with a juvenile. Text me when you grow up.*

I didn't need their shit.

I really did not.

It seemed I wasn't going to get my way on that.

Because Matt finally broke his silence.

He did it to text, *When you're acting like a bitch, leave Sash out of it.*

I did not reply.

I also sold nary an item until Madison came in. And the first thing I did when she arrived was rush out to grab a bite to eat and a coffee for both of us just so I could get some time to sort out my head.

I ate lunch at my desk, and I did not sort out my head.

From the drawer where I locked my purse, I unearthed the file a man apparently named Rhys Vaughan (though, who was named that? it was so perfectly kickass, it sounded like something a bunch of romance novel readers would come up with) had amassed for me.

I chewed on my Safeway sushi (which wasn't half bad) and leafed through the file.

This Susan was really very pretty.

But she hadn't led that great of a life (serial killer kidnapping her aside, she lost her mom young, and the reason that happened was so impossible to fathom, I blocked it out instantly).

I had to get back to Madison, so I put the file, with Vaughan's card, back in the drawer, locked up and hustled out.

We fortunately had things pick up around three, so I was pretty sure I covered Madison's salary that day (at most).

But my phone, which I left in my office for obvious reasons, was awash in notifications when I returned to it.

Sasha: *That wasn't nice.*

Matt: *You should apologize to Sash. She isn't in this thing with you and me.*

Mom: *How about you, Sasha and I do some wedding gown shopping while I'm in LA? Fancy a weekend trip?*

Dad: *I'm feeling Wagyu. Would you like to join me Thursday for dinner at Capital Grille?*

Judge: *Do you have greenspace for Zeke, or do I need to come prepared?*

Also Judge, though later: *You okay?*

Last from Judge, and this was what did it.

What made me decide.

Duncan told me you and your sister had a thing. Call me if you want to talk.

So somehow (probably because she was up there, living with them, and Duncan worked at home a lot so he could be close to Mom, especially in the mornings), between Sasha being a brat and Judge's last text, Duncan had learned she was pissed at me, and for some ungodly reason, he'd shared this with Judge.

I did not want this to be my life.

"I do not want this to be my life," I said out loud.

However, when I said the words out loud, it wasn't the fight with Sasha and Matt that I was talking about.

As I realized this, I felt them.

They hurt.

I hated them.

I avoided them *at all costs*.

As such, I had practice in how to keep them at bay.

So when the tears threatened, I steeled myself against them, pulled out my laptop and got to work.

Once I'd read every section of the Kids and Trails program, it wrote itself, really.

I found some images to support the look I was suggesting, penned two strong messages we could send with a signup appeal that hinted at a funding appeal, broke those out into two loose outlines, even provided some scripting.

And then I emailed them to the addy Judge had programmed into my phone when we were at Dad's for dinner.

This included a note that I dashed off deliberately, like it was the last thing I had to do at the end of a long day.

J-

Sorry, can't do Wednesday or Saturday but this needs to get going.
I drafted a start.
If we could continue through email for the time being, I'd appreciate it. To
that end, just send your notes in a reply.
Hope you enjoyed your Monday,
-Chloe

With that, I shut down my laptop, locked it up, did a walk-through to make sure all was good for the next day, the doors were secure, and I set the alarm before I walked out to my car and drove home.

And with iron will, through all that, I did not think of a thing.

Except what bottle of wine I'd open when I got home.

Judge

"She seemed high maintenance to me."

Chloe was the new definition of high maintenance.

Judge took a sip of his beer and smiled at the starry sky.

When he finished the sip, he said to his buddy Rix, who had his own beer and was lounging in his wheelchair at Judge's side by the railing on Judge's deck, "Shut the fuck up."

"Probably takes an hour and a half just to do her hair," Rix kept on.

"If it looks like it has every time I've seen her, I don't give a shit," Judge replied.

"She'll spend half your money on makeup alone."

"Good she makes her own then."

"Though…that ass…"

Rix let that hang, and the crinkles at the corner of his eyes stated how he knew that got under Judge's skin even if Rix didn't look at him, just sucked back some of his own beer as he stared at the sunset.

"That isn't funny," Judge warned.

That was when Rix looked at him, all fake innocence. "It isn't?"

"Fuck you," Judge returned.

Rix suddenly stopped giving him stick and started studying him.

He then diagnosed, "Man, you got it bad."

"She's gorgeous. Dresses great. Is funny. Smart as hell. Got her own thing going with work. Gives back. So yeah…" He shrugged, totally down with this concept. "I got it bad for Chloe Pierce."

"Your dad is gonna love her," Rix said carefully.

Judge shifted in his seat.

"Your mom is gonna detest her," Rix went on.

"How 'bout I have an actual date with her before we get into the parents," Judge suggested.

"I don't know why, considering you've met all of hers, and work with the step one."

"And they're damn fine people," Judge returned.

Rix shook his head, took another slug of beer and cautioned, "She's gonna be work, bud."

Okay, now Rix needed to piss off.

"I've been around her where she hasn't been pushing me away twice, Rix," he shot back. "And one of those times, I had to coax her to stop pushing me away while we were having it. We got to know each other a little. We had fun together. She doesn't have my ring on her finger. Christ. Chill."

"I just know you," Rix noted.

"I know you do, but you don't know her."

"Yeah, I know, even though I spent hours with her at a party where it wasn't like there were five hundred people there and she didn't meet me," Rix pointed out.

"She was pushing me away. She's hardly going to stroll up and introduce herself to my best bud when she's avoiding me."

"And at that time, you hadn't even let on you were interested and she was jacking you around already."

Judge kept quiet so he wouldn't lose his shit and say something he didn't want to say.

Rix twisted his torso to fully face Judge and continued, "Listen, I can see you're pissed at me. But you gotta know I'm not sayin' this shit to set you off. I'm also not saying it to dog her. But you got a type… and you repeat a pattern."

"Let's not talk about this," Judge suggested.

"We been out here thirty minutes and you've looked at your phone ten times because the woman has not reached out all day."

Judge said nothing.

Though it hadn't been ten times.

Three, tops.

"That's shades of Meg *and* Kimberly," he carried on. "And Jess was far from above yanking your chain."

"Chloe has a business to run."

"She knows you're into her and she knows, because you are, she can bust your balls."

Yup.

Rix could piss off.

"Just because you got a thing for heads-up-their-asses pieces of work, Rix, do not land your shit on me," he clipped.

"At least mine don't make me drive two hours before they fuck me over," Rix shot back. "And they wait until they've given me at least one orgasm before they decide to try to lead me around by my dick."

"You do not know this woman," Judge returned.

Rix nodded once. "You're right. I don't. I know *you*. And all I'm saying is, be careful. That's it. The thing now is, you're as pissed as you are about my message because you know I'm right. And you've put yourself out there."

He had.

But so had she.

"She's not who you think she is," Judge told him.

"I hope you're right," Rix replied. "What you need to get is that not every woman who's just your average, everyday woman who doesn't have some lofty ambition or some massive trust fund or some other gold-plated stick up her ass is gonna turn out to be like your mom."

Judge returned his attention to the night sky.

His black and brown brindle shepherd mix, Zeke, shifted up from his place lying on a folded blanket between them to sit on his haunches and butt Judge's hand with his muzzle.

His boy felt his daddy's pain when mentions of Judge's mom reared their head.

Judge massaged Zeke's neck.

"I'm not being a dick," Rix said quietly. "I'm being a friend. I got good parents, both of them. I have no clue what it's like to have a dad like your dad, who's on your ass to make more of yourself. And a mom like your mom."

Rix didn't put any definitions on Judge's mom.

But he'd met her.

She called herself a free spirit.

Judge called her a functioning alcoholic and drug addict.

Nope.

Strike that "functioning" part.

Regardless that bar was low, "functioning" was what he wanted her to be.

The brutal truth: she was just an addict.

"I'm just saying, turn the tables, and what would you say to me, Judge?" Rix asked. "You'd look after your boy. You'd say the same damn shit."

"I don't see you shacked up with the woman of your dreams."

It came out before he could stop it.

And before he could do anything about it, Rix tossed a hand to his stubbed legs and returned, "I did. She just couldn't deal. So she took off. None of them can deal, Judge. They like my big dick and what upper body strength means with the way I can use it. They're not such big fans of me walking on my hands to the bathroom when I don't wanna dick with my wheelchair or put on legs. What's your excuse?"

"The word hasn't been invented for the kind of woman Peri is," Judge said low.

"She was normal. She met and fell in love with a man who became not that man. So she took off. She tried. But it wasn't on Peri."

It was Judge this time who twisted fully to Rix as he demanded, "Are you fucking kidding me?"

Rix threw forward his shoulders. "I've come to terms with it."

"Saw her in Sprouts the other day."

Rix's jaw bulged.

He *so* had not come to terms with it.

"She tried smiling at me. I flipped her the bird," Judge finished.

At that, Rix's lips spread wide in a huge white smile. "Seriously?"

Was *Rix* being serious?

"Dude, she fucked you over," Judge bit off. "Of course I'm serious."

"Think about it, man. Am I not better off without her?"

He absolutely was better off without that weak, cowardly bitch.

"You're a pain in the ass when you get all Zen," Judge mumbled.

"You do PT after a double amputation, learn to race a wheelchair, handle a handcycle and get used to new legs and running blades. Zen's the only way to go."

"Fuck you for being superhuman, then."

Rix let out a longsuffering sigh at how awesome he was. "It's always been the way."

Judge chuckled, but he didn't miss how quick Rix looked away and how he further hid what he was feeling behind another sip of beer.

Yeah.

Peri was a weak, cowardly bitch.

"I know you want to, check your phone," Rix invited to the blanket of midnight-blue, starry sky.

He'd turned his sound off, but he didn't get a vibration for a text.

Still, when he flipped the phone over, he had a notification he hadn't noticed.

An email.

From Chloe.

"She emailed," he muttered, opening the mail.

"Okay, maybe she isn't a player," Rix muttered back.

But he was wrong.

"What the fuck?" he asked his phone.

"Oh shit," Rix replied.

"She's blowing off Wednesday." He started opening attachments. "And Saturday." The attachments loaded, began coming up, and he skimmed. "And she did all the preliminary work on the project."

"That'll save you some time."

He looked to Rix. "And she says she wants to move forward through email," he glanced at his phone then quoted, *"for the time being."*

Rix did not look at all happy that he was right.

Judge returned to his phone, reread the message, and then pulled up his text string with Chloe.

"Right, hothead, take a breath," Rix advised.

"Fuck that," Judge gritted.

"Suit yourself, but you're gonna regret it."

He looked to his friend. "I broke through. And now she hands me this shit?" He waved his phone in the air.

"What makes you like her?" Rix asked.

"I told you. She's funny and—"

"Bullshit. What makes you like her, Judge?"

"I told you, man."

Rix leaned his way.

"Bullshit," he clipped. "She's different. You told me that after New Year's. Why?"

"There's something…"

Judge couldn't finish.

"You don't understand it yet?" Rix asked.

Oh, he understood it.

"She's vulnerable."

Rix's considerable muscled bulk landed back in his chair as if the power of what Judge said shoved him there.

"Lady in White Satin is vulnerable?" he asked with sheer disbelief.

"Don't give me shit."

"She's the visual definition of a maneater."

"She's also carrying the entire weight of her ludicrously famous, once worldwide-celebrated for the functional healthiness of their love, but now very broken family on her shoulders."

Rix winced before he replied, "Well…fuck."

"Uh, yeah," Judge concurred.

Rix had nothing to say to that.

Judge did. "There's more to it, I know it. She can't share because she can't be sure I won't buy a new car by selling it to some rag. That's a whole new version of alone we don't get."

"*I* don't get," Rix corrected. "You being Jameson Oakley's son, AJ Oakley's grandson, I think you get it. Or you get it more than me and maybe more than most folk she could meet. Does she know who your dad is?"

He nodded. "She asked if she needed to sign an NDA."

"She knows who your dad is," Rix murmured. Louder, he asked, "Does she know you got enough money to buy a fleet of Cherokees?"

Judge looked away.

"Well...fuck," Rix repeated. "You haven't told her she has nothing to worry about with that shit?"

"I want her to trust me because she trusts me. Not because my dad has offered to lay enough money on me I could buy a city block in downtown Phoenix and my granddad declared I'm the only 'real man' left of the Oakleys, so he's cut everyone else out of his will."

"Fun times for you when that old guy kicks it," Rix observed on another chug of his beer. And when he finished swallowing it, went on, "That happens, that family of yours is gonna land on you like the pile of stinking shit they are."

"Probably a decade of lawsuits." Judge chugged his own. "But they can have it. I have no interest in sucking more blood from the earth to perpetuate the cataclysmic damage of fossil fuel."

Rix grinned and tried to joke. "Because you'll already own a city block and then inherit the state of New York when your old man kicks it?"

Judge shook his head in disgust.

Rix chuckled.

But then he got serious again. "Vulnerable?"

"Yes."

"Man, I'm not sure you should go from finding the ones that want to take over the world and drag you along with them to hold their purses and eat their scraps to ones you gotta fix."

"Protect," Judge corrected.

Rix gave him a look.

Yeah.

It wasn't one or the other, it was both.

Fix and protect.

Like he'd failed to do with his mom.

Zeke settled back down between them with a groan.

Judge looked to his phone and then he typed in, *That email. Not cool.*

He sent it.

"Shit," Rix whispered.

Judge kept typing.

See you Wednesday.

He sent that too.

Nothing all day, but only a few seconds passed by, and he got something back with that.

I have something on.

He immediately texted, *Liar.*

No wait at all and then, *Something came up. And incidentally, how rude.*

Nothing came up except you had some time to work yourself up about how much you like me. Suck it up. We're exploring this. Zeke and I'll be hungry when we get there, but he'll need a bathroom break. Pizza's on you, I'll bring the beer. Order it to be there by six thirty, just in case I hit traffic and to give Zeke plenty of time to find his perfect spot.

I won't be here, Judge.

Your ass better be there, Chloe.

What'll happen if it isn't?

Obviously, via text, he couldn't tell if that was sarcastic or curious.

Knowing her, it was both.

Though she'd only let the sarcasm show.

You don't want to find out.

You're terrible with a threat.

No, if you're not there, I'll tell Duncan I can't work with you and I want you off the project.

Radio silence.

He sucked back some beer.

Zeke fell to his side and stretched out.

His phone vibrated.

Not. Gentlemanly. AT. ALL.

And there it was.

No way in hell was she going to give Duncan a headache, and through him, her mother, and through her, her father.

She'd bleed herself dry before she did that.

Regardless that he wasn't fighting fair and he knew it, Judge grinned at the midnight blue with its sparkling pinpricks outlining the purple-black ridge of mountains before he threw back the rest of his beer.

"Want another?" he asked Rix.

His friend drained his own, held out the empty and then grunted.

That meant yes.

Judge grabbed Rix's bottle, pushed out of his chair, avoided the firepit he'd lit to keep them warm in the chill mountain air and headed into his townhouse with Zeke coming out of repose to be at his heels.

But he didn't miss Rix's parting shot.

"Let the games begin."

Oh yeah.

Too fucking right.

In his life, he'd experienced the agony of defeat.

Way too fucking often.

But this one he was in to win.

CHAPTER 14

THE PIECES

Chloe

*I*t didn't bode well that it was physically painful to play Wednesday evening so I would be at the very least twenty minutes late to meet Judge at my place (in the end, checking the clock on my dash, it was twenty-three minutes).

However, it wasn't just pain, it was agony as I drove down my street, seeing him standing on my front stoop, a cute medium-size dog that was absolutely some kind of shepherd breed (or mix) with brindled fur and tongue-lolling happy grin on its adorable face sitting next to him, and on the other side of the stoop, a small cooler, probably filled with beer.

As he watched me drive by, Judge didn't look happy.

I wasn't happy either.

I suspected we were both thus for entirely different reasons.

I headed around back where my garage was, pulled in, parked, grabbed the pizza I'd personally picked up from Federal (I didn't ask, indeed, we hadn't texted since Monday night, but I went with prosciutto and date), along with the paper bag containing the wedge salads, my purse, attaché, and I walked into my house.

I put the food on the island and dropped my purse and case before I headed to the door.

Incidentally, not going directly to Judge leached massive reserves from my iron will.

I used more arranging my face in a part bored, mostly displeased expression before I finally opened the door.

"Hello, Judge," I greeted.

"Chloe," he replied. "Just to say, I know your head's twisted up with something, but my time on this earth is as limited, therefore just as precious as yours. You fucking twenty minutes of it away that I'll never get back is not okay. Even with this shit we got going on between us, due to the fact your head is twisted up, I'll remind you, not that I don't know what I want, that is still not okay."

In my frame of mind, although this was fair, and I deserved it, it was not a great place for him to start.

"I'll remind *you* that I didn't want to have this meeting," I retorted.

"And I'll remind *you* you don't got a choice."

Before I could say anything further, he clicked his tongue, his dog jumped up, body wagging with excited friendliness, and they both came into my house.

The dog was on a lead.

I did not want to like that Judge wasn't one of those people who just assumed, due to his love for his dog, that everyone should love it, but more, abide it willy-nilly in their space.

I did not trust people who didn't like animals.

That said, I did not like people who had some mistaken sense of entitlement that everyone should put up with their pets wherever they, as an animal owner, bringing along said animal, decided to be.

If it was genuinely a companion pet, that was one thing.

If it was your hyperactive springer spaniel that jumped on my leg while I was buying a sweater at Neiman's, that was another.

Judge having his dog on a lead gave indication he got this vital nuance of socially responsible pet ownership.

And as I said, I didn't want to like it.

(But I did.)

I wandered in with them and asked, "Did your dog find his perfect spot?"

"He's good," Judge muttered. And then he exacerbated my earlier concern about this new knowledge regarding Judge that I liked by asking, "You okay with him off the leash? He can hang out back, he's not destructive. Or I can keep him tethered to me. He'll be cool."

I did not want to be dying to greet his dog.

(But I was.)

"You can let him off," I replied.

"He'll come to you if I do," Judge warned.

Oh, I knew that already. The dog had his eyes trained to me and was in full body wag.

I refused to show my desperate desire to get my fingers into that soft fur.

Because it was a cute dog.

But also because it was Judge's dog.

"That's fine," I replied casually.

Judge bent and let the pooch free.

He came to me.

My love of animals and lifelong conditioning had me squatting to make myself less threatening, but also welcoming.

After a couple of get-to-know-you sniffs, I got a snuffle in the ear and a lick on the neck.

I fought my smile but didn't fight giving him a thorough head rub.

"Zeke," Judge said in a soft voice I immediately tucked away somewhere sealed tight, never to be remembered again.

The dog looked over his shoulder at his daddy.

"No, boy, enjoy. I'm telling Chloe your name," he said to his dog.

I'd noticed he was precious about this, and as such, hadn't offered it up until then.

It felt like a gift.

I refused to consider it a gift.

"Do you want water?" I asked the pup, rather than his dad.

"That'd be good. I have a travel bowl," Judge said, and I noticed for the first time he had a backpack hanging over one shoulder.

I got out of my crouch and we sorted that. Judge put the extra beers in the fridge. I got out plates, cutlery, and napkins. Judge opened two bottles. I unearthed the salads. All this was done in silence, like a comfortable, practiced dance.

It was torture.

Judge flipped the top of the pizza box over.

He then inquired, "What the hell is this?"

I wanted to laugh.

I did not laugh.

"Prosciutto, date, arugula, ricotta, pecorino and balsamic vinaigrette," I rolled off like I was a bored server.

Judge tried to lighten the atmosphere, delivering through a crooked (but still dimple-producing) grin. "Couldn't get pepperoni and sausage?"

"Do you not like what I got?" I asked coldly.

His grin died.

Something inside me shriveled.

"Yeah," he muttered.

Zeke came up and sniffed my feet.

It wasn't Zeke's fault I couldn't have his dad.

So I took time for more rubs, these full body.

Zeke licked my wrist.

Quiet, behaved, affectionate, crazy adorable.

Perfect.

Totally Judge's dog.

"Just stop when you're done giving the love. He's good at taking the hint."

Of course he was.

But I didn't want to stop.

I really did *not*.

I stopped.

Coming out of my crouch, I caught Judge's eyes on my heels, a look in them I never wanted to go away.

I sealed that up tight too, focusing instead on the fact I should change.

However, I wasn't going to.

I was going to get this done.

As fast as possible

"Let's work and eat at the coffee table," I said efficiently, but in a way that it was an order, slipping my laptop out of the attaché.

"Works for me," Judge replied unnecessarily, since nothing else was going to happen.

Nothing.

At all.

Ever.

My stomach clutched.

We loaded up salads, even though, for my part, eating it might make me sick. We grabbed beers, even though, for my part, I'd prefer to slug gin from a bottle. And Judge took his backpack to the coffee table, thankfully picking one of the armchairs flanking it, rather than the couch, where I wanted to sit, and I didn't want him to give indication he wanted to sit by me or have the awkwardness of me avoiding him.

Zeke seemed uncertain as to where to position himself. In the end, he proved how good a dog he was, politely, selecting sitting by his father as his place to beg for people food with his eyes.

We settled and Judge began, "Chloe—"

I cut in. "It'd be good to start with where your issues lie with my draft proposal."

"Chloe," that was somehow both sharper and warmer.

My gaze cut right to him.

And I said what I had to say.

"As it's obvious I didn't make myself clear, I'll do it now. We're not doing this," I declared. "You were right. After you left, I spent some time thinking about it. And yes, I find you attractive. Yes, we had a nice time this past weekend. But you're an employee of Duncan's. Duncan is soon to be my stepfather. As such, when it doesn't work out with us, it'll be messy. I don't do messy. And I don't make my family put up with messy."

His brows had bunched as I spoke, and he shared why with his, "When?"

"What?"

"*When* we don't work?"

I puffed a you-should-know-this-already mini-breath out of my nostrils.

And then I shared what he should know.

"I'm far too young to get seriously involved with a man. You're settled in Prescott. I love it there, but I have no intention or desire to move there. Frankly, if my boutique takes off as I hope it will, I'll be opening more, eventually moving back to LA. So, since this doesn't have the prospects of a good end, but it *does* have the prospects to make things awkward for people I care about, including me, I see no reason for it to begin."

That was a lie.

All of it, most especially the last.

But also about LA.

I'd been far away from my family for a good long spell when I was in France.

That wasn't going to happen again, not unless it was them that moved, and they did it to a place I didn't want to be.

Furthermore, I loved Phoenix. There was something...*unfinished* about it. Young. New. It was sprawling and impersonal in the sense you could be private, feel that privacy, but it was still friendly. There was culture. Class. History. Just the existence of the Biltmore Hotel and The Gammage made Phoenix somewhere I wanted to be.

In LA, I knew people.

In LA, my mother was the deposed queen.

In LA, I felt like a nobody.

Here, I was just me.

Judge cut into my train of thought.

He did this saying, "Fine."

On this word, I came back to the room and our conversation with a razor-sharp focus on his neutral face.

Not carefully neutral, or overly neutral, or affectedly neutral.

Genuinely neutral.

He was fine with us not going there, not angry.

Just...

Neutral.

Oh my God.

What had I thought this was?

I was an attractive woman. I was, indeed, interesting. I had a famous family, and that made me more interesting. I did not want for male attention.

He saw me, I saw him, sparks flew, something came of that, but we'd only had a day and a half where it was something we were both exploring.

Through it, and especially recently, I was adamant about not going there. I'd behaved badly on more than one occasion. The email had been an appalling idea. Judge was right, it was uncool. It wasn't like we had anything to break up, but that was ill-mannered and detached and Judge didn't deserve that.

Then there was my most recent speech.

And he was good with that.

He was no longer here to talk me into more exploration of what could be us, not after I'd laid it out, making no bones about it.

He was "fine" with that.

With utterly no warning, it happened, besieging me in a way I couldn't ignore.

So I dumped my salad on the coffee table and stood abruptly.

My movement was so sudden, Zeke lost interest in the bacon on Judge's wedge and his head whipped around.

Judge's also snapped back to look up at me.

"I need to change out of these work clothes," I said, my voice breathy, wrong. "This won't take long, but I've been in these clothes all day. My feet are killing me."

"All right," Judge said slowly.

Too slowly.

I didn't notice.

I had to get out of there.

So I did.

Humiliatingly, I dashed from the couch and ran up the steps.

When I got to my room, I closed the door without turning on a single light, and I stood in the darkness.

I would not cry.

I would *not*.

"I'm not going to cry," I whispered, elbows bent, wrists loose, shaking my hands in front of me.

I needed to get it together.

I needed to change clothes.

I needed to put on something comfortable, not stylish, or overtly attractive.

I didn't think I owned anything like that.

I ran to my closet and threw on the light.

I'd only been in the dark for seconds, but that light blinded me.

In that flash of sightlessness, my mind filled with Judge and his cute, well-behaved dog and his cooler on my front stoop.

Waiting for me to come home.

Waiting for me.

Call me if you want to talk.

"God, God, God," I panted, something itching in my throat, crawling over my skin.

My clothes came in focus, and I began to clack hangers around indiscriminately.

But your brother and sister should know you've got your own baggage to unpack.

My eyes started stinging.

What I mean is, I'll shield you as best as I can.

I swallowed.

It hurt.

God, how it *hurt*.

Until you shared what was behind your big speech and I could have been there for you in whatever way you might've needed me.

I stopped clacking hangers and wrapped my fingers over my mouth, worried I was going to be sick.

I then covered my face in both of hands, closed my eyes tight, scrunching with the effort.

Susan Shepherd's picture flashed in my head.

This was followed by the memory of Matt telling me to go fuck myself at Duncan's New Year's party.

Then another, of Sasha during her beach volleyball days, long and lithe and tan, hitting a spike that won the match, and turning a sunny, victorious smile Dad's way even before she ran to her teammate to give her a hug.

On to Mom in that beautiful, floaty lilac gown that she'd eventually given me. Dad dapper and so very handsome in his tux at her side. The perfect couple. Perfectly beautiful. Perfectly happy. It was the first time (but not the last) that I could remember them saying goodbye to us before they were off to attend the Oscars.

From that, I went to Duncan's face, the gratitude, the stark need— a need to know me, a need to connect with what was hers, what she made—the first time I met him and told him I was Imogen's daughter.

Then to Dad asking me to Capitol Grille because he had no one else to go with.

I swallowed again, and almost gagged, my nose plugging up with a wave of consuming emotions.

"Pick an outfit and get it together, Coco. Just an outfit, and getting it fucking *together*, Coco," I verbally lashed at myself.

I dropped my hands.

Deep breath.

Right.

Another.

More hanger clacking.

This time, with determination.

I picked a rosy-hued jogger and slouchy top ensemble.

I kicked off my heels. Peeled down my skinny jeans. Tore off my blouse.

Gone were the accessories.

I donned my outfit.

I bunched my hair in a clip at the back.

And I faced the door.

I was Chloe Marilyn *fucking* Pierce.

My parents had gotten divorced.

A man I trusted betrayed everyone I loved.

Including me.

But I had everything I needed and nearly everything I wanted, from the three pairs of shoes I lost my mind and bought in a fog of euphoria at being around Judge and seeing how much Tiffany liked him, not to mention how much he liked her, to the bottomless depths of love I had from friends, family, and the new family I had in Duncan, Sullivan and Gage.

I had nothing to complain about.

I would be fine.

I would be fine.

On this thought, I squared my shoulders, sniffed the final remnants of unshed tears away, sucked in the biggest breath I'd ever taken, and headed downstairs.

Judge did not hide he was watching for me when I came down.

"You good?" he asked.

There was concern there. Kind concern.

No piercing looks or anything deep muddying his eyes.

He'd given it a go with me.

I made things clear.

Like the decent man he was, he was backing off.

Now, I was just a human who'd run off, and he was a human who gave a shit about other humans.

That was all.

And it *killed.*

To answer him, I told the biggest lie I'd ever uttered in my life, and we could just say there were a fair few that tested the limits of such modifiers as "little."

This one was flat-out propaganda.

"Yes, I'm great," I replied, and with two sets of male eyes on me, I resumed my seat.

"Cool," Judge said quietly. And then he said, "The ideas you sent were great, but gotta warn you, you're not gonna like my feedback."

Fabulous.

He kept going.

"The thing is, the power of the message is both of them delivering it together, rather than footage of them hiking different trails solo and having jumps between them as they share it. This isn't just about nature. It's about doing stuff with your friends. Rallying them, getting outside and being active. I know it's tough for you to have to put them together, but it's the way to go. And I can guarantee you, no shade on what you did, it was good work, but Duncan is gonna nix your idea, and from how he was talking, I think Tom would too."

"You're right," I sniffed. "Wishful thinking."

Judge nodded. "Though, maybe as they talk, we can have them jump to different trails. I've made a budget I think will fly, definitely it'll be covered by what the campaign brings in without the percentage of expense versus net gain being screwed. The season isn't right for easy travel right now, there'll be snow in Colorado, Utah, anywhere else with picturesque trails that are close, and they, like you, probably want this done and behind them. But we can do Arizona, some spots in New Mexico might be good, and definitely California. I'm sending the budget I mocked up to you now."

My laptop chimed with a new mail.

I pulled it up.

It was his budget.

From there, Judge kept talking, eating, sipping his beer, stroking his dog, getting up to grab slices of pizza, and except for the sustenance part, it was all about work.

Only about the project.

And I learned something else I didn't like (but I did).

He was astute, savvy, creative, reasonable, responsive, knowledgeable and passionate.

It hadn't occurred to me there was a reason Duncan picked Judge to run the only charity program River Rain Outdoor Stores put their brand on.

But there was.

I'd dealt with more than my fair share of people working in non-profits.

Judge was better than half of them and could easily compete with all the rest. Even the executive directors of nationwide programs.

I didn't know if Duncan understood what he had in Judge.

But regrettably, I did.

In an hour and a half, we had a rough script, general blocking, a tweaked budget, a draft travel itinerary and shooting schedule, and Judge's stuff was packed in his backpack, his quiet, sweet dog was on his lead, his cooler in hand, and I was trailing them to the door.

He turned at it and said, "Email me when you can meet on Sunday to scout locations."

Excuse me, *what?*

"Sorry?" I asked.

"We're gonna need to hike the trails and decide locations. I'll do the research into what might be viable for LA and New Mexico, if Duncan signs off on this budget. But when we present to them, I want to have something visual to show them."

A flutter of panic trembled around my heart.

"Can you not do that yourself?" I requested.

"Chloe, that's gotta be you," he denied. "I can do the scripting, budgeting, projecting and messaging, but the visual shit is not my thing."

That made sense.

However.

"Okay, then I can go alone."

"Who's going to film you?"

Film me?

"I—"

He interrupted me before I even began.

"Right, get over it," he ordered. "It's not a big thing. We gave it a go. It was promising. You don't wanna go there. I'm down with that. I got a program to run and a world-class athlete has hitched his wagon to it. We've never had this huge of an opportunity. I'm not gonna fuck it up. It's your family's name and face, you're not gonna fuck it up. What happened, happened. It lasted a minute. Now it's done. We both can be professional, do our parts, together and separate, and get it done right. I'll email my address. Meet me at eleven at my place on Sunday. We'll do the hike, scout some spots, take some footage, and then I'll build the presentation for Tom and Duncan to sign off on. You in with that?"

It's not a big thing.

You don't want to go there. I'm down with that.

What happened, happened... It's done.

"Chloe?"

I jerked myself out of my head.

"Yes. Fine. Eleven. Email your address."

"Come prepared to hike," he pushed. "We're not going to hit a spot that looks dangerous or difficult, but we'll be out in nature and the sun. And it could be chilly."

"I've hiked before, Judge," I stated coolly.

"Right. Okay, we're good then." He tipped up his chin. "Thanks for the pizza. Later." With that, and before I could even stretch out a hand to give Zeke a goodbye pat, or say a word of farewell to his dad, Judge shook the lead, made a kiss noise, and murmured, "C'mon, buddy."

And that was it.

They were out the door.

I stood in it for several seconds, watching them walk to his Cherokee before I realized I was doing it.

Then I closed and locked the door.

I stared at it and declared, "I'm not going to fall apart."

I did not fall apart.

I tidied the pizza and beer bottles, then put the dishes in the washer. I packed up my laptop in preparation for the next day. I poured myself a glass of wine.

After I accomplished all that, I headed upstairs, brushed my hair, twisted it up again, pushed it back with a band, cleaned my face and slathered on a mask.

I read for half an hour as I sipped my wine.

I then took off the mask, moisturized, brushed my teeth, took the clip out of my hair and twisted a silk scrunchy in it. I walked my wineglass back down, rinsed it, turned out the lights, made sure all doors were secure, then I went upstairs and climbed in bed.

Lying there, wide awake in the dark, then and only then did I allow myself to fall apart.

And when I did, I was unsurprised I didn't crumble away.

Instead, I shattered to pieces.

CHAPTER 15

THE ALLIES

Chloe

*T*he next day, I was inventorying the floor, checking to see we had browse availability of all sizes that were in stock, when I heard, "Excuse me."

I turned and then smiled at a woman who was probably around my mother's age. Great hair, fantastic pair of glasses, curvy figure, *fabulous* outfit.

She was also carrying two peach bags with black handles, and in bold, feminine script of gold foil written across the sides, my store's name, Velvet.

"Can I help?" I asked.

"Mi-Young, your manager, told me you were the owner," she said, tipping her chestnut-with-champagne-highlighted head toward the checkout desk where Mi was standing.

"I am." I turned fully to the customer. "Is everything all right?"

"I just wanted to say, I drive by this store all the time. I noticed your windows months ago, but since I'm driving by, I never got the chance to really look at them. Even if I did, I would just expect it was another kind of store."

I wasn't sure by her demeanor that I wanted to know what kind of store she thought it was.

Even if she was carrying two bags containing my merchandise.

"I met someone for lunch down the way," she went on. "Walked by, and saw you had a curvy model in your window. I couldn't believe it. I came in, and then I couldn't believe what I found."

She seemed to have found a lot. I'd noticed her perusing and spending a good deal of time in our changing rooms.

And her bags were filled to the brim.

"I'm hoping your bags mean you found some things you adore," I remarked.

"I did. And I found all of it in my size," she stated.

She couldn't know this, and I wasn't going to tell her outside what she experienced. But I didn't stock designers who didn't go up to at least 3X and size twenty-four.

I smiled. "I'm so pleased."

"Your clothes are stylish."

"I'm glad you think so."

"You don't get it. Shops like this..." She shook her head. "Your things are edgy. Chic. Current. For the most part, I find things that Bea Arthur would wear on *Golden Girls*. It's okay, but it definitely tells me to act my age. I just don't understand why my age has to be defined as waiting-for-my-grandchildren-to-be-born."

"It doesn't," I replied firmly, sticking to only those two words, because if one got me started on this subject, I could rant on it for days.

And never get me started on the term "plus-size."

I loathed it.

Women were women. There was no reason to segment them.

Label them.

Legs came in different lengths it was necessary for fit to note how a hem might fall.

But there were not "normal-sized" women and "plus-sized" women.

There were women.

The end.

"I know, and I'm glad you do too," she replied. "I'm delighted to walk in a shop and not have to hold my breath that some styles I like won't come in my size, and as such, won't be for me. I'm thrilled that it's all mixed together. Even your jewelry, which a lot of the time at other places doesn't fit around my neck, or my wrist." She lifted one of her bags. "Yours does."

I kept smiling. "One of our lovely associates helps me make certain that everything we carry is inclusive."

I was alluding to Jocelyn, who was on staff, but doubled as our body positive model on social media because she was a size 20, but mostly because she was *fabulous*, and she knew it.

Incidentally, I sold staff the merchandise at cost, and in most cases, let them pick what they wanted me to order before I purchased it for the store, so I could make sure they'd have the pieces they wanted, and they were wearing them fresh when the stock was on the floor.

Albeit most stores gave a discount, I had two students on staff who wouldn't be able to afford it, even on a discount.

So at cost it was, and no skin off my nose, the rest of the clothes were being ordered regardless, throwing more pieces in only increased my status with my suppliers.

It was a tried-and-true system to have your associates attired in your apparel.

I'd tried it, and it held true.

The customer nodded and carried on.

"Eloquii and Lane Bryant have some great clothes, and Nordstrom has a nice curvy section. But most of it is online. I like to shop. Try on. And the clothes are separate. Either completely different stores, or clothes for me are in another section. Like, people like me need to be hidden away. Like, the people not like me don't want to be rubbing shoulders with me when they shop. They don't want to look at me. And they definitely don't want to think that something they wear might be something I'd put on my body. It makes me feel like a pariah. Like I should feel shame when I'm shopping. Shame about my body, shame about wanting to look good. I love shopping, but it's sometimes hard, and there are times it even makes me sad. I actually have friends I don't shop with anymore because it's uncomfortable. Their clothes aren't in my section, and vice versa."

"I'm glad you weren't sad in Velvet," I said quietly.

"I wasn't, not at all," she asserted. "You're young, you're slender, so beautiful, so you can't even begin to know what it means..." She cleared her throat. "Like I said, I have friends. A lot of them. In every shape and size. Those other stores..." She lifted both bags this time. "To quote a pretty woman, mistake. Big mistake. *Huge*." She grinned at me. "See you again sometime soon."

"I hope so," I replied. "And when you return, ask for Chloe or Mi. One of us is always here, and we'll take personal care of you. And if you give us a heads up, we'll have a bottle of champagne waiting."

The woman actually got tears in her eyes before she dipped her chin, gave me a trembling smile, and walked out of the shop.

I watched her go, thinking how beautiful it felt I gave that to her.

As well as how badly I needed what she just gave me.

I then finished the section I was working and started to head to the back to grab some sizes to restock.

"Hey," Mi called before I cleared the floor of the store.

I turned to her. "Hey."

"That lady made your week," Mi told me.

She didn't.

She made my month.

Best thing that'd happened so far, considering the good parts with Judge were blown to smithereens by the fact we lasted "a minute" and he was happy to move on.

"As in, she bought that red leather jacket, among a *ton* of other things," Mi explained.

I turned to our red section and saw the only red leather jacket that we'd had left—a size 20—was gone.

That had been a hot item that I was pleased, in Phoenix, I took the chance of stocking two in each size, rather than one. I'd sold all the others at full price, which was $850. I didn't want to discount the last. It was a good markup, a tidy profit.

Add that to another bag and a half worth of stuff and yes, maybe she *did* make my week.

It felt better that maybe I made hers.

"We need to do more marketing around our size ranges," I noted, thinking about that conversation, and how maybe testimonials, or even customer models on professional shoots, were possible ways to go.

Tell them their friends could come to the shoot. Have select items on hand for a discount.

"That's hard, Coco," Mi replied, cutting into my buzzing mind.

It was.

Because our new customer had not lied.

An extended size range appealed to women who were size 14 and over.

It had the opposite affect with the others.

That said, 68 percent of women were size 14 and above, 25 percent of all online shopping was browsing for curvy size clothes, and again, 68 percent of "plus" consumers were interested in partici-pating in fashion trends.

And I would repeat, one shouldn't get me started on how I felt about dressing mature women.

Hint: Unless she enjoyed the freedom of caftans and jersey sets and flowy kimonos, she should embrace whatever style she wanted.

However, the golden goose marketing strategy for Velvet was one that appealed to millennials, Gen X, and people of all sizes, not to mention all colors.

As yet, my experience was, such a strategy didn't exist.

But if it did, I was determined to find it.

"We can brainstorm," I told her, then shared, "I'm heading back. There are things to restock."

Before I took two steps, Mi called, "Chloe."

I turned to her again.

"You okay?" she asked.

No, I absolutely was not.

"Of course," I answered.

She tipped her head to the side, her sheet of gleaming ebony hair tipping with it.

"Sure?"

"Absolutely."

I began to move away again.

"You haven't said a word about Judge. Not since you texted me you were still with him at five on Sunday," she noted.

"We saw each other last night," I told her.

She brightened.

"We worked on the project. We have a solid plan. It's good. We also decided not to see each other in that way. Too messy."

Her face fell.

"It's okay," I outright lied.

"I thought he was really nice, and Jacob super liked him."

He *was* nice and *super* likeable.

It was also *very* nice my best friend approved of him and strangely, even better her boyfriend got on with him.

Women could be hoodwinked by men (with the men doing the hoodwinking).

Other men could often see through that.

"He works for my soon-to-be-stepdad," I pointed out.

"He's very into you," she returned.

He'd seemed to be.

"And you seemed very into him," she carried on.

Hmm.

"If it didn't work, it would be uncomfortable," I noted.

She now appeared confused. "Are Duncan and Judge good buddies?"

"They work together," I reiterated.

"I thought Duncan was the CEO of the chain and Judge was the director of their kids' program."

"That's right."

"They work side by side every day?" she asked dubiously.

"They see each other every day."

"There's like, hundreds of River Rain stores across the nation," she declared.

"I think that number is actually something like seventy-seven," I corrected.

"What I'm saying is, they both have important jobs, but you shouldn't hold back because it's not like Judge is Duncan's assistant or the VP of buying. He runs a program that's somewhat independent of the stores. Even if they work in the same offices, there are probably a lot of people who work there. It's unlikely they interact day to day."

"What *I'm* saying is, we're not that into each other."

Mi-Young read my tone and her lips pursed, pushing up into her nose.

It was cute.

It was provoking.

It told me she knew I was in a mood, she was not going to deal with me in this mood, but this conversation wasn't over.

"Can I go grab that stock?" I asked fake-sweetly.

"Be my guest," she returned, taking my sweet to the highest heights of fake.

I shot her a bored look.

She flicked her sheet of perfect hair.

God, she always won in a catfight.

I did my best to move away at a cavalier pace.

But I feared I looked like what I was.

Escaping.

"I'M FEELING...LOBSTER," I ANNOUNCED THAT EVENING ABOUT TWO seconds after the server walked away from our table with our drink order.

I hadn't even looked at my menu.

"Of course you are," Dad murmured, sitting on the other side of the booth from me, grinning down at his menu, looking gorgeous, as always.

Tall, lean, fit, athletic, dark, with patrician features that had more than a mild hint of roguishness.

Dad did not have the look of the knight in shining armor.

He had the look of the prodigal son.

Every girl knew that was not the smarter choice, but it was the better one.

He'd been a heartthrob as a breakout teen star on the tennis circuit.

He'd become a heartbreaker when he'd grown up.

And that (no prejudice, truly) had never died. I saw the fanmail his assistant had to sort through every month. It was not a joke.

And just like Mom's, it could get unnerving.

I allowed him time to make his selection (I really was feeling, and ordering, lobster, so I didn't bother looking) and to put down his menu before I asked, "And how are you, *mon père bien-aimé?*"

He smiled. "I'm well, my beloved daughter, how are you?"

"Perfect," I chirped.

His face clouded.

"Oh Christ, what's going on?" he asked, likely because I never (ever) chirped, then, before I could answer, he presented another question. "Is it your mother fixing you up with Judge Oakley?"

It seemed odd that he'd use both Judge's names.

"I'd heard the kids ribbing you about things during Christmas," he went on. "Though I had no idea who he was then, since he was only referred to as Judge. When Gen shared what she was up to, I told her it wasn't a good idea. But then you showed and went outside with him, and you two seemed close when we were having dinner."

We had?

"And he's a good kid," Dad carried on. "Far as I know, he has been his whole life."

I blinked.

"Sorry? His whole life?" I queried.

"Yeah, I met him when he was…" Dad had to think on it and then he said, "Four, five. You weren't born yet. Or maybe your mom was pregnant with you, or about to be. Around that time."

What…the…*fuck*?

"You…*know*…Judge?" I pushed.

Judge hadn't mentioned this.

Neither had Dad or Mom.

"'Know' is a stretch," Dad answered, his gaze never leaving my face. "Though I know his father, Jamie."

I drummed my fingers on the table and glared at him.

"What's with the patented Chloe Death Stare?" he asked. "Are you seeing him?"

"No." That hurt to say, but I pushed through it. "But it would have been nice if you," *or Mom*, "had shared you'd met him before."

"Once, when he was four. That said, Jamie speaks of him a lot," Dad stated. "You're not seeing him?"

"No," I bit off.

"Too bad," Dad mumbled.

Of course Dad liked Judge.

Of course.

I kept at him. "Mom didn't mention you'd met him either."

"I'm not sure she would know. She was still doing *Rita's Way* back then. She was at home in California. I was in New York doing a fundraising thing. That's how I met Jamie. There was a ball the night before the match. He introduced himself. It was the next day during the match I met Judge."

Hang on a moment.

"Wait, *during* the match?"

"If you Google it, there might be pictures," he noted. "The crowd loved it."

Good Lord.

There were pictures of Dad and Judge on a tennis court?

"He wandered out on the court," Dad went on.

And there it was.

Yes.

There were pictures.

Dad kept speaking.

"He'd grabbed one of my rackets before anyone noticed he was out there. The crowd started tittering, he nabbed a ball and lobbed it at me. I had another racket in my hand. We had a five-minute play match. He won. Natural backhand, by the way."

"He was *four* and had a backhand?"

Dad shrugged. "Saw me use it and emulated me. Almost picture perfect. It was uncanny. I told his dad to get him lessons."

"Judge didn't mention this," I murmured, thinking it was absolutely something you mentioned.

Maybe even in your top five things to know about this person you were making out with copiously.

For instance, *Say, when I was a toddler, I played tennis with your dad.*

Or, *I beat your father in tennis. I was four.*

"I'm pretty sure he doesn't remember it," Dad said. "At least, he didn't mention it."

Seriously?

"Even if he doesn't remember, I can't imagine his father doesn't have a picture of him playing tennis at four with the Great Tom Pierce," I drawled. "Or hasn't told that story a thousand times since that day."

Dad's lips quirked at my title for him, but they did this as he studied me closely.

"Or, say, *you* might have mentioned it," I kept at him.

"He didn't grow up with his dad, honey."

Oh Lord.

Judge hadn't mentioned that either.

"Jamie married his high school sweetheart," Dad continued. "I met her that night. She was gorgeous. And totally vacant. Seen it before, Valium trance. She was zoned out."

Oh my *God.*

"Big scandal." Dad shifted in his seat. I'd know why when he said uncomfortably, "Jamie cheated on her. But honestly, until very recently, I didn't know if she divorced him, or he divorced her. But it was the latter."

I stared at him.

Judge hadn't shared any of this.

Then again, I didn't ask.

I'd been all about me.

All about pretending I wasn't attracted to him.

All about my Cooking Club. My friends. My brunch. My shopping.

My issues.

And, I had to admit, my varied tests for him.

All of which he had passed.

I had asked the five top things about him, and I could understand why one didn't choose to reveal in that short discourse, "My dad cheated on my mom and then we split New York City."

He'd been very attentive, inquisitive, he seemed to enjoy meeting my friends, being at my side as I lived my life.

But he'd never volunteered a single thing.

"Jamie and I were more than acquaintances," Dad told me. "But we weren't quite friends either. We were in that in between. Until, I should say, recently."

Until recently.

"Why recently?"

"He called after Sam did what she did on that gossip show."

Wonderful.

But that made sense.

Judge's cheating father called my cheating father after my father's cheating became public.

We'd quashed it.

Still.

"He had some advice to share," Dad said carefully.

"Well, good." I reached for my water. "It's nice to have friends who understand."

"Right," Dad said quietly.

I sipped my water.

Mercifully, Dad returned to the subject at hand.

"When Judge didn't say anything, I didn't mention meeting him when he was young because his relationship with his father is strained."

More I never bothered to find out.

Dad kept speaking.

"Jamie didn't want to lose his boy, Chloe, but he did. The divorce was acrimonious. Out there. Picked over. Ugly. And the ensuing battles were lengthy. She fought for custody. She fought for money. She won. Then she kept fighting at every turn. It's my understanding she moved with Judge back to Texas, where she and Jamie grew up. It's also my understanding things did not go well there, and Jamie was not happy she'd moved his son that far away from him. He was less pleased that she used every dime she won in the settlement to keep Judge from him, when she wasn't using it for other things. And even worse, how it ended up that the only father figure Judge really had was his granddad, AJ."

"He shared all this with you?"

Dad nodded. "Recently, yes, after I phoned and told him I was working with Judge. Did... *Judge* not share this with you?"

"We're not that close," I prevaricated, not meeting his eyes as I put my water down.

And I didn't ask, I thought but didn't add.

Then again, Judge had reasons to keep things from me too. Private things his family didn't want public.

Though, this all sounded like it happened out in the open.

Which was worse.

Way worse.

"Jamie remarried," Dad continued. "Not the woman he'd cheated with, another one. A couple of years ago, she died of breast cancer. I met her too. They were very close. Been married nearly two decades, but they acted like newlyweds."

Much like you and Mom, before that turned to shit.

Though I found it interesting he mentioned *not the woman he cheated with*.

I wasn't sure how that was relevant.

Though I was sure how Dad saying it was relevant to me.

The server came with our drinks.

It was a gin-themed night.

G&T for dad, Pink Lady for me.

We ordered our appetizers (another theme, I was having lobster bisque with my lobster) and the server moved away.

Dad lifted his glass my way. "Here's to the prettiest girl in the world."

That always got me.

Thus, I smiled and tipped my glass his way. "Here's to the best dad in history."

He returned my smile.

We drank.

Then Dad launched in. "Are you not interested in him?"

Yes.

Dad liked Judge.

Or maybe partly it was that, and partly it was the fact he really did *not* like any of the artists and assholes I'd previously dated.

Hesitantly, I reminded him, "He works with Duncan."

"Duncan was in on this setup, honey," Dad pointed out.

I closed my mouth.

"All right, I'll let it go," Dad relented. Such a soft touch, Tom Pierce. "I'm just going to say one thing."

Not totally soft, though.

I rolled my eyes.

His lips tipped up as he watched me do this.

But he got serious when he said, "You seemed very comfortable with him."

Oh Lord.

"I've never seen you that way with a man."

Oh Lord!

"And, I don't know what you two were talking about outside, but he was hanging on every word you said."

I looked away, unable to take staring at my father while he said these things about the man I could not have.

"I don't think Duncan would mind if you wanted to go out with him," Dad finished.

I was still trying to hide from my father at the same time as I was in the same booth with him when something hit me.

I looked directly back at Dad.

"What other things was she using it for?"

"Pardon?"

"Judge's mother. The money. You said, 'when she wasn't using it for other things.' What other things was she using it for?"

My father didn't answer at first.

And when he spoke, he still didn't.

He asked his own question.

"Are you sure you're not interested in Judge?"

"Dad, just answer me."

"I'm uncomfortable doing that if you intend to see him. Although it's widely known and would be an easy deep dive with a simple Google search, much of what I told you is his to tell. Especially that."

"We're not seeing each other, and we won't be."

"Are you certain?"

"Yes," I gritted.

"Why?"

Because he's marvelous, and what happens to me when I get used to that marvelous? When it's my life? When I count on it being there every day? And then he breaks my heart? I don't have a childhood sweetheart to rediscover.

I'll be lost.

Alone.

And broken.

Naturally, I said none of these things to my dad.

"He's not my type," I said instead.

"Please know this is coming from an honest, loving place when I say, I'm not certain that's a bad thing."

I clicked my teeth in irritation.

Dad ignored that.

"I'll finish that by saying, if you're attracted to him, you should consider it. Life is a risk. But you win nothing if you don't risk anything."

"I'm putting that on your coffee mug this Christmas," I kidded.

There was thoughtfulness in his eyes even as he smiled at my reference to Sully and Gage's Christmas presents to us all: personalized coffee mugs, most of which had things we'd said that they'd thought was hilarious on them.

The one they'd given me didn't go with either my office or home décor.

But at home, red with black lettering that said, I'M GOING TO HAVE TO GET YOU IN HAND, one of the first things I'd ever said to Gage, it was the only one I drank from.

"Now, as promised, enough about that," Dad finally ended it.

"So, tell me about Judge's mother and the money," I kept at it.

"Maybe you should reflect on why you want to know so badly," he muttered.

I needed no reflection.

I knew why.

It just didn't matter.

"I can hear you," I singsonged, and when he gave me a knowing smirk, I went on, "And that isn't telling me."

Dad looked me straight in the eye and said, "Belinda Oakley is an addict, Chloe. Her settlement was millions, child support was thousands a month. Judge went to university at eighteen and never came back, so child support ceased. She still should have had enough to live on very comfortably until she died. But now, she lives in a town outside Dallas and works as a waitress in a diner. It's cliché. It's also the terrible truth."

"Good Lord," I breathed.

"This gives indication why Judge never went back," Dad remarked. "Now, in all fairness to Judge, even if you two aren't going to become an item, you still have to work together on our project, and this isn't right. Enough. Let it go and let's enjoy dinner."

I nodded absently.

I was absent because I was thinking.

I knew Judge's father was a billionaire, I did not know he was from Texas.

I knew nothing about the mom.

Or this AJ granddad person.

And now I wondered if Judge had been okay with me making it plain we weren't going to carry on because he had a moment to think about what a self-centered harpy I was.

My bisque came along with Dad's shrimp cocktail.

We ate.

We had father-daughter time.

I settled in the knowledge that at least one night this week, my father wasn't home, alone, knowing his ex-wife, the love of his life was loved up in the mountains, looking forward to planning a wedding to another man.

I attempted to make our time jovial and fun for him, even if I couldn't quite stop being distracted.

Dad was a dad and, indeed, the best father in history.

So, at the evening's end, before he helped me into my car, right after he kissed my cheek, he whispered in my ear, "Take a risk, give him a chance."

I pulled my head back and looked into his beautiful eyes.

Eyes he'd given me.

I then smiled but said nothing.

I just got in my car, and he watched me drive away.

As I was driving home, my phone buzzed with a text.

It was somewhat late, not too late, still, I was surprised.

I was more surprised when I checked it after I walked into my house.

It was from Gage.

Buckle up, we're hanging out this weekend.

This made me smile because Gage was a good time.

He was young (nineteen), but sweet and still pliable.

I had many things to teach my green grasshopper.

This weekend (or at least Saturday) was the perfect time to pick up our lessons.

I was putting down my clutch and turning on a light when another text came in.

This also from Gage.

Because you need brother time seeing as Matt's being a total dick.

Oh dear.

I was about to reply, but I got another text.

From Sully.

Now, Sully was an entirely different kettle of fish.

His text proved it.

FaceTime, now.

And then my phone rang with a FaceTime call.

"*Merde*," I bit, rearranged my expression to severe and took the call. "Sullivan, do I need to explain why women don't like to be treated as on demand?"

He had no response to that.

He had other things to say.

"You know, it's not my deal. I barely know your dad, though he seems a cool guy to me. It's their deal. I'm not butting into that. But fuck this shit with Matt being an asshole to you."

"Sully," I whispered.

"No," he clipped. "And you know, Sasha needs to get her head out of her ass too. I've been through a divorce. I get it. It sucks. It's out of your control and everyone is hurting, and it's not in your control to make that stop either. You don't lash out when that shit's going down, especially at each other. And by that, I mean siblings. Gage and I were always tight, but during the divorce, we got tighter. Because we were looking out for each other. We didn't plan it or talk about it, we just did it. Because we're brothers. You seem like you're always wearing armor. Impenetrable. But anyone who cares about you knows that's for show. So they should know your armor has vulnerabilities. And they sure as shit shouldn't use that knowledge to aim a kick at your soft spots."

I said nothing.

But what I thought was, my new brother had just gone through a breakup, a Christmas blow his girlfriend had landed right before he'd flown home to be with his family, and Sullivan was undoubtedly still wounded from that.

When I'd first seen him after he'd returned home, it didn't say much about me, but I'd wanted to find her and put Nair in her shampoo bottle.

To start.

However, this occurrence made me vow (and this phone conversation cinched it), when Sullivan found the one he thought was actually the one, I was putting her through a test of fire only the most pure of heart would survive.

And she had better pass with flying colors.

Or I was poisoning her.

I'd do my time if caught (though I would never get caught).

But Sully was only going to have the best.

For the rest of his life.

"And don't be pissed at me for wading in," he ordered. "We're family now, Coco, and I am not fucking down with Matt taking his shit out on you and dragging Sasha in to help him do it."

"How do you know about this?" I asked.

"Yeah, let's talk about that. What the fuck with you not calling?"

I was quiet again.

"Matt was over, we were having some beers," he belatedly answered. "Sasha called, and he put her on speaker so we could all talk together. They started in on you, and I laid them out then asked Matt to leave. Sasha was a mess. But fuck it. She's old enough to know better."

Sully was one year older than her, so he'd know.

Not to mention, he was correct.

"You asked Matt to leave?"

"Did you tell him to talk to your dad?"

"Yes."

"And that's it?"

"For the most part, to my recollection."

"And he's pissing and moaning about that? If Gage was carrying a grudge for...fucking...ever, I'd tell him to sort his shit too."

It was then I realized.

He was a firstborn, the responsible one, the protector.

The same as me.

I had someone who got it.

I could not talk to him about Susan Shepherd. I could not rope him into maybe (or discuss the merits of maybe not) getting involved with that with Dad. And as such, I couldn't discuss the pros and cons of making a call to the mysterious Rhys Vaughan. And because Sullivan was so protective (case in point, this call), I couldn't tell him about Vaughan at all.

Dangerous mystery man who lands a file on me that the only thing it didn't include on my father's lover was her bra size, then he shows at my shop exuding menace and making me wonder if he's who James Bond was after, or who Bond wished he was...

Sully would lose his mind.

And absolutely I couldn't talk to him about Judge.

But I could talk to him about this.

"Obviously, I need a cocktail to fully commit to *my* pissing and moaning about how infantile my brother and sister are being."

Sullivan's lips twitched and he replied, "Obviously."

Even though it was much later in Indiana, I went to the kitchen.

Sully kept talking.

"You should know, Gage is coming up this weekend. He says he's taking you 'on the town.' Prepare to party in someone's garage."

I started chuckling.

But I felt better than I had in days.

"And I want you to think about coming out for a visit," he carried on.

"To *Indiana*?" I asked, aghast.

He laughed. "Yes, to Indiana. I'll take you to Harry's. And we'll drive down to Indy. On tours, they take you in a van around the track at the 500."

"This is not a selling point, Sullivan."

He laughed more.

I made my cocktail.

And yes, as we chatted, it started seeping in.

Feeling loved.

Looked after.

Not alone.

Understood.

Definitely.

I felt better than I had in days.

But when it was over.

When it was dark and I was in bed, a bed that was empty, save for me.

I didn't feel better at all.

CHAPTER 16

THE LUNCH

Corey

Three and a half years ago...

CHLOE HAD PICKED THE RESTAURANT.

But of course she had.

He'd heard about it.

And what he'd heard, it was superb.

They had a two-top table. He'd arrived before she did, selecting the chair on the outside that would face the booth bench on the inside that sat against the side wall.

He made this selection not only because the lady should get the better seat, but also so people could look at her, and with Chloe being Chloe, they might not notice Corey at all.

He saw her in the gold marbled mirror above the bench seat, making her way to the table.

Dark hair falling in waves and curls over her shoulders. A pair of oversized, cropped jeans with wide hems that displayed to their utmost her brown crocodile pumps. An asymmetrical cardigan that buttoned on a slant to the tip of her shoulder, had long, slouchy arms, and some added bit that fell off the back on one side to wind around and dangle down the other arm like a shawl. It ended above her waistband.

She had on sunglasses with very small oval lenses sitting horizontally, just barely covering over her eyes.

And last, deep red lips.

"*Bonjour,*" she sang from behind him, right before she made his side.

She put her hands on his shoulders and leaned in from behind to kiss his cheek.

As she rubbed at the lipstick she'd left, murmuring, "*Ça va,* Uncle Corey?" Corey's annoyance at her shifted to the point it almost entirely evaporated.

Once she'd erased her mark, she tossed her small bag on the bench before she tossed herself in it, her hair gliding and bouncing as she moved, her body lithe as only young people's bodies could be.

His gaze went back to the mirror.

Every man in the room had eyes to her.

He sighed before he greeted, "Hello, Chloe."

She looked fed, well, though her skin was pale. It was late autumn in Paris, not the warmest season.

However.

"I'm so glad you're here," she declared. "I haven't seen anyone from home in *ages.*"

"This would be because you haven't been home in over two years."

She lifted a hand. "Uncle Corey." She flicked out that hand toward a window. "*Paris.*"

Corey was who he was.

Therefore, as relieved as he was to see her looking her normal self (except the LA fashionista having two years of France injected into her bloodstream turned her into a fashionassassin), he didn't fuck around.

"Your mother and father are worried sick about you."

Her lips thinned before she asked, "Are you here to enjoy lunch with your favorite niece or are you here to get in my face for my parents?"

He didn't answer.

He noted, "And according to your sister, you've had a recent breakup. *Another* one."

To his astonishment, after he brought that up, she turned her head away immediately, her jaw going solid.

Corey paused, examining her profile.

And he realized, whoever this latest one was, it hurt.

"Talk to me," he ordered.

She faced him again. "Can we just have lunch?"

Fortunately, for her, the waiter arrived.

They ordered drinks and starters and the waiter moved away.

"Share," he essentially repeated, declaring her brief reprieve was over.

She made a huffing noise.

"Chloe," he said warningly.

"You're a pain in my ass, Uncle Corey," she replied.

"Do I have to harm someone?" he asked casually.

For a second, she simply stared, her lips parting.

Then she whispered, "What?"

"Has someone hurt you?" he demanded.

"It's not a big deal," she said quickly and waved a hand in front of her. "He wasn't that important."

Corey made no reply but did not release his hold on her shades.

She tried to change the subject. "What are you getting for your main?"

"I had meetings in London," he began. "I had meetings in Stockholm. And I have meetings in Johannesburg. I have delayed those last to be here, right now, with you. So do not waste my time by lying to me."

She looked stunned.

"You changed your plans because—?"

"Because your family is worried about you and—"

"You're my family," she finished for him softly.

Though that was not what he'd intended to say.

And hearing her say it, the exertion it required for him not to display the effects of the feeling of his chest caving in nearly put him in a catatonic state.

But he managed to avoid it and recovered through his silence.

Their wine arrived.

The waiter was long gone before Chloe said quietly, "He made me the other woman."

Another blow landed on Corey, this being the look on her face, not close to hidden by her sunglasses.

But more, the small sound of her voice.

Chloe was not small; she'd never been small in her life.

Whoever this man was, he'd made her feel small.

Corey made an instant decision.

He not only needed to harm someone.

He intended to.

"Pardon?" he asked menacingly.

She took her glasses off, tossed them on the table and reached for her wine.

After a sip, she returned her attention to him.

And her gaze was haunted.

Indeed.

Someone would feel that pain.

"I didn't know he was married," she shared. "He's young. Not, like, seventeen or anything. He's twenty-four. But he's been married two years. I had no idea. I went to a party, and they were there. An acquaintance of mine who didn't know I was seeing him told me who she was. He saw me and freaked *out*. But in a very French way."

She shook her head, disgust mixed with anger that did not hide the pain in every centimeter of that movement.

And then she continued sharing.

"He called me later. That same night, if you can believe. Pretended not to know me when someone introduced us at the party, then I'm home, like, ten seconds and he's calling me. When I lost it on him, he told me to stop overreacting. It was fine. He had deep feelings for me and there was no reason we couldn't carry on. Yes, he actually said that and no, I still can't believe it even though it happened a week ago. I asked if she knew about us, and he said there was no need for her to know. *No need for her to know.* Who thinks that way?"

Corey didn't answer that question.

He presented his own.

"You cared about him?"

"He's..." Now just a sad shake of her head. "He takes these *amazing* photographs, Uncle Corey. He's...when his attention is on you, it's like you're in his lens. The focus. It makes you feel...it's special."

But yet, it wasn't.

She took another sip of wine, set the glass down and said to it, "I was really happy with him. I felt something...I don't know what it was. Then, when I knew what kind of person he was, it all turned ugly. Dirty. Every second we shared. Every word we exchanged. And worse," she lifted her gaze to his, "I half wanted him to talk me into persisting."

"Because you were falling in love with him."

Her attention dropped back to the wineglass.

No.

She wasn't falling.

She'd already done that.

Christ, his throat burned.

"Chloe, look at me," he ordered.

Her gaze drifted back up.

"Never put up with anything from anyone that makes you uncomfortable, makes you feel wrong, makes you question the woman you are, or makes you go against who that woman is in her soul. Especially if any of that is coming from a man."

The small voice returned, and Corey felt it in the back of his teeth.

"I thought, with him, I had what Mom and Dad have."

And that made Corey's mouth fill with saliva.

"That is rare, what they have," he forced out. "But you'll find it."

"Right, right, I have to kiss a lot of frogs," she muttered, watching her fingers twist the stem of her wineglass this way and that, bored with the metaphor that had probably been suggested to her one way or another with every boy she'd liked or boyfriend she'd snared.

All Corey could think about was the word "frog."

The day they'd met Imogen, Duncan had thrown a frog at her.

She'd been incensed.

Years later, they were in love.

"Chloe," he called, and she again focused on him. "There is a man out there who will worship you. Not because he's intent to make you feel special. Because he understands to his bones that you already are."

Tears shimmered in her eyes.

He gave her time and was unsurprised when she conquered that emotion.

"Do not think another moment about this piece of shit," he advised. "Live your life being you, and one day, you'll run into him, the man you're supposed to find. And you know yourself so well, you'll recognize him instantly. He won't slip through your fingers, Chloe. And whoever that man is, he would eat a bullet before he made you feel dirty. But until then," he picked up his own glass and tipped it her way, "have fun with what's on offer. That day he's in your life will come soon enough."

He took a sip and did not dwell too long on the fact that her bright smile that was accompanied by bright eyes made him feel exactly how he felt when he'd earned his first billion.

They had lunch.

He insisted on driving her back to her flat and then going up to inspect it.

It looked like it'd been dressed by an award-winning Hollywood set designer.

This Corey found unsurprising too.

He knew she'd been working in an exclusive boutique on the Rue Saint-Honoré, doing this now going on a year and a half. He also knew that her parents were augmenting her income, because she didn't make much money (and he'd just added to that, slipping an envelope with several thousand Euro next to the undoubtedly-bought-used, but that only made it stylishly retro espresso maker in her kitchen).

However, he should have known they had nothing to worry about with Chloe, at least not with all the trappings of life, and the trimming of it.

Her heart, well, that was different.

She walked him down to his car, and before he folded into the back seat, she got up on the toes of her pumps, kissed his cheek and said into his ear, "Thanks for dropping by Paris."

Dropping by Paris.

When she rolled back, she was grinning at him as only Chloe could, showing nonchalant gratitude about a gesture that took two of his assistants three days to successfully shift his entire schedule so that he could make it.

Nonchalant in tone or not, her point was made, and the true depths of gratitude she felt were unhidden in her eyes.

He tilted his lips up for her.

Then he angled in his car.

She stood on the pavement as his chauffeur glided the car away.

Once they'd made a turn, he pulled out his phone.

It rang and then a deep voice answered, "Vaughan."

Corey's lips were absolutely not tilted up when he asked, "Rhys, how long will it take for you to get to Paris?"

"I can be there by the morning."

"Good," Corey replied. "I have a job for you."

CHAPTER 17

THE HIKE

Chloe

ow...

As I ambled down the sloping walk to Judge's front door, I did it trying to focus on the townhome development I'd already fully taken in as I'd driven through.

And not because it was small, even though it was.

It was because I could be convinced Judge had been consulted by the developers while they were designing it (yes, it was that perfect for him), and therefore it was fascinating to me.

I'd counted, and there were five lines of five townhomes, all of them inclining up steep rises and dotted over a rather large, densely treed area. The buildings were situated in ways that you had neighbors in another set of homes, but they weren't all that close.

And the entire area around them was natural.

No tennis court, swimming pool, or play area.

These homes were for people who wanted to live in nature,

perhaps in a community not far from others, just not a bustling one. And people who didn't want land they had to maintain but did want space and views that were gorgeous.

Indeed, the area was so uncluttered, whoever owned the covered snowmobiles and uncovered four-wheelers were apparently required to keep them where they sat, down close to the road, which was at least a hundred yards from the first set of townhouses.

Judge's building was at the top.

And he had an end unit at the top of that.

Which had the best view of them all.

I walked from my car toward the path to his door, thinking of this at the same time trying to prepare myself for the day (most especially seeing and then spending time with Judge). And with all of that, I was trying to wipe my mind clear of not only the research I'd done the last two days whenever I'd had the chance to do it, but the fact that I'd done it at all.

Yes, I had seen pictures of Judge as a little boy with my dad on a tennis court.

They reminded me how ridiculously gorgeous Dad was when he was young.

They also showed me how adorable Judge was when he was a toddler.

I had further seen photos of Belinda Oakley, his stunner of a mother. Strawberry blonde hair, ice-blue eyes and freckles that proved there was a God, because only God could dot those so perfectly across her upturned nose.

These pictures, however, included two mugshots that showed her at times when she was a fair bit less than stunning.

And last, there was Andrew Jefferson "AJ" Oakley, a second-generation oil baron who'd sired four children on his first wife, a woman he scraped off when she was in her early forties. He'd since married three others, all in their twenties, including his current wife, who was younger than me by a year.

She was twenty-three.

He was eighty-seven.

According to AJ, he was well aware of the age discrepancy, what it looked like on all accounts, and the small fortunes he had to pay when he was ready for a new model.

"In one way or another, a woman is always a whore. One thing I can say about these gals, they're honest about what they want, they got ambition, and they're willin' to go the extra mile. Gotta hand 'em that."

Yes, he'd said that.

And yes, he'd said it between wives two and three, and regardless that he had, he'd earned another one after that.

Apparently, AJ Oakley had a personality nearly as big as the vast amount of acreage he owned, was notoriously opinionated, loud-mouthed, mulish, chauvinistic, old-school, and as such, he was roundly hated by anyone who had no reason to stick their nose up his ass.

His first son and vehemently touted heir, Andrew Jefferson the Third, took an inebriated fall off a yacht on which he was partying somewhere off the coast of Greece, struck his head along the way, was not noted missing for hours, and washed ashore days later.

He'd been thirty-nine.

All Andy's life, up to his death, his doting sire had dismissed his laddish behavior as "any real Oakley will be sowin' his oats until the day he dies" (which, in Andy's case, was prophetic).

Andy died competing with his father in one area, and that area was absolutely not AJ's aggressive tactics to remain a wildly successful tycoon by any means necessary.

No, when Andy had died, he was in the midst of his third divorce and engaged to his fourth fiancée.

Not quite finished with branding the family name stamp on his offspring, AJ's second son was named Jefferson Billings Oakley, Billings being AJ's mother's maiden name.

But he was called Jeff.

He was also frequently referred to by AJ as "the Waste of Space," and by frequently, I meant that I read an article from last year where AJ again did just that.

On Jeff's part, he'd spent a fair amount of his life earning this moniker, including, in his early thirties when he'd done some time after, in a drunken, coked-up haze, he'd pistol-whipped to within an inch of his life some poor barkeep in a busy honkytonk who'd had the audacity to tell him to hang on a second for his drink.

The sentence Jeff had served for this assault was four months.

The barkeep lost an eye, partial control of the left side of his face, full use of his right hand, but he gained the ire of AJ when he'd lodged a civil suit for damages.

"Probably asked for that whuppin', tryin' to make a dollar off the Oakleys," was AJ's supposition.

In his one court appearance, the victim's one attorney faced off against AJ's five.

Needless to say, he got his ass beat again.

AJ's third child, a daughter, Patricia, clearly the second most intelligent of the bunch (if not the first), had moved to New Zealand when she was nineteen, and she never looked back.

His fourth, Jameson Morgan, Judge's dad, had been entirely dismissed by the whole family, except his mother, whose maiden name he was granted as his first, her mother's maiden name his second.

She reportedly adored him.

This earned him the erroneous reputation of being a momma's boy. Or at least the erroneous part of that was that it was bad to be as such, because apparently, he was. And in so being, he'd made sure she lived like a queen after his father disposed of her. And at her end, he was photographed with a tear running under his sunglasses while attending her funeral five years ago.

Considering Jameson was the only one with a brain and any grit (outside Patricia), he essentially told them all to go fuck themselves, moved to New York upon graduating from UT at twenty, became a stockbroker and eventually made enough money he could buy and sell his father and all his family's vast holdings ten times over.

In that mix, there were various wastrel grandchildren of AJ's who he publicly despised and had no problem sharing that with anyone who asked.

And there were a number who did.

Including the copious reporters who dogged his every step because he was so good for a quote that would rile up feminists and/or the liberal left, or, frankly, anyone with any amount of civility or modicum of good breeding. His shenanigans didn't only drive clickbait to articles, retweets of AJs exploits were off the hook.

He was so famous for all of this, I was surprised I'd never heard of him.

Then again, I viewed Twitter only for videos of pandas and baby huskies running through huge piles of snow (and the like).

Indeed, AJ despised all his offspring, except Jameson, who had nothing to do with him, Patricia, who also had nothing to do with him, and the "chip off the old block," his beloved grandson.

Judge.

If he thought Judge was a chip off the old block, he'd either not been around him in a while or dementia was setting in.

And as he was an octogenarian on the wrong side of that mark, I wasn't being cruel in noting that last possibility.

Judge somehow (magic?) had escaped all of this (at least in the press), even though his name was noted frequently (he was now AJ's vehemently touted heir).

If he was mentioned otherwise, it was as Jameson's "estranged son." And on a variety of Google searches, I'd noted there were far more pictures of Judge with Duncan than there were of Judge with his father or grandfather (even though there were some...with both).

Jameson and Belinda's divorce was, as Dad mentioned, picked apart with utter glee, as the press liked to do with beautiful, rich people who had fallen into heartbreaking times (Jameson, predictably, was also immensely attractive—more rough-hewn and wolfish than his son, but nevertheless exceptionally handsome).

In what was available to read online from back in the day, or what was resurrected due to the public's captivation by the mighty or beautiful who fall (in other words, people were still writing about it, and I did not have the time to watch them, but in my research I discovered there was both a short hour and a half documentary and a news-magazine show about it), I learned it was no secret that Belinda had a drinking problem. Further, it was wildly speculated she did vast amounts of cocaine and popped any pill going.

As to why, outside having an addictive personality (and/or a cheating husband), no one knew, because either Jameson's people had a chokehold on the spin, or what came across was actually true. That being it was widely reported, even if it was he who cheated on her, that he was the wronged man. The somber husband who had been "besotted" with his wife and "forced" to look elsewhere when she did not accept his many pleas to get help.

Yes, but of course this flew two and a half decades ago.

And apparently, it still did now.

This was, I would admit, helped along by the fact that Jameson clearly adored his second wife, Rosalind (I hadn't had time to fully fall down that rabbit hole, but this was so clear, the little time I had for it made it so—indeed, there wasn't a single picture of them where they didn't seem to be ridiculously into each other, and these pictures spanned decades).

Judge's parents had separated when he was five, and he'd grown up "the poor tyke, not really knowing his daddy, and forced to live with that bitter husk of a woman who is his mother," an alleged direct quote by AJ.

To put a fine point on it, Judge's upbringing had been a shitshow, with a mom who was apparently a junkie, a dad who had slightly less money than God (and that god was my Uncle Corey) who "fought for him," but still somehow never managed to win, and a grandfather who might just be Satan incarnate, who butted his nose in whenever it suited him.

Obviously, I failed spectacularly in keeping all of this off my mind as I strolled down Judge's path.

Equally obviously, his big windows had many views.

Including to my arrival.

And therefore, the door opened when I was three feet from it.

My heart stuttering, I looked up, but my gaze snagged on a massive chest that was not Judge's.

Up further I went and saw his best friend, Rix standing there.

Well…

Fabulous.

"Hello," I greeted.

"Hey," he grunted, looking me top to toe, his sensuous lips (something I could note now, being up close to him) becoming an irate line. He twisted at the waist and shouted. "Yo, man, she's here!"

I stopped at the door and lifted my hand his way when he turned back to me. "You're Rix, I'm—"

"Know who you are," he cut me off to say, then he ignored my hand and left the door open as he turned and walked away.

His gait on his prosthetics was triflingly ungainly.

His ass was everything.

I heard a screen door open, claws on floor, and then I saw Zeke.

I hadn't stepped over the threshold before he ran to me, tail wagging, and stopped on Judge's indoor mat, now with whole body wagging.

I crouched to give him a full head and neck rub, murmuring, "Hello, beautiful boy."

He panted and lolled his tongue.

At least one male in this house welcomed me.

I saw movement, glanced up, and there was Judge.

Rix had a younger Frank Grillo vibe to him, big, built, tough, rough and ready.

Judge was sun and dirt and pine and moonlight and forest rains and gentle breezes.

He was beer on the deck and pepperoni and sausage on pizza and conversations that were entirely teases that were endearingly annoying and annoyingly endearing and strong hands with long fingers that were tailored to wrap around yours.

He was warm brown eyes and soft brown hair and that perfectly angled tilt of your head when you wore heels and you wanted his mouth on yours, then got it.

Rix could probably wrestle a bear.

Judge could walk through the forest and not startle a doe.

As I crouched there, petting his dog, gazing up at him, I wanted him so badly, I feared it was imprinted on my DNA.

And I had to find a way to get over it.

"Is she a vampire? Does she need an invitation to walk into a house?" Rix's voice came from inside.

And suddenly, I remembered who I was.

With one more thorough sweep of Zeke's ears, head and neck, I straightened, walked in and said to Judge, "Hello, Judge."

"Chloe. You hit a River Rain store before you showed?" he asked, eyes traveling down my body.

Message clear.

My outfit was spectacular.

However, I already knew that.

Slim hiking pants in a deep gray-green, a long-sleeve, thin thermal in a muted bright yellow-green and a hooded featherless vest in olive.

Strapped over me was a medium size crossbody that had tucked inside a hat, gloves, my phone, license, a KIND bar, and some antibacterial wipes. And I carried a carnation pink Hydro Flask.

What could I say?

My new brothers and soon-to-be stepfather were nature lovers, and I loved them.

I was also Chloe Marilyn Pierce, so I didn't do anything not kitted out to absolute perfection.

Therefore, when my life included Duncan, Sullivan and Gage, I'd purchased several items to create a limited wardrobe for this specific type of occasion.

And although I did this in a River Rain store (of course), I didn't do it before I showed at Judge's.

Therefore, I answered Judge coolly with a "No." I then turned my attention to Rix. "And you said earlier when I introduced myself that you know who *she* is, that being *me*. So please, have my leave to use my name. It's *Chloe*."

Rix scowled at me.

And when he did, I had to admit to being slightly scared.

"Rix is gonna be our camera guy," Judge shared.

I thought Judge was going to be our "camera guy."

Therefore, we didn't need a "camera guy."

However, if Judge needed a buffer (why he would need this, I had no idea, he was *fine* with us not being anything), I wasn't going to discuss that part.

I turned and looked up at him. "Did Rix get the memo that we were only together *a minute* and therefore there is utterly nothing for him to be a cad about?" I asked acidly.

At first, Judge's head jerked.

Then his brows edged down.

After that, something openly dawned on him.

This led to his polite but impersonal gaze warming exponentially (alas).

And to end this conglomeration of fascinating emotiveness, he appeared in pain, the kind you had when you were trying very hard not to laugh.

The fourth one was difficult to withstand.

The last nearly impossible.

Even his deep voice was choked with humor when he asked, "Cad?"

"I could use a far less polite word," I suggested drily.

"That's all right, I think we got it," Judge muttered amusedly.

I glared at him. Then I glared at Rix (who was still scowling at me, incidentally).

I then looked down at Zeke, who was sitting between me and Judge, and not scowling at all.

"Please tell me you're coming too," I said to Zeke.

"Of course he is," Judge answered for Zeke.

"Thank God," I said to the dog.

He licked his chops, noticed my sustained attention, and got to all fours to offer the body wag again, since all indications were it earned him pets.

He was right to go for it.

I bent to scratch his head.

But I did it tilting mine back to look at Judge (who was watching me...could it be? ...*affectionately*. What on earth? No, I didn't want to know) and demand, "Are we doing this?"

"Yeah," Judge replied. "We'll take my car."

Oh no we wouldn't.

I was limiting our time together to the absolute least it could be.

Thus, no riding around in cars with them, and when we were finished, I was leaving him and going home.

That was to say, going directly to Duncan's (and Mom's now, I guessed) for dinner.

Then I was going home.

I straightened to declare, "I'll follow."

Judge shook his head. "We're all going to the same place. There's no need for you to drive."

"I'll follow."

"Chloe—"

I stared into his eyes and said low, "I'll *follow*."

His expression shifted again, contemplative, and something else.

Something I looked away from because I understood it, even if I didn't.

Remorse.

"You get to ride with me," I told Zeke.

That made Rix enter the conversation. "No, he doesn't."

I leveled my gaze on Judge's friend. "I'm sorry, but he does. He's exceptionally well-behaved, and I'm afraid it concerns me, his being around you. I don't want anything to rub off."

Rix's eyes widened in shock at my insult, or anger, I had no idea and didn't linger to find out.

Judge grunted with the effort not to guffaw.

"Leash?" I demanded of Judge.

"By the door," he told me.

I twisted, looked, moved that way and took it off the hook.

Then I called to Zeke, patting my leg (something I didn't have to do, I had the leash, he was already bounding to me), "Come, *mon chou*, let's get some fresh air."

Zeke was in concurrence with this, I could tell. He was very good as I put on his lead. And he was very good as I walked him to my car to sit in it and await Judge pulling out of the garage that was a level below the rest of his house, built into the incline of the mountain.

And I managed to do this without thinking once about the glimpse of perfect vista I saw off his deck from the wall of windows at the back of his house. *Or* the manly, rustic décor in his home that looked inviting and comfortable. So much so, I wanted to invite myself into it and get very comfortable.

Therefore, we were ready when Judge backed out in his Cherokee, Rix in his passenger seat.

And then we were on our way.

CONSIDERING MY EARLIER HYPOTHESIS THAT RIX COULD WRESTLE A bear, I shouldn't have been surprised that he could keep up with Judge while hiking.

What was vexing was that they both openly (if not verbally) expressed surprise that I could.

"She probably does spin classes or something," I caught Rix up ahead, walking beside Judge, saying to Judge under his breath (loudly) after we'd been hiking a trail for a good fifteen minutes.

To which I, coming up the rear, said (also loudly), "I wouldn't be caught dead in a gym. Too many people there to work out, no interest in admiring my outfits."

Judge turned his head away from Rix and grinned huge at the vista.

Even in profile, it was a sight to behold.

Rix glowered over his insanely broad shoulder at me.

The vista was so gorgeous, it clearly caused Judge to temporarily lose his mind, because at this point, he declared, "Zeke and I are gonna go on a quick run. He's dying for it. We'll be back. But while we're gone, you two learn to get along."

And with no further ado, Judge twisted and reached long, tugged Zeke's lead from my hand and took off running.

Although it was clear that our pace was driving Zeke around the bend (so being a good dog dad, it was a moral imperative for Judge to give that puppers what he needed), I halted entirely, such was my shock that Judge left me with a man who really did not like me.

For what reason, I did not know.

It wasn't like I left Judge at the altar (an unfortunate thought, because it brought up the next one, which was Judge looking handsome in a bespoke tuxedo, surrounded by walls made from trailing white wisteria, waiting for his bride).

"We're not gonna get this shit done if you just stand there," Rix informed me.

I came out of my Judge-in-a-tuxedo-among-wisteria trance and focused on Rix, who had also stopped about five feet ahead of me on the trail.

I didn't start moving again.

I asked, "Can I please understand why you have a problem with me when, until very recently, I've never met you?"

He turned his black-haired head to look up the path where Judge and Zeke had disappeared, he then looked back at me.

After that, he simply raised his thick brows.

"I'm sure your good looks and defined muscles allow your Neanderthal act to work on some women, but I'm afraid I must inform you, I'm evolved, and therefore require speech. Full sentences if you're able," I stated.

"We're gonna be honest?" he asked, walking back to me. "Then here's the honesty, sweetheart. I'm sure with your looks and that ass and that attitude, you expect men to drop like flies. And I bet that's a fun game for you. What I'm not a fan of is when my boy," he jerked his head to the trail, "does it, and you crush him under your four-hundred-dollar heel."

"Excuse me," I returned, wholly affronted. "I don't have shoes that cost four hundred dollars. At least not ones with heels on them. They cost *far more* than that. However, I will admit, my flip-flops cost something around that zone. But they're Valentinos, and I wouldn't use them to crush bugs."

"You're a piece of work," he muttered, beginning to turn away.

"You don't know what I am," I retorted.

He stopped turning and got that scary look again.

"You think he hasn't been dicked around?" he asked.

"You think he's the only one?" I shot back.

That made him even angrier, *much* angrier, and he didn't hide it.

"Are you standing there, after you kicked him in the teeth three days ago, telling me that *he* dicked *you* around?"

"I didn't kick him in the teeth," I snapped.

He got close to me, lifting a hand and tapping his head with his fingers before throwing it out in disgruntlement, all while growling, "Christ, he's so fucking gone for you, he can't fucking see straight. He waits months for you, *months*, you give him a taste and find him lacking. And I don't even fuckin'," he leaned closer into me, *"know* what you're lookin' for, if you find *Judge* lacking. But you do and you kick him to the curb. And you don't think he's gonna feel that? You think, because he's got a dick, he doesn't have emotions, and when you toy with them, it isn't gonna mess him up? Well, you're wrong."

"I didn't toy with his emotions," I fired back.

"Bullshit," was his stellar retort.

"We haven't even had a date," I reminded him. "And I shared how this would get messy and we should abstain. Now, clearly Judge has told you a different story, but *he* was not the *slightest* upset that I came to that conclusion. I will quote from him directly that he was *fine* with that and I needed to *get over it* because it didn't last *a minute*, and now we need to focus because we have a job to get done."

"You are far from dumb, woman, you cannot have missed how deep he's in it for you."

"Well, Rix, since you just met me, you couldn't possibly know how much *deeper* I was in it for him."

He clamped his mouth shut.

Unfortunately, for some unhinged reason, I did not.

"It's none of your business, but this," I tossed my arm to the trail, "is *torture* for me. To be around him. To see him smile. It's *killing me.*"

"Then why—?"

"I can't take the chance."

"What are you—?"

I got in his face and whispered fiercely, "You love with a love like that, it *becomes you.* And then when you lose it, you *fade away.* He's the kind of man you love like that, Rix. I know it *to my bones.* And I can't take that chance. I can't take the chance of loving like that, then losing him and fading away. So it's good he's fine with us not going there. Because in the end, I'd be lost to him, and that scares the hell out of me."

He stood there, close, staring down at me, his eyes burning.

God, what had I done?

I stepped away, smoothed down the front of my vest, gathering myself, and then requested in a calm voice, "Now, if we could get along from here on out and you would refrain for both Judge and my sakes, but especially Judge's, from telling him what I just shared, we can finish this task, and all enjoy the rest of our Sundays."

"I'm sorry, darlin'," he said gently. "But if you think I'm not gonna tell my boy what you just said, you're crazy."

God.

What had I done?

"He won't care," I asserted.

"You're wrong about that."

"I think you might not have the latest details," I said helpfully.

"I think I just got all I needed."

God!

What had I done!?

"If you don't promise right now not to tell him, I'm going to turn around and leave," I threatened.

He didn't promise.

He advised, "Whatever's causin' you to think like that about love, you gotta work it out with someone, Chloe."

"And I suppose that's Judge," I said bitterly.

"Well...yeah," he said like I was dense.

"Did you not *just* hear me?" I demanded.

"Determined to think you were a cold-hearted bitch," he said, talking to himself, but doing it staring right at me. "And here you are, something else entirely. Fuck, he saw it. I totally didn't."

"Rix," I bit sharply.

"It's impossible to protect yourself your whole life from love," he shared.

"Would you care to bet?" I asked.

"Then tell me, what kind of man are you gonna find?"

"Who says I need a man?" I queried.

He shook his head slowly. "Sweetheart, who're you kidding?"

After my deranged speech, that was a good question.

And this "sweetheart" was entirely different from the last.

It was like a snuggly blanket on a cold day.

Maddening.

I huffed.

His lips quirked and then, "So, answer my question."

I tipped my head coyly. "Who do I think I'm kidding?"

"And she's back," he muttered, his dark eyes lighting. Then he said, "No, the one before."

He wanted to know?

To get this insanity done, I'd tell him.

"I will find a man who could do his worst, and I'll be totally fine to walk away."

"In other words, a man you don't love."

I nodded curtly. "I might find two of them."

Another lip quirk and, "Right."

"Do we have an accord?" I pressed.

"I'll give you this, I won't tell Judge until we get what we gotta get done today done."

"No," I parried. "Until I'm driving away."

"You got it."

"And...I've been gone at least fifteen minutes."

"Now you're pushin' it, sweetheart."

Ugh.

I clicked my teeth.

He bared his in a smile.

Could I make that bargain?

This means you don't have to leave now, and you have more time with Judge.

Without me willing it to do so, my hand pushed out.

And my mouth said, "Deal."

He took it, dwarfed it and squeezed too hard, though I didn't think he meant to, I just wasn't sure he knew his own strength.

"Deal," he grunted.

But there was no lip quirk.

He was smiling.

Enormously.

Lord, help me.

Now what had I done?

CHAPTER 18

THE RELEASE

Chloe

*A*fter the preliminary torture of the day with Judge was done, I drove up to Bowie's massive manse wondering what became of that iron will I was so very proud of.

I was a quivering mess.

This was partly because, after Judge and Zeke rejoined us, regardless of my attempts at assuming an attitude that should have formed a layer of hoarfrost over my entire body, Rix had morphed to good-natured, playful, and generally acting like I was his adored lost little sister found.

It was tremendously appealing.

It was also excruciatingly annoying.

I never settled my gaze on him without it being my patented Death Stare.

He acted like it was cute and even chucked my chin once while I was giving it to him.

As I said.

Annoying.

This, I could handle, if Judge had not demonstrated his best buddy openly liking me had made his millennium.

In other words, neutral, courteous Judge had vanished.

Once he'd returned from his run, he became the Judge I knew.

Teasing. Funny. Attentive. Affectionate.

I caught him staring at my ass (sexily), my breasts (appreciatively), and I caught this because not only didn't he hide it, he'd done it meaning to get caught.

He'd done it meaning to show how deeply he was attracted to me.

And not once, not twice, not thrice, but *seven times* (oh yes, I counted) while we were in one of the three spots he'd selected where we would film portions of our message (I played Dad, he played Bowie) that we read off sheets of paper Judge had printed out, he not only touched my body, he touched my hair.

He tucked it behind my ear.

He pulled some away from where it became stuck on my lips after we were hit by a mountain breeze.

He flicked it over a shoulder.

And once, he got close to me, and instead of putting his arm around me as he had been doing (and it would reveal too much to pull away, so I didn't—see? Total...*torture*), he trailed his hand up my back, gathered the lot of it and held it in a ponytail with his fist.

Yes.

He did that.

Like we were together and that was his wont.

When it was *not*.

No matter the shield of ice I put up, he flirted with me outrageously *the entire time*.

It.

Was.

Agony.

But even as I was enduring it, I knew the worst was yet to come.

I was right.

I was not in my car driving away for ten minutes before my phone blew up first with calls, then with texts.

I didn't even have to look (and thus, I didn't) to know that, as promised, Rix had shared.

The good news was, during our time together, I'd dropped the falsity that I was going straight home. They had no idea I was headed to Bowie's.

So if, say, Judge wished to make some grand gesture and seek me out (and knowing what I knew of Judge, and how deeply he was attracted to me, and how deeply he now knew I was attracted to him, this was precisely what he would do), he'd be headed the wrong way.

Regardless if dinner with Mom and Bowie was a good hiding place, I wished I hadn't arranged it. I needed to go somewhere (perhaps Mi-Young and Jacob's? or, perchance, a remote cabin in Siberia?) and pull myself together.

Rediscover the true Chloe and then fortify her.

But, I told myself, a good way to do this was being with family.

And although there were niggles that probably would never go away that was nostalgia I couldn't shake about what had once been, there was also great beauty in being with Mom and Bowie when they were together.

Seeing Mom happy again.

Seeing how madly Bowie loved her.

Not to mention, feeling how much he cared about me.

And I'd done my due diligence, so I knew Sasha was hanging in Phoenix with some friends.

The coast was clear.

I let Bowie's beautiful piece of this earth with his sprawling house and the mountain backdrop with the big lake start to penetrate as I parked in front.

I got out, let myself in, and over the cacophony of dogs racing to me to say hello (Bowie had three, Shasta, a husky, Rocco, a tripod silver receiver, and Killer, a peekapoo), with forced joviality, I called, "*Bonjour*, I've arrived!"

I gave love to Shasta and Rocco but scooped Killer up into my arms as I walked through Bowie's massive foyer and into his equally massive great room, looked right, toward the kitchen, and saw Bowie and Mom in it, doing as they often did, cooking together.

I did not stop to consider what they might be cooking, seeing as it was a couple of hours until dinner time.

I didn't do this because Sasha was on a stool at the island.

Damn it.

For a moment I had hope. Hope that Mom told her I was up from Phoenix, so she'd returned in order to chat matters through with me.

Although she could dig into things, Sasha was normally mellow, and she generally hated conflict. She also tended not to hold grudges, had her piques, then got over them.

Nevertheless, upon sight of me, her eyes narrowed, and her lip curled.

Well, that hope was dashed.

As I approached, I ignored my sister and asked the room at large, "How's my beloved family?"

"Good, darling, that's a cute outfit," Mom said, coming my way.

She gave me a double cheek kiss when she arrived, gave Killer a head scratch then headed back into the kitchen and Bowie was there.

Both Killer and I got a big hug and Bowie said in my ear during it, "Martini?"

When he slightly pulled away, I smiled up at him and replied, "Gasping."

His lips twitched, he released me and muttered, "On it."

I moved to stand at the island and greeted, "Sasha."

She returned the coldness with, "Chloe."

My mother was a renowned actress.

She was also a fantastic mother.

Thus, she did not miss this stiltedness.

Bowie was relatively new to our lives.

But he was a father.

Thus, he didn't miss it either.

They exchanged a glance.

"Everything okay with you guys?" Mom asked.

"Peachy," I lied.

"Liar," Sasha said under her breath.

I pulled up the Death Stare and aimed it at my sister.

Mom turned from whatever she was doing at the stove, and Bowie twisted away from the martini he was preparing to mix, both aiming their attention toward the island.

"What's going on?" Mom demanded.

"Nothing," I declared. "We're having a slight tiff. Détente for this lovely dinner with Mom and Bowie, though."

"Always the drama," Sasha said with a verbal roll of her eyes.

"How about we not make our issue Mom and Bowie's, hmm?" I suggested to her.

"What issue?" Mom pushed.

"It's nothing," I repeated.

"Says you," Sasha stated.

I sent the Death Stare her way again. "Should I leave?"

Like she had claim to Bowie's house, she replied, "That'd be good."

"*Sasha,*" Mom snapped.

Sasha turned her attention to our mother. "She's bossy and she thinks she knows everything. She's always been that way, it's never been fun, we've always hated it. But Matt and I are grown up now and it's *way* getting old."

It took a lot to bite my lip and not float a retort to her "grown up" comment, considering the woman two feet from me was twenty, nearly twenty-one, jobless, aimless and living off her trust fund.

That was, she was doing that when she wasn't mooching off her father, her mother or her mother's fiancé.

"Chloe, what now?" Mom sighed.

And at that, I turned my stare to her, not the Death Stare, a stunned one.

Mom didn't miss that either and noted, "You *do* bring a lot of drama. This isn't something you don't know about yourself."

"You know, maybe I *should* go," I returned.

"Honey, no," Bowie entered the conversation, and his eyes on me were not accusatory. They were sharp and concerned. "Are you okay?"

No.

I was *not*.

"I've had a long day and I don't need this," I stated honestly.

"Again, drama," Sasha mumbled.

All right.

Enough.

Instead of saying to my sister, *Actually, I have a job I work fifty plus hours a week. And I'm volunteering my time to do something for the social outreach arm of Bowie's store. So I've been hiking all day as only part of my efforts to prepare a presentation for that project. We won't get into the emotional situation it is with Judge that I've had to ride all day. In other words, it's not drama. I'm physically and emotionally exhausted. But let's talk about what you've done this week, this month, and, say, the past two years.*

I wanted to say that.

But even if I was angry at her, I loved her, and because now was not the time to broach that, I didn't.

Instead, I decided it was, indeed, time for me to go.

"It's not me acting like a spoiled brat," I replied, giving Killer one last stroke before stooping and dropping her to the floor. "I'm off. We'll do this some other time."

And with that, I turned and started toward the door.

Again, it wasn't about drama.

I had to get out of there.

Because I was shaking.

Actually *shaking*.

With fury and a lot more besides.

I couldn't do this, not now. Not after the day with Judge, and Rix (and Zeke).

I couldn't do it at all, not after...

Everything.

"Chloe, don't walk away from this. Whatever's going on, you two need to work it out."

This was Mom, and I could tell she was following me.

I didn't break stride as I replied, "Maybe later."

"She couldn't suck all the attention to herself if she didn't attempt a grand exit."

This was Sasha.

"Sasha, stop it."

Mom, getting pissed.

"She's all over Matt to work things out with Dad," Sasha, who I could tell also had moved, but her voice was distant, so she wasn't following, but she'd adjusted her position to watch me leave.

And hand her shit to Mom.

"Chloe." Mom was using her Mom's Voice. "Wait."

I opened the door, turned at it, and I was right.

Mom was maybe three feet away, Bowie wasn't far from her, and Sasha was across the foyer, standing in the entryway to the great room with her arms crossed on her chest and an ugly expression twisting her face.

I looked to Mom. "I'll call."

"I know that Matt's breach with your dad is hard for all of us, and I know you always come from a place of caring, but how about you let your dad and me worry about that?" Mom suggested.

"Oh no, not Chloe," Sasha called. "She has to stick her nose into everything, tell everyone what to do, how to think, how to be. She even turned Sully and Gage against Matt and me."

I mean, *seriously?*

Was she five?

The dogs had started moving with agitation around us, Rocco and Killer coming in and out of the opened door, but Shasta remained outside, barking.

I ignored all of this, such was my fury at my sister's crap.

"Sully and Gage are in this?" Bowie asked.

"Not really," I evaded.

Vaguely, I heard a car door slam, and another one, and Bowie shifted so he could crane his neck to look out the front door.

Sasha dropped her arms, moved forward, and said to Bowie, "They totally are." Then to me, "You dragged them in with your bullshit version of what's going on."

Now who was lying?

"I did nothing of the sort," I snapped.

"And you know, Matt and I get it. Where you're coming from. Why you're so staunchly on Dad's side," Sasha declared.

"Sasha—" Bowie tried to cut in.

"And you should thank us," Sasha went on resentfully, after coming to a stop fully entering our tableau by the door. She too, glanced out the door before looking back at me and saying, "For not telling Sul and Gage why you get it. How you know exactly what it's like to be a cheater. Because with that married guy in France, you *were* one."

Mom went still.

Bowie went still.

I suffered a death blow.

And through it, I whispered to my sister, "You know that's not right."

She did.

She totally did.

I saw the guilt and shame fill her face the instant the words left her mouth.

This was because I'd cried my heart out over the phone to her after that happened to me.

And I knew she hadn't forgotten a second of it.

It didn't take the resurrection of Freud to diagnose she was dealing with her own shit.

And I cared.

I really, *really* did.

I also worried.

A whole lot.

But one thing I knew was never to bury someone else in my shit.

And never to allow someone to bury me in theirs.

And she'd just done that.

Buried me under her shit.

In front of Bowie.

I told Mom (almost) everything, so Mom already knew about it.

But she said that *in front of Bowie*.

"We're done," I proclaimed, my voice stone cold.

The wave of concern from Mom and Bowie's direction hit me so hard, it was a miracle I didn't fly sideways.

Sasha's face became a mask of fear.

And I completely lost my renowned cool.

"We're done!" I shrieked.

"Chloe!" Mom cried, reaching to me.

But I whirled and swayed to a halt before I even began to beat my retreat.

Because Judge and Rix were standing in the open door, staring at me.

They'd heard.

God!

They'd heard!

I planted a foot and then launched off it, racing around Judge and down the front steps.

"Chloe!" Mom shouted.

I got to the door of my car, and I ripped it open, absently noting the Cherokee parked behind it.

Before I could position myself in it, my door slammed shut in front of me.

"Baby," Judge whispered in my ear.

That one word, his tone, it slid from my ear over my scalp, my face, into my eyes, blinding me, filling my mouth, muting me.

My knees buckled.

The world melted away.

His arm clamped around my belly.

"Judge." That was Bowie's growl.

My hair flew when Judge pulled my crossbody over my head and my body jerked when he tossed it.

"Drive her car to my place," he ordered, probably Rix.

"Gotcha."

Yes, Rix.

"Judge." Again, Bowie.

"I got her." Judge.

He was pulling me to the Cherokee.

"Chloe, Coco, Chloe, God, that was…it wasn't right. God, I'm so sorry. That *so* wasn't cool." Sasha, up close.

To me.

"You need to step away from her." Judge, polite, but steely. *"Now."* No longer polite, furious, impatient.

Demanding.

Reaching beyond me, he pulled open the passenger door to his Jeep and whistled to Zeke, who jumped out. Then he practically lifted me into the seat.

I tried to do the seatbelt, but my fingers felt numb, and it flew out of my grasp.

So Judge nabbed it, leaned in and did it for me.

"Darling." Mom, agonized.

"I think she needs some time, please." Judge, respectful.

"Come here, honey." Bowie, to Mom.

A sob.

Sasha.

My door closed.

I watched my Evoque roll away, Rix behind the wheel, Zeke in my passenger seat, head out the window.

And then we were going, and I didn't look to the side, where I knew Mom, Bowie and Sasha were standing.

We cleared Bowie's drive, and I stared at the back of my car, finding it strange it was there, and I wasn't.

"You with me?" Judge asked.

"I'm not a cheater," I said through stiff lips, not tearing my gaze off my car. "I didn't know he was married. I ended it the first moment I could when I found out."

"Give me your hand, baby," he ordered softly.

I kept my hands in my lap.

"Okay, we'll be home soon," he relented gently.

Home?

I didn't ask.

Eventually, after an interminable, silent drive, I watched Rix pull

my car into Judge's drive and idle until Judge opened the garage door.
He then pulled in.

Judge did too.

We all got out.

I stood between my vehicle and Judge's, wondering why Rix had
parked my car in Judge's garage, also not knowing what to do.

Rix and Judge did the handoff of my bag, and I heard Judge
murmur, "Take Zeke?" and Rix reply. "Yeah." Then Rix again, "Turned
her ringer off, man. Her phone's blowin' up." And Judge, "Thanks."

Then I had my chin caught between the side of an index finger and
the pad of a thumb.

I looked up.

At Rix.

He said nothing, but the kind look in his eyes unraveled the only
part left knitted together inside me.

My lips quivered.

He stroked my chin in an affectionate gesture, a gentle squeeze to
the tip, as he moved his fingers away.

Then he was gone, my hand was in Judge's, and he was pulling me
inside.

I was right.

His fingers…

Tailored to fit my hand.

We went up some steps, and he dumped my bag on a counter in
the kitchen and then let me go and was all about turning on lights
against the waning sun of a winter afternoon.

Distractedly, being fully in it, I noticed his space was far more upscale
than I expected it to be. It was also far roomier than the outside indicated.

A trick of architecture. A façade for safety's sake.

Outside it was Nothing to See Here.

Inside, it was a mountain home fit for the vehemently touted heir
to the dual thrones of the Texas and New York Oakleys.

Judge was suddenly standing right in front of me.

I tipped my head back to look at him.

"Do you want a drink?" he offered.

"I researched you."

He made no noise and showed no reaction.

"You played tennis with my father."

"Yeah, Dad called yesterday. Guess they talked. He told me. I was too young to remember."

"I researched you," I repeated like he didn't speak.

"Chloe, baby, you're kinda freaking me out," he said softly.

"He left me," I whispered.

"That guy who cheat—?"

"He left me all alone. All alone to take care of them. All by myself."

"Who, honey?"

"Uncle Corey," I croaked.

And that was when I totally lost it.

I had no idea how I got from where I was standing with Judge to being tangled in him lying side by side on one of his leather couches, my face shoved in his throat, sobbing.

But when I finally surfaced enough from the emotion that had dragged me under to be aware of anything but it, that was where I was.

That said, my surfacing wasn't about rescue. It was about gasping for air, because the emotion still had hold of me, trying to tug me back down.

"Mom and Dad were golden. Shining. *Ethereal*," I blubbered against the skin of his throat.

"Yeah," he said quietly.

"I lived my life knowing that was *mine*. Mine because I basked in their glow. Mine because one day, I knew I'd have that same thing."

Hazily, I felt Judge's body tighten.

But I needed to say the words, let them out, so that hold would loosen. That hold that had been constricting its death grip, inch by inch, day by day, from the minute Uncle Corey took his own life.

I needed it to let me go.

I didn't know if I'd survive as the me I knew me to be if it swept me back under.

"But Dad cheated on her."

"Christ, baby," he groaned, gathering me closer, tangling his long legs tighter in mine.

I tipped my head back, and he dipped his chin to catch my watery eyes.

"I'm so mad at them, both of them. Mom too, for not finding a way to work it out. And as crazy as it sounds, I might be *more* mad at Mom. Dad did not do right. It is not okay what he did. I'm not saying that. But he was destroyed. *Destroyed.* And she was always on us about forgiving. About understanding why people do the things they do and not being too hard on them. And this man that she loved and adored, who she gave children, spent half her life with, she just throws him away? And then throws Bowie in his face?"

Judge said nothing, just stroked along the nape of my neck.

"I know that's judgy and even childish, her pain is not my own. It isn't my place to make that call. And it's an ugly trait some women have, placing the blame on a sister's shoulders when it is *so* not a woman's burden to bear. Especially with what he did. And I want so badly to be happy Mom found Bowie, and part of me is, but I miss them." A sob tore up my throat. "The bottom line is that I miss my mom loving my dad." Another catch and he shoved my face into his neck again.

"Just cry it out, Chloe," he urged gently.

"I can't...I have to...I have...have to release," I whimpered.

"Do what you need to do," he replied, giving me a squeeze. "I got you."

I got you.

I cried harder.

But I spoke through it as I did because I couldn't stop.

"What she said, Sam, Corey's ex, wh-what she said on that sh-show, he did that. Uncle Corey. He did that to M-mom and Bowie. I kinda knew, all my life, he had a th-thing for her. Everyone knew he wa-was cutthroat. But I had no idea he was that *evil.*"

"Yeah. That was seriously messed up," Judge concurred.

"But he was...we all forget, because of that. B-because of how ugly that was. Because of what a shock it was to...to learn about that. We forget, he was always th-there. For all of us." I gulped. "Especially me."

"All right. All right, honey," Judge crooned.

"He was...he was...I'm him."

"What?"

"Me," I pushed my head back against his hand and he caught my eyes again. "I'm Uncle Corey."

"You are not," he growled.

"No." I shook my head against the toss pillow we were lying on. "He taught me to be like him."

"Chloe—"

"The good parts. The strong parts." My lips trembled. "The loving parts."

"I don't get—"

"He loved her so much, Judge, and he couldn't be close all the time. So he groomed me to take care of her and all that was hers. To be his proxy."

"That's you, not him," Judge stated firmly. "That's who you are."

"Sully said I wear armor."

I was jumping all over the place.

But Judge was right there with me.

"You do that," Judge agreed.

"But it has vulnerabilities."

Judge said nothing.

"And...and...people I love shouldn't aim at those vulnerabilities."

A darkness that was even more scary than a glower from Rix shadowed his eyes, and he enunciated every word clearly when he replied, "No. They. Should. Not."

He was thinking about Sasha.

"I'm talking about Uncle Corey."

"Okay, but we'll also be talking about what kind of relationship you have with your sister, because, straight up, she either extricates her head out of her goddamn ass or we're gonna have issues. And by that I mean her and me. No fucking way is she gonna get away with that shit again, I'm there, or not, and I got no problem informing her of that."

It was my turn to say nothing.

He misinterpreted my silence.

"You think it's not my place. But when you pull yourself together and get a good look around at where you are right now, and *how* you are right now, you'll understand it fucking is."

"I'm scared about how much I feel for you," I blurted.

He blinked.

Before I could lose my nerve, I whispered, "You terrify me."

I didn't miss his moves this time when I suddenly found myself on my back with Judge flat-out on top of me.

And I felt as well as heard the rumble of his, "That shit you spouted at Rix."

"If Mom didn't have Bowie..." I let that lie.

"Honey," he smoothed my hair away from my face with both hands then kept them woven in the strands on either side of my head, "this is not about your mom losing your dad, it's about you losing him."

"I haven't. He's there. He's hurting. He fucked up, but—"

"The golden dad who could do no wrong. *That* is who you miss."

I shut up.

Judge spoke.

"I don't know what went down, none of my business, and we can talk through why I'm gonna say this to you, but it's none of yours either. What happened between the two of them can't help but affect you, but the truth of it is, it's theirs. And from what I know about both of them, if either of them knew you were struggling with it this way, it'd kill."

He was so right.

It would.

"And I don't mean just get over it," he carried on. "I mean, if you'll let me help, we'll work to get you to a place of realizing they both love you like crazy, your brother and sister too. And what happened between them has no bearing on how they feel about you."

He was so right about that too.

He also wasn't done talking.

"Specifically, as for your dad, what you gotta get is, he is the same man *to you* as he always was. Steadfast. Loyal. Loving. You'll never see this, but you need to know. When he heard you come through his back door, and he knew you were there, I swear to fuck, I don't think I've ever seen a man I'd describe as beautiful. Your dad knowing you were gonna be close and soon, *that* was beautiful."

Oh my God.

Another sob ripped through me.

Judge moved his thumbs to catch the new onslaught of tears as they fell down my temples.

When I got a (kind of) lock on it, Judge said gently, "I would never let you fade away."

My lips started quivering again.

"I don't know what we got ahead of us, baby, but no matter what, I would never, ever let you fade away. The thing is, you wouldn't let that happen either. You are a lot stronger than you think."

"It's a ruse," I whispered.

"Horseshit," he fired back. "You're hurting right now because you lost your grandma, the foundation of your family, and Szabo all in blow after blow after blow. You instinctively turned your focus to making sure everyone else was all right, and you didn't look after you."

I did this.

I did as Uncle Corey told me to do.

But he was supposed to have my back.

Then he took himself away from me.

"No worries about that," Judge continued. "You got me now, and we'll see to that. But a warning, doll, as of now, that focus is shifting. They can sort their own shit, we're gonna look after you."

We're gonna look after you.

Damn it, it was going to happen again.

I was right, it did, and I lifted my head and shoved it into the side of his neck to hide my latest assault of tears.

He pressed me back down to rest on the pillow and angled so I could have my hiding place and he could run his nose along the side of my neck.

That felt so nice, I could concentrate on it and eventually (again, but a lot faster this time), I got it together.

And when I did, I said dejectedly, "I miss him."

He lifted his head and got it on the first guess.

"Szabo?"

I nodded.

"You miss him, and you miss who you thought he was, and found out he wasn't when he did your mom and Duncan so dirty."

I nodded again.

He got an odd look on his face before he asked, "Does it occur to you what you saw as grooming was something else?"

"Like what?"

He shook his head, like he was trying to figure something out, and he talked it through while he did it.

"I've heard a lot about Corey Szabo. Some of it wasn't so good. But nothing negates the fact he wasn't just a genius. He was canny. Loyal as fuck. To your mom, especially. And he had a will of steel."

A will of steel.

"So maybe," Judge went on, "he saw himself in you and like attracts like. So could it be he wasn't grooming you? Could it be that he just admired you? Or more importantly, he saw those qualities in you, and the other ones besides, and he just really loved you?"

"He totally loved me," I admitted softly, and Rhys Vaughan sprang to mind.

Only Uncle Corey, as a parting gift, would leave someone he loved a tool she could wield to do what she needed to do for those she loved.

The only thing she'd ever want that she couldn't get herself.

That was what he'd left me.

I didn't share that though.

That was for later.

(Maybe.)

But it occurred to me then, giving me Rhys, it was more than just a gift.

It was keeping his promise to me.

It was giving me back what I'd lost when he took himself from me.

It was giving me someone to take my back.

"He loved me a lot," I finished huskily.

"Did you love him?"

"He was family."

Warmth hit his gaze. "Then of course you miss him, baby."

"Yes," I whispered.

Warmth hit his entire face, he bent his head and touched his mouth to mine.

He then lifted it and declared, "In case you didn't get this, I am not fine at all with us not being an us."

One could say I got that.

I pressed my lips together.

Judge did not.

"It wasn't hard to sense your hesitancy, that something was messing with you. I thought I could play that. Then, at your pad on Wednesday, you laid it out, and I pretended I didn't give a fuck. You stood up and freaked me out, though I thought for sure I'd called your bluff with the look you had on your face before you took off upstairs. But you just did what you said you were going to do. You changed clothes, came back, and you were totally over it."

Oh Lord.

"And that fucking stung."

Hmm.

"So, being a guy, instead of feeling hurt, I got pissed. And at this juncture, I hate to have to share that, if certain buttons are pushed, I can be a hothead."

Well then.

"And so I spouted my own shit. Which obviously hit the mark, but you were behind your armor, so I couldn't tell."

Damn.

"And then you didn't reach out, at all, and I knew you were serious.

I'd read it wrong. You weren't into me. Or I didn't do it for you. Or whatever."

Fuck.

"But this morning, I knew you were full of shit when you made that remark, throwing in my face my own words about us lasting a minute, and I realized I had to get my own head out of my ass."

Well...

"And I felt like a motherfucker that I'd left you hanging for so long after I said that crap I did not mean."

The remorse.

God, he was so sweet.

"You'd barely started your car to take off before Rix filled me in on your convo."

Ugh.

"And here we are."

We were that.

Right here.

With him flat out on top of me.

"So, let's get some shit perfectly straight, yeah?" he declared.

Oh dear.

"Judge—"

"Nope, quiet and listen."

I shut my mouth and narrowed my eyes.

He grinned.

Then he said, "I like you. A lot. I think about you. All the time. I barely know you, and I know I want to explore a future with you. You fascinate me. You turn me on. You piss me off. You make me laugh. You're completely predictable, and you surprise me all the time. I could stare at you for hours, but I'd rather kiss you for days. I can't wait to be inside you. I want to know everything about you. Zeke digs you. Rix thinks you're the total shit. I want you immersed in my life. I want to dig deep into yours. I know I could fall in love with you because that's already happening. So *this* is happening, because I know you feel all that too, and we're done with you pushing me away. We're doing this."

As if that declaration wasn't enough (which it was), he kept speaking.

"I can't make any promises. I can't heal that hurt that's making you skittish to open your heart. All I can do is be steady for you as you do that work yourself. And as you do it, then beyond, promise to give everything I got to protecting you against those who would fuck with you, including your sister..."

Well then.

It seemed clear Sasha had far more to contend with than just me holding the grudge I had just decided to hold for at least a month.

Her bigger challenge was going to be winning Judge.

"...and guarding your heart, and Chloe, honey, I swear to fuck, I'm gonna do just that."

That heart he'd promised to guard was beating a mile a minute, I could feel it slamming against his chest.

"So?" he pushed.

There was only one answer to that question.

And I gave it.

"Fine."

He went still a moment.

He came out of that stillness when he burst out laughing.

The richness of that washed over me, and I basked in it gleefully.

For a second.

And then Judge lowered his head and kissed me.

I enjoyed basking in that *a whole lot more*.

CHAPTER 19

THE WILDCAT

Judge

*H*e was expecting it.

The soft knock that came at his door after he and Chloe made out, then he'd made her comfortable and got them a couple of beers. They snuggled in his couch and discussed the totality of the shit she'd been facing with her brother, her sister, her mother, Duncan, her dad and her Uncle Corey.

She went to clean up, came back, snuggled again, and they got into what to do for dinner.

A conversation she fell asleep during, passed out so bad, if she wasn't curled into him, she would have spilled her beer.

He was used to witnessing emotion draining a woman, grew up with it, so he'd been ready to set her up, make her comfortable.

And after he tucked her under a blanket on his couch, he made the decision to throw together some tacos, which were quick and good.

He'd gone to the kitchen to get that going in order that it'd be ready to finish up when Chloe was ready to eat when the knock sounded.

Now, he went to the door and opened it to who he expected to see.

Duncan was standing there.

After he gave a chin lift to Judge, he inclined his head to see in as Judge pushed him back and stepped out.

He wasn't holding Duncan back.

He was letting Chloe sleep.

Duncan probably sensed this, wanted it for her too, and therefore didn't fight it.

Before Duncan could ask, quickly, Judge said, "She's fine. She's good. She cried a lot and she'd been holding too much in. She let it out. She's sleeping it off now. When she gets up, I'll get her fed. Take care of her. You can tell her mom I've got her covered."

Duncan nodded, and it felt good he didn't even give a hint he questioned Judge's last.

He said instead, "Everyone's been calling."

"Rix turned off her sound."

Another nod and, "By everyone I mean my boys, Hale—"

Judge was confused at that name, confused and alert.

Who the fuck was Hale?

"Hale?"

"Another adoptee of the Pierce family. Corey's son. Chloe grew up with him. Treats him like a brother."

Judge relaxed.

"In between her mother sharing how furious she was, trying to get Coco on the phone, and then digging into Sash again, Sasha sent some texts," Duncan continued. "And my guess is, those she texted sent some of their own."

"Good your woman had words," Judge said angrily.

"I think you understand, but I gotta be sure you do, this is rocking my family, Judge." Duncan jerked his chin to Judge's house. "She's their pillar. She crumbles, it's all gonna go to shit."

"Then it's gonna go to shit," Judge stated, his voice filled with shards. "She thinks the world of you, do you know that?"

It was gruff when Duncan answered, "Yeah."

He thought the world of Chloe too.

Good.

"So her sister saying that shit about that married guy in front of you tore her apart."

"Sasha explained that wasn't what—"

"Yeah, she knew it wasn't what she was making it out to be and it still came out of her mouth. In front of her mother. You. Me. And that woman saw me and Rix walking up to the door. She lashed out in her own pain knowing just how deep that blow would go, and she still fuckin' dealt it."

Now, Judge's voice was rocky, that was how pissed he was at the memory.

"Again, Genny is on that," Duncan reminded him. "And I'm not at that point with them, Judge, I've been in their lives mere months, but I had a few things to say to Sasha too."

Excellent.

"I didn't need to say them, though," Duncan went on. "She feels like hell she did that."

He didn't give that first fuck.

"Chloe's tenure of holding them all up is done, Duncan."

Duncan sighed.

After hearing that, Judge remarked, "I think I'm understood."

"You are. But she's a part of this family, and we all need to rebuild with what we have now. And it goes without saying, she's a big part of that, it's just the way it is, the way *they* are, but it's also the way Chloe plays it."

Maybe so.

However...

"She's worn herself out with that effort while they all wallowed in their own issues. It's time for the rest of them to boss the fuck up."

"Those are almost Sully's exact words," Duncan muttered, and Judge wasn't surprised.

He liked Sullivan Holloway unreservedly. He was a solid guy and always had been for as long as Judge had known him. Even when he was a lot younger.

Duncan focused more fully on Judge and went on, "You and her—"

"We're happening."

Duncan's lips twitched before he pressed them together.

"Do you get that, Duncan?" he asked.

"I don't think I need it explained, bud," Duncan answered.

"No, what I mean is, for her," he jerked his own head back toward the house, "she needs this family rebuilt too. It's everything to her. It being fractured has torn her apart. She's been suffering a lot of blows for a long time and keeping her chin up through them so everyone else can have their shit. And no shade on Genny, or Tom, they had their own issues they were dealing with. But it doesn't negate the fact Chloe's been swinging in the breeze with this, alone, no backup, making it easy on them to deal with their own shit. What you need to get is, she's got backup now."

"Thank fuck."

At this response, the tension ebbed out of Judge.

Duncan's voice was quiet when he said, "It is not lost on her mother that she's suffering. And Chloe confided that directly to me. We've been worried. I cannot tell you…" He lifted a hand, pulled it through his hair, dropped it. "This brings relief."

Judge didn't want that for them, any of them, but all the same, he was glad to hear they'd not been entirely clueless.

The door behind him opened.

He twisted and watched Chloe slip out.

After she'd hit the bathroom to clean up the mess her crying jag had made of her makeup, she'd come out and most of it was gone.

She was as gorgeous as ever.

Now, a little puffy-eyed from the weeping and the sleeping, she was the same.

He knew she would be, puffy eyes and all.

Even so, his tension came back at her appearance, only to slide away again immediately as she sidled up to Judge then pressed against his side, wrapping her arms around his middle.

Jesus.

It felt like his fucking soul let out a breath.

He glided an arm around her shoulders.

Duncan took them in, his mouth curved.

"Hey, Bowie," Chloe murmured shyly.

"You okay, honey?" Duncan asked.

She nodded, her cheek moving against Judge's pec.

"Your mom's worried. Sasha is—"

Judge cleared his throat.

Duncan's chest heaved with a held back laugh before he kept on, "Everyone's worried."

"I'll call Mom."

"By everyone I mean Sully, Gage, Hale…and Matt."

Fuck.

"I'll connect with Sullivan, Gage, Hale. I'll do that soon," she promised. "But I need space, Bowie."

In other words, Matt could fester in the situation he'd wrought by dragging Chloe through his shit and then blaming it on her.

Yes.

She'd been thorough when she pulled it together and then gave it all to Judge.

And he liked Sully and Gage more than he already did, and he'd liked them both a lot.

For his part, Gage had driven up from Tucson to "show her a good time" last night. He did this by taking her out to some club he could only get into because he had a fake ID, and then he used his allowance to buy her drinks and watched her purse while she danced.

But her blood siblings, they were another story.

"I'll see to that," Duncan promised.

"Tell Mom I'm okay, though, yes?"

"Of course, honey." Then he looked to Judge. "She doesn't drive down the mountain tonight."

Chloe tensed at his side.

"Absolutely not," Judge agreed.

"I—" Chloe didn't quite begin.

Duncan cut her off by saying, "Come here just real quick, honey."

Chloe didn't protest further. She pulled from Judge, and Duncan folded her tight in his arms.

Judge shifted just enough to see the expression on her face was relieved, content.

And suddenly, Judge felt the same.

Duncan had to say no more, the hug said it all, so he kissed her cheek, broke their hug and ordered, "Eat. Rest. We'll see you soon."

Judge reclaimed Chloe, and Duncan clapped Judge on the arm, dipped his chin and sauntered away.

Judge felt Chloe's head move and looked down at her to see her looking up at him.

"I have to work tomorrow, Judge."

"So wake up early to get down the mountain."

She scrunched her face.

He bent and kissed her nose.

When he lifted away, she didn't hesitate to educate him about something important.

"There will be times you doing something that sweet will allow you to get away with being ridiculous. A very early morning on the line is not one of those times."

"Sure it is," he disagreed.

She glared but rearranged her face to watch and then wave as Duncan drove away in his Tesla SUV.

When the night swallowed his taillights, Judge guided her inside.

Straight to the kitchen.

There, he gave her a squeeze and let her go to get on with dinner, because he was starved.

She reached for her bag.

"You touch your phone, I'll take it from you and throw it over my deck."

That got him another glare.

"I'm not sure I'm a fan of this bossy," she declared.

"They can stew in the pot they cooked up and tried to boil you in," he said, dumping the ground beef in the skillet.

"That's quite the metaphor," she tossed at him.

He shot her a grin. "You're not gonna get poetry from me either, doll, but you won't go wanting to understand what I mean." He paused then, "Or how I feel."

She rolled her eyes, but she did it with lips curving.

She then explained, "I wasn't going to connect with Sash...or Matt. But Mom needs to know I'm good and Sully might do something severe, like charter a plane to get to me or go over to Matt's and punch him in the face. He's overprotective, that one. I'd weed that out of him, but it's immensely attractive and will serve his future partner well, once I've decided she passes muster."

Judge burst out laughing, his relief complete because she was herself again.

He noticed her lips were again tipped up as she finished reaching for her phone.

When he saw the screen light up, he also saw it filled with notifications.

Shit.

Before she got into it, he said, "I want you spending the night."

Her head came up, and her eyes found his.

He made himself clear.

"In my bed, next to me. Where I can be close to you. No sex. That's going to be only ours, and I don't want the memory of our first time clouded with something ugly. But I also don't want you driving down in the dark, or after a big trauma and crying jag. It'll worry the fuck out of me."

She left that a moment, her face soft, her eyes gorgeous, but she said, "I really do need to open tomorrow, and I am not a morning person. Further, my *toilette* is not swift. I'd have to be out the door by five and I don't fancy that."

Only Chloe would describe getting ready as her "*toilette*."

"Are you overrun with customers on a Monday morning?" he asked.

She looked like she was assessing that.

Then she said, "No."

"Can you open a few hours late and it not detrimentally hit your bottom line?"

She didn't have to assess that. "Yes."

"Is there anything scheduled, a meeting, deliveries, that you have to be there for?"

"No."

"So are you spending the night with me?"

She smiled. "Yes."

"Come here, baby," he murmured.

She came to him.

He rounded her with an arm, and she kept her face tipped to him so he could take her mouth.

He did that, the beef sizzling, and he kept doing it, because the beef could burn for all he cared.

If it did, he had more in the fridge.

But now, he finally had her there, at his side, in his home, after she let it all hang out.

He needed to see to his woman.

When she was fully melted into him, he released her mouth and paid attention to their dinner.

But he didn't let her go.

It was possible they looked ludicrous, but he didn't care about that either as they shuffled around the kitchen attached, Judge making taco meat and getting stuff they'd need out of the fridge, whooshes coming from Chloe's phone as she dealt with the fallout of her sister's nasty.

He knew when she gave him more of her weight that he had her attention back.

And that was when he asked, "How much research did you do on me?"

She stilled.

He laughed and looked down at her.

"It's okay. It's cute. It proves how totally into me you are."

It took her a beat, but she wisely decided to let that slide.

Unfortunately, she did it to say carefully, "Your grandfather seems like quite the character."

He didn't break their gaze when he shared straight out, "He's a dick. I detest him. Even though I've said this to his face more than once, he considers it indication I'm a 'real man' who 'knows his own mind and has the balls to speak it,' instead of the reaction I'd like it to have. Him getting out of my life for-fucking-ever."

"I sensed this would be the way you felt about him," she murmured.

But he did not miss her pressing closer.

She then said to the simmering taco meat, "As much as I, too, want to know everything about you, I think you should not only share all of this in your own time, but also, we've had enough excitement for one night."

"My mom's a functioning addict with the 'functioning' part of that being pretty dicey."

Her head jerked back, and her eyes locked with his.

"No time like the present," he said.

"Judge—"

"Let's get it out of the way, yeah?"

A brief hesitation, then she nodded.

Yeah.

"I do my absolute best to steer clear of her because she's a fucking mess," he said dispassionately. "I've learned not to get dragged in, but it's still hard, because she's my mom. Though, only because of that. Anything else I might have felt for her has been leached out through years of cleaning up her puke, putting up with her ranting about my father, when she was the one who cheated on him first, and generally our home being devoid of any parental guidance at all. The only thing she put her absolute all into, outside of making certain there was always booze, pot, pills and coke in the house, is keeping me from Dad."

"She cheated first?"

He nodded. "Apparently, Dad had repeatedly called her on her consumption, not only of booze, but blow and other pharmaceuticals. When she refused to admit she had a problem, something she's committed to, to this day, he attempted a tough love route. He cleared the house of all of that and cut her off financially. She couldn't access cash at all, which wasn't a problem. He paid for everything, and she didn't need for a thing. Or want for one. Except the thing she needed most. Which she got by fucking her dealer."

"*Judge*," she breathed, full-on pressing into him now, her hand coming to his stomach to flatten tight to the muscles there.

He shrugged, set the spoon aside and reduced the heat on the meat.

"Judge," she called.

He looked down at her again.

"How do you know this?" she asked.

"She got drunk and told me. Then I called Dad, and he'd been protecting me from it, so he was pretty pissed she let it slip. But he confirmed. By the way, when I learned this, I was fourteen."

"*Mon dieu*," she whispered.

He shrugged again.

Her eyes narrowed on him.

He gave her a squeeze.

"By the time he supposedly cheated on her, he'd already asked her for a divorce and had made moves to see that through. She fed it to the media he had another woman, when they were living in the same house while she was supposed to be sorting herself to move, but they were separated. She was lashing out. And I suppose in the end that was a good thing for Dad. It was the final straw."

Chloe was staring up at him in horror.

Judge moved to allay that.

"It's gonna sound cold, but I honestly don't care about any of this anymore," he told her. "I can't say it's comfortable when she's around. I find her trying or irritating or embarrassing. But she doesn't come around often, and I don't go to her. She's no fun, obviously, but she's also locationally close to Granddad, and he's to be avoided too. Problem with him is that he has a sixth sense of when I'm close. And then he's there and she's enough. The both of them..." He shook his head.

"I find it difficult to believe you're this cavalier about all of this," she remarked hesitantly.

"Sadly, one day, you'll find out. They both are family. And although we're not close, family is family."

"Yes," she said softly. "Family is family."

He gave her another squeeze.

"I'll warm the tortillas," she whispered.

He let her go.

She didn't go far, only standing on his other side to turn on the griddle he'd put out and then she opened the bag of tortillas.

"Do you want the cheese melted on yours?" she asked.

"Sounds great."

She got to work.

He prompted, "I know you wanna ask."

She tipped her head back to look at him. "Ask what?"

He didn't tell her what.

He just gave her the answer.

"Dad and I aren't tight. He wants it. He always has. She blocked him at every turn. He also thinks what I do is a lark. He was okay with it at first. Now I'm old enough, according to him, he thinks I need to get serious about my future. By serious, he means getting out of this hick town and making a shit-ton more cash. He even offered me the seed money to start my own thing, whatever that might be. Called it an early inheritance. He has more of Granddad in him than he'd ever admit. But it's seriously there."

"Hmm," she hummed.

She was right.

Hmm.

"So, he reaches out," Judge continued, "and has been doing that often from the time I went to college to establish some kind of relationship we never really got to have when I was growing up. And it wasn't like I never got to see him, or never spoke to him when I was younger. He had visitation rights he fully took advantage of. It's just that Mom went out of her way to limit that as much as she could. And she didn't succeed in much in her life, but she succeeded in that."

After he gave her that, Chloe just stared at him.

So he kept going.

"Dad and I started building something. It was good. But it stalled because I dig what I do. Even though I'll likely move on, and when I do, it'll be to something where I'll move up, make more money, take on more responsibility, learn new things, it'll be in the not-for-profit sector. Something for kids, or the environment, or social responsibility."

He was far from relaxed after laying all that last out.

And her response was exactly why.

"I don't understand that."

"Why I'll stay in charity?"

She shook her head even as she sprinkled cheese on a tortilla she'd just flipped.

"No, not that. You're exceptionally skilled at what you do. Obviously, I don't want you leaving Bowie anytime soon, but as we were working, I saw you as an executive director of an independent organization. Something large. Maybe national." She looked up at him again. "Frankly, and I won't tell Bowie this, but you're wasted on Kids and Trails. It's not big enough for you. It's clearly been good to cut your teeth on, but with your talent, you've outgrown it. As far as I can tell, reading the website, your annual report, working with you, you did that a long time ago. Plates?"

Mutely, because he was stunned silent by her words, not to mention distracted by the warm feeling building deep in his chest, he jerked his head to a cabinet.

Chloe reached.

And kept talking.

"Unless you branch out. Say, Kids and Trails has another arm, Kids and Conservation. Or Kids and Cleanup, where you take them out and show them what littering or non-recycling does to the landscape, and they help clean it up. Or Kids and Heritage, taking them to Native American reservations to learn stories of the people who were here before us. How they used the land, venerated it, took care of it, how they do that still."

Judge remained silent, in awe of her and tracking every word out of her mouth, cataloguing it and filing it away to consider later.

"So not that. Your dad. I don't get that. He's filthy rich. How did he not find ways to get to you?"

When he didn't answer, she stopped what she was doing with the plates, cheese and tortillas and turned back to him.

"Judge?"

He cleared his throat.

And said, "Because Granddad wanted me to himself, but if he couldn't have that, he wanted me in Texas. Dad could have crushed Mom, but Granddad got involved, and he fights dirty. In the beginning, I was caught in the crossfire. To save me, particularly from the media feeding on the custody battle, and Granddad feeding that media, in the middle of all that being me, Dad had no choice but to back away."

Her face paled.

"It's okay," he said.

Her face got red.

"It's okay, honey," he reiterated.

"You mean to tell me," she began slowly, "that it wasn't only your mother who fought tooth and nail to keep your father from you… your father, who sounds like the only functioning one out of that bunch, outside your grandmother, who's dead…your grandfather did that too?"

"Look at me, I'm fine. I survived."

"*Are you kidding me!*" she screeched abruptly.

Judge went solid.

"Oh my *fucking* God!" she yelled.

Judge stared.

"This…is not…to be…*tolerated!*" she shouted.

"Baby, calm down," he urged soothingly.

"Fuck calm," she snapped.

He blinked.

"Did you want to see more of your dad?" she demanded.

"Like you said," he started cautiously, "he was the only functioning one of the bunch. But yeah, I mean, he's my dad." Considering her reaction, he wondered about the wisdom of adding his next, but since they were getting this out of the way, he did. "I didn't spend a lot of time with him, but he was the only one I felt safe with the entire time I was growing up."

She took a beat with that then literally shoved him out of the way.

Yep.

Shoved him out of the way.

Then she ripped the wooden spoon out of his hand and took over dinner.

And she did this raving.

"Well, no. No way. Not on your life. That is *done*. I mean, you must do what you must with your mother, the *bare necessities*. She did birth you after all."

She was slamming around meat, tortillas, cheese was flying, opening the salsa, clicking the top off the sour cream container.

"But that grandfather of yours. And that uncle?"

He hadn't even mentioned Jeff.

But Jeff was a fuckup and creepy to boot.

Judge had learned a long time ago to stay away from Jeff.

Obviously, though, her research had been thorough.

"No. No way," she repeated, slapping meat on a cheesy tortilla. "And your dad is going to have to get over it. You're good at what you do. You love doing it. If he's not okay with you doing that, he can *fuck off*." She twirled the wooden spoon in the air and taco juice went flying. "*C'est fini.*"

"Baby, you loaded half a pound of meat on that one tortilla."

Her head snapped back, and her fiery eyes caught his.

"Are you not hungry?"

This.

Fuck.

It was *this*.

This was why they all leaned on her.

Because when Chloe Pierce loved you, she fought like hell to protect you.

And she did it like a wildcat.

He pulled the plate out of her hand, set it aside, took the spoon from her other hand, tossed it in the skillet, pushed the meat and the griddle from their burners and turned them off.

Then he maneuvered her back to the counter and pressed her to it.

"Judge, dinner will go cold," she snapped, her hands on his chest, pressing.

"I...am...absolutely...fine...with...my...crazy...fucked-up...family," he stated.

She gazed up at him.

"I live my life, and I don't give a fuck what they think of how I do it."

"Okay," she said quietly.

"So you can stand down."

Her eyes got big, and she sucked her lips between her teeth.

"Yeah?" he pushed.

She let her lips go and he knew by the way she said the one sylla-ble, "I—" she was not at one with his *Yeah?*

"Chloe, this..." he waved a hand between them, "is me looking out for you, not the other way around. Don't lose the weight of carrying the others only to pull me on your shoulders. I don't need you to carry me."

"You might."

"I don't."

"Maybe eventually."

"But not now."

"What I'm saying is...*Judge*," she drawled his name slowly, it was cute, and hot, "it goes both ways, or it doesn't go at all."

"You gonna let this shit go you got in your head about Mom, Dad and Granddad?"

She lifted one shoulder. "If you say you're good, then okay. Yes. I'll let that go."

He examined her face, looked deep into her eyes, and then he gave in. "Okay."

She then examined his face, looked deep into his eyes, and asked, "Really?"

"Yeah."

"You'll share the load if there is one, or let me carry it, whatever the case may be."

Share, sure. He was down with that.

Carry it?

No way in fuck.

"Yeah," he somewhat told the truth, somewhat lied.

Her brows drew down. "You're lying."

He grinned. "Totally not." *Though partially, yes.*

She didn't quit her examination, one hundred percent not believing him, so he threw her off the scent.

"You throwing the drama was hot as fuck."

Her head ticked.

Then she rolled her eyes and clicked her teeth.

"We need to have our official first date so we can make love after it and get that out of the way so I can fuck you," he declared.

Her cheeks pinkened, her eyes darkened, her body slackened into his, but her mouth was all sass.

"I'm not a sex-on-the-first-date type of girl," she sniffed.

"Then it's good we're essentially on what I'd consider our seventh, though I kinda think that time in Wild Iris is a semi-date, so seven and a half."

"Seven and a half?"

"Wild Iris. New Year's. The meet the parents dinner at your dad's."

She hmphed and said, "That wasn't a meet the parents."

"Did I sit down to eat with *all* your parents?"

She hmphed again but said no more.

He fought a grin and kept going.

"Cooking Club. Brunch. Wednesday. Today's hike. Tonight. Seven and a half."

"None of those were dates."

"C'mon, baby," he murmured. "Seriously?"

She couldn't even lean into her claim for a full second, he knew that when her gaze skidded from his.

He grinned and asked, "Are you a sex on the eighth and a half date girl?"

She looked back at him. "Don't be annoying, Judge."

"Thursday, you're letting someone else look after the store, because Wednesday, you're driving up, we're going on a date, and you're spending the night. That'll be our first time. Saturday, I'll come down to you, I'll have Zeke with me, and we'll stay until Sunday evening. That'll be when we fuck." He paused. "A lot."

She licked her bottom lip.

He dipped and caught it between his teeth.

Then he licked it and against it, prompted, "Yeah?"

"Okay," she breathed.

"Wanna eat?"

"Yes," she lied, gaze lowered, eyes to his mouth.

He touched it to hers, and before he was lost, and took her with him, he let her go.

"One thing you can say about today," she began as he started to rescue the food by sorting out the gargantuan taco she'd made in her snit. "We'll soon find out if I can't trust you, or you can't trust me."

He grinned at her. "Luckily, I totally trust you, and I know you can trust me."

It was then, it happened.

His life changed.

The world changed.

Everything changed with the look in her eyes.

A look she got right before she replied…

"Yes, *chéri*. Luckily."

CHAPTER 20

THE WISTERIA

Chloe

I woke when the bed moved.

My first semi-coherent thought was to grab hold of Judge and not let him get out of it. Keep him close to me, just him and me, the world outside could take care of itself.

Just him and me.

For the day.

The week.

Forever.

Bliss.

But when I stretched out my arm, I came up empty.

I felt something land on my hip.

"Hey, sorry to wake you, but real quick, then I gotta go and you can go back to sleep," I heard Judge say softly.

I rolled to my back, toward the sound of his voice, and opened my eyes.

There was light coming from somewhere, his bathroom? The hall?

But it was dim.

Nevertheless, I saw he was dressed, and his hair was still drying from a shower.

Right.

What was happening?

More importantly, how did I make it stop?

"Sleep as long as you like," he was saying. "I put a new toothbrush head out for you. Use my electric one. There's bacon staying warm in the oven. If you wanna make some eggs or a bagel to go with, go for it. Coffee is Nespresso. You know how to work a Nespresso?"

He'd been up long enough to cook bacon?

"There isn't a coffee machine I cannot master," I said, my voice still drowsy. "That said, you clearly missed it in the warm glow of food and friendship during Cooking Club, but I, too, own a Nespresso."

He grinned, his dimple made an appearance, and I suddenly wasn't drowsy at all.

"Rix brought Zeke home this morning."

He did?

Already?

At this hour?

That was lunacy.

"He's good," Judge went on. "But if you wanna let him out before you go, he'd love you forever."

"I already have his devotion," I pointed out.

Still grinning and, "Yeah. Also, I set a key out for you just in case and put the garage door opener in your car. It's on the seat. Plugged your phone in to charge, you forgot to do that last night. Please just be sure to turn off the oven before you go."

I pushed up to my behind and noted, "This all seems alarmingly like a farewell."

"It isn't. It's an 'I gotta get to work,'" he corrected.

"I'm alarmed about that too." I gazed out his windows at the dark and then turned my attention back to him. "It's still night."

"It's seven a.m."

"I'll repeat, it's still night."

He started chuckling.

Then he committed the cardinal sin of leaning in and attempting to kiss me before I'd brushed my teeth.

I turned my head away.

"Baby," he murmured.

"It's morning."

"There is no time I'm not down with kissing you."

I kept my chin in my neck, my head as far away from him as possible as I looked back at him. "That's very sweet. It also isn't going to happen until I brush my teeth."

"I gotta go and I want a goodbye kiss."

"It isn't goodbye. It's 'you have to get to work.'"

"Right, yeah, forgot." He was back to murmuring, but now it was filled with amusement.

"Wait until I brush my teeth. Then we can kiss, and I can convince you to go to work late."

"I'm never late."

I had no doubt he wasn't.

I tipped my head in challenge.

"You'd be worth being late," he allowed. "Absolutely. And I don't think Duncan would give a fuck, especially not today. But Chloe, I kiss you, *really* kiss you, in my bed, neither of us is going to work today."

This explained why he didn't give me but a peck last night after we'd settled in.

I clicked my teeth, vexed because he was right.

Not to mention, uncertain why that was a bad thing.

"Quick kiss," he said, and before I knew what he was about, he'd pressed his lips hard to mine.

I could allow that, closed mouthed, which was as far as he went.

He pulled away, whispered, "Text me when you leave. And text me when you make it home."

"Fine," I huffed.

"You're a pathological cuddler," he announced, apropos of nothing.

I stared.

Then I asked, "Sorry?"

"You chased me around the bed all night."

"I did *not*," I stated coldly.

I mean, *hardly*.

"You *so* did. I woke up once because we were both almost falling out."

"That didn't happen."

"It did."

"It did *not*."

"Whatever," he muttered, stole another quick kiss, then got off the bed and walked to the door.

Yes, the light was coming from the hall.

Plugged your phone in to charge, you forgot to do that last night.

This man, this sweet, thoughtful, handsome, caring man was falling in love with me.

"Judge," I called before he arrived at it.

He turned.

"Do you like wisteria?" I asked.

"What?"

"Wisteria, the flowering vine."

"Is this code for something?"

"No."

"Is it crucial you have this information before I go to work?"

"Yes."

"Then I'm a little scared to say I don't know what it is."

"I'll text you photos."

I heard his soft chuckle before he said, "Look forward to that."

He turned again.

"Judge," I called.

He turned back.

"Thank you…for last night."

His expression lost its humor and became so beautiful to behold, I nearly had to look away.

Obviously, I did not.

"Just glad it happened when I was close," he replied.

I was too.

"Sleep, have breakfast, and be careful going down the mountain," he bid.

I nodded.

"Talk to you later, baby."

"Yes," I replied.

He gave me a sweet smile and turned away again.

"Judge," I called.

He turned back and lifted his brows.

He wasn't amused, impatient, or edging toward irritable.

He was attentive and waiting for me to say what I had to say.

This wasn't a test.

I just didn't want him to go.

But if it had been a test, he would have done what he'd always done.

Passed with perfect scores and extra credit.

"Can't wait for Wednesday," I whispered.

He stood there a second, two, three.

Then he was across the room, and I was up from the bed, in his arms, and he was kissing my morning-breath mouth.

Not closed.

I forgot I had morning breath and kissed him back.

When he was done, he murmured, "I can't either."

He then gently laid me back in his bed, slid away the hair that had fallen in one of my eyes, pulled the covers over me, and, after giving me the most beautiful smile in history, he walked out of the room.

IT's PRETTY.

This was Judge's text response to my sending him three pictures of white wisteria, one of purple, one of pink.

We would be doing white, of course, but one must explore other options just to be certain one's vision was as superlative as one thought.

Just pretty? I replied.

The muted noise that sounded when someone opened the door to Velvet beeped, and I looked up from where I stood at the checkout desk to see Mi-Young heading my way.

"What are you doing here?" I asked my friend a very good question, since it was her day off.

"Have you lost your mind?" she asked back.

My phone binged.

I looked down.

It's VERY pretty.

Ugh.

Men.

Mi rapped the checkout desk with her knuckles to get my attention, something I gave her.

"Are you texting him?" she demanded.

"Yes," I told her.

"Happily? Flirtatious? Not finding inane reasons to push him away anymore?"

I gave her a Death Stare.

It dissipated upon impact.

This was because Mi had a Death Stare vaporizer. I would never admit it, but this was probably one of the reasons she became my best friend.

She took no shit, not even from me.

"Happily," I gritted.

She gave me an approving nod then launched in.

"So, you write me seven, and I'll note that I counted them, very long texts that had me scrolling for half an hour. Texts that included details of Sasha behaving like a little bitch..." She waved her hand in my face. "I know, she's not my sister, I can't say that, but in this instance, I'm going to, because what she did is not okay. Judge was there. He heard. Your adored stepdad was there. He heard. Sasha herself knows you agonize about that to this day, even if it wasn't your fault. You didn't know that married guy was such a magnificent asshole. Then you finally come to terms with your uncle's death, face your feelings about your parents' divorce, and pull your shit together about Judge, *and you spent the night with him*, and you're asking me why I'm here?"

"I had wondered why you hadn't responded to my texts," I remarked.

She dropped her head back and stared at the ceiling.

My phone binged.

Why is this important? Judge asked.

I had a ready response to that.

(In other words, a lie.)

No reason.

"Chloe," Mi called my name.

I focused on her and stated, "Judge and I made dinner together."

"I feel with the way you said that, congratulations are in order, but I've no idea why," she replied.

"We did it attached. He had his arm around me, and he didn't let me go. We shambled around the kitchen like we'd been tied together by an enchanted rope. It was utterly ridiculous and the most romantic thing a man has ever done in my life."

"Seriously?" Mi breathed.

There it was.

I was not in a Judge Daze.

I was correct.

That *was* romantic.

"I mean, how sweet is that, especially after all you'd just been through," she went on.

I knew how sweet it felt.

And the definition of that level of sweetness had not been invented yet.

"He says he's falling in love with me."

She gaped.

"Yes," I concurred with her response.

"He laid that out *already*?"

"I'm right now assessing his opinion about wisteria."

She gaped again and whispered wonderingly, "Your wedding flowers?"

As you could see, she was totally my bestie. She knew everything, including the fact my wedding was already entirely planned.

Down to the wall of wisteria.

(Though, color options were not set in stone.)

I nodded and shared, "He thinks they're 'very pretty,' which is likely just a man's response to flowers, or him knowing why I'm asking and he's trying to get a rise out of me."

Mi leaned into the counter. "I'm so glad you got your head out of your ass about him."

"I'm so glad I have a friend who would come into her place of business on her day off to talk about him, even if she says things to me like I had my head in my ass."

Perfectly Mi, she didn't back down. "Well, you did."

"Shall we move on?" I suggested sweetly.

"Yes, let's talk about what you're going to do about Sasha. Because Matt's damage isn't new. This Sasha thing, so out of character."

That was it precisely.

Completely out of character.

"She's called and texted, I've asked her to give me some space. She's promised to try."

"Yeah, like right about now, she should endeavor to go to Mars."

Hmm.

I looked down and twiddled with my phone.

"Hey," Mi called.

I caught her eyes. "Bowie was standing right there, and Judge was walking up. She saw him."

"I know," Mi said softly. "You told me."

"That's mean girl, Mi. Sasha isn't a mean girl."

For a moment, Mi's face was soft with sadness and understanding, then it got hard, and she said, "Oh no you don't."

"Don't what?"

"Feel sorry for her when she lashed out at you like that. Feel sorry which means letting her off the hook and then giving her your time and patience and wisdom and anything else you have to give to help her pull herself together. Coco, seriously. All this stuff going on with your family didn't happen when she was six so it's understandable when she throws a tantrum. She's a big girl. She needs to grow up and start acting it."

I felt my lips thin because she was correct.

And this was a one-two punch, because I had a feeling Judge would be disappointed if I gave in this soon to my sister, who, I could tell by her texts and voicemails, really was suffering for what she'd done.

"You're wavering," Mi accused with narrowed eyes on my face.

"I'm going to forgive her, we both know that."

She shook her head. "Somehow, this world is careening toward being a place where there are no consequences. You throw some comment out on social media to some person you don't know and will never meet, shady or critical or downright cruel, and you just go on with your life. Not realizing there are real people out there who suffer because you couldn't just scroll on by, you had to lay out the nasty. There are absolutely no consequences to millions of people every day spreading a layer of negativity, or even hyper-negativity over something a vast majority of us use. That festers and breeds and it's filtering into real life. Where we think people in our spheres don't have feelings. That the world revolves around us and our opinions. But it does not."

"My sister is hardly treating me like some influencer who she's not fond of their look."

"No, she isn't. But first, if you don't like an influencer's look, pass it by. There is absolutely no need to make a mean comment about it. And second, you're a real person in her life, someone who matters, someone she loves, so what she did is far, far worse, Coco, and some-how, she has to learn she can't do it again. She doesn't just get to say something and think she can scroll on to whatever's next. Her words caused harm. She needs to account for that."

"So it's on me to teach her that lesson when it hurts me to do it?" I asked.

She did a one-shoulder shrug. "Only my opinion. But, yes."

Marvelous.

"Sadly, Judge agrees with you," I sniffed.

"I knew I liked him."

Speaking of that particular devil, my phone binged.

I looked at it.

Bullshit. It's either wedding or you're angling for me to plant some at your house. Give it up.

I rent, I replied. Then, before he could read anything in that (like the truth), I whooshed off, *As you know, it's far too soon for wedding talk.*

His reply was almost immediate, and even just getting the words, I knew they were dripping with disbelief.

Are you angling to garden at my house?

As if.

Me?

Garden?

"Are you still talking wisteria?" Mi asked.

"No," I lied.

"You are so full of it," she muttered, but at least she didn't sound angry at Sasha anymore.

Mi thinks I shouldn't give in too early to Sasha's apologies, I told Judge.

Again, almost immediate, *Mi's right.*

Bluh.

Then he sent, *I knew I liked her.*

Ugh.

"I decided in the heat of it yesterday to hold my grudge for a month with Sasha," I told Mi.

"I vote two," she retorted.

Well then, I wouldn't share that now I was thinking only a day.

My phone binged again, a text from a number I didn't know.

It said, *We're not doing some stupid-ass mutual bachelor/bachelorette party horseshit.*

Who is this? I demanded.

Who else? Rix. And no mixed shower. I'm getting my boy drunk off his ass the night before and buying one gift. That's it. And I speak for all his male friends on this.

My back straightened.

Because one thing that was non-negotiable about my wedding (actually, it all was, but this was ironclad).

My groom was not going to be hungover on the big day.

"What's going on?" Mi asked.

"Judge's friend Rix is staking claim to a non-mixed bachelor party and refuses to come to the shower."

"Oh my God," Mi said, both horrified and miffed.

Oh dear.

We haven't even had a date! I snapped to Rix.

And before I could turn my attention to my friend, Mi pulled my phone out of my hand.

I blinked at her then watched as she took two steps back and started double-fisted maneuvers, my phone in one hand, hers in the other, her thumbs moving over the screens of both.

"What are you doing?" I inquired, but only because I didn't want to face my suspicions as to her actions.

"I'm negotiating since we're going to a strip club for your bachelorette party too, so might as well all go together," she said, absently handing back my phone even as hers whooshed with a text.

Yes, this confirmed my suspicions.

"Mi—"

Not looking at me, still looking at her phone, she raised a hand my way and waggled a finger at me, shushing, "Shh."

And there was another whoosh from her cell.

"It is not good at this juncture for you two to put this pressure on me and Judge," I stated firmly.

Her phone binged, she read it and then looked at me. "He wants to know if we can arrange crash pads down here in Phoenix for about twenty of Judge's buds. I think we can handle that. You have a guest bedroom. I have a guest bedroom. And your mom has at least three."

"Mi!" I snapped.

"You brought up the wisteria," she returned.

My phone sounded.

I looked down at it.

From Judge, *I have high standards, baby. Maybe we should take the bachelor-bachelorette thing to Vegas?*

I refused to feel the relief I actually felt that Judge had high standards about the gentlemen's clubs he'd accept (as, naturally, I did too).

I also refused to feel the relief that it was clear he thought this was fun and wasn't terrified about such discussions before we'd even officially been on a date.

Instead, I put together a group text that included the current offenders, upon which I declared, *I've ceased talking to all of you for at least a day.*

Mi giggled.

Rix texted, creating two chimes in my ears, *No worries. You shouldn't be in on the planning anyway.*

Mi giggled again.

On our personal string, Judge cajoled, *I hope that doesn't include me.*

It especially includes you. You gave my number to Rix.

Mi had her own whooshes and chiming, and she declared, "Rix is coming to the next Cooking Club."

Dear Lord.

At this point, I did the only thing I could do.

I programmed Rix into my phone.

And said to Judge, *Go back to work.*

Finally, I gave my attention to Mi and drawled, "Impressed with the outfit you threw together to come in for unscheduled girl time."

She swished her hips and her short zebra print skirt floated, beautifully paired with a mustard turtleneck I knew had no sleeves, with a baby blue cargo jacket over the top.

"This old thing?" she replied.

It wasn't old, she bought it last week.

Call you tonight, baby, Judge texted.

I sent a gif of Marie from the *Aristocats* tucking herself into bed.

"Jocelyn will be here in fifteen minutes," Mi announced. "When she gets here, let's hit Joyride for lunch."

My stomach decided I needed some Mexican street corn.

My heart decided I needed some unadulterated girl time with my bestie.

"Yes, let's," I agreed.

My phone signaled one more time.

From Judge.

God, you're cute.

I wasn't.

But he was for thinking that.

"IT'S NOT MY DECISION, IT'S NOT MI'S, IT'S YOURS."

It was late that evening.

I was wearing a pair of pink silk pajamas with red piping on my body and a hydrating mask on my face.

And Judge was in my ear.

"Do I think she should squirm a lot longer, yes," he said, referring to Sasha, who we were discussing since I told him what Mi had said earlier. "But she's not my sister and what she did, she didn't do to me. It's your call. It's always been your call."

"So if I made a date with her for brunch on Thursday before I came back down to Phoenix, you wouldn't be upset?" I asked.

"Chloe, honey, you have to do what makes you feel right. If it's gonna upset you to draw it out, or add stress, then sit down and talk to her."

Interesting.

"You made it sound like you'd be disappointed if I did that. Let her off the hook too easily," I noted.

"Babe, there is you and there is me. I met her at the New Year's Eve party, and she seemed bubbly and nice. And I saw her yesterday, when she was neither. I don't know her. And right now, I don't care about her. I'm sorry, but not even a little. I care about *you*. So if confronted with her, am I gonna be a dick to her? No. Am I gonna be pissed at you that you do what you feel you need to do for you, her, your family? No. Am I gonna be wary around her and protective of you when it comes to her? Yes. Absolutely."

I sat with that a second.

And then I said quietly, "I really like you, Judge Oakley."

"I'm so fucking glad you do, Chloe Pierce, I could howl at the moon," he said quietly back.

We each let the other have that.

And then Judge said, "Speaking of Thursday, if you're thinking of staying longer, can you arrange for someone else to open up on Friday and spend the night then too?"

My heart fluttered at this opportunity and I didn't even consider the possibility of telling it to behave.

More time with Judge.

Another night with him in his bed.

And hopefully, a lot more than a peck on the lips.

"It's just that I spoke with both Duncan and Tom about our progress," he continued. "They're down to go over what we propose for the project, and if we do it, it's gotta be ASAP. Your dad's heading to Australia for the Open very soon."

Damn.

He did color commentary for all the majors.

He'd mentioned that at dinner.

How had I forgotten?

"If you want to get it out of the way," Judge carried on, "Thursday is a good time. But if you want me to try to get them up early, say, right after lunch so you can have brunch with your sister, then you can get home without having to drive at night, I can arrange that too."

"Mi opens on Friday, so I'll stay Thursday too, and we'll do the meeting."

"Awesome," he said, his voice low and warm, that tone having nothing to do with the meeting with Dad and Bowie (I was definitely going to get more than a peck on the lips). "I'll send you the finals of everything so you can approve it."

"I'm sure it'll be perfect."

"Nothing's perfect, baby, but we can give it the best we got."

That was so true, I was ordering a coffee mug for him the next day with that on it.

Once that was out of the way, we talked about everything under the sun (or right then, the moon) and then we talked more.

Too late, both of us sleepy and barely holding to consciousness (something I deemed only slightly less romantic than making dinner attached), we had no choice but to bid adieu.

Judge's phone call was what woke me the next day.

It was so much better than my alarm (which was classical music, so that's saying something) it was not funny.

And we talked again Tuesday evening while I packed to go back up, Judge teasing me throughout that I had a quota of only one bag he'd carry up the stairs for a two-night stay.

I decided to get ready at his house for work on Friday, just to push my overnighter beyond capacity so I'd be forced to bring two.

And as my getting-ready game was extreme, in the end, I was definitely at two.

I received the same wakeup call Wednesday.

I did it knowing, that night, I'd see him again.

I was way beyond playing it cool.

I couldn't wait.

And I didn't consider the possibility of putting the effort into caring that I couldn't.

I did not hide it from Judge (who didn't hide it either).

And honestly?

That was the most romantic of all.

I selected an outfit for our date from my own store, it took no time to do so, I knew precisely what it should be.

The perfect date outfit for Judge Oakley.

A man who might not care about wisteria.

But that didn't matter in the slightest.

Because he cared about me.

CHAPTER 21

THE PETALS

Chloe

*T*he second time I woke in Judge's bed, I did it for the same reason as the first.

The bed had moved.

My eyes fluttered open even as I reached, coming up empty, then watched, in shadow, as Judge got up, and he in his pajama bottoms silently made his way to the bathroom.

He didn't turn on the light until he'd closed the door.

I snagged his pillow, claiming it, curling full body around it, letting the smell of him hit my senses, and I stared through the dark at the bathroom door.

My date outfit was a bust.

Not because Judge didn't think it was cute, he did.

No, because last night, when I arrived, he was standing in the doorway to the garage as his garage door opened after I hit the remote.

I pulled in, shut down my Evoque, got out, and he didn't move from his spot.

"Hello," I called, shifting to the backseat door to grab my things.

"Touch your bags, I'll spank your ass."

I stopped dead.

"Come here," he ordered.

"I see someone had an early cocktail of bossy," I remarked.

However, I did this moving his way considering (and this likely came as no surprise) I was not a female who turned down a man carrying her bag for her.

When I cleared my car, his gaze gave me a top to toe, though he lingered on the toe part.

"Nice outfit," he said offhandedly.

I stopped in front of him, not surprised he was in jeans and an attractive, hunter-green button-down. Thus, I was right in expecting our date wouldn't be formal because that just wasn't Judge.

"Please tell me this date involves food, because I'm starved."

"Sorry, doll," he whispered, "I get to eat first."

This confused me.

A lot of things were confusing me, since he was lounged in the doorjamb, arms and ankles crossed and unmoving.

That unmoving part including not touching me or, say, *kissing me hello*.

"Is Zeke here, one, and are you frozen in place, two?" I asked.

At these words, he unfroze, his hand darting my way, catching mine.

This wasn't a sweet holding of hands.

This was a capture and tug.

As in, his fingers were tight around mine and I was being hauled into the house and up the stairs.

More confusion.

A good deal more.

"Judge!" I snapped.

We hit the landing by the kitchen, didn't hesitate, and he dragged me through that floor to the main stairs.

And we started up them.

My confusion cleared.

"Judge," I whispered.

As with the first, the second time I said his name, he didn't respond.

He didn't say anything until we were in his room.

He had a great bedroom. Large with a fireplace across from the foot of the bed that was made of an interesting mix of gray and brown bricks that went all the way up to the vaulted ceilings. Ceilings that were covered in tongue-and-groove.

There were also these incredibly interesting low, wide, six-drawer dressers tucked in on either side of the fireplace that were made of distressed wood, and their handles looked like the old-fashioned leather grips from suitcases.

Further, there was a chair and ottoman tucked in the corner on what, on our first night sleeping together, had been Judge's side of the bed.

An iron and wood chandelier hung from the center of the ceiling.

And it was clear he simply bought the mushroom comforter, tan sheets and mushroom edged in navy and tan euro pillow shams (as well as all the accoutrement, including shammed standard pillows and a downy cream throw folded at the end) from a display in some department store (I would have done some mixing and matching, but it very much worked).

He had a wall of windows and small balcony off my side of the bed, a TV hanging over the fireplace, a large complementary rug covering the wood floor, and on the wall, a magnificent, slightly impressionistic painting of a white horse bounded on the canvas in bold, primary colors that represented a forest.

And now, there was a fire burning in the fireplace.

But more...

The wood mantel above it, the dressers, the bedstands were all covered in various size cream candles. All of them lit. The ottoman had a brass tray on it, on which there was an ice bucket filled with champagne and two flutes.

Last, on my nightstand, there was an extraordinary bouquet of the palest pink roses I'd ever seen, and profuse petals of the same were scattered all over the bed.

Profuse as in, they almost covered it.

Champagne.

Roses.

And petals.

It was clichéd.

It was sappy.

It was *everything*.

I had a long moment to take it in before Judge's hand in mine manipulated me to standing in front of him, then he walked forward, forcing me to move back.

"I got a spread downstairs all laid out," he said quietly, eyes to my mouth. "I'll bring it up later."

"Okay," I whispered.

The backs of my legs hit the bed and we stopped.

"Wracked my brain to come up with something special enough for you for our first date," he murmured, still talking to my lips.

Oh God.

"Judge."

I'd never heard my voice that way, it was quivering with emotion.

He lifted his gaze to mine.

"There was nothing," he declared. "And this is hokey as fuck, but I didn't want some restaurant doing all the work. For you, I wanted the effort to be all mine."

Oh God.

My *God*.

There was no way to fight this time.

My eyes filled with tears.

His hands spanned my waist. "Now, I know I should feed you. But I can't wa—"

"If you don't kiss me immediately, I'm going to expire."

I was going for authoritarian, but my voice was still quaky.

His mouth quirked. "Can't have that."

"Judge," I snapped.

He made me wait no longer.

He kissed me, taking me down to the bed.

I landed in the scent of Judge and roses and honestly, it was God's perfect bouquet.

His kiss was soft and languid and deep and wet.

His body was warm and hard and weighty.

And this, all of it, was exquisite.

When I pulled his shirt out of his jeans to get my hands on his skin, he broke the kiss.

"You wore the boots," he murmured.

I absolutely fashioned my entire outfit around the Jennifer Chamandi booties I'd worn when we first met.

And it absolutely meant the world that he remembered them.

"Mm," I hummed.

"So my baby can be corny too," he whispered, the words meant to be a tease, but his expression, his tone were anything but.

"I'm bronzing these boots," I informed him haughtily to hide how deeply all this was affecting me.

Because I knew how special he was. I knew how special he could be to me.

But I didn't plan for him to get even *more* special.

"Thank fuck," he replied.

My brows inched together. "Thank fuck I'm bronzing these boots?"

"Thank fuck every woman I was ever with blew it, so I'd end up right here, right now, with you." He touched his mouth to mine. "The best," he touched our lips again, "for last."

For last.

No wonder he didn't panic at the wisteria discussion.

"You haven't even had me yet, *chéri*," I pointed out.

"Are you the best?"

"Of course," I replied.

"Yeah," was all he said.

Yes.

That was all he said.

And then he kissed me again.

And he meant what he'd said.

All he'd said.

He intended our first time to be making love.

And as often as the heat he was building in me, the need, made me try to tip things to go faster (much faster), Judge kept it slow.

He kept us at tasting. Caressing. Uncovering. Stroking. Revealing. Exploring. Listening. Whispering.

The fire crackled, and with each move, the crush of petals would send up an aroma of roses.

This wasn't *making* love.

He'd already created it.

We were just basking in it.

So, obviously, that made the heat increase, the need build.

And then the other thing he'd promised, that he would eat first, happened too.

I was so in the zone, warm naked skin against warm naked skin, the taste of him in my mouth, the feel of him on my fingers, the scent of him and roses in my nose, it was almost a surprise when his lips slipped across my belly as his hand pressed my legs wide.

And he shifted down.

Other things about what we were doing shifted then too.

Enormously.

His mouth wasn't tentative, and it wasn't about discovery.

It was a bottom to top lash with his tongue dipping deep in between, and I stilled in response to the wonder of it.

It wasn't just that it felt amazing.

It was a claim.

It was a brand.

The sultry feeling of my limbs slid away.

Judge tossed my legs over his shoulders in preparation, a move in and of itself that had me bracing.

And then he *ate*.

Now *that* was just *amazing*.

In but moments, I had an arm over my head, elbow bent, hand in the comforter, pushing me down on him, but Judge also had both his arms wrapped around my ass, pulling me down as he sucked and he licked and he nipped and his tongue thrusted.

God, Judge Oakley made love with his hands.

But he fucked with his mouth.

"Honey," I whimpered.

He took one arm from around me, tucking his hand behind my knee, pushing it up and to the side, spreading me wide.

Oh *God*.

He then drew so hard on my clit, my entire body convulsed. I was pre-orgasm instantly.

And I couldn't wait.

He lifted his head, but so I wouldn't feel his loss, he slid a finger inside me, slowly stroking.

Oh yes.

"You don't come without me inside you, Chloe, and I don't mean my finger," he growled from between my legs. "Can you take more?"

No.

"Yes," I gasped.

It was hot and amused when he asked, "Are you lying?"

"No," I said.

Yes.

He kept his finger inside me as he rolled my other leg off his shoulder and surged up over me.

The instant he caught my eyes, I pouted.

He grinned.

After an outward stroke, the inward one was two fingers.

My eyes went hooded.

"I want us to come together, baby," he said.

"I want that too, Judge."

Eventually, perhaps the next round.

"Come together and *come together*. You can come in my mouth later."

Oh my God.

I was squirming, what with what his fingers were doing, what his mouth had done, the vision of the breadth of his muscled shoulders and that handsome face all I could see.

Then there were the candles, rose petals, the awaiting champagne.

I didn't need him talking dirty.

I used my hands on him, anywhere I could touch him, and ordered, "Then get on with it."

"I wanna eat you more."

"I want that too."

"You were about to go."

"I was not."

I *so* was.

He started chuckling.

"Judge!" I cried.

He slid his fingers out but then used them to circle my clit.

That was such delicious torture, I arced up into him.

Not fair!

"Fuck, didn't think you could get more beautiful, but there it is," he groaned.

My hands were now moving on him desperately, trying to pull him to me.

"Change my mind, gonna make you come and watch," he said gruffly.

I rubbed against his fingers, my own diving into his hair, and I used this hold to pull me closer to him.

"Come inside," I breathed.

He added a thumb and gave me a gentle pinch.

At the rocket of sensation that blasted through me, I mewed, and my hand fisted in his hair, my hips moving frantically.

Judge turned his head to watch the work of his hand and murmured encouragingly, "Ride those, baby."

"Judge," I gasped.

His eyes came to mine.

I felt my pussy contract at the heat in them.

"You're magnificent. Predictable and totally a surprise," he growled.

"Come inside."

"Keep riding."

At this point, I was not above begging.

So I did.

"*Please*, come inside."

He put more pressure on and my head fell back.

"There we are," he whispered, righted my head, kissed me deep, then he shifted.

Using a knee to press my legs apart, he knelt between them, took his fingers from me, reached under a pillow and pulled out a condom.

Yes.

I sat up to get my hands on him, my mouth, but ran into a hand in my chest that pushed me back down.

"Judge."

"Lie back."

"*Judge.*"

He ripped the condom open with his teeth and then I was glad I was up on my elbows because I could watch him roll it on his lengthy, thick, hard cock.

I hadn't gotten a good look at that hefty dose of Judge's beauty.

I gave myself that as well as taking in his long torso, the veins popping in his biceps and forearms, the vee of muscles that acted as guideposts to treasure.

That was where my eyes were resting when he fell forward into both hands on either side of me, did a push-up and kissed me in the middle of it with an added tongue sweep before his gaze locked to mine, and he whispered, "Guide me home, Chloe."

I didn't make him ask twice.

I found his cock, wrapped my hand around it, watching his jaw clench at my touch, his eyes darken, feeling a surge of power at his response, and I brought him home.

I drew my hand away, and without hesitation, Judge slid all the way in on a single, slow, leisurely stroke.

And then he was a part of me.

He was mine.

Lord, I might start crying again.

When he'd filled me, taking him, having him, instinctively I wrapped my legs around his lower back.

I did that tight.

Like a vise.

A claim.

My brand.

He stilled.

I needed him to move.

And I wanted us to stay just like this forever.

"Taste good, honey, feel better," he murmured.

I didn't say anything. I couldn't. I was feeling too much.

I just held on with my legs and lifted my hand to his face.

I touched his cheek, his temple, his jaw, running a fingertip along the edge of his beautiful bottom lip.

"Chloe."

I looked from his lips to his eyes.

"Why is everything about you perfect?" I asked.

He'd been holding steady, buried inside, connected to me.

With that, it seemed he turned to stone.

And then there was champagne in a bucket on the ottoman and rose petals under us, candles flickering, firelight dancing in the room.

The perfect scene for Judge and me to learn each other intimately by making love.

But we did not finish how we started.

We finished fucking.

He dropped his mouth to mine and took it in a shocking, bruising, savage, *sensuous* kiss that stole my breath away, this as he slammed inside with a velvety brutal pound that made me see stars.

Oh yes.

I panted against his tongue.

He broke the kiss and ordered, "Unlock your legs."

"No," I denied.

"Unlock your fuckin' legs, baby."

I didn't.

He slid completely out.

I unlocked my legs.

He then knifed up but only so he could flip me to my belly.

Oh yes.

This time he didn't gently prod my legs apart, he kicked them apart with his knee.

Then he lowered himself onto my back, and he was inside again, another long but far from languid stroke, he was thrusting deep.

I whimpered against the bedclothes and tucked my ass in his groin.

He took one of my hands, laced our fingers, and shoved them under my body, holding tight to me and giving himself leverage to fuck me harder.

Something he did.

His other hand he drove under me, going right for my clit.

Heaven.

"Judge," I whispered.

He bit my shoulder, my neck, my earlobe, each sting sharp and demanding, possessive and carnal.

I shuddered underneath him.

"Honey," I gasped.

"You feel that?"

Oh yes, I so did.

"Chloe, baby, answer me," he grunted.

I ground my ass up into his groin and panted, "Yes."

"Who takes care of who?"

Oh my God.

He wasn't talking about what I thought he was talking about.

"Judge."

"Who takes care of who?"

It was building, too fast, his beautiful cock banging into me, his finger rolling deep, his weight bearing down, our hands linked, the smell of him, the throb his teeth left behind.

"*God,*" I breathed.

"Who takes care of who?" he demanded.

He was…

He was taking care of me.

"Not fair," I pushed out.

"This is it."

"Not fair," I repeated, fainter, God, I was *this close*.

"One way or another, baby, this is *always* gonna be it."

"You're a cheat," I forced out.

"You're a liar," he whispered in my ear. "We *so fucking work*."

I had no retort because there wasn't one.

He was right.

But regardless, my head snapped back, slammed into his shoulder, and it obliterated me as I came.

God, trembling and mewing underneath him, my orgasm refused to let go and my breath eventually caught and held.

And held.

And *held*.

Suspended in Judge.

Judge and me.

La petite mort.

My hand was let loose, he slid out, lifted up, tossed me to my back, latched on to my hips, dragged me up his thighs, and I opened my eyes as he plunged back inside me.

Oh my.

I got to watch.

His gorgeous face was dark, his concentration was entirely focused on my face, and his hips were pistons, driving in so hard and fast, even if he had a grip on my hips, I had to clamp my thighs to his sides to hold on.

"Judge."

"Don't come again, baby, I'm close, and I don't want to miss watching yours."

I wanted to see, but with the way he was fucking me, I didn't know if I could carry out his demand.

My eyes moved down his wide shoulders, his bulging pecs, his tipped nipples, to his flat stomach, the valleys and plains of his abs, his slick cock moving in and out of me.

Okay, no, I definitely wasn't going to be able to hold out.

"You're beautiful, honey." I lifted my gaze to his. "I want to touch you."

"I want to watch you take my cock."

Oh my God, now I wanted that more.

I whimpered.

"Yeah," he grunted his agreement.

I clutched him the only way I could.

"*Yeah,*" he groaned.

I lifted both hands over my head and pulsed into him.

"The best," he growled, let go of my hips, dropped to me, his eyes capturing mine, his gaze vague with sex and lust and oh so much more, he rumbled, "for last."

Then his head shot back, his neck muscles strained, his hips drove into mine, and I watched the beauty of him being swept away.

It was a toe-curlingly smooth move when his climax started to leave him and he collapsed and rolled, both at the same time, so I ended up on top, but I never really took his weight.

And then he clamped both of his hands on my ass so we didn't even inadvertently lose connection, lifting his knees so his still-hard dick slid in that little bit more.

I bent my knees too, for the same reason.

I also puffed a happy breath against his neck.

He squeezed with both hands.

We both came down, quietly, together.

Then he explored, raising his head to nuzzle my neck tenderly with his lips, his fingers gently digging into my crease, one going up, one going down, meeting our union. His other hand slid up my spine and into my hair.

That was when I raised my head.

And griped, "That was totally no fair."

He grinned, unrepentant.

"Just because you're stronger than me and have otherworldly hip strength, don't think you can take over during sex," I warned.

"Otherworldly hip strength?"

"Um…were you *just there*? You could power a train."

His body shook with humor.

My eyes narrowed.

"I think the definition of being able to take over anything is being stronger than someone else," he teased.

"We take care of each other," I shot back.

He clasped a handful of my ass. "Oh, you took care of me, Coco."

"Don't call me Coco for the first time when I'm exasperated with you," I retorted. "It's sweet and I don't feel like thinking you're sweet right now, Judge Oakley."

"Baby, you quit breathing for thirty full seconds while you came. I thought I'd have to stop fucking you so I could resuscitate you. How can you be pissed right now?"

I planted my hands in his chest and tried to push off.

Only to find myself on my back again with Judge pinning me.

In this, I lost his cock, which was a shame. But nature always eventually took its course, so *c'est la vie*.

I sensed I'd get it back.

"I thought we were going to make love," I accused.

"You were the one that screwed that pooch."

Me?

I had control over the proceedings exactly zero seconds the entire time.

Therefore, I demanded, "How…*precisely*…did I do that?"

"You called me perfect. Being all perfect and gorgeous yourself, that thick mane of hair all over my bed mixed with rose petals, wet, tight pussy all greedy, those eyes of yours I feel in my balls even when we're not naked, I won't get into how much I like your tits, and that fucking ass. With all of that, you say shit like that, what'd you think was gonna happen?"

"I would assume you'd have more control," I sniffed.

"You assumed wrong." He then changed the subject, declaring, "We're totally doing this rose petal thing at least once a week. Having those caught in your hair while you're getting fucked is all kinds of hot."

"It isn't special if we do it all the time, Judge," I pointed out.

"So you think it was special?"

There was a tinge of earnestness in that.

God, he was.

He was actually perfect.

"Don't fish," I fake admonished, but my tone was full of affection. "You know this was impeccable."

His face warmed.

But his mouth still teased.

"You haven't even seen my charcuterie board, babe. I got like, five kinds of cheeses and tons of different nuts and olives, and there's some peppers, and I rolled up the meat myself. And I made cereal treats but with Fruity Pebbles and extra marshmallow, and they *rock*."

That sounded amazing.

What was more amazing was the effort he put into it.

For me.

"Are you going to feed me with your fingers?" I asked.

He did a body shrug which was just a shrug, but since his body was flat out on mine, I felt it all along my length.

It felt nice.

"Sure."

Hmm.

"I get top next time," I announced.

"We'll see. You hungry?" he evaded.

I was, as I'd said earlier, starved.

I was more so now after our recent activities.

However.

"I get top next time, Judge," I pressed.

"We'll see," he repeated, bent, touched his mouth to mine, and cut off all further discussion on that topic by lifting away and saying, "I gotta let Zeke out and get the food. If you open that champagne while I'm gone, you're not getting top for at least six months."

I gave him the Death Stare even as every iota of brain power homed in on the words *for at least six months*.

He ignored my glare, reached to grab his throw blanket and tossed it over me before he rolled off the bed.

Then he strolled to the bathroom to deal with the condom.

I found out later Zeke had been corralled in Judge's home office, just to be sure he didn't interrupt us. When we went at each other again after champagne, charcuterie and Fruity Pebbles treats (I did not get the top, by the way, however, Fruity Pebbles treats did "rock"), Zeke was as he always was.

Completely behaved, lying by the bed until Judge exhausted me and left me to take the food we didn't eat back down to the kitchen.

The last thing I remembered from last night was moving like a zombie as I put on my panties with hazy ideas of finding and pinching a T-shirt of Judge's to sleep in, giving up on that and collapsing back into bed. Then Zeke sensing the all-clear and coming to cuddle me.

I cuddled him back.

And now was the next morning.

I watched the light go out in the bathroom, meaning Judge was coming back.

And when he did, I was getting the damned top.

"Scoot, Zeke," I called softly to the dog lying at the foot of the bed while I uncurled from around Judge's pillow and righted it.

Zeke's head was up, eyes aimed at the bathroom, but it turned to me for a split second before he hopped down.

Such a good dog.

Judge returned, sliding in bed and reaching for me.

I let him claim me, his arms gliding around me, pulling me half on him, as he asked quietly, "You awake, Coco?"

I loved my nickname, mostly because I only allowed those I cared deeply about to use it.

I *adored* it coming from Judge.

I moved full on him and tucked my face in his neck.

I kissed him there. "I'm awake."

"Wanna shower together?"

That'd be nice.

Just…later.

I kissed his throat. "In a minute."

His arms around me spasmed as he caught my meaning and he started to roll us.

I clamped on his hips with my legs and pushed up to sitting astride him.

Judge, who did not at all fight fair, pushed up too.

I took a page out of his book, put a hand between his pecs and ordered, "Lie back."

"In a sec," he muttered, his lips landing on my chest.

I wrapped the fingers of both hands around his neck and squeezed. "No. Now."

He tipped his head. "Now who's sucked down some bossy?"

"I'm going to suck something," I shared.

That something I intended to suck was already stirring under me, I knew how pretty it was, I knew how good it felt, so I was looking forward to it.

"Judge, lie back," I demanded impatiently.

"We don't have a lot of time, baby, and when you got your mouth wrapped around my cock, I want you to take your time."

This was something to consider.

Sadly, in noting it as something to consider, I lost concentration on what I was doing.

Therefore, I found myself on my knees facing the headboard and Judge's hand was moving my arm so he could wrap my fingers there.

His other hand was moving somewhere else entirely.

"Judge," I warned.

He straddled my calves. "Fast fuck now, you can blow me tonight," he said in my ear.

Unfortunately, this had the result of gathering wet between my legs.

Or *more* wet.

"Judge."

He pulled my panties over my ass and ordered, "Tip."

Oh *God*.

"Ju—"

He tweaked my nipple.

That charged through me and my head fell back to his shoulder.

"There's my girl," he murmured, pressing his hard cock to my ass.

"That's not where that goes," I pointed out.

I didn't want to admit I sounded like I was semi-panting, but I was.

He grinned against the skin of my neck, then kissed me there, this before he reached to his nightstand for one of the condoms lying there.

"Best hold on tight," he suggested.

I'd already learned that.

He prepared.

I tipped.

Judge dipped.

And I forgot all about blowjobs when I got him back.

I held on to the headboard.

He held on to two delicious parts of me (well, one, the other one that ran low, he did other things to).

And we fucked fast.

It was Judge and me.

So in other words, it was sublime.

CHAPTER 22

THE NORMAL

Judge

*T*here were certain things you knew right off the bat you were going to remember for the rest of your life.

Early that afternoon, sensing Chloe, looking out the window of his office and seeing her swanning through the cubbies that formed the workspaces that resided on the upper floor, he was going to remember.

Chloe wearing a flowy, high neck, pink blouse with big sleeves, tight jeans, and high-heeled brown pumps, her eyes on him, Judge was going to remember that.

Remember that beautiful woman walking right to him.

Remember what she was wearing.

Remember in that moment, he knew how she tasted.

Remember in that moment what she'd sounded like just hours earlier when he'd made her come.

What she felt like, slick and tight around his cock.

The way she'd looked when she had her gaze locked to him and called him perfect.

The way her eyes filled with tears when he explained why he did something dorky, covering his bedroom in rose petals and candles, but it meant a lot to her, why he did it.

No.

To his LA reared, France dwelling, droll, sophisticated, well-spoken, well-traveled, successful Chloe, something that completely sappy meant the world.

He would remember all that as he watched the smartest, classiest, most fashionable, loving, funny, sexy, beautiful woman he'd ever met walk toward his office.

Walk toward *him*.

Because she was *his*.

But he hoped he forgot the look on her face.

He was at the door before she hit it and he pulled her in when she led with, "I'm going back to holding a month-long silence with Sasha. I might extend it to two."

Once he got her in, he closed the door and sat her down in the chair facing his desk.

He then rested half of his ass and a thigh on the edge and ordered, "Talk to me."

She fiddled with the strap on her small bag that was in her lap, head bent to it, and told it, "She apologized profusely. She feels terrible about it. It hurt to watch her even talk about it. And she said she wants the opportunity to apologize to you too."

"Wasn't me she laid out," Judge reminded her and then asked, "Why aren't you looking at me?"

She tipped her head back and shared, "I didn't get into it. And she didn't either."

He was confused. "Wait, what? I thought you just said—"

"Her being lost. Wandering between Phoenix and here. Doing nothing. When she was complaining about me to Mom and Bowie, she said I was bossy and acted like I knew everything."

Judge felt his jaw tighten.

Chloe kept going.

"So I didn't go all big sister on her and point out *why* I thought she did what she did. Or *why* I thought Matt was doing what he was doing. Or simply *why* they might both wish to reflect on their behaviors and figure it out for themselves. Instead, I just listened to and accepted her apology. And then she wanted to talk about you and if you showing and rescuing me means we've finally started seeing each other. And she was all fake cheery about the fact we are. Acting like she didn't pick a fight when I repeatedly tried to get her to lay off. And then she took it to a point that crossed a line that meant she should reflect on this for a spell before we sat down and put this behind us. Frankly, if I wasn't me, and I'm not saying I'm everything, but I think I'm being really nice to talk this soon about moving beyond this. She purposefully hurt me. And all her sunny, happy, Sasha crap was all such fucking bullshit, Judge, I wanted to scream."

"So you don't want to keep distant from her because you're pissed, you want to do it because you're frustrated," he boiled it down.

"I want my sister back."

She returned her gaze to her purse.

And the thing, right then, Judge decided he disliked most of all on this planet was seeing Chloe Pierce's head bowed to anything.

He reached to the bag, slid it out of her hold, put it on his desk, then took both her hands in his and pulled her to her feet.

He then pushed to sitting fully on his desk, spread his legs and positioned her between his thighs. He dropped her hands and liked it when she lifted them to rest on his chest.

He put his to her hips.

With her standing steady on her feet, which he felt was much more natural for Chloe, he said carefully, "You should always feel free to be yourself."

"I'm not sure, since she noted she and Matt *always* hated how I *always* knew everything and told them what to do."

"I have a stepsister, didn't grow up with her, so I don't know this kind of stuff. But isn't that the way all big sisters, or big brothers, are? I mean, you are who you are, it's not like you held her or Matt at gunpoint and forced them to do your bidding." He squeezed her hips. "She was transferring, honey. This isn't about you. She was just trying to get her licks in."

"Well, she succeeded."

He already knew that.

He just didn't know how bad it was.

"This is not an I told you so," he began. "But I do encourage you to take a second and think about where this went. Because from my viewpoint, you sat down with her way too soon. It wasn't just that last shit she said that bit deep. She got under your skin. You needed to get your feet firmer under you before you sat down with her."

When she didn't say anything, though she looked like she was taking in what he'd said, he continued.

"And while you're thinking of that, think about the fact you put Sasha's needs before your own. That kind of selflessness is a beautiful thing, but it can also be damaging. I think you already knew it was too soon for you, but you were looking after her. I'm angry at her for what she did to you, but that isn't leading me to say this to you. It's the fact you ignore your vulnerabilities in order to allay those of people you love. Yes, I think Sasha might have needed more time to think about her own actions and the consequences of those. But I reckon she already knew you'd eventually forgive her, so if she had to wait another day or a couple of weeks, it wouldn't be so bad. Mostly, I think it'd be good for you to learn you don't have to give up bits of yourself for others. You can keep yourself steady, and still take care of the people you love."

"I hate you're right," she stated, staring him direct in the eye. "But you're right."

There it was.

She was smart enough to know she couldn't know everything. She wouldn't always make the right calls. There were always things to learn.

But the fact she copped to it right away, looking him in the eye?

Predictable.

And surprising.

"It's more, though, Judge," she said. "Even if she was intentionally meaning to hurt, I think there was honesty behind some of the things she said, and *I* need to reflect on that." She lifted a single shoulder and went on, "Maybe there will be times I can continue to be the big sister, but I've thought it, Mi said it out loud, and the truth is, she and Matt aren't kids anymore. They need to take responsibility for their actions and emotions. My main drive is to fix, nurture, guide. But I have to think on if that's my job anymore. Because at this point in their lives, it might not seem like that to them. It might just seem like meddling. Or worse, judgment."

"Yeah," he said quietly.

"So it's time to bite my lip and let them be who they are."

She looked like those words caused her pain to say.

Which meant he was grinning when he repeated, "Yeah."

"You think this is funny?"

"I think it's amazing how deeply you care for the people you love. And how hard it is for you not to interfere in their lives so they'll be happy."

"Hmm," she hummed irritably. Then she asked, "You have a stepsister?"

"You didn't learn that in your research?" he teased.

"No," she said bluntly.

He nodded. "Dad's second wife, she had a daughter from a previous marriage. I'm actually not surprised you didn't know about her. Dad's really protective of her, keeps her under wraps."

"Name?"

"Dru. Drusilla. It's apparently a family name."

"And?"

His body started shaking at Chloe's interrogation, though it felt hella good she was determined to know all about him.

"And...I like her. She's nine years younger than me, so twenty. Her dad is a twat, which means she thinks of mine as her real dad even if her father refused to allow Dad to officially adopt her without paying through the nose for it, something Dad agreed to do, the price just kept increasing. Eventually he and Rosalind, his wife, decided that he didn't need it to be official for him to be Dru's father. So they told the guy to go fuck himself, and even now, after Rosalind is gone, they're tight. Probably because, since she was little, they were a family."

She was studying his face closely before she asked, "Are you okay with that?"

"With what?"

"With this girl being close to your dad?"

"You trying to invent ways to look after me?" he joked.

She didn't come close to cracking a smile.

So Judge rounded her with his arms and pulled her closer, dipping his head to hers as well as his voice. "I'm good, Chloe. I can't say I know Dru real well, but I like her. I think she'd also like me to be more brotherly, but she lives in NYC, and I live here, and Dad and I have baggage, so that isn't easy. Dad adores her, she calls him Dad, so that says it all about how she feels about him, and the bottom line is that every kid needs parents who adore them, blood or not."

"Including you."

Yup.

Inventing ways to look after him.

"That didn't entirely work out for me and I'm okay with it," he reminded her. "It was what it was and now my life is how I want it. So it's all good."

She didn't believe him, he could tell.

"Okay, you want a problem you can sink your teeth into?" he offered. "Rosalind died too young. Dad wasn't rocked by it, he was crushed by it. He lives his life but he's not even close to dealing with it in a way he can move on. So someday, when you meet him, you can take him in hand."

Her eyes lit at the prospect.

Which obviously made Judge burst out laughing.

When he quit, she was glaring at him.

"Do I amuse you?" she asked.

He bent in and touched his lips to hers.

"Constantly."

There was a knock on his door.

Chloe twisted and Judge leaned left to see his volunteer coordinator, Alex, peering in the window.

He jerked up his chin, and she opened the door.

"Mr. Pierce is here," she said, her eyes darting between Chloe and Judge.

Gently, Judge pushed Chloe back a step, jumped off his desk, and introduced, "Alex, this is Chloe, my girlfriend. She's also co-chairing this project with her dad, Tom Pierce. Chloe, this is the Volunteer Coordinator of the Kids and Trails program, Alexandra Sharp."

"Hello there," Chloe greeted, her voice smooth and rich and just the sound of it was intimidating, add the outfit and her manner, forget about it.

Alex, smart, dedicated, passionate, but shy and introverted, was intimidated.

"Hey."

He was looking at Alex so he didn't see it, but he felt something coming from Chloe.

To ascertain what it was, he looked down at her to see her gaze riveted to Alex, and even in profile, he saw that gaze was calculating.

She'd noted the intimidation, and she didn't like it.

Maybe it was because Alex was cute and petite and curvy, along with that smart, dedicated and passionate that Chloe didn't know about yet. Introversion was what it was, a part of who you were. Shyness often stemmed from other things, and he had no doubt Chloe knew that.

So she intended to get a handle on it.

Though, maybe it was something else.

But his woman was locking and loading, ready to roll, he felt it.

Doing this approximately five minutes after she committed to butting out of her siblings' issues.

As such, he asked, "Are you serious?"

She jerked, rearranged her face and looked up at him.

"What?" she inquired with sham innocence.

"Yo, Alex," he heard Rix say, this dragging his attention from his woman.

And he saw Alex scurrying out of Rix's way like he'd surprised the hell out of her as he rolled into the doorframe.

This meant Alex slammed into the door.

Rix didn't seem to notice.

Sometimes, Rix wore his prosthetics. Lately, since he'd just introduced them to his cadre of mobility choices, so he was training on them and getting used to them, when they went for a run together, Rix wore his running blades. Sometimes, he was in his chair.

There were often obvious reasons for his decisions. Rix had a highly mobile chair, so he could go on hikes in it, but usually, he wore his legs. But he rarely wore them to work.

Judge had no clue why he'd choose one or the other.

He didn't ask. He thought it was too personal.

If Rix wanted to share, he would.

If he never did, that was his prerogative.

So he was just about to greet his bud, who had important things to input, therefore he was going to attend this meeting, when he felt the back of Chloe's hand brush his.

This was because she swayed.

His attention went back to her.

Oh shit.

He turned to Rix.

For a second, he didn't get it.

Then he took in both of the people in his office door and he did.

Oh shit.

"Yo, Chloe," Rix greeted Chloe as Alex stared at him like she didn't know if she should get on her hands and knees and genuflect or if she should tackle him in a way that Chloe and Judge would need to give them the room. Rix looked up at Judge. "We doin' this, or what?"

"Alexandra," Chloe drawled her name, wrapping it around her tongue like it was a delicious treat.

A delicious treat Rix should try.

"Are you attending this meeting with us?" she queried.

"Uh...yeah. I'm, uh...taking notes."

Alex was a mess because she was trapped by the door and Rix's chair and couldn't get away from him.

Jesus Christ.

How had he not seen this?

"Excellent. I wish to know *all about volunteering* for Kids and Trails. I know!" Chloe clapped. Judge pressed his lips together. Rix's brows drew down over his eyes. "How about, after the presentation, the four of us go to a late lunch?"

"Babe," Judge growled.

"I already ate lunch," Rix said.

"Me too!" Alex nearly shouted, her voice pitched so high, even Rix swung his head to look at her.

Rix knew her. They worked for the same company. She worked closely with Judge. Rix was close to Judge. He often helped with the Kids and Trails program.

But outside of understanding she existed and them sharing the same spheres on a frequent basis, that was as far as it went.

And now, with Rix's gaze on her, something Alex was studiously avoiding, she was in hell and her blazing cheeks shared how hot it was.

Damn.

Chloe was not to be thwarted. "Perhaps another time. We'll plan. *Soon.*"

Judge waded in. "Your dad's here, babe. Let's get this party started."

She looked up at him. "Let's."

He widened his eyes at her in a *stand down* gesture.

She tipped her head to the side in a *I'll do as I wish* gesture.

"Sorry…oh! Sorry!"

They both looked to the door.

Rix and Alex were doing a dance where Alex was trying desperately to escape, attempting to do this squeezing past him, which only caused Rix the inability either to shift in further or reverse, so he could get out of the way without running into her.

"Stand still," Rix growled.

Alex played a statue it pained Judge to witness.

Rix backed out, looking ticked.

Fuck.

"Sorry," Alex muttered miserably, dashing away from him to finally make good her escape.

Fuck.

It was impossible for Rix to avoid his change in life circumstances. And it wasn't something he'd lived with for decades. It had only happened a couple of years ago.

That said, it was Judge's opinion that, even if there were blips, and he was concerned some of them ran deeper than Rix was letting on (at least to the point of sharing with Judge), he handled things incredibly well.

He wasn't totally adjusted, emotionally, mentally (even though he was physically).

But as far as Judge knew, he was good.

It was when people acted like he was an invalid, a different sort of person you were uncomfortable around or needed to be painfully polite to, it visibly pissed him off.

And Alex was that way a lot.

Now Judge knew why.

He reckoned it was one of the reasons, once they got over their tiff, Rix liked Chloe quickly and unreservedly.

He was not a disabled man to her.

He was a man to her.

Alex was being awkward because she was into Rix.

Rix just saw the awkward and that made him angry.

Which of course made matters worse for Alex.

Christ.

"Mm," Chloe hummed as she caught his hand and they moved to the door.

He knew with that *Mm* she didn't know Rix or Alex well at all, and she'd still sussed all this out.

"Let it go," he ordered under his breath, moving with her to follow Rix who was rolling toward the conference room.

"Let what go?" Chloe asked, eyes fixed on Rix, and in front of him, a scampering Alex.

"She's not his type," he told her the truth, slowing their gait so they'd fall back, and Rix wouldn't hear.

That was when she looked up at him. "Not his type?"

"No."

"You mean adorable, and although lusciously curved, his strength is such, he could, perchance, when she was trying to run away from him, likely catch her, throw her over his shoulder, or, say, toss her on his bed? That's not his type?"

Rix liked leggy, which Alex was not.

He liked ass, which Alex had in abundance.

He also liked blondes, which Alex was not.

But any man liked a lot of hair, and Alex had that, though it was a reddish brown. A shiny, healthy, reddish brown she wore up in a ponytail most of the time, but Judge had seen it down and it was something.

Rix was also an outside guy. He exclusively saw women who weren't only down with hiking, camping, kayaking and the like, they were seriously into it.

Alex's shrine was the out of doors. Sometimes, Judge thought she got itchy when she had to be inside too long. She took a walk on her lunch hour every day, and if they had a working lunch at some restaurant, she always piped up and asked for outside seating.

And they weren't this type of bros, but things slipped, and he sensed Rix was probably even more dominant in bed than Judge was.

Alex was so shy, not to mention somewhat obsessive compulsive, it was just a guess, but probably a good one that she needed a man to take control so she could let go.

So a little thing with lots of hair and a round ass he had to chase, expend the effort to break through and then toss on his bed who maybe would complain Rix didn't camp often enough (when he did it all the time)?

Fuck.

Even if Judge liked this, he'd lived through Rix losing the love of his life along with his legs.

Rix was not the kind of man who wanted for company.

That said, getting laid by a man like Rix, and taking on a man who lost the career he was dedicated to, the woman he was going to marry *and* his legs in the expanse of a few months, and what all that might mean to the now and a future wasn't as attractive to most women.

He worried Rix wouldn't have the patience for Alex.

And he knew Alex's reserve and timidity would be hard to break through.

So he wasn't sure either of them were ready for this.

Especially Rix.

"Stop it," he ordered.

All Chloe did was again hum, "Mm."

He let it go because they were walking hand in hand into the conference room.

Chloe only let him go when she greeted her dad, then Duncan.

They then sat down to do their presentation, and he was not surprised they knocked it out of the park.

With barely any discussion, they got the greenlight.

And during it, Rix, who'd not only visited a lot of forests in his previous occupation, as noted, he was an avid outdoorsman and liked to travel, gave his spiel about the trails in Cali and New Mexico he thought would work for the additional footage, including doing a slide presentation of pictures he took when he was in those places.

With Alex hanging on his every word.

Oh yeah.

Shit.

LATE THAT NIGHT, JUDGE DID HIS BEST TO LET CHLOE HAVE TIME before he took over.

He went the extra mile.

But her mouth was so sweet, eventually, he couldn't hack it.

So when she was on an upward glide of his dick, he caught her under her arms, hauled her up his body…then to her adorable noise of frustration, he rolled them so she was on her back in his bed, and he was on her.

He then reached to his nightstand for a condom.

"I wasn't done," she huffed, even as she opened her legs for him, and his hips fell through.

"You were done," he pointed out the obvious.

"Judge—"

"Coco," he put his mouth to hers, "quiet."

She gave him the stink eye, even if it was completely invalidated by her hands grabbing his ass.

Which meant he was fighting a smile as he dealt with the condom.

Then he slid inside her.

Christ.

That look on her face, the same she had last night, when he first took her...

Fuck.

He started moving.

She anchored him to her with a long leg wrapped around his back.

Even so, he whispered, "Hold on."

And the smile he got at that nearly made him come.

He didn't.

Not until she did.

And then he let himself have it.

And as with anything with Chloe.

It was spectacular.

All of it.

CHAPTER 23

THE CALM

Judge

wo days later...

"I CAN'T EVEN..."

Judge had no more words.

Regardless if he did, he didn't have it in him to give them.

This was because it was an imperative to shovel the scrambled eggs Chloe made him in his mouth.

She sat with him at her island, ate lazily and watched as he wolfed his food down.

She was wearing a smirk.

She knew how good those eggs were.

"It's better if you prolong the pleasure," she said with purposefully ironic timing.

He had one bite left.

He ate it.

Tender. Fluffy. Rich.

The best eggs he'd had in his life.

Only then did he ask, "How did you make those?"

"You don't want to know," she answered.

"I wouldn't ask if I didn't want to know."

"Then I made them the French way."

"And that would be?"

She picked up a piece of bacon, also perfectly crisped, and broke it in half. "A squeeze of lemon, cooked slowly, whisking constantly, in one tablespoon of butter per egg."

Holy fuck.

"Did I just eat...?"

"Three tablespoons of butter?" she finished for him when he couldn't go on. "Yes."

She then casually dropped half of her bacon into Zeke's open mouth.

Zeke instantly bowed his head and crunched.

"Babe, I don't feed Zeke bacon," he told her.

"I'm sorry?" she asked, then bit into her half of the rasher.

"I don't feed Zeke bacon. And I never feed him at the table."

"I didn't feed him bacon," she outright lied to his face.

He fought laughter and shared something she knew. "I just watched you do it."

She turned her gaze down to Zeke. "Did your favorite woman in the whole wide world feed you bacon?"

Zeke, already having devoured the treat, got up on all fours and did a full body wag that could be taken as a no.

But mostly it was an *I worship you because you're you...and you give me bacon.*

She patted his head and looked to Judge. "See?"

"Now you've got my dog lying for you."

"I'll speak for both Zeke *and* myself as I share we're gravely insulted."

She was not.

A glance at Zeke and he wasn't either.

Judge grabbed his own rasher, muttering, "It's good you rock a blowjob."

"Please, Judge," she drawled. "You're with me because every other woman you've been with fell at your feet then bored you to tears, and I was hard to win, not to mention I'm insanely interesting."

He was caught between laughing and being deadly serious when he said, "I'm with you because yesterday, you shared you'd arranged it with Mi that you'd have every Thursday and Sunday off, and you'd be going into work late on Friday. Therefore, if I wanted you, which I told you I do, and I'll confirm that now, I could have you in my bed Wednesday and Thursday. And then you said I was free to be here from Friday to Sunday, should I so wish. And I so wish. But you should know, not one woman I've dated who lived in Phoenix put herself to that trouble for me. Arranged her life so I could have her in my space and I wasn't the only one in a fucking car driving back and forth all the time."

She stared at him, those beautiful brown eyes working hard as she took in all he said and all it meant.

"That or they were ambitious, which is good, but when they felt their careers were more important than mine, or what I did wasn't serious, but what they did was, it's bad," he continued.

Chloe remained silent, her gaze not once leaving his face, but it flickered, and he saw the wildcat rearing.

But he wasn't done.

"Or they came from money, and we can just say that Sasha might have fucked up because she's struggling with some issues, but I've learned to know a spoilt bitch when I see her, because I dated one, and she took two years of my life before her mask slipped, and Sasha is not that."

He could almost hear the growl of that cat reverberating through the room.

"Or they fell at my feet and bored me to tears," he finished. "Though, I didn't know that last part at the time. I do now that I know you."

It took a beat for her to wrangle control of the she-beast within before she said softly, "More fool them, but very fortunate me."

"Stop being sweet," he replied in her same tone. "I haven't recovered from fucking you yet, and I'm pretty sure my arteries are clogging with butter as we speak."

He watched her pretty lips twitch.

She then turned her attention to the last rasher of bacon on her plate, broke it and dropped half in Zeke's waiting mouth.

With her gaze to Judge, she chewed her own idly even if it was also challengingly.

He didn't say a word.

Judge was active, and Zeke was active with him.

They'd both work it off.

Though, Judge would have more fun with some of the ways he'd do it.

But giving in meant Chloe would have what she wanted.

Spoiling Judge.

And spoiling Zeke.

And one thing he was all in to do, if it was within his power, was to give Chloe what she wanted.

A WEEK AND A HALF LATER...

JUDGE SMELLED IT ON ENTERING HIS HOUSE AFTER WORK.

Heaven.

He found her and his dog in the kitchen.

Chloe was cooking.

Zeke was idolizing her.

He counted himself lucky when his dog deigned to come to him to say hello when he showed.

But Chloe gave Judge a one finger up motion and said into the room, "I'll call and arrange the appointments, but I have to talk to Judge before I do that."

"All right, darling," her mother said from the speaker of her phone which was sitting on the counter.

Zeke moved out of the way, and Chloe moved in.

He got a peck on the lips and then she said to her mother, "He's just home. We'll talk and I'll text you later. I'll confirm the rest when I see to it."

"Sounds good. Tell Judge I said hi."

It was a little wild that, in his kitchen, over a speaker, Imogen Swan was telling him she said hi.

It was an odd contradiction, but the woman he knew as Genny doing it wasn't wild at all.

"You can say it yourself." Chloe had moved to the oven and was peering in. "You're on speakerphone."

"Hey, Genny," he called.

"Hello, Judge. You're home, I'll let you two alone. Maybe we can all have dinner soon?"

"That'd be awesome," Judge said.

"I'll plan it before you head off to LA," Chloe said.

"Excellent. Have a good night, you two. Love you, Chloe."

"Love you more," Chloe replied, did some kissing noises, then terminated the call.

"Hey, baby," Judge belatedly greeted.

"Hello, *chéri*," she replied.

"What are we having for dinner?" he asked.

She'd moved to the counter where there were the makings of a massive green salad which was not what he was smelling.

"Tartiflette," she declared. "And salad," she finished unnecessarily.

He hit the fridge for a beer, asking, "What's tartiflette?"

"Bacon, potato, and cheese casserole made with onions."

Okay...

That was what he was smelling.

"Your cooking is gonna kill me," he bullshitted, since he could dive into that smell headfirst, so he couldn't wait to shove it into his mouth.

"Regardless that they eat alarming amounts of bread, cheese and butter, the French are exceptionally healthy. This is because their food is fresher, it isn't overproduced, overprocessed, or injected with things that aren't good for you that, once consumed, will also swim in your body. And they don't have as much fast food. Last, they're not consumed with the idea of low fat, as Americans are, but without fat, the flavor is gone, therefore we cover that up by adding ridiculous amounts of sugar. Many fats are good for you as your body actually needs them. Sugar, it doesn't need, but we eat a lot of it, and the way food is processed adds even more. To wit, regardless of the contents of this meal, although it isn't a bowl of spinach, it's not going to kill you."

He'd turned from the fridge, beer in hand, to watch her deliver this speech.

And when she was done, he spoke softly.

"I wasn't complaining, baby. I was teasing. Your cooking is the shit. And for the record, I don't eat fast food. I also go organic."

"I perused your refrigerator. I noticed," she sniffed.

"Are you pissed at me?" he asked, watching her closely.

"No," she returned sharply. "I'm being snippy because Mom wants me to go to LA in the next couple of weeks for a very long weekend, meaning arrival on Wednesday and leaving Sunday. This so I can be with her while she has meetings with some people so she can decide who's going to design her wedding gown. And first, I'm trying to be happy for her and in a space this will be fun for all, when I *am* happy for her. Delighted. Beside myself for her and Bowie. But I'm also...not."

Shit.

Yeah, she was always pulled both ways with that, and it understandably messed her up.

"I get that," he replied quietly.

"Adding to that, she wants Sasha there, and since this is a girls' thing, a family thing, a mother-daughter thing, but also because Sasha has nothing better to do, she'll be there."

He kept his mouth shut but nodded.

She carried on.

"And I'm trying to get into *another* headspace where I won't be vexed by the fact that Mom will probably buy Sasha's ticket when I won't allow her to buy mine, even though she'll offer, because she's a mother. I won't accept, because I have a job and pay my own way considering I'm an adult, and as such, Mom and Dad's responsibilities for caring for me financially are done. And Sasha has a trust fund, which was given to her, but she also mooches off Mom, Dad *and* Bowie. *A lot*. None of my business, as we've discussed. It's still infuriating as all hell."

"I get that too," he said, and he did.

Not his business either, but that was uncool.

"And while Mom's in LA working, since most of the filming will happen in Phoenix, meaning she might not have to be in California very often, she and Bowie haven't decided yet about where she'll-slash-they'll stay the time she has to be there. Buy some condo or loft or small property and have it for all of us to use if we're there. Or stay in hotels. She can't really know until she understands how much time she'll be there. So, for now, Hale's letting her stay in Uncle Corey's house. That being the house where he killed himself."

"Holy fuck," Judge interjected.

She nodded, sharply, and kept speaking.

"And Mom's determined to face that and memories of Corey, taking Duncan with her. But I'm not ready for the one, two, *three* punch of Mom diving into plans of getting remarried, having to spend time with Sasha and facing Uncle Corey's death house, because I'll be staying there too."

She stopped talking, but before Judge could say anything, she added one more.

"Oh, and I don't want to be away from you. Wednesday through Sunday is exactly our time together. And it's a few weeks down the line, but losing that time with you doesn't thrill me."

Since she seemed done, he opened a drawer to grab his bottle opener, saw to that, and sucked back a sip of beer as he moved to her.

Then he set it aside and pinned her to the counter, leaning into her, hands on the edge of the worktop.

She didn't move or make a peep, and this was no surprise. Judge had noticed she liked being pinned, and not just sexually (though she liked that most of all).

She liked it when they were watching TV.

When they were sleeping.

And times like now.

He didn't know if it was a safety thing. Her world was chaotic right now, and if he narrowed it down to just them, it soothed her. Or if it was something else.

He just liked doing it, so he was grateful she liked it too.

"It's a little weird she's staying where your uncle...did what he did."

"You're being very sweet," she whispered. "But he committed suicide. Judge. It isn't a dirty secret, and not only because he was who he was, so it literally is not secret but worldwide news. And as much as I miss him, it was also his life, so it was his decision. He had demons. He could no longer battle them. So he took his own life." She cupped his jaw then dropped her hand before she finished, "What I mean to say is, it's okay to say the words, honey."

He nodded. "So then, it's a little weird she's staying where your uncle killed himself."

"Yes, it is," she agreed. "Hale wants to sell, but Mom is pushing against it. It's bizarre. Both Mom and Dad are more parent to Hale than Uncle Corey or Sam ever were, but it seems really strange to me she's butting her nose into that. I don't understand why."

"You might find out."

Her gaze went skyward, and her lips murmured, "*Merveilleux.*"

His poor baby.

"Is this what you had to talk to me about?" he asked.

Her gaze came back to him. "Yes."

He didn't get it.

"Why did you need to talk to me about all that before you finalize plans with your mom?"

"Because I need to know if you're all right for me to go."

Judge stood perfectly still.

"Are we here...already?" he asked cautiously.

That was when she jolted, looked down and to the side, and tucked her hair behind her ear.

She also was about to push through the pen he'd caged her in, but he caught her by saying, "Hey."

She stopped moving and slowly, her gaze came to him.

"I assumed. It was wrong. I'm thinking ahead. Going too fast," she rattled this off quickly.

"Chlo—"

"And I probably should have, you know, not expected you wanted me up at your house two nights a week. You seemed pleased. And now I feel that maybe—"

"Baby, chill a second, yeah?"

She clapped her mouth shut.

"Just to confirm, I'm there. I guess with all this, you're there too. I just think we need to take a second and be in that."

"You're there?" she asked softly.

"Fuck yeah," he answered, not softly.

Her eyes lit.

Christ, she was gorgeous.

But since they were doing this…

"That means exclusive, Coco. We're there, but we're still new. Even so, I'm not down to share."

"Me…" She cleared her throat. "Me either."

"Good," he murmured.

"Good," she whispered.

They didn't take their eyes off one another, and hers were so bright, it felt like they warmed him.

Right to the bone.

She then brought it up.

"We should get tested. And I can look into something for birth control. I haven't been…active so I'm not on anything right now."

"We'll do that."

"Soon."

He felt one side of his mouth go up at how quickly she said that.

"Soon," he agreed.

"I'm sorry I was grouchy about my cooking, *mon beau*, I know you were teasing."

"You letting it all hang out on my couch a couple of weeks ago doesn't make it all go away."

Some of her brightness dimmed, she rested her hands on his stomach and said, "Yes."

"I don't think I have to say it again, but I will. I'm here for you. It's not just my job as your man, it's my privilege."

She clicked her teeth but didn't attempt to hide she got off on that.

He grinned.

"As for LA, go. You probably figured this out, but my job includes travel. It happens mostly in the summer, when we do the vast majority of our hikes, but I wanted Rix to take me to New Mexico where we'll be shooting. We can do that while you're in Cali."

"Perfect," she whispered.

He took in her gorgeous face in his kitchen with the smell of the dinner she cooked for him filling the air.

But he decided not to give it to her, not now, he didn't want to wake the she-beast with Chloe skating through a vulnerable place.

This being getting into the fact that not one of his girlfriends made dinner for him in his kitchen.

In their own?

Yes.

Making themselves at home in his and what that communicated about how they felt about him?

No.

So yeah, she was very right.

Perfect.

"Zeke been out?" he asked.

"We took a walk about an hour ago. You have nice neighbors."

He grinned again.

"When's dinner?"

"It should be done in about ten minutes, but it can rest."

"I'm hungry."

"Good."

"Coco?"

"Yes?"

"I like coming home to you."

That got the bright back.

And more.

She threw her arms around his neck, pressed deep even as she slid up to her toes, and kissed him hard.

They made the salad together while the tartiflette rested.

It tasted just as it smelled.

Awesome.

———

THREE WEEKS LATER...

HE WAS ON HIS DECK WITH THE BEER, THE WANING SUN, HIS DOG, HIS phone, a bag upstairs in his room needing to be unpacked after his return from New Mexico and the vague idea of grilling hamburgers when his phone went with a FaceTime call.

Chloe.

He answered and saw she too was on a deck, the sun shining far more brightly on her since it was reflecting off an ocean, and her hair was swaying in a gentle breeze.

She looked stunning.

Who said California girls had to be blondes?

"Hey, gorgeous, how's it going?" he greeted.

"Hello, *chéri*," she replied, but said no more.

He smiled to hide his concern. "So...how's it going?"

She'd been there since Wednesday. It was now Saturday.

She'd warned him her time would be a whirlwind because they were beginning the wedding preparations with her mom (something Genny, and Chloe concurred, said had to be started by the selection of the gown—no other plans could be made until the gown was decided, which reportedly was frustrating Duncan, who was down to marry her wearing boots and jeans and flannels by his lake, but Genny wanted to do it up big, and Judge saw that—they'd waited a long time for this celebration).

But also she'd be busy because she was "home."

She had friends to see, and they all had old haunts they wanted to visit. Not to mention, Hale was in town so there was family time.

He'd received a ton of texts.

But this was the first time they spoke.

He'd been busy too with Rix, hiking trails and making decisions on locations.

But even so, it made him twitchy.

That feeling came from them being apart when, since they got together, they were *together* and spent a lot of time in each other's company.

It also came from her being there.

With Sasha.

In that house.

And LA, where she said she wanted to end up living.

"It…well, my mother never ceases to amaze me," she said as her opener.

"Explain," he ordered.

Her expression shifted with amusement before she did as told.

"We're everywhere here, Judge. Us and also, even though Uncle Corey wasn't a very *there* dad, Hale."

He didn't get it. "Right, now explain that."

"He has pictures of us. *Everywhere.* If you didn't know him, you'd walk into this house and think we were his family. His kids. His wife. Though, Dad's all over the place too. He…"

She took a second.

He gave her that second.

"He really loved us," she shared. "And I think that's why Mom doesn't want Hale to sell. This is like a temple to the people in his life Uncle Corey cared about. That being Hale, Mom, Matt, Sasha, me, my grandparents, I mean Mom's folks, and also Dad."

"Shit, baby," he murmured.

"I've been here, of course," she continued. "And I saw some photos, but I hadn't been here in years. They multiplied. By *a lot*. When we were kids. Teens. Sasha playing volleyball. Matt playing tennis. Me behind the wheel of the convertible he owned that I loved that he let me drive all the time."

This had to be a lot to process.

"How does that make you feel?" Judge asked.

"There's more."

He said nothing.

She did.

"He had three photos on his desk. The desk where he killed himself. Mom never saw them. At least, she hadn't for decades. The first time she did was when Bowie came with her when she hit LA. She asked Hale about it and he said he'd seen them before. Not on that desk, but other places, like in his briefcase, or tucked in a bunch of pictures on his credenza at his office. Those frames moved around with him. Hale didn't think he took them everywhere with him, but he'd seen them more than once and not in the same places. He asked about the man in them he didn't know, and his dad just said, 'He's an old friend.' But he never said more."

Judge knew where this was going.

It went there.

"One was a picture of them when they were kids. All three of them, Mom, Bowie and Uncle Corey. Mom said it was during one of Corey's late-night birthday parties Gram and Gramps used to throw because his parents were...well, *not right*, and they never celebrated Corey being alive."

Shit.

"The other one," she continued, "was Mom and Bowie, when they got back together the first time, back when they were in their twenties. Mom was sitting in Bowie's lap and they had their arms around each other, smiling big at the camera." Pause. "At Corey."

"Right," he muttered.

She finished it up.

"And the last was a picture of Bowie and Uncle Corey. Mom says she took it. They were in high school. Kicked back in the flatbed of a truck at a drive-in theater. They'd just had a popcorn fight. Bowie and Corey were covered in popcorn and," another pause, "they were laughing."

"That must have been hard for your mom to see," Judge remarked. *And you*, he didn't say...yet.

But she shook her head.

"No, it was...she told me that Bowie was all set never to forgive him. But he saw those photos, probably the last thing Uncle Corey looked at before he died, and it happened. I guess Bowie kind of lost it. But Mom said it was good. A release. Of the pain. And it was a reminder, of how good of friends they were. What he did will never be forgotten, but there is no way anyone, even Bowie, could walk through this house and not see the love Uncle Corey carried in his heart."

Abruptly, she stopped talking, and although he could see her face, she turned away from the camera.

He gave her the time she needed.

She got it together and came back to him.

"For me, it changed things," she said, her tone different, pensive. "Seeing that picture of all of them together as kids, then of Mom with Bowie back when they had their whole lives ahead of them, I...I..." She took a second then, "I'm sad about what happened with Mom and Dad, but something clicked, Judge. Seeing that photo, I think I finally got it. The fullness of their love story. Mom's with Bowie. And now I'm genuinely happy for them and not just because I love my mother and I want her safe and settled, and Bowie is wonderful. Because, this is going to sound strange, but it's a simple fact that they were meant to be."

"Yeah," he said carefully, because this had to have been a rough emotional road to travel.

But it was obvious to him as an outsider, just being around Duncan and Genny, not to mention knowing the story, that they were that.

Meant to be.

"So we had our meetings with some of the designer's reps and we're having fun and I mean it, honey. I'm having fun. This is exciting. Mom is ecstatic, and I love that she wants to make it a big thing to celebrate them finally having this. And I feel honored to be a part of it."

"I so fucking dig that for you, Coco," he replied.

"It's even making being around Sasha cool."

Well, shit.

"So that isn't going as well?" he asked.

"I don't want to say this, but I think the truth is, after she did what she did, and while she's still not connecting with anything or anyone really, I'm not sure we'll be the same."

Yeah.

Shit.

"But Matt called and talked to Mom," she carried on. "She put him on speaker, we all talked to him, and he asked to speak to me privately. I took the phone, and we had a chat. He told me he was being a dick, apologized, and shared he was contemplating. He had plans with some friends for spring break, but he secured a job this summer at a large animal vet clinic outside Prescott and he's going to think about sitting down with Dad and talking things through."

"That's good."

"Yes."

"So this is all good."

Her lips curved. "Yes." Her lips stopped curving. "But I miss you."

Right there, no hiding, she gave it to him.

"Miss you too, but you'll be back tomorrow, and I'm picking you up from the airport."

The curve returned. "Yes."

"How's being back home?" he asked, far from unaware that the question made him tense.

"Sorry?"

"Being back home, in LA."

"I can't wait to *really* get back home."

Judge blinked.

He then noted, "I thought you loved LA."

"Why on earth would you think that?" she inquired.

"Because you told me you planned to move back there."

He saw the phone jostle, such was her surprise at that memory.

And then she admitted, "I was lying."

It took a beat.

And then Judge roared with laughter.

When he was done, she had another small smile on her face, but it was cautious when she asked, "Were you worried about that, *chéri*?"

"Well, yeah," he stated the obvious.

"I'm so sorry," she whispered.

"Don't be. I'm not worried about it anymore."

"Sure?" she pressed.

"Sure, honey," he promised.

Her face warmed.

They talked, and Judge ascertained she was telling the truth about something important. She seemed peaceful, happy, not weighed down by anything.

That was good, and he felt better when she eventually had to let him go so she could finish getting ready because they were all going out to dinner.

But before she did this, she said, "I left you a welcome-home-from-New-Mexico present in the kitchen."

He was smiling, but surprised, when he replied, "You did?"

"Yes, *mon beau*, nothing big. Just a little something. It's in the cupboard with the coffee mugs."

Judge immediately got up to go see what it was, and when he did, Chloe hurriedly said her goodbyes, like she didn't want to be on the call when he saw what she'd given him.

Which made him even more curious.

He noticed it right away when he opened the cupboard.

A green coffee mug with yellow lettering that said, NOTHING'S PERFECT, BABY, BUT WE CAN GIVE IT THE BEST WE GOT.

The sight of it hit him right in the throat.

He'd seen her drink from hers at her place and he'd asked after it.

She'd then told him the coffee mug story, how everyone in the family had one, given to them by Sully and Gage at Christmas.

Now he had one.

From Chloe.

Obviously, this made him feel even less twitchy.

A whole lot less.

But he didn't feel exactly right until around the same time the next day, when he was standing in Sky Harbor Airport and he saw her walking toward him from the concourse.

And Judge wasn't feeling perfect until she skip-ran the last fifteen feet and threw herself in his arms.

One week later...

"Hot guy delivery!" Mi shouted as she escorted Judge into Chloe's office.

So he was laughing when he walked in.

Chloe was behind her desk, her laptop open, and she looked like she was scowling at it.

Her head came up as he stopped with Mi at his side, but Mi did a sideways bow with hands out his way, "I present thee with the finest thing in our store."

Chloe was now smiling as she got up, skirted her desk and drawled, "Sadly for our customers, he's not for sale."

"Tragic," Mi said, then winked at him, turned on her foot and said as she was leaving, "Several of them witnessed his entry. I need to hold back the hounds. Ta ta!"

And off she went as Judge called after her, "Later, Mi."

"Later!" he heard from the hallway.

When he turned back, Chloe was right there.

He saw her looking gorgeous, dressed impeccably, but he couldn't stop himself from taking in her office.

Because it was *tight*.

But also, it looked like a starter office for an up-and-coming retail magnate.

"Nice digs," he noted when his gaze came back to her.

"Thanks." She threw that word his way indifferently, as if her office wasn't shit hot, then asked, "Is everything okay with my car?"

He was there, picking her up, because it was Saturday, she had to work, he did not, and he'd taken her car to be serviced that day.

"All good," he answered.

"Excellent. So why aren't you kissing me?"

He looked down at her. "Because I'm recovering from the one-two punch of how fuckin' awesome your store is and how much more awesome this office is."

He'd dropped her off that morning, but he hadn't come in.

Now he'd seen it, and he was seriously impressed.

"My store is *far* more awesome than this office," she sniffed, though the softness of her eyes told him his compliment registered.

He smiled.

Then he asked, "Why were you trying to get laser beams to shoot out of your eyes at your computer?"

She glanced back at her laptop, and when she returned to him, the scowl was back. "We open applications for Fabulous Foot Forward after we complete the round before. I try to keep up with them and prioritize them so when the time comes to make our selection, I'm not overwhelmed."

"That's smart."

"And we just finished with our last candidate, and she was amazing. But the time is coming nigh for us to begin again."

"None of this is explaining a scowl," he noted.

"Any kid that signs up gets to go hiking, Judge. Mi and I have to select one woman a quarter, only four a year, out of hundreds of applicants. I think it would be easier and less painful to flay myself alive than whittle each quarter's applications down to one."

That was when he put his arms around her and murmured, "Rough, baby."

"Torture," she mumbled.

Christ, she was something.

"Can I help?" he offered.

She wasn't focusing on him, her mind was on applications, but at his offer, she did that, and said, all breathy, "What a nice thing to say."

"Babe, I'm in the business, so I like to think I know a thing or two. And it isn't as close to my heart as it is yours. I might be able to be more objective."

"You'd do that?"

He kept his arms around her even as he shrugged.

She melted into him, tipping her head back in invitation.

"We still need to talk about your office," he announced.

Her brows shot together. "Why?"

"You said that LA wasn't a thing, but this office says you're serious."

"Of course I'm serious." There was a slight snap to that, and he got that, because what he said didn't sound good.

"Serious about expansion," he clarified.

"Oh, right, well...yes." She tipped her head to the side. "Is that an issue?"

"No, just that..."

He didn't finish.

She squeezed him with her arms.

And when he still didn't say anything, she pressed by saying his name, "Judge."

He moved his arms so he could wrap his fingers around either side of her neck.

"Okay, Coco, the thing is, it's awesome as fuck, what you created. It's very you, it's very cool. I'm hella impressed. And I think we both get this is something, what we have. We're exclusive. It got real fast, and we were both down with that. But you need to know, I want a family."

"So do I."

He stared down at her.

"Having a business doesn't preclude having children, Judge," she said, a little snap to that too. "My mother had one of the most enviable careers in Hollywood, and she had three, she never quit working, and she was a very hands-on mom."

"I...that's great. Great news, honey."

She was glaring at him, but abruptly, that glare shifted.

And she whispered, not soft, or sweet, but pissed.

"What did those women do to you?"

Shit.

"Nothing," he lied. "I'm just glad we're on the same page with that."

"Judge."

That time, his name was a warning.

So he gave it to her.

"The last one, Meg, said she wanted kids, and maybe she does. But she led me to believe she wanted them sooner, not later. She wanted them later. I want them sooner."

"Of course. You don't want to be ninety and raising children," she scoffed. "And she *can't* be, unless some miracle of science elongates a woman's reproductive years exponentially. Which I hope and pray does not happen, because I want children, but I'm also living for the day I don't have to bother with the cramps and cravings and mood swings of having a period."

Judge was staring again.

So her eyes got squinty.

"I see this hurt you," she bit out.

"I'm *way* over her, Chloe," he assured.

"I know that, Judge. Still. You do not lie about that to the man in your life. Things happen. Opportunities arise. Minds are changed. But I sense she lied so she could keep you when she knew, if she told the truth, she wouldn't keep you."

After they were over, and he thought about it, he'd sensed that too.

"Yeah," he grunted.

Her cheeks started to pinken.

"Tame the cat, baby, she's gone," he told her. "The reason I was quiet after you said what you said is because I assume you want to start early too."

"Yes," she stated shortly. "When I'm forty I want to be teaching my daughters the importance of facials then leaving them with a babysitter to have date nights with my husband, not changing diapers."

He came in right when she finished speaking. "So we click on that too and it means a fuckuva lot to me."

"This means you're happy?"

"No. It means I'm super fucking happy."

"So again, why aren't you kissing me?" she demanded.

He grinned.

Slow.

Then he glanced over her shoulder at her desk.

"Judge."

Another warning.

"We'll be quiet," he whispered.

"Judge."

That wasn't a warning.

It was breathy.

"You gonna lock the door, or am I?" he asked.

She licked her lower lip.

Judge didn't mess about with locking the door.

Then he went back and kissed her.

A lot.

And he did that all over.

CHAPTER 24

THE SETTLING

Judge

 *ne month later...*

THE MEN SAT BY THE FIRE UNDER THE NIGHT SKY.

Judge, Rix, Duncan and Tom.

And Judge did it thinking he never got used to how many more stars there were in the sky when light pollution didn't drown them out.

He did it also thinking how he wanted to extend Kids and Trails to include overnight camping trips so the kids could see this. He wanted to show them the wonder of it and how the human footprint didn't just affect the earth, but also the heavens.

"Right, give it up."

This coming from Rix took his attention from the sky and his kids to the man at his side, where Rix was sitting in a camp chair in front of the carefully contained campfire they'd built.

Duncan and Tom were sitting across from them.

They were back in New Mexico, shooting the final segments for the video.

They'd already done Prescott and California, and Chloe had come with them to both, including the latter, but when they were there, she'd insisted he stay with her in town at her favorite hotel, the Chateau Marmont.

This he'd done.

And that hotel was the shit.

Elegant and almost painfully cool.

Very Chloe.

Though, during the day, instead of hitting things in the city, she and Genny had gone hiking with them to watch the segments being filmed.

This was the last bit they had to do, and for this one, the women had stayed home.

It was not lost on Judge that this was his woman's decision for a reason (and maybe her mother's too).

The men had decided to camp, and it wasn't that Chloe didn't want to camp. She'd told him she was down with that idea (even if she'd never done it before, though she had slipped in, "Have you ever glamped, *chéri?*" so he had a feeling he was going to have to ease her into the hardcore stuff).

No, it was that she wanted him to bond with her two dads.

"Give what up?" Tom asked.

"Not you, Duncan," Rix said, talking to Tom but nodding to their boss. "You call him Bowie. Chloe and Harvey do too. What gives with that?"

At this question, Judge straightened in his chair because he was keen to know this too.

He'd asked Chloe about it, but she'd only said, "That's Bowie's and Bowie's alone to give."

Which only made him more curious.

However, Judge had noticed that Tom had also started calling him that.

He didn't in the beginning.

But after the Cali shoot, he did.

There was something meaningful in that.

Judge sensed it was like the coffee mug thing with the Pierce-Swan-Holloways.

It meant you were in.

And make no mistake, Judge wanted to be in.

He knew his assumption was true when Tom was the first to speak, and he did it in a shutting-this-down tone.

"I think that's—"

"It's okay, Tom," Duncan said low.

Tom had moved to protect whatever this was for Duncan.

But Duncan's gaze was on Judge.

Judge glanced at Tom and saw him smiling at the fire.

Yep.

Whatever this was, if you had it, it meant you were in.

Duncan announced, "When I was a kid, my dad made me kill a deer."

Both Judge and Rix sat even straighter in their chairs, because unlike Duncan, who did not partake of the hobby, but approved of hunting for game control, under the tight supervision of licensing and quotas, neither Rix nor Judge did.

In a big way.

They were both anti-gun and anti-hunting.

Vehemently.

So this was a shock.

"I didn't want to do it," Duncan went on.

Okay then, that wasn't a shock.

"My dad thought it was a rite of passage for a man," he continued. "And I later had sons. I would learn there are a variety of rites of passage for boys, and undoubtedly for girls. But making a child kill a living being he does not have any interesting in killing is not one of them."

Everyone around that campfire was silent and Tom was no longer smiling.

"I got a doe on the first shot," Duncan carried on. "And Dad made me gut her with a bowie knife where she lay. She was beautiful. She was also still warm with life."

"Jesus, fuck," Rix muttered, not hiding his revulsion.

"It marked me," Duncan declared.

It would. It was marking Judge and he hadn't even been there.

"I'm sorry, man," Judge said, totally getting that, but not understanding why Duncan would allow himself to be called Bowie by his loved ones if this was the story behind it.

"I went to Genny after it," Duncan kept going.

When that came out, Judge glanced between Duncan and Tom, and he felt his skin prickle when he saw it.

Tom had his head turned, was staring at Duncan, and it was all there to read in his expression that was lit by firelight.

The understanding.

The amity.

Judge would never fully comprehend the foundation of it because he'd never put Tom through asking about it.

Maybe it was knowing who Genny was and how she could be that person for a man, or a boy, even when she was a girl.

Maybe it was getting why Duncan went to her, the depths of emotion he must have felt for her, though they were much younger. And knowing from that them being together was somehow meant to be, even if that meant Tom and Genny weren't.

Maybe it was both.

But it was there.

And Judge respected it a fuck of a lot, because a man had to love a woman in a serious way if he could settle into the knowledge she had who she needed, she had what was meant to be, and that was not him.

"I wasn't close to my dad," Duncan shared, taking Judge from his thoughts. "He wasn't a good father. He wasn't a good man. But he was very proud of me for doing that. I was sickened by it. So, obviously, I didn't get why he was proud of me. He told me at the time, standing over me as I gutted that doe, that I was going to be known as Bowie from then on."

Okay, now Judge was even more confused why he'd allow people to call him that.

"And I told Genny later that he was right. I was. I was Bowie and always would be Bowie. Because I didn't want to go hunting. I didn't want to shoot that doe. I did it so I didn't have to take any shit from my father. I put her life ahead of my fears of dealing with my dad, who could be volatile, but he wasn't violent. And I was going to be Bowie because I never wanted to forget the consequences of not standing up for my beliefs."

"Jesus, fuck," Rix whispered, his tone much different now.

Comprehension.

And respect.

"And I never did. I also never hunted again," Duncan concluded. "It infuriated my father, and I paid that price. The price was hefty. But it was a price I'd learned I was willing to pay."

Judge noted that Tom was now slumped in his chair, but not having folded into himself.

He'd settled in.

Comfortable.

At one with the idea that the man at his side was the man in Genny's life.

Which was huge and Judge couldn't wait to tell Chloe about this. She was coming to terms with what was becoming of her family, and this would set her mind even more at ease.

"My loved ones call me that, people I'm tight with," Duncan continued. "And if you want, I'm inviting you both to do the same."

Holy fuck.

He felt Rix's gaze so he looked to his friend.

"But remember," Duncan kept going, and they turned back to him, "when we're at work, we're at work. Harvey calls me Bowie, but Harvey is to me what he is to me and people get it." He pinned Judge with his eyes. "You're seeing Chloe, people will get that. But just be aware. This is important." He swung a hand out to indicate the campfire, the story, and what he'd just given to Rix and Judge. "But work is work."

"You don't have to say that, man. We get it," Rix said quietly.

Judge jerked up his chin to indicate Rix was right. They got it.

Duncan nodded.

"It was, you know," Rix said.

Everyone focused on him.

"It was what?" Duncan asked.

"A rite of passage," Rix told him. "Though not the one your father expected. I hate you had to do that. I hate that doe had to go down. But since then, you've saved forests. You've blocked building on important land. You've stood strong between The Man pushing to sprawl and spoil, desecrate and destroy, steal and appropriate, and you've put a stop to it. You became the man you were going to be that day, Duncan. And if that doe was sentient, and she understood what was to come for you, my guess is, she would have felt her sacrifice was worth it."

Duncan stared at Rix for so long, not only Judge but Tom shifted in their seats.

And his voice was gruff when he replied, "You're right, Rix. Thanks."

At his tone, Judge knew, Duncan still felt that doe's death. He still felt the bite of regret, and it was far more than a sting.

But Rix in Rix's way alleviated it.

Maybe not totally, but a little.

"Don't mention it," Rix muttered like it was no big deal what he said, when it was.

Duncan had to know he'd become that man, because he was that man.

But it never hurt to know other people saw it.

Tom grinned at Judge.

Judge grinned back.

"Did someone bring the makings for s'mores? Because if they did, it's time for those and Bushmills," Rix declared.

"On it," Judge said, pushing up from his camp chair, because he one hundred percent packed marshmallows, chocolate bars and graham crackers in his backpack.

And he knew Rix carried in the Irish whiskey.

ONE WEEK LATER...

"SO, *MAMAN*, YOU'VE SPENT QUITE A BIT OF TIME IN NEW YORK CITY," Chloe declared.

Judge watched Genny's brows knit together as she looked at her daughter across the table at Steak 44, where they were having dinner in Phoenix.

"Uh, yes, my darling daughter," Genny replied. "As you know since we've been there shopping together on no less than two dozen occasions."

Of course they had.

Judge smiled to himself and reached for his beer.

"And you have many friends and acquaintances who live there," Chloe went on.

Hand with beer arresting in mid-air, Judge looked to his woman.

"Out with it, Chloe, what's this about?" Genny, unsurprisingly knowing her daughter was up to something, demanded.

"I am in search of a woman of a certain age who is either divorced, or widowed, smart, stylish, has an excellent sense of humor, and most importantly, is adjusted. In other words, no psychos, no stalkers, no drama queens, unless they're the benign yet fabulous kind, like me, of course, and no vultures," Chloe decreed.

"Chloe," Judge warned under his breath.

She turned his way and tipped her head to the side.

"Why?" Genny asked suspiciously.

Yep.

Totally knew her daughter was up to something.

His woman looked back to her mother and bald-faced lied, "No reason."

"You do absolutely nothing for no reason," Genny returned.

Judge grunted with the effort to hold back his laugh and that was when he caught Duncan looking at him and silently doing the same.

Judge finally took a sip of his beer.

"I just have a friend there who not-so-recently became a widower and needs a slight... *prod* to start socializing," Chloe lied again.

"She's talking about my father and she hasn't even met him yet," Judge supplied, regaining Chloe's attention and her sharp, "Judge!"

"Chloe," Genny said slowly. Her uttering her daughter's name was also openly beleaguered.

"*Motherrrr*, have you *seen* Jameson Oakley?" Chloe asked.

"I met him once briefly a long time ago when I was with your father. So, yes, I've seen him," Genny answered.

"Then you know he's rich and hot and very single. It's a total waste," Chloe returned.

"How about you let Judge's father decide when it's time for him to start dating again?" Genny suggested.

With zero shame, Chloe immediately turned to Duncan and demanded, "How would you feel right now if I let Mother decide when it was time for her to start to open her heart again?"

Judge had learned that Chloe had interfered rather significantly in Duncan and Genny's reunion.

He wasn't God. He had no idea, if she had kept her nose out of it, if they'd all be sitting together right then.

But since they were, the happy couple across from them, and Chloe being at his side, he'd never tell her this, but he was glad as fuck she did.

"Love you, sweetheart, but leave me out of it," Duncan ordered.

This was translated as he felt the same as Judge, but he wasn't going to side with his woman's daughter for a variety of reasons.

Chloe clicked her teeth in such annoyance, she also tossed her hair with it.

Judge didn't swallow back the chuckle that caused.

Which meant Chloe glared at him. "I'm not being amusing."

"Yes, you are," he refuted.

"How about this?" Duncan intervened. "Maybe you meet the man before you start running his life. And I suggest that because, from experience, I've learned that meeting you makes a man powerless to do anything but give you whatever you want."

At that, Chloe verbally huffed, but it wasn't annoyed even a little bit.

"Gotta admit, he's right," Judge muttered.

And that earned him a look from his woman that was so far from a glare, it wasn't funny.

At that juncture, Genny announced, "Your grandmother has a lot to answer for." When Judge looked at her, she explained to him, "Chloe is a creature of my mother's making. I'm officially declaring it right now that I take absolutely no responsibility for it."

"And my beloved grandmother would be wild with delight at this acknowledgement because she put a good deal of work into it," Chloe added.

"Then I'm sorry she's gone so I can't thank her," Judge put in.

Now *that*...

That got him a look that was so warm and tender, seeing it felt like she'd pressed her hand hard against his heart.

"You were right," Genny said, which meant Judge had to tear his eyes away from Chloe's glowing, happy, gorgeous face.

But Genny was talking to Duncan.

"Yeah, I was," he agreed.

"*Rude*," Chloe chimed into their private conversation that wasn't exactly private.

And when she did, Genny turned directly to her daughter and laid it out.

"Duncan told me the man who won you would have to be some kind of man, because you were going to turn his world upside down," her gaze slid to Judge, "and he was going to love it."

Judge didn't move.

Because Duncan was right in what he said.

But it wasn't only Judge who loved it.

It was Genny too.

Approval from Imogen Swan.

From Genny.

From Chloe's mom.

Christ.

That hand in his chest didn't leave.

And it felt fucking fantastic.

"*Ma mère chérie,*" Chloe said quietly.

She loved it too.

Duncan cleared his throat.

Judge reached for Chloe's hand.

They linked fingers, but it was Chloe that took it under the table and rested their hands on his thigh.

"Now, stay out of Jameson Oakley's love life," Genny demanded.

Chloe's gorgeous, happy face turned into a gorgeous, pouty face.

Judge chuckled again, which bought him another glare.

It didn't deter him from leaning in and kissing it.

And when he was done, the server was there with their food.

JUDGE HAD CHLOE'S WRISTS IN HIS HAND AT THE SMALL OF HER BACK, his thighs splayed wide because he was astride hers, and he was pumping inside her, hard.

"Judge," she moaned.

"Don't fucking come," he ordered.

"*Darling.*"

She was going to come.

Judge pulled out.

"Judge!" she protested.

He let her wrists go, shoved a hand between her legs, cupped her sex and hauled her up to her knees.

"Down at the front," he demanded when she made a move to come up to her hands.

He took her in as he always took her in when she was positioned like this. He liked her like that, bowed before him, his strong, meddlesome, take-care-of-everyone-and-everything Chloe all his to play with.

His to take care of.

Whisper soft, he touched her clit.

"More," she murmured.

"Take it," he commanded.

She didn't hesitate.

She rubbed against his hand restlessly, her beautiful ass moving, his fingers slickening even if they weren't inside, she was that wet.

"Judge, I need to come, honey," she whimpered.

He pulled his hand away and said, "Turn around."

Again no hesitation, she did, on hands and knees. And when she was facing him, her head tipped back, eyes coming to him.

Fucking hell, she was hot.

"Mouth open, baby," he said softly.

Her expression grew hungry, her eyes dipped to his dick, and she opened her mouth.

He positioned, thrust in, she took him, and her wet on him, and she sucked hard.

Yeah.

Hot and sweet and beautiful and *life*.

All Chloe.

He put some effort into gathering all her hair in a fist, alternating watching her swallow his dick and staring at the long length of her beautiful neck, those soft, dark baby hairs at the base of her scalp curling against her skin, liking all of that so much, it didn't take long before he had to pull out.

Her head shot back, and she offered, "I'll swallow, *chéri*."

He knew she would, she'd done it before. She dug driving him over the brink and drinking that down.

And he liked her doing that.

But not tonight.

"Tonight you ride," he told her.

Her eyes blazed, he let her hair go, and she nearly tackled him to get him to his back.

This meant Judge was smiling when she climbed on top, took him inside, and she *rode.*

He watched, and it took work, but he went at her clit as she bounced on his dick, and she got there before he blew.

The second he did, she collapsed on his chest, and he felt another jet gush out of his cock when his body accepted her weight, her tits crushed against his chest, and her hair flew all over his neck, jaw and shoulder.

After he came down, he called softly, "Baby," and she lifted her head for him.

With regret, Judge brushed her hair away from his neck and chest, skimming it over her shoulder, then he held her gaze as he touched his finger to her lips.

This was a thing he'd introduced a few weeks ago, a thing Chloe took to like she took to everything Judge did, in bed and out of it.

So she sucked his finger into her mouth, tonguing it and coating it, before he slid it out, and she stayed seated on his still-hard cock as he moved his hand to her ass and slid the finger she'd wetted to the second knuckle up her ass.

She was hot and tight, and they both knew he'd eventually take her there, even if he hadn't yet.

But this was something else.

It was more than sex. More than intimacy. More than connection.

It was all that, for certain.

It was also claiming.

She was his everywhere.

She wanted him to know it.

And he wanted her to know that he loved having it.

As if to make that point, not moving her body an inch, she shifted only her head to kiss the underside of his jaw before she settled into his shoulder and melted further into his frame.

"You good?" he asked unnecessarily.

"I'm fabulous, *mon beau,*" she murmured contentedly.

He stroked her gently in her ass and her pussy contracted around his softening cock.

He did this before saying, "I ever do anything that you don't dig, you tell me, baby."

"I need it."

Not knowing where that came from or what it referred to, Judge blinked at the gleaming hair on top of her head.

"You need...?" He let that trail.

She lifted her head again and looked down at him.

Her eyes caught his but fled to the pillow beside him before she stammered, "I need you to...I need...to be yours."

He still didn't get what was happening, now not understanding why she couldn't look at him when she said that because it wasn't news.

"I need you to be mine too, honey," he said softly. "And I need to be yours as well."

Her gaze came to his.

"No, Judge, I need you to..." A long hesitation before she declared, "Take over. I need who you are. *How* you are. In bed."

"Right," he murmured, watching her closely, because she said this like it was an admission, but they'd been fucking a lot for a while now, so what she needed was far from lost on him.

"I don't, that doesn't mean..." she said that fast, but didn't finish.

"Chloe, baby, I hope you get I get off in a big way for you. We're hot as fuck. I need you to be like you are too. I don't care you assert yourself, that's hot too. But I'm a control guy, and the fact you get off on that works for me. *Huge.*"

She seemed to relax.

But Judge didn't like it that she'd been tense in the first place.

"It isn't a weakness to enjoy giving up control," he told her.

"I know, I just..."

Again, she didn't finish.

"You just what?" he pushed, sliding his finger out and wrapping both hands around her waist to communicate she had his full attention, what she was sharing mattered to him and he wanted her to share it so he could fully understand it.

"I just don't want it to become a burden."

There it was.

When she gave him that, he wrapped both arms around her.

Then he rolled them so she was pinned, kept her in the curve of one arm, but came up on his other elbow.

Only then did he say, "Baby, stop dooming us. We're not good, we're great. In *all*," he pressed his hips into hers to make a point, "the ways we can be."

"Okay," she said, but that word was almost timid.

He didn't like that, it was not Chloe at all, so to get her out of it, he grinned at her. "If I have a physical day, and you want a ride, I got no problem lying back with you throwing a leg over and doing the work. But I think we both know, the norm is gonna be what it's been, and I am *way* down with it."

"You...the..." She looked to his forehead, took a second to get her shit together, then she gazed right into his eyes and declared, "The sex is fantastic, Judge. I love who I am when I'm in bed with you. But it's so much more. It's *so much more*. And that—"

"Trips you."

She pressed her lips together and nodded.

"You're scared," he noted.

"Judge—"

He dipped his face so his nose brushed hers.

"Chloe," he growled, "again, *stop dooming us*. You're right. We are. We are *so much more*. Live it. Be happy in it. Because so many people do not have this, but we do, right now, at dinner earlier with Gen and Duncan, this morning when we were brushing our teeth side by side in your bathroom, tomorrow morning when we do the same. Stop looking back and stop fretting about the future. Doing that builds nothing in the now. Which is where we are. It's always where we are. It's impossible to be anywhere else. And I, for one, fucking *love* being here."

She gazed up at him, her heart in her eyes, which meant Judge's slid up into his throat.

She then touched his check, ran her thumb along his lower lip.

And then she said, "Okay, Judge."

Time to move them past that and into a new now.

"You leaking?" he asked gently.

She nodded.

"You or me?" he inquired after who was going to take care of that.

"Me," she answered. "I'll be right back."

That was when he nodded, dipped, kissed her deep and thorough, then broke it and rolled off.

She went to the bathroom to clean up.

He went to his pajama bottoms to put them on.

Zeke, who'd been hanging on the dog bed on the floor that Chloe bought him (which was a pink faux fur that looked like a sheepskin, but that hid it was orthopedic memory foam—a bed that Judge had decreed upon sight Zeke would reject, but he'd immediately been disproved because Zeke loved it), joined him in the human bed.

Chloe came back, grabbed panties and a nightie, put them on and climbed in with her two boys.

They each turned out their lights, met in the middle and snuggled with a dog on their toes.

"Mom likes you," she said quietly into his throat.

"I'm likeable."

"I like you too."

Judge grinned into the dark. "Good, because I like you."

"We're so corny," she sighed.

"Not sure corny likes her man's finger up her ass right after he shot a load up her pussy. That's more aptly described as hot...and tight."

She pulled slightly away (slightly) and slapped his arm. "Judge! Don't be vulgar."

Judge kept grinning and declared, "I'm buying lube."

"Oh my God," she said, totally fake harassed because she said it settling back into him. "You're insufferable."

"And you're gonna get your ass fucked."

She shifted against him.

"Had that before?" he grunted, not wanting to know if that was a yes, but needing to if it was a no.

"No," she whispered.

Fuck.

That would always only be his.

Instead of howling his elation, he stated, "You don't like it, we'll stop."

"I like everything you do."

Yeah, she did.

He pulled her closer and was grinning again.

"We've done it," she declared.

"What?" he asked.

"We've managed to make assplay corny."

For a second, Judge did nothing.

Then, his arms convulsing around his woman, he burst out laughing.

ONE WEEK LATER...

IT WAS THE NEXT SATURDAY NIGHT AND JUDGE WAS DRIVING THEM AWAY from dinner at her dad's house.

It had become a thing.

They'd fallen into a variety of rituals.

Wednesday, up in Prescott, Chloe showed after she drove up from work, and since she usually arrived between seven and eight, he either had dinner waiting for her, or they went out.

Sometimes, Rix met them out. Sometimes, a few of his friends met them out. Sometimes, it was just them.

Thursday night, Judge came home to her cooking.

Friday morning, she made the massive sacrifice of getting up early and getting ready with him. He made the massive sacrifice of not telling her every time how adorable she was in her grumpy morning moods.

She went down the mountain.

He and Zeke went down it nine hours later.

Friday night was date night, no exceptions. Dinner. Maybe dinner and a movie. And then home, fuck and sleep.

When she worked during the day Saturday, he and Zeke took runs or hikes around the Phoenix area. Chloe would sometimes leave a grocery list that said, *If you have the time and inclination, chéri...* (he always did). He met with friends who lived in the Valley. And he always ran the vacuum, top to bottom in her house before she got home, so Zeke didn't leave her with a layer of fur everywhere that she had to clean up.

She came home, and they often went out with her friends. They also had their Cooking Club at Mi and Jacob's, which Rix drove down to attend (and he'd stayed with Chloe and Judge). The next Club at Chloe's, Rix came to as well. The next was that following week, and they'd decided on a change of plans, with Chloe spending the weekend at his, and Rix, Mi and Jacob cooking in his kitchen, with Mi and Jake spending the night.

In Phoenix, on Saturdays, they might also meet Genny and Duncan for dinner like they had the weekend before (if they were in town).

Or, more often, went out to dinner with Tom or to his house to eat.

Like tonight.

Sundays for them were sacrosanct. Time in. Sleeping in. Cooking together. Eating. Fucking. Zoning out in front of the TV. Sometimes reading together.

No chores. No errands. Just togetherness.

Judge woke early Monday so he and Zeke could get up to Prescott.

The only blip in this was when he had to take a trip to a new school they were introducing the program to in Denver, so he could go to an assembly, talk to the kids, pitch the program and get recruits.

They'd been together four months.

Chloe gave more than any girlfriend had before.

It still wasn't enough.

This was an issue, because if it wasn't enough already, it was only going to feel more that way.

And he had no desire to move to Phoenix.

She'd confessed LA was out, but she did not say she'd lied about not wanting to move to Prescott.

Shit was eventually going to get real, and that was going to be sooner rather than later.

Because he hated to leave on Monday morning, she didn't even try to hide she hated it too, they were going to be apart only three days and not even full days.

And they both thought it sucked.

Because it sucked.

So, yeah.

It was going to get real.

Soon.

But right now, she was unusually quiet.

He gave her that until they were on Scottsdale Road and he was done giving it to her.

"Where's your head at?"

"He's lonely."

Tom Pierce adored his daughter, and Judge could not deny that it felt super fucking good that Tom liked Judge for his girl.

He not only showed it on a variety of occasions, at one point, a few weeks ago, when Chloe had excused herself to go to the bathroom, he'd shared it straight out.

"You are not what I expected," he'd said. "And that's a good thing. I won't betray her confidence by telling you something it's hers to tell, but I'm pleased she's finally with a man who cares more about her than whatever he's convinced himself is more important than the woman in his life. Nothing is more important than that. I've heard the road's been rocky. I won't speak for Sasha, she has her work to do after she behaved the way she did. But you should know, it brings me relief Chloe isn't carrying it all on her shoulders anymore. She has someone who will help her bear the weight. Or help her to understand, she can choose to lose it when she's ready."

Yeah.

That was what he said.

So yeah, that felt fucking great.

Nevertheless, Chloe was correct.

Tom was lonely.

…whatever he's convinced himself is more important than the woman in his life. Nothing is more important than that.

Yup.

He might have come to terms with the fact that Genny was with Duncan and that was a good thing, he was still totally lonely.

And still kicking himself in the ass.

"I have…something to tell you," she said.

"What?" he asked warily, since he wasn't a fan of the way she was speaking.

It was hesitant, unsure, and two things his Chloe was not was either of those.

"Uncle Corey left me something."

"Sorry?"

"He left me something. After he died."

Okay, now he got it.

She was always iffy when she talked about a man she knew as loving and supportive, but he'd betrayed them all in a hideous way it was impossible to wrap your head around.

"Right," he replied. "What was it?"

"A person."

He wasn't expecting *that*.

"A person?"

"A…I don't know what he is."

He glanced at her and prompted low, "Chloe."

"I think he's…I don't know, he's too…*sinister* to be just a detective. I think he's a fixer."

She had his full attention before.

She had that wired now.

"What are you talking about?" he demanded.

"When we get home, I'll show you. I didn't know he was amassing it, nor did I ask for it, but he gave me a file. On...well, Dad."

"Jesus Christ," Judge bit. "Are you serious?"

"Yes."

"What's in this file?"

"It isn't exactly about Dad. You see, I hired someone myself to...*look into*...Dad's lover. The woman he cheated on Mom with."

"Christ, Chloe," he muttered.

"But they were...they covered their tracks. My investigator could get no leads. But, we can just say, Corey's man found everything about her and gave it to me."

Judge said nothing because he couldn't believe what was coming out of her mouth and he was trying to wrap his head around it.

"The thing is, that's not Dad...to cheat. She has to be something special. And I thought—"

"You thought you'd find her and fix them up like you interfered with Genny and Duncan."

What she did with Genny and Duncan was cute because it worked out great.

It could have gone a totally different way though.

Like this could.

"I didn't *interfere*," she shot back. "I'd categorize it more like a...*nudge*."

Like she wanted to "prod" his father into "socializing."

Fucking hell.

"Regardless of the outcome, I'm not sure Genny would feel the same way. Duncan dotes on you, and he's beside himself Genny is back in his life. But if you weren't you, Duncan might not feel that way either."

He knew she'd turned to him when she said his name.

"Judge."

"Burn that file."

"Judge!" she snapped.

"And tell this guy to take a hike."

"I didn't *ask* him to help. I actually don't know how he knew I was looking for her. Unless he's...keeping tabs on me."

"Fucking shit," Judge bit. "Are you serious right now?"

"Judge, don't overreact. This is *very* Uncle Corey."

"Don't overreact when you tell me some *sinister* fixer is keeping tabs on you and giving you files on people in your dad's life he took pains to keep private?"

"It doesn't sound good when it's put that way," she griped.

"That's because it's *not* good, Chloe."

"I think I should call him," she stated snootily.

"Do not do that."

"Dad can't have dinner every Saturday with one of his daughters."

"Like your sister, and your brother, your father is a grown-ass man who can sort out his own life. And newsflash, doll, if he was sitting right here, he'd tell you the same thing."

"Sasha and Matt's issues are not the same as Dad's. Sometimes people need a little...*push*."

"This is a very bad idea," he told her, then something occurred to him. "Has this guy given you info on me?"

"No. Which I assume means Uncle Corey would approve of you, and obviously, I must concur."

"So your research on me was your own."

"Totally."

At least there was that.

"Is this all he's done?"

"He sent the file and dropped by the shop to...I guess mostly to introduce himself. This was months ago. Before we even got together. I haven't heard from him since."

"Maybe he'll fuck off himself," Judge muttered.

"I'm not sure I want him to," she replied. "Dad's lover lives in Phoenix, and I've wracked my brain, but I can't for the life of me figure out how to arrange for them to run into each other, or something. It would be best if there was a damsel in distress situation, Dad would be all over that. But she's irksomely...*together*. I sense this Rhys guy has skills where he can help."

Judge took a deep breath.

Then another one.

Then he said, "Chloe, baby, honey, listen very closely to me. Are you listening?"

"Yes, Judge," she sighed, already knowing what was coming.

He gave it to her anyway.

"Do...not...contact...this...man...or...meddle...in...your father's... love life. Are you hearing me?"

"I *am* hearing *and* listening, Judge. I just don't know if I agree with you."

Judge grew silent.

Chloe didn't.

She blew his argument to smithereens.

"You aren't close to your father, like I am. You still love him, like I do my own. And it's base to throw something in your face at any time, but especially during a charged discussion. However, I will remind you that you gave me free rein to meddle in *your* father's life. You did this because you're concerned he's not coping with the death of his wife. Now tell me, why is it okay for me to interfere with Jameson Oakley, and not Tom Pierce?"

"I was kind of kidding," he prevaricated.

"You were not," she called him on it.

"Dad needs a shakeup. And I'll point out, you haven't even met him so the danger of you *nudging* him is very low."

Though, he suspected that wouldn't stop her and he knew this due to the conversation they'd had with her mother and Duncan just last weekend.

"*My* dad needs a shakeup too," she retorted. "And I'll point out, you *have* met him, and you cannot argue that he's wretched."

He wouldn't use the word "wretched."

But he couldn't argue that.

He wouldn't say Tom was wallowing.

That said, the man had made a massive mistake, lost what was most important to him in this world, and that did not often find a quick recovery.

"Give him time," he coaxed.

"I have," she returned.

"Chloe."

"Judge."

He gave it a beat.

Then he lowered his voice meaningfully and repeated, "Chloe."

She didn't respond to that.

He heard her humph though.

That was often indication she was giving in.

In this instance, he fucking hoped so.

"I'll look at the file when we get home," he allowed, though only to read it to find things to use in it as more fodder to get her to shred it.

"Thank you," she said shortly.

He shook his head at the road, regardless of the fact his mouth was smiling.

Any man would want a woman with a big heart.

But Chloe's?

It just might kill him.

He pulled out and looked into her eyes.

She read his look and knew she could do anything.

Anything.

She didn't take him to his back.

She forced him to angle up so she could turn to her stomach.

And then he pushed all the way up, because she kept her front down, but came up on her knees, presenting her ass.

And her pussy.

Judge took hold of her sweet ass in both hands and gave himself some time to watch her take his cock, her body rocking and then surging back to meet his thrusts.

Then he got busy, curling over her and diving in with his fingers.

He gave her an orgasm and then she pushed up on her hands, knowing he got off on that too. Tossing her hair back, letting Judge see the dark waves and curls sliding over her skin, her ass slamming into his groin, her pussy pulsing around his dick.

When he was close, Judge shifted position so his knees were between hers and grunted, "Up."

She pushed up to sitting on his dick. And angled together, he pounded her down on him as he powered up inside her, one arm slanting across her chest so he could wrap his hand around the side of her neck, the other hand full of one of her tits.

He listened to her breath catch with each thrust, felt her fingers curl around his wrist at her neck, her other arm reaching back to grab as much as she could of his ass.

And that was when he exploded, shooting inside her.

She rode him through it, her head dropping back to his shoulder. He turned his and grunted his orgasm into her skin.

Christ, she was everything in bed.

And just everything.

As it was receding, Judge opened his eyes, gazing down the length of her body. Her full tit almost too much for his hand, her trimmed bush sheathing his cock. He felt her soft hair crushed to his chest, all over his shoulder. And his dick twitched inside her.

They fucked everywhere. Her bed. His bed. Her couch. His. Her shower. His. On the basin in her bathroom. On his. He'd dropped to his knees in her kitchen and eaten her out. She'd dropped to hers in his and sucked him off. They'd fucked on her desk at her office. They'd fucked in his car after they got back to it when they took Zeke walking on a remote trail.

They fucked in the morning and they fucked at night. They fucked all day on Sundays, and it wasn't usual, but it happened where she'd wake him up in the middle of the night to fuck her, or he'd do the same.

Hell, they didn't make it out of her foyer when he brought her home from her trip to LA, they'd been so desperate to go at each other after they'd been apart. And that had been repeated in his entryway when he got back from New Mexico and Denver.

They couldn't get enough of each other.

And staring at her beauty sitting on his dick, he knew they never would.

Chloe loved looking at him and didn't hide it. Her face grew hungry whenever she'd see his cock. But even dressed and out doing shit, he'd catch her eyes on him, and she wouldn't look away. She'd smile softly, and the fact she liked what she saw shined right from her eyes for him to see.

She loved his dog and her family.

She cooked like a fucking dream.

She liked to hike. She enjoyed being busy. She knew how to relax.

She'd traveled and wanted to do more. They'd talked about vacations they dreamed of taking and they'd planned one in a break from his travel that summer (it was glamping, and he was looking forward to it).

She had a stack of books she wanted to read, it got bigger, but she made her way through them.

She was ambitious and fully supported the fact he was the same, but it came of a different variety.

She dressed great and she loved kissing him, and if he didn't pin her down at night, she chased him around the bed.

She was it.

She was his.

This was it.

This was theirs.

This was forever.

He wasn't in love with her.

It was easy for a man to fall in love with a woman like Chloe Pierce.

No.

He loved her.

Bottom line, heart, guts and soul, *loved her*.

This was it.

She was it.

Forever.

"Honey?" she whispered.

"Yeah?" he answered.

"Okay?"

Fuck yeah, he was okay.

He kissed her jaw, shoved his face in that long, graceful neck and gave himself a minute with all he'd just realized.

Then he pulled her off his dick, but he kept her in his arms.

"Am I clean up duty, or you?" he asked.

She twisted slightly and he lifted his head to catch her gaze.

But he couldn't catch it, it was roving his face.

It finally settled on his eyes.

"Judge, are you okay?"

He was fucking perfect.

"Absolutely."

She got it. Immediately. She either heard it in that word or saw it in his eyes, or both.

Because her eyes melted, her body did too, and her mouth got soft.

And it shimmered between them.

What he felt.

And she felt too.

"Clean up together," she whispered, like speaking louder would shatter the moment, but she didn't want them to disconnect.

Not now.

He moved out of bed, dragging her with him and lifting her in his arms.

He saw her eyes get wide at the gesture, but she simply slipped her arms around his neck and held on as he carried her to her bathroom.

Message clear.

That being he agreed.

This was their moment, and nothing was going to shatter it.

She let him clean him from her pussy and he let her wipe her from his dick.

They bumped into each other as he pulled on pajamas and she put on panties and a nightie.

They slid in bed, one right after the other.

Judge turned out the lights.

Zeke jumped up, did a little roaming, then settled in at their feet.

In that time, Judge had gathered Chloe close.

"Judge?"

"Yeah."

She didn't say anything.

Well, she did.

She kissed his throat.

He pulled her closer and tilted some of his weight into her.

"Go to sleep, baby."

"All right, *mon beau*."

She kissed his neck again.

Judge Oakley thought little of his life. He'd learned a long time ago that what was done, was done. When he was young, it was out of his control, and he knew instinctively he simply had to keep his shit together and survive it until the day he could get out.

When he hit Phoenix and his time was his own, his life was his own, and the people who had been in it were far away, he felt a freedom that was so unreal, so precious, he latched on to it with everything he had.

And he'd vowed he'd never let it go.

He'd emotionally let *them* go, but he'd never let that freedom go.

His first day in his dorm at ASU, Judge considered the first day of his life.

The rest of the life he'd lived was just one thing.

Over.

But this night, this night Judge understood was something new.

It was the first night of the *rest* of his life.

And he was grateful for the whole of his life also for one thing.

It brought him right here.

And in that moment, Chloe in his arms, his dog at their feet, shit for her having evened out, and knowing they loved each other without that word passing their lips, Judge was seriously fucking looking forward to the rest of his life.

He did this calm and happy having no goddamn clue that the deeper you bury your past...

The more brutal it is when it comes back to haunt you.

CHAPTER 25

THE STORM

Judge

he next morning…Sunday…

HIS PHONE RANG.

They'd both had the same ringtone, but Chloe changed hers so they could tell them apart.

And that was his.

Waking them both up.

On a Sunday.

He twisted at the waist, reached out, found it on the nightstand, and hit the side button so the ringing would stop.

Then he curled back into Chloe.

She snuggled closer, shoving her face in his throat.

She kissed him there.

Judge had learned what that meant.

It meant she wanted to get fucked.

He hadn't even opened his eyes.

But he was smiling.

His phone rang again.

That was when his eyes opened.

It was also when Chloe's body stiffened.

He tipped his chin down as she looked up.

They shared a glance before, wordlessly, he twisted again, reaching for his phone.

She'd had a charge pad waiting for him the second time he'd stayed over. It was the same kind he used at his house, plugged in and resting on his bedstand.

She'd put the one she bought him in the same spot.

He took his phone off the pad and looked at the screen.

His dad was calling.

"It's early," Chloe whispered, staring at his screen, seeing the time.

At any given moment, Jameson Oakley knew what time it was in pretty much every corner of the world.

He wouldn't mistakenly call at six-thirteen on a Sunday.

He wouldn't call at all that early on a Sunday.

Unless something was up.

He turned his gaze to Chloe, took the call and put the cell to his ear.

"Hey, Dad," he greeted warily.

"Judge," Jamie Oakley said, his voice heavy.

No.

Weighty.

Christ, it weighed so much, some of it landed on Judge.

He'd heard his dad sound like that once.

When Rosalind had passed away.

Judge turned onto his back, pushing up on the pillows against the headboard, hauling Chloe with him.

"What's going on?" he asked.

Chloe wrapped her arm around him, held tight and pressed close.

Zeke moved from the foot of the bed and pressed close too, on Judge's other side.

"Son...*shit.*"

Judge sat up straighter, gut twisting, hoping like fuck whatever this was, it was not about Dru.

Zeke's head popped up.

"What's happened, Dad?" he demanded.

"Last night...yesterday...they found her." An audible sound of a forceful blown-out breath as Judge held his own on the word "her." "Goddamn it, son, a friend of your mom's found her last night. She'd overdosed. She was, I'm so sorry, Judge, by the time anyone got to her, she was already gone."

Judge didn't move.

"Judge?"

Judge said nothing.

"Judge!" That was sharper, authoritative, meant to be heard and obeyed.

He stayed still.

His phone was slipped from his hand and he heard, "Mr. Oakley? This is Chloe Pierce, Judge's girlfriend." Pause and, "Yes, that's right. What's happened?"

He felt her jolt against him when she heard the news, felt her push up farther.

Then she said, "Okay, right. What now?" Pause and then, "Yes. You've sent a plane? Okay. Yes." Pause and, "No, can they divert? He's in Phoenix." A shorter pause and, "*We're* in Phoenix." Another and, "Yes. Thank you. Yes. I'll handle it. He's...reacting right now. I'll get him to call you when he's had some time to let this sink in." One last pause, "All right. Of course. We'll see you soon. Thank you."

Then there was a clatter of phone to nightstand, and she was straddling him, his face in her hands.

"Baby, you with me?" she called.

She'd overdosed.

"Judge, honey, are you with me?"

She was already gone.

"Judge, darling, you're worrying me."

"I assume I'm required to attend the funeral?" he asked.

She blinked.

Then she said, "Yes."

"Dad's sent his plane?"

"Yes."

"Now?"

"Erm...yes. I...of course. He's meeting us there. In Dallas."

"Right," he muttered. "I'm all she's got so I should probably sort that shit."

He then lifted her off him, tossed the covers from his legs, and knifed out of bed.

Zeke jumped off with him and followed, close to his heels.

He was in the bathroom preparing to use the toilet with Zeke as his witness when she arrived.

"Baby, I'm about to take a piss," he told her.

They spent a lot of time together, and it wasn't like they closed the door anymore when that went down, but she didn't tend to keep him company, and vice versa.

"Are you all right?" she asked.

"Sure, though I'd be better if I could empty my bladder."

She hung on that a beat before she nodded and made a kissing noise to Zeke.

In the past months, Zeke had defected to his beloved Chloe. Judge didn't mind, he totally got that.

But now, Zeke wasn't moving.

"C'mon, baby," she cajoled, "Daddy needs some privacy."

It took a second, but when Zeke looked up to Judge and he jutted his chin toward Chloe, his dog trotted to her, and they both walked out of the room.

He did his thing, including brushing his teeth, and when she came back, he was in the bedroom, having pulled out his overnighter that he'd left there and hadn't touched for weeks. He hadn't because he didn't use it much anymore. After she made the herculean effort to clear a couple feet of space out of her closet and a drawer and a half, he'd packed heavy a few times and left a bunch of shit at her house.

She had two mugs of coffee in her hands and no Zeke. This meant she'd either fed his pup and he was busy scarfing, or she let him out in her small back yard. Food or outdoor time were the only things that kept Zeke out of Chloe's sphere, or Judge's.

Her eyes went to the bag on the bed.

She came to him.

He took the coffee, also a sip.

She said, "I'll call Rix and ask him to stop by your place and bring one of your suits when he comes. You don't have one here. But you do have one, yes?"

"Rix?" he asked.

"Yes. Rix."

"What do you mean, when he comes?"

She stared at him.

And hesitantly, she said, "When he comes to Dallas. For you."

"He doesn't have to do that."

Still hesitantly, she replied, "This isn't a 'have to' situation."

"It is for me, it doesn't have to be for him. If you can, I'd like for you to come. It'll get meeting Dad out of the way. Not great circumstances, but one thing Jamie Oakley is good at is a crisis. You'll see him at his best. But if you don't want to come, I'll get it. I'll only be gone a few days."

Her mouth opened.

Shut.

It opened again.

Shut.

Then she stated, "I'm calling Rix and getting him going. He can drive down here and fly to Texas with us. I'll also call Sasha. She can come get Zeke. He can stay at Mom and Bowie's."

"Chloe, baby, really, Rix does not—"

"If you think for a second he won't want to be at your side through this, you're mad. He will be hurt and offended if I don't call, and he isn't asked to come."

That was probably true.

Judge gave in. "Okay, but I'll call. It'll probably take you longer to pack anyway."

He then moved to his phone.

He didn't make the call because she made her own.

His name.

He looked to her.

"You're concerning me," she announced.

"Why?" he asked.

"Why?" she parroted.

"Chloe, I told you, whatever I felt for the woman who was supposed to be my mother is gone. Not even gone. It was never there. She wasn't that person to me. If she wasn't out of it, she was partying. If she wasn't partying, she was mean and bitter. Maybe not to me, but life done her wrong, according to her, when that was bullshit. Even as a kid, I knew that. *She* made fucked-up choices. I couldn't get away fast enough, and I never looked back. It sucks she's dead. It would have been nice if she'd eventually gotten herself in hand. But I lost hope a long time ago she'd do that. I gotta get her in the ground or whatever. She probably didn't make any plans, something legal that would share what she wanted. Maybe Dad knows. But once that's done, it's done, and we'll get it done and come home."

"When you first heard, you completely blanked out," she reminded him.

"I was shocked. It's not every day someone calls and tells you your junkie mother overdosed and she's dead."

"Judge," she whispered, part rebuke at his callous phrasing, part surprise he'd phrase it that way.

"Babe, you'll get it when you get there. How messed up it all is. But really, now that I'm over the shock, I realize it isn't a shock at all. And I'm good."

She didn't say anything for a few seconds before she asked, "Do you have a suit?"

"Yeah."

She nodded, moved to her nightstand and tagged her phone, probably to call Sasha, her mom, or Mi.

Judge decided to give Rix ten more minutes to sleep and went back to packing.

ANOTHER THING JUDGE WAS GOING TO REMEMBER HIS ENTIRE LIFE.

Being behind Chloe as she emerged from his father's private jet.

She did this sliding on her sunglasses, tucking her bag under her arm, then gracefully reaching a hand for the railing to the steps.

The wind was whipping her hair around her head, pressing her black button-up shirt to her torso. The bottom half of her was covered in pink trousers that had a sheen to them. They were cuffed at the ankle. Black belt, black pumps.

Black shades.

She was top to toe cool, and glancing beyond her as he emerged behind her, he saw his father on the tarmac, and he didn't miss an inch of all that made Chloe Pierce.

Jamie was wearing sunglasses too.

Even so, Judge saw the approval was immediate.

Completely unsurprising.

When he made it to his dad, Jamie pulled him into a hug.

Jameson Oakley gave him his height, something Judge's granddad didn't give to his son. That came from Judge's grandmother, who had been as tall and cool as Chloe, just fair.

No, AJ Oakley was a stout bulldog of a man who told everyone he was five ten when he was barely five eight.

Though, since he was always wearing a cowboy hat, no one would know.

"Shitty circumstances, but good to see you," Jamie muttered in his ear.

"Yeah," Judge replied, pulled away and claimed Chloe.

"Dad, Chloe Pierce. My girl."

She put out her hand and Jamie took it. "Mr. Oakley, nice to meet you."

"Jamie, darlin'," his dad replied.

Even if the man had lived in New York City for three decades, that Texan drawl hadn't quite disappeared.

"Jamie," she allowed, taking her hand back, tucking some blowing hair behind her ear, and standing strong with her other arm around Judge.

"Rix, man, pleased to hear you could come," Jamie greeted Rix, giving him a handshake and pounding him on the shoulder with his other hand.

This was something Jamie knew beforehand since Chloe had programmed his number into her phone, and along the way, had kept him abreast of their travel plans.

"Jamie," Rix replied.

His dad turned to Judge. "Right, got you all a car. We've got suites at the Rosewood. Do you want to get settled in or...head out and maybe see your mom?"

"Do you have your own car or a driver?" he asked back.

"A driver for now. But—"

Judge didn't let him finish, he encompassed Chloe and Rix with the same look. "You two go with Dad to the hotel. I'll go out to Lucas and start looking into shit."

Lucas being his hometown.

Or the one he grew up in. It was a great place with great people and he still had friends there.

But it was never really home.

To his command, he got two versions of the same answer.

A low, "No," from Rix.

A sharp, "I don't think so," from Chloe.

But Chloe took it further.

Turning to his dad, she said, "We'll check in and settle in. Judge needs food. And then, will you come with us to the funeral home?"

"Of course," Jamie murmured, watching her closely now.

"Babe—" Judge started.

"Shush," she shushed him without even looking at him. Her attention was still on his father because she wasn't done with him. "I'd like to know where AJ Oakley is right now."

Jamie shifted, and Judge saw it.

She had his approval on sight.

She had his attention when she got bossy.

He was understanding right now she'd have his admiration in about thirty more seconds.

"He's aware this has happened, but I can't say where he is right now."

"We know he's aware," Chloe retorted. "He's called Judge no less than fifteen times since you phoned, seemingly incapable of understanding Judge knows he's calling because his name comes up on the screen, but he doesn't want to talk to him, which is why Judge hasn't picked up. I assume you're going through your own emotions right now, but someone needs to tell that man to back down. When and if Judge wants to see him, that's Judge's decision. It always is, but now, it definitely is. So who's going to share this with him? You? Or me?"

Rix moved and Judge looked to him to see he'd slightly turned his upper body away, but fully turned his head.

Probably so no one would see him laughing at this appropriate but still inappropriate moment.

"Although I would very much like to witness your end of a phone call with my father, I'll take care of that," Jamie told her.

"Fine," she said tersely, glancing away and noting the staff were bringing their bags. "Then let's move this along." She tipped her head back to Judge. "And you're eating, *chéri*."

"Whatever you say, General."

Her lips pursed in annoyance.

He bent and kissed them.

She allowed this, but when he lifted away, she was right back to his father. "He refused breakfast and wouldn't eat anything on the plane. Fortunately, Rix was there, and he kept the attendants busy servicing his *every* need."

Jamie made a pained noise as her meaning wasn't even close to veiled, a noise very similar to the one Judge made as he swallowed laughter.

Rix entered the conversation. "Uh, excuse me, but that was private."

"If you wanted it to be private, you shouldn't have been *so loud*," Chloe shot back.

Rix shrugged. "She was pretty."

"Does the level of their attractiveness correlate with the level of your racket?"

"Well...yeah," he replied.

"You are not to be believed," she retorted.

Rix grinned.

She clicked her teeth then turned back to Judge. "Are you okay to drive?"

"My mom died, I didn't."

The hilarity he knew she'd forced, and Rix had played along with to elevate the mood, evaporated.

"I think I want Rix driving anyway," she said gently.

"I know Dallas, he doesn't."

"He can hear fine, so he'll follow directions."

"Whatever," he said, then to his dad. "Keys?"

"The fob is in the car."

And the car was a Jaguar SUV into which Jamie's airplane staff were currently loading Rix's chair.

"You're shotgun," he told Chloe.

"You should sit up front to direct Rix."

"He can hear fine, baby, if I'm up front or in the back. You... are...shotgun."

She nodded immediately.

With nothing further, Judge moved to the car.

His woman and friend followed him.

His father, though, stood and watched.

———

JUDGE WAS UNSURPRISED THAT THE SUITE THEY WERE GIVEN HAD TWO bedrooms, one off each end of a large living room area that also had a four-seater table and massive bar.

Chloe undoubtedly advised his dad that the accommodations needed to be such that Rix wasn't too far.

She was totally overreacting, but this was her gig. It gave her something to do. Something to turn her mind to. Something that made her feel better.

And Judge was all for that.

They were barely in with their bags before there was a knock on the door.

Judge stood back and wondered, as they both moved quickly to the door, if Rix and Chloe would duke it out as to who would get to open it.

Rix glowered down at her and won the Protect Judge Battle.

At least this round.

Chloe stepped back.

Rix opened the door.

"Hey," a woman's voice said, "you're Rix."

"I know," Rix replied.

But Judge knew that voice and called, "Come in, Dru."

She came in, her eyes darting around the room quickly, but coming to a rest on Judge, her mother's flame red hair startling him, like it always did, before it settled in how damned pretty it was, and *she* was.

She moved his way, and when she got close, only asked, "Okay?"

He opened his arms.

She fell into them, hers wrapping around and holding tight.

Something happened in his throat, so he cleared it.

"If you don't want me here, I'll take off," she said to his chest. "I get it. I totally do. But I wanted to be close to Dad."

"You're family, doll," he murmured. "Of course you need to be here."

She held tighter.

"That's Judge's sister," he heard his father say, obviously he'd come with her. "Dru."

"Hmm," was all he heard from Chloe, so he looked her way.

She had her arms crossed on her chest and was assessing this situation, but he could see she was leaning toward complete acceptance of Drusilla Lynch.

"My girlfriend is about to force feed me," he lied to Dru.

She tipped her head back to look up at him, her brows inching together.

"You hungry?" he asked.

"If you're not hungry, you shouldn't eat," she advised.

"Wrong," Chloe called.

Judge kept his arm around Dru's shoulders, so she kept one around his waist as she turned to the sound of Chloe's voice.

It kept coming.

"Hello, I'm Chloe, and you're extraordinary. Your hair very well may be the meaning of life. And that hug was incredibly sweet. But Judge needs food. Even if it's something light."

"I'm on it."

That was Rix and he was, considering he was at the phone with the room service menu open.

But Dru was staring at Chloe.

"She doesn't bite," *anyone but me,* "promise," he told his sister.

"Are you sure?" Dru stage whispered.

Chloe's lips twitched.

"I'm sure," he answered.

"Yeah, we'll have the cobb salad, extra plates, two turkey clubs, cut each of those into four pieces, two Reubens, again cut into quarters, three orders of truffle fries and," he stopped, looked around the room, and finished, "two pecan tortes, two praline cheesecakes and two flourless chocolate cakes. With a ton of forks."

So much for light.

Judge's attention moved from Rix to Chloe, to see her gazing with approval at their friend.

Dru rested some of her weight into his side.

He squeezed her shoulders and caught his father staring at them with a look on his face that Judge quickly turned away from.

And the gang was all there.

Checked in.

Key cards in hand.

Rental with the valet.

Judge had a mental checklist of what needed to get done. It'd probably take a couple of days to do all of it. But those were three things he ticked off the list.

Next, eat.

Then get on it.

Lay his mother to rest.

So they could all get the fuck out of there.

———————

JUDGE WENT IN TO SEE HER ALONE.

He did this because he didn't know what state she'd be in, and if Chloe saw her at all, he didn't want her to see his mother looking like shit.

She didn't.

She'd been cleaned up and put in a casket probably one of Jamie's assistants selected, but he knew his father had a hand in it.

It was an iridescent blue.

Her favorite color.

She looked like her, except dead.

And a lot more tranquil than he'd ever seen her, even if she was passed out.

He didn't take long with her, but he did tick finding a funeral home and dealing with the casket choice off his mental list.

He should have known his father would get things in hand.

As he walked out, in the short hall outside the small, private viewing room, he ran into that same man.

"All right?" Jamie asked.

"Have you seen her?"

Jamie looked beyond him to the door Judge had just cleared.

Like his dad, Judge got his grandmother's height. Judge also got her brown eyes.

His mother's were a light gray-blue.

His father's were a clear sky blue.

Now, those sky-blue eyes were troubled.

"No," Jamie answered.

That one word was rough.

Damn.

"Do you want to see her?" he asked quietly.

Jamie turned his gaze to Judge. "You go on out with the oth—"

"I'll go with you if you want to see her, Dad. We should…as insane as it all was, if you strip away the shit parts of it, us being together is all she ever wanted."

Jamie studied him. Nodded. Then took in a visible breath.

Judge clapped him on the shoulder, turned around and opened the door, leading them through.

The room was small. There were two enormous sprays of gladiolas behind the casket. A good choice, neutral cream that would go with anything put before it. A short bench sat against one wall and two chairs rested a few feet from the front of the casket. Places to sit and reflect with room to stand and gaze.

As it had been when he left it, the door to the casket was up, and you could see her lying there.

Judge flinched slightly at something he hadn't noticed before.

The inch and a half of gray roots in her hair before the faded red-blonde she got from God in her youth, a bottle later in life, started.

Even constantly wasted, in one way or another, she'd always managed to retain beauty.

"Good genes, buckaroo," she'd say, pointing to her face…

Or his.

Judge wondered when the last time was his father had seen her.

He also wondered what kind of blow this was, both the women Jameson Oakley loved dying before they even got close to the age of sixty.

They moved to stand at the casket, Judge positioning so he could see his father and keep a finger on that pulse.

Jamie didn't look away from Belinda.

Then, abruptly, his dad said, "She didn't want to come to New York."

Oh shit.

"Dad—"

His father's eyes were tormented when they looked to his son. "She was a Texas girl through and through. Dirt under her feet. Wide open spaces. She was a force here. New York made her feel small."

"It isn't your fault."

Jamie looked back down at Belinda Oakley. "You love her?"

Judge was confused. "Who? Mom?"

His gaze rose again to Judge. "No. Chloe."

"Yes," he stated with zero hesitation.

"Then get ready, son, because you will take on every hurt she feels. Every bump she sustains. Every blow that lands. When she's sick, you'll feel ten times sicker that you can't heal her. When she's sad, it'll feel like torture that you can't move a mountain to make her happy again."

Judge stood still, staring at his father, not only because Jamie knew what he was saying, and he knew it down to the depths of his soul, the agony was written all over his face, and Judge felt that agony with his father.

But also because Judge knew he was right.

Judge couldn't even hack Chloe bowing her head with the upset of dealing with her sister. He'd made her gain her feet and her equilibrium.

He couldn't imagine enduring any of what his dad had endured.

"I know it wasn't my fault," his father continued. "But it will never stop feeling that way."

"I want us to be closer."

It just came out.

And Judge knew in that instant it did because it needed to.

And it was a long time coming.

Jamie's head jerked. "Pardon?"

"I want us to be closer, and I want to be closer to Dru. I love my job, Dad, and I'm ready for more, but it will be in that same field. It's who I am. It's what I do. I'm good at it. I'll want to contribute to a life that makes Chloe happy, and I just want more for myself, so I'll need to make money for me, for her, for us, for the family we'll eventually make. But you need to get over it, and when I say that, I mean you really do. Because if you don't, Chloe will make that happen. And trust me, you don't want to go there."

Jamie's mouth quirked and he nodded. "I'm sensing that about your girl."

"She's close to her family," Judge carried on like Jamie didn't speak, getting it out because it had to be said. "We have dinner with her mom or dad all the time. I want that. I want to give you to her. And I want you for myself."

Jamie visibly swallowed before he remarked, "It's my understanding she's Tom and Imogen's daughter."

Judge knew what he was saying.

"She has a nest egg they've given her, but she's ambitious. She'll make her own way. There's what we do to feed our own needs, but it all comes together in the middle, which will be us. I'm not saying I need to support her. I don't have to support her. But I do. And I will. Do you get that?"

Jamie nodded again.

"Doing this, with her here," he dipped his chin to his mom, "I'm not being a dick. She fought you because she never stopped loving you. If she didn't give a shit, she wouldn't have given a shit. But I got done a long time ago with my life being about her and her choices. I hope wherever she is, she wants me to have what I want. I hope when she was around, some part of her she didn't let show wanted that too. And she knew, deep down, I always wanted to be with my dad."

Jamie's jaw clenched.

"So, can you get over it?" Judge pushed.

"I fucked up," Jamie declared. "I did it trying to guide a son who'd already become a man. You think I have an issue, but I don't. I wanted to contribute to your life. I wanted you to understand you could come to me for advice. I wanted you to know I want the best for you. The bottom line I didn't get across is that I want you to be happy. That's it. If what you do makes you happy, that's it."

"But you said—"

Jamie interrupted him.

"I did what I did in my life, and I was driven to do it because I had a deep need to prove my father wrong, and then rub his nose in it, and not stop. That got in my way when I finally had a line to you, and I didn't know how to be your father. That was all I knew. Pushing is not guiding. Judging is not offering wisdom. I learned that when you pulled away. But you don't have anything to prove to me, Judge. I've always been proud of you."

I've always been proud of you.

Jesus shit.

His jaw jerked sideways and up.

And then he and Dad were hugging.

"I've always been proud of you," Jamie whispered in his ear, his voice hoarse.

This time, Judge swallowed.

They held on.

And they did that a long time.

Belinda Oakley lay silent beside them.

But it wasn't lost on Judge that what she'd threatened happened.

Over her dead body he'd be with his father.

Judge just didn't know what to do with that.

"I LOVE THIS," CHLOE WHISPERED TO HIM.

She was lying on top of him.

It was late by the time they'd had lunch and gone out to Lucas to check in with the funeral home, deal with some of the details (his dad did know what his mom wanted, and after a memorial, she'd be cremated).

They decided to return, have dinner, and chill out before they went back the next day, to the house where Judge grew up. The house Jamie had bought for them. The house Belinda nearly lost countless times and would have if Jamie or AJ hadn't stepped in to make sure she, but mostly Judge, wasn't turned out into the street.

After dinner, they all hung in the living room of Chloe, Judge and Rix's suite, Dru drinking wine, the rest of them sipping bourbon.

Eventually Jamie drifted away. Then Dru followed him. And Rix said he had to hit the sack.

So Chloe and Judge moved into their bedroom, prepared for bed, and that brought them to now.

Judge had just told her about his conversation with his dad.

"You seem okay," she noted.

He gave her a squeeze with the arms he'd had light around her.

"I told you, I am."

She was back to whispering, like Jamie was still in the other room. "He's wrecked."

"I know," Judge whispered back.

She lifted a hand and tracked whatever pattern moved her on his cheekbone, temple, along his hairline, jaw.

Then she said, "Love just doesn't die."

Duncan and Imogen.

Corey and Imogen…and Duncan.

Tom and Imogen.

Jamie and Rosalind.

And Jamie and Belinda.

No.

Love just didn't die.

"Baby," he murmured.

Her gaze went to her finger at his jaw to his.

"Thanks for taking over."

She assumed a mock severe expression. "You take the fun out of being bossy, because you're so easy."

He gave her a small smile.

She pushed up and kissed it.

When she pulled away, she tried to hide the concern that had dug deep in her eyes, and she failed.

So he threw her something.

"Can I ask a favor?"

If it was possible, not even a nanosecond passed before she said, "Anything."

"I don't know if they can do things like this, but can you call the funeral home tomorrow? Ask them to dye Mom's hair so it's...right. No one's going to see her before...they finish things for her. I just can't have her—"

"First thing in the morning, honey," she said softly.

"Thanks."

She touched her mouth to his again then moved away, his asking a favor doing nothing to alleviate her worry.

"I'm totally okay," he said again.

"All right, *mon beau*," she whispered.

She didn't believe him.

He sighed.

Then he rolled her to her back.

And he gave her something she could believe in.

And he gave it to her good.

CHAPTER 26

THE FURY

Chloe

he next morning...Monday...

"JUDGE'S WHOLE 'I'M TOTALLY COOL' ACT IS FUCKING CREEPY AS FUCK."

"Hmm," I hummed to what Rix muttered to me under his breath as, ahead of us, tentatively, Jamie followed Judge, who was not tentative at all in walking up to a highly dilapidated, but obviously it had once been a rather nice, large, ranch-style home.

It was out in the middle of nowhere.

However, I might be wrong, but it seemed like that wasn't the intention when it was built.

That said, I could see from a property that veritably screamed *I don't give a shit!* why no one else would build anywhere nearby.

Looking at some of the siding that had slipped, the peeling paint around the eaves, the yard that had long since given up any hope of being a yard and was a tangle of knee-high weeds and scrub, I grabbed a stranglehold on my temper.

Because Judge grew up here.

My glorious Judge grew up in a home where the woman who owned it, the mother who had charge of him, didn't even bother to mow the fucking lawn.

"Has he ever talked about her with you?" I asked Rix, also under my breath.

"Mentions. Not much. He's shared about his life. Talks about his grandfather more, but not much about her. Or he says shit, but not about how he felt about her. She was just the woman who gave birth to him who he had to put up with until he left."

This was the same thing he gave me after he'd explained some things that day stuff exploded between Sasha and me.

"I've met her though," Rix remarked.

I stopped dead.

Rix stopped with me.

"You have?"

He nodded.

But his expression was dark.

"She'd come to Prescott. Judge would pay for her to do it. Obligation. She'd be on about healing breaches and talking things through. What she really wanted was money. He was gone, she was fucked. No more child support and the granddad stopped propping her up."

That startled me.

"Propping her up?"

He jutted his chin. "Yup. She pissed away any money she could get her hands on. Settlement went up in smoke on the legal battles. Child support was gone before she even got it with dealers she owed money to and tabs she had at bars. She'd remortgage the house, it'd go into arrears. Once Jamie got sick of doing it, probably in hopes she'd be evicted and he could pounce on Judge, AJ stepped in, so she wouldn't be evicted, and Judge wouldn't go anywhere."

Rix stopped talking.

I didn't start walking.

"Babe?" he called.

"Just a second."

"Woman," he got closer, "you can't blow a gasket when our boy in there is going for an Academy Award with his performance."

"I'm not going to blow a gasket."

"Your hair is about to catch fire."

"Don't be dramatic, Rix," I scoffed.

"The temperature of the entire state of Texas just amped up fifteen degrees because of your attitude. Lock it down."

I rolled my eyes.

But his gambit was well played.

He amused me enough, I didn't "blow a gasket."

It was close, though.

"Let's just get this done," I murmured.

Rix again jerked up his chin in assent and walked by my side.

However, we both reared back in unison several feet from the opened front door.

The smell wafting out was unspeakable.

"How long was she dead before they found her?" I asked in horror.

"That isn't dead body smell," Rix said, taking my hand, clearly for fortification purposes. "That's not cleaning your house for fifteen years smell."

I wanted to know, but at this moment didn't ask how he knew what dead body smelled like.

"Was she a hoarder?" I whispered as we inched forward.

"No clue."

With trepidation, we walked in.

The good news, Belinda Oakley was not a hoarder.

The bad news, Rix's estimate on when this house was last cleaned was off substantially.

By about a decade.

It was clear she drank.

And smoked.

Not only marijuana, but cigarettes.

A lot of them.

Overflowing ashtrays were everywhere, ash and butts spilling out on surfaces and on the floor. There was a thick layer of dust you couldn't only see, you could see how thick it was because there were swipes, fingerprints and smears wherever someone had touched.

Everything had a brown/gray pall on it, likely from the smoke, but also simply dust, dirt and grime.

The cigarette odor mingled with a pot scent and that loitered with spilled booze and lingering vomit smell. This wrapped around the overall aroma of neglect, spoiled food and rotten milk.

I had a highly honed sense of smell.

It took everything not to gag.

Judge and Jamie both stood in the midst of it all, tall and straight—so very obviously father and son it was uncanny (also quite adorable)—staring around the place.

It took effort, but as I glanced around, I peeled back layers and years.

As laid testimony outside with this decrepit but still expansive family home, at one time, the bones of the house, including the furniture and blinds, had been stylish and attractive. The walls might once have been a soft peach. There were pops of color in what could once have been cobalt blue and shamrock green armchairs. A now faded, perhaps once vibrant red couch. There were pieces that were Nordic, solid, good quality, Scandinavian design.

'90s chic.

But it was all now worn, stained, nicked, or just plain grimy.

I peered through the large living room into a massive kitchen that was open to the space but had been cut off by overhead cabinets that would, to any design-scheme-minded person in the early aughts, have been removed to create a true great room.

And I saw that the kitchen was an absolute pigsty. I could barely look at it, it was in such a state.

I wanted to move no further into this hellhole.

I actually wanted to grab my boyfriend and walk right out.

On these thoughts, my gaze fell on some windows at the back. Through the yellow tinge staining the glass, I saw a pool that was undoubtedly a health hazard. It hadn't seen chlorine or a pH test in at least a decade. In fact, it had so been taken over by weeds, scum and rainwater, it could be described as a pond.

A fetid one.

But there were rotting loungers around it that had once been quite lovely. A table and four chairs with a skeleton of an umbrella impaling it. A rusted charcoal grill that had fallen on its side.

"Judge."

Rix's low, clipped utterance of his name made me shift my focus to my man.

And my desire to flee faded as something much stronger took hold.

"Where was she found?" Judge asked, probably his dad since Rix and I didn't know.

Though I could answer because Jamie couldn't tear his eyes off it.

"The couch," Jamie said, his tone guttural.

It was a piece of furniture I'd already glanced at.

I gave it my full attention then and noted it was clearly not only where a lot of the living occurred, because the ash and dust were unsettled, chip bags and fast-food wrappers scattered about, pill and booze bottles everywhere, and a mirror with heavy white residue on it was within close reach on the coffee table. But also, a lot of recent activity had occurred there, undoubtedly when the police or paramedics dealt with her.

Jamie looked to his son and asked, "Was it like this when you lived here?"

From the expression on his face, that guttural tone did not indicate he was upset poor Belinda ended her days in such filth.

He was livid his son might have grown up in it.

"No," Judge replied. "I cleaned."

He cleaned.

I processed that, but my eyes narrowed on him.

His expression was odd. I couldn't put my finger on it.

And his voice was blank.

Like he was not here, seeing what we were seeing, smelling what we were smelling, standing mere feet from the spot where his mother died.

"*Chéri*," I called.

He didn't look at me.

"Judge." I tried again.

And that was when it happened.

He bent to a side table, picked up a large, clearly heavy, glass ashtray, and cigarette ends exploded like a foul firework. Then the ash burst and began streaming in a gray cloud as he viciously threw it side arm through a window.

I jumped at the sound of shattering glass filling the air.

"Honey," I breathed, starting to move to him, but Rix's hand still in mine stayed me.

"*Are we seeing this shit?*" Judge roared.

Oh God.

Rix pulled me to his front, let my hand go and wrapped both his arms around my chest.

Judge turned to his immobile father.

"Are we?" he demanded. "Are we seeing...this...*vile shit?*"

"Son," Jamie murmured.

He made a move to close in on Judge but stopped when Judge also moved.

And another ashtray flew through the window, ends tumbling, ash choking the air.

After that, a liquor bottle flew, and I heard it smash outside.

A coffee cup went next. One that had been sitting so long, when the contents escaped, they slithered out as sludge, splatting on the floor and wall with a sickeningly wet slap.

Another empty bottle trailed after that.

"I cannot believe *this fucking shit!*" he thundered.

"Honey," I called.

He whirled on me but really on us because he said to Rix, "Get her the fuck out of here."

"Bud, no. We're here with you through this. Let it out. Let it fuckin' *go*," Rix encouraged.

"Get her out," Judge gritted.

"You know more than me she won't go."

"*GET HER OUT!*" Judge bellowed.

Tears filled my eyes at the fury saturating his face.

I'd never seen Judge look like that. Not once.

I didn't even know Judge *could* look like that.

Rix didn't move a muscle.

Jamie reached out to his boy, saying with forced calm, "Judge—"

"What the fuck was the matter with her, Dad?" Judge asked him.

Jamie's arm fell.

"I don't know, buddy," he answered quietly.

Judge threw out a hand. "Was she okay with this?"

"I don't know," Jamie repeated.

"How could she be okay with this?"

Jamie's voice got stronger. "I don't know, Judge. Now, take a breath."

"I can't fucking *breathe* in here, Dad, can you?"

"Maybe we should step out," Jamie suggested. "All of us."

"What'd she OD on?" Judge asked.

I was relieved Jamie didn't push an exit and answered immediately.

Because Rix was right.

My man needed to do this.

Here and now.

"Vodka and tranquilizers."

"Yeah, I remember those fucking nights. *Fuck!*" Judge shouted.

"What do you remember about those nights, man?" Rix asked right away.

I put my hand over his at my chest.

He just wrapped his fingers around mine and held on.

With what was to come, I would forever be grateful that he did.

"I don't know, Rix, bein' fuckin' eight and terrified the bitch wouldn't wake up," Judge answered.

Oh God.

God, God, God.

With that opener, as was the only way it could be, it got worse.

"Shaking her, pulling her off the couch, out of bed, throwing water in her face," Judge went on. "That was vodka and valium night. Cocaine and tequila was all kinds of fun," he said snidely. "She'd be so goddamned jazzed, dancing around, the only time she fuckin' cleaned, she had so much energy, she didn't know what do with it, because she was so coked up, it was a wonder her brain didn't explode."

Rix's fingers tightened in mine.

Judge kept speaking.

"She'd make me dance with her. Wake my ass up and yank me out of bed so I could dance outside with her under the stars. She'd build a fire in our Weber and I was scared as fuck she'd tip it over and it'd start a brush fire and catch the house. She'd dance and laugh and call some boyfriend, who was usually kitted way out with his own pharmaceuticals, and he'd show. I could go to bed then because she didn't want me around when she fucked him in the living room on the couch where I watched TV. And in the hall outside my bedroom door. Fuck all night, loud and crazy. Then they'd pass out, so I had to get up, half dead because I'd have no sleep, and get myself to school."

He looked to the couch.

"Vodka and valium, I should have known," he snarled. "I shouldn't even have had to ask."

I jerked in Rix's arms when suddenly Judge jolted violently, turning on his father.

It was only then I saw, and right on the heels of that, *felt* Jameson Oakley's blinding fury.

Rix did too and edged us back two steps.

"Don't take this shit on," Judge growled to his dad.

"How did I not know it was that bad?"

"Don't take it on," Judge repeated.

"I had court ordered representatives come and inspect this home *six times*," Jamie declared.

"Dad, do not take this shit on."

"How didn't I know this?" Jamie shouted.

"Granddad paid them off, and I couldn't leave her, Dad. I'd clean up and hide shit because I couldn't leave her. I wanted to live with you. But if I did, who'd take care of her?"

"*Not you!*" Jamie exploded with such force Rix pulled me two more steps away. "*Not fucking YOU!* Jesus fucking Christ," he swore, wandering away from his son, tearing his hand through his hair. "Jesus...*fucking Christ.*"

"Dad, I got out."

Jamie pivoted to him. "You were with her for twelve years."

"Once I was fourteen, fifteen, I was never here. My friends' parents knew how it was. They looked out for me. She'd lost hold, that's when I could go spend more time with you. I was always somewhere else. You know that. I told you."

"Who gives a fuck, Judge?" Jamie bit out. "Who gives a fuck? Do you know how Dru grew up?"

"Dad—"

"Her father was a different kind of piece of shit, and she went to private school and she got a diamond tennis bracelet for her sixteenth birthday—"

"Dad, don't—"

"And we were all busy, Dru with her music and Rosalind with her practice and me with work, but Rosalind demanded we sit down as a family at least three nights a week, so we sat down as a—"

"Dad, stop."

"And you were listening to your mother get fucked? Coming to me two weeks every summer, every other Christmas, every other spring break, and that was all I got to give to you?"

"You had me more later, Dad," Judge reminded him quietly.

"And that was all I got to give to you?" Jamie repeated.

Father and son grew silent.

Jamie broke it.

"I wanted to give more to you."

"Stop it, Dad."

"I wanted to give you tennis lessons and take you sailing—"

"Dad, stop it."

"I wanted to be a father to you."

"Dad," Judge whispered.

"Time to go." Rix was whispering too.

He was right.

Jamie's voice had fractured on that last statement.

Rix and I hurried out the door.

We were barely down the three front steps when Rix grunted. "Come here."

"I—"

"Sweetheart."

I protested no further.

I fell into his arms, and I let the tears flow as quietly as I could, because if Judge heard me, he'd come, and this was not about me.

When I could speak, I asked, "Did you know it was that bad?"

"Nope," he answered, tucking me closer to his wide chest, that syllable a rumble of feeling that beat into me.

"God, Rix."

I said no more.

"Yep."

He understood.

He then tensed.

I did too, tipping my head back to look at him.

But he had his attention focused beyond me, to the road.

Wiping under my eyes, I twisted to look.

A very big white truck was headed our way.

"Three guesses," Rix muttered.

"Oh no," I whispered.

"Chlo—"

I tore from his arms and marched down the cracked walk.

Rix was on my heels.

We stood at the end of the cement that should have been dug out years ago and replaced with attractive pavers, me at the tip, Rix behind me, and watched AJ Oakley arrive, park and hoist his old man's ass out of his ridiculously large truck.

We then watched him saunter our way on his short, slightly bowed legs, like he owned this house, the land around it, and the entire state of Texas.

He was in cowboy boots.

With a white cowboy hat on his head.

I would have selected black.

I'd recently spent quite a bit of time in a place where there were real cowboys, and they could set even my city girl's heart to tripping a faster beat.

This man?

"I'd like you to turn around, get in your truck and drive away, please," I called.

AJ looked from me, to Rix, took in Rix, and wisely halted his progress.

"You wanna tell me who you are?" he asked Rix.

Not little ole me.

Rix.

Rix didn't make that first noise.

"I'm Chloe Pierce, Judge's girlfriend," I answered.

AJ's aviator-sunglassed gaze swung to me.

"Well, always knew m'boy had good taste," he drawled, his shades giving me a once-over.

Disgusting.

"I'll repeat, I'd like you to leave."

"Now, gal, I think you know there's been a loss for this family, and my guess, you're here, then Judge is here, and I'd like to see he's okay."

"It's my understanding that *you know*, as your son made this request, that he and Judge need some time to process what's happened without unnecessary interruptions."

"I *do* know that," he retorted impatiently. "I just don't give a shit."

I didn't give a shit that he didn't.

"The funeral is Wednesday at three," I shared. "You can see Judge and share your sorrow at his loss then." I finished pointedly, "Be informed, we will not be holding a reception after."

AJ had just that much patience for me, I knew, because when he was at the end of it, he started forward again, not having an issue walking through the weed infested (snake infested?) lawn.

Rix didn't have a problem shifting into it either, and he did this to block AJ's path.

AJ came up short and peered up at Rix.

"And who might you be, big fella?"

Good Lord, did he study tapes of JR Ewing so he could act this much of a cliché?

"The lady shared plans for Ms. Oakley's service and asked you to go," Rix rumbled, and even though I wouldn't admit this to him, I was already halfway to adoring him. That sped me the rest of the way. "I 'spect we'll see you Wednesday around three."

"And *I'm* askin' *you* to stand aside," AJ said.

But before Rix could answer, a dread noise sounded.

The door to the house opening.

AJ stretched his neck to look around Rix.

I released a frustrated sigh.

I then turned and moved as quickly as my silver python Tom Ford ankle-wrap padlock pumps (that I lamented I'd worn that day for a variety of reasons) would take me up the walk.

"We're taking care of this," I announced.

Both Oakley men were out of that damned house.

That was the good.

The bad, I had eyes on Judge, who had his on Rix and his grandfather.

A fatal error in judgment.

I should have had eyes on Jamie.

He took off like a shot, and in high heels, and with shorter legs, and utterly no intention to wade into that "grass," I had no hope.

Fortunately, Judge's legs were as long as his father's.

He wasn't scared of snakes (like Jamie wasn't).

And Rix was there.

Rix got to Jamie first, a gentle butt of the chests and a quiet, "You don't wanna do that."

Okay, yes.

Adored that man.

It was just the moment Jamie needed to get a handle on himself. He stepped back, eyes locked to his father, and Judge, quickly prowling through the weeds, took his back.

"Go home, Pop," Jamie demanded.

"Now, Jameson—" AJ tried.

"I'm buying the gulch," Jamie announced.

Judge went straight.

Something very much not happy wafted from AJ.

My eyes shot to Rix.

His came to me.

I raised a brow.

He did a slight shake of his head.

Damn, he didn't know what that meant either.

"I'm *starting* there," Jamie went on.

"Now, Jameson—" AJ repeated in an entirely different tone.

"Tell Jeff to get his shit straight," Jamie warned. "I won't be covering his ass like you do."

"Jam—"

"You, I'll make sure you're taken care of in your final years. You can live in that house." Jamie jerked his head to Belinda's house. "I'm sure your latest wife will enjoy making it suitable for the two of you."

"You mistake the way things are, Jameson," AJ stated.

"I know exactly the way things are, Pop," Jamie returned. "I've known it for a long time. The only thing that held me back was Rosalind. She said life's too short for ugly emotions like payback and revenge. She was right. Her life was." An exceptionally timed pause then, "Mine isn't."

AJ said nothing, but he didn't take his shades from Jamie.

"You left the door wide open, you old fucking fool," Jamie said in a low, terrifying voice I was instantly fond of.

"It's your boy's legacy," AJ snapped.

"Don't worry, I'll keep it intact for him," Jamie assured.

They went into a staring contest that I knew Jamie would win.

I was correct.

AJ turned his gaze to his grandson and said, "You look good, boy."

"Thanks, Granddad, but maybe you should give me and Dad some space, yeah?"

My man, so polite. So respectful. Even in these trying times.

I smiled, and I didn't care that it was smug.

AJ glanced through me, took in Rix, then back to Judge.

"See you Wednesday."

Fabulous.

He ambled off and none of us moved, just watched as he got in his truck, did a three-point turn in Belinda's drive, and rolled away.

Immediately, I turned to Judge and called, "Darling, get out of that jungle. You've no idea what's slithering in those weeds."

"Baby, I got boots on."

I glared at him.

He studied me, his lips tipped up, then that disappeared when he looked at his dad.

"What was that about?"

"Please don't talk about this when you're so far away. I can't hear you," I stated.

I could.

I just wanted Judge, and Rix, and Jamie out of that grass.

Because, honestly, anything could be in it.

All the men, being gentlemen (even Rix), shifted to the walk.

I met them and we huddled.

Jamie shared.

"Your grandfather is in trouble."

"Financial?" Judge asked.

Jamie nodded.

"Serious?" Judge pressed.

"Maybe not," Jamie allowed. Then continued, "If he had time. Which he doesn't. And I didn't want to crush him. Which I do."

"Dad," Judge said quietly.

Jamie shook his head. "No, son."

"Dad," Judge clipped.

"Were you in there just now?" Jamie asked in another voice I instantly adored, ominous and angry.

"He's an old man," Judge pointed out.

"The wells dried up under his tenure. If he was smart, he'd have gotten into wind or solar. He has the land for it. He wasn't smart. No gambler is smart, Judge, and he's the worst kind there is. One who doesn't know when to fold."

"Dad, your entire career is based on gambling."

"My career is based on data and projections and calculated risks I, and my clients, understand. Those risks have levels, low, moderate and severe. You wade in severe. You embrace moderate. And you play the long game with low. That is not what your grandfather was doing. Cap that with paying ten million to every woman he bought after he wants to throw them away because he regards females as accessories that reflect on his manhood, rather than as the people they are. Women who needed thirty-thousand-dollar handbags and eighty-thousand-dollar earrings just to stomach sleeping with him. He's pissed away that legacy he likes to brag that he's giving you. He's leveraged to his cowboy hat, Judge. His debtors are unhappy, and the point has come they're willing to take anything they can get. He's got no choice but to lose the only real asset he has left. The land. And he's going to be losing it to me."

"That'll kill him," Judge stated.

Jamie's response was silent.

And eloquent.

He merely turned his gaze to the house behind us, then back to his son.

"Right, as much as I'm enjoying Bobby finally getting his back from JR in a Real Oil Barons scenario, this place is shit, and I need lunch," Rix declared. "So we need to go get Dru and find somewhere that has a mountain of food. And booze. There's nothin' you want here, Judge, and since there isn't, there's no reason to be here. So let's get the fuck out of here."

"That wasn't Bobby versus JR, that was Bobby versus Jock," I educated Rix.

Rix turned to me. "Whatever."

"Or not Bobby, Gary. He was the smart one who got the hell out of Texas and went to Knots Landing," I carried on. "Though, that had its own troubles."

"Who cares, Chloe?" I didn't get to answer that he should get his soap opera metaphors correct before Rix asked another question. "Are you hungry?"

"I'm always a tad peckish," I replied.

Rix looked to Judge. "It's good she's gorgeous, bud."

Judge was staring at me.

He explained why by inquiring, "Have you been crying?"

"No," I lied.

"You have to know your makeup is messed up."

Damn!

I pulled my purse off my shoulder and dug in it for my compact.

"We're definitely getting out of here," Judge proclaimed. "We are definitely getting Dru. And we're definitely getting drunk. I don't care if it's only eleven."

I gave up on the compact because I was at one with that plan and I could fix my makeup in the car.

We started moving out, Judge commandeering my hand when he did.

I pulled on him to hold us back, and when the others were what I hoped was out of earshot, I asked, "Are you okay?"

"We'll talk later."

I stopped.

He stopped with me.

"I'm okay," he answered. "Dad's okay. I'll tell you about it later. Yeah?"

I nodded.

He bent and touched his mouth to mine.

Then he guided me to the car and opened my door for me so I could climb inside.

I didn't get right to fixing my makeup.

I looked at the house with its sprawling Texan vistas on all sides.

I'd seen only a portion of the inside, there was a great deal more that I didn't discover, and I didn't wish to.

But there was a great deal more.

Bedrooms. Perhaps a den. A home office.

Then there was that pool.

Jameson Oakley had bought that house for his ex-wife to raise their son in, with good furniture, plenty of room, a big kitchen to cook holiday and birthday meals in, a place for him to have pool parties with his friends out back.

He had then been blocked at every pass, and lied to, stepping back because he thought it was best for his son.

When it was not.

He should never have quit fighting.

But he did.

That could not be changed.

As Judge said, now was now.

Father and son were together.

They had a future.

And as Jamie drove us away from that house, sitting beside Judge in the backseat, I reached out to take his hand and vowed that was the last time he'd ever visit.

His future was bright.

And he was going to live it.

Free of that past.

CHAPTER 27

THE FAMILY

Chloe

*L*ate that afternoon...

"I'D BE SCARED OF SNAKES TOO, CHLOE," DRU DECLARED.

After a gargantuan meal of some Tex-Mex food (heavy on the Mex) at Judge and Jamie's favorite restaurant, this accompanied by copious beers for the men (except Jamie, who was driving), margaritas for Dru and sangria for me, we were back in what I had decided was our safe harbor hangout.

The living room of Judge, Rix and my suite.

Jamie was finding a place very close to my heart considering he made clear that he didn't bother with mini bars.

Instead, he'd placed a call and ice buckets filled with bottles of beer, a carafe of margaritas, another of sangria, heavy old-fashioned glasses and a bottle of Blanton's had been delivered to the room.

It seemed the Oakley men had taken my "always a tad peckish" comment as a challenge.

I'd eaten so much food at the restaurant, I didn't need to eat for a week, and I couldn't imagine anyone else would either.

Even so, Jamie had also had a large cheese plate, fruit and crudité platter, and some bowls of nuts, olives and pickles brought up.

As far as I was concerned, we were set for the night.

Especially considering Judge and I had one couch, and I got to lie on my back on it with my head on his thigh, his legs stretched out, stocking feet on the coffee table.

Dru and her dad were on the couch opposite us, Dru curled up in a cute red-headed-girl ball in the corner, Jamie stretched out just like his son, with Rix in one of the two armchairs at the ends, facing the coffee table and couches.

I was not drunk, but I was so mellow, and so happy that Judge was with this small group of people who cared about him, who had not used him as a pawn or neglected providing him loving care, and he was away from that house, I did not care the men were handing me guff about being scared of Belinda's lawn.

I had no qualms I was scared of that lawn, because it was scary.

They were the ones who needed to have their heads examined because they were not.

"I suppose only a true man is one that's survived a dose of venom," I drawled.

"That's part of it," Rix said, chugged some beer, then added, "You also gotta tame a lion, drink your weight in whiskey without puking and carve at least three dozen notches on your headboard. And don't give me that look." He aimed that last at me at the same time pointing my way with the neck of his bottle. "I didn't make the rules."

Judge was chuckling.

"How many notches do you have, Rix?" Dru asked boldly.

Jamie, as any good daughter-dad would at the topic of notches discussed with his girl, be she twenty or fifty, dropped his head.

I fought a smile.

"A gentleman doesn't tell," Rix said.

"About five dozen," Judge said.

Dru laughed, and even though she wasn't much younger than me, there was still a girlie hint to it.

It was sweet.

It was also indication she'd grown up protected, nurtured, and with loving care.

I liked her and I liked that for her.

But I loved that Judge did the same.

She clearly adored her "big brother," and Judge had been correct. She wanted more.

For Judge, there was no competition or resentment there.

That said a lot about him and gave even more to her.

And I was glad Judge was going to put effort into folding her further into his life.

A knock sounded on the door and Rix's gaze came right to me.

I tensed to move.

He shook his head and got up.

It was then I noticed both Dru and Jamie had the same silent discourse, one that Dru had won and was also rising.

I was very much beginning to love that girl.

"Stay still, sweetheart, I got it," Rix muttered to Dru as he moved to answer the knock.

I looked up at Judge, who was staring at the door.

"He wouldn't come here, would he?" I asked, meaning his grandfather.

His gaze came down to me. "He does anything he wants. But there's also Jeff. And he does anything he wants as well, and it might seem impossible, but most of the time, it's even less appropriate than what Granddad gets up to."

Marvelous.

"Well, hey," Rix greeted, the surprise and friendliness in his tone making me push up enough to see who was there.

And then I stared in shock as Dad, Mom, Bowie, Sully, Gage, Sasha and Matt came through.

"Holy fuck," Judge whispered as we all made moves to rise from our seats.

Once they'd all filed in, Bowie took the lead.

"We're not here to intrude, Judge. We're just here to...well, *be here.* For you."

"Family," Mom piped up.

I noted Jamie had made his approach, and Dad was greeting him with a man hug.

"We've got our rooms and we can entertain ourselves," Bowie went on. "Until the service on Wednesday."

"But if you need anything in the meantime." Mom was staring hard at Judge.

Something I had not yet noted.

I talked with my mom a lot, about everything, and once Judge and I got together, that was included in our everything.

And from the time I placed a short phone call to her yesterday morning to tell her what was going down, I'd continued sharing.

I suspected, however, that Dad had filled in a few blanks.

And honestly, I was proud I'd kept it together. I was worried and I'd cried in Rix's arms, but I was pretty pleased with myself that I'd kept a lid on my own emotions that had a schizophrenic range. I'd done this to be available in any way that might come about (like calling the funeral home that morning about his mom's hair) when Judge needed me.

However, the way Mom was gazing at Judge—giving him that Mom Look that was keen on the scent of an injured cub—how I could tell she was barely holding back, her need was so deep to reach out for him.

And then my gaze skipped to Bowie, who I didn't think had taken his eyes off Judge from the minute he entered the room.

And I knew it was them, Mom and Bowie, who had arranged this.

For me.

For Judge.

Because...

Family.

That was when I lost it.

I didn't even know I had until both Judge's arms had wrapped around my head and my face was in his chest, where I pressed it, sobbing.

"It's been a lot," I heard Dru say softly.

The room was quiet for long, torturous, embarrassing moments during which I could not find it in me to get it together before I heard Gage's voice coming my way.

"You done gone and broke Coco," he said, then I was out of Judge's arms and in Gage's. He rocked me side to side with exaggeration, saying, "Stop being a dork, you big dork."

"I'm not a dork," I cried into his neck.

"You're totally being a dork, and it looks like a frat party in here. But you still *totally* need more booze," Gage replied.

Mortifyingly, I let out one of those laugh-cries and pulled my face out of his neck.

"I doubt any frat party has Blanton's and camembert."

"It does when *I* throw it seeing as I'm the son of an outdoors tycoon and stepson of high-falutin' millionaire Hollywood actress and...whatever I am to your dad, the best tennis player in history."

"First, please tell me you have not joined a frat," I demanded.

"As if," he said. "So I'll change that to college party."

"Good," I returned. "Now did you just say high-falutin'?"

He grinned down at me and asked, "Does it help if I tell you I don't know what camembert is?"

"It's cheese."

He gave me a mock serious look. "Well, I need to know all about that."

I smiled at him.

This lasted half a second before I was tugged away by Sully, and he did this while he said to his brother, "Don't hog her. Jesus."

"You're just jealous because I got there first and made her stop crying," Gage retorted.

"Whatever," Sully muttered, while hugging me hard.

God, I seriously loved my two new little brothers.

"Sullivan," I greeted.

"Cocoroco," he replied.

"Aren't you supposed to be graduating soon?" I asked a question I knew the answer to, because Judge and I had plane tickets to attend those festivities. And these included Sully vowing to take me to Harry's (a bar just off campus that apparently couldn't be missed) and threatening to make me ride in a van around the Indianapolis 500 track.

It was going to be Judge and my first trip together as a couple.

Woefully, this one bumped it from the top spot.

"Fortunately, my dad, who pays my tuition, not to mention for other things, like plane tickets to Dallas, thinks it's crucial I learn priorities."

That was fortunate indeed.

There were then general greetings which mostly boiled down to hugs all around for Judge and me, some introductions, and then I was left with Sasha and Matt.

It was Matt who did it, towing me to him and pulling in Sasha too.

In our huddle, Sasha met my eyes.

"You okay?" she asked.

"It's just been..." I used Dru's words, "a lot." I hesitated then, "I'll tell you later."

That earned me a sunny Sasha Smile that was not fake at all.

And my relief at experiencing it was extreme.

"We'll be talking about you blowing town with your guy when his mom passes and not fucking calling...*either of us*," Matt grumbled.

"I called Sash," I defended.

"To look after a dog," Matt returned.

"Hmm..." I hummed.

"Matt, lay off. Coco is dealing with a lot and you're being a meanie," Sasha reprimanded.

"Jesus, did you just say meanie?" Matt asked her.

"I was shying away from asshole," she retorted.

I burst out laughing and felt both of them look at me.

Matt pulled us tighter together.

Sasha reciprocated.

So I did the same thing.

"Never again," Matt whispered.

Oh God.

I loved my brother.

I looked him in the eye, then Sasha. "Never again."

Sasha's eyes were bright with tears and her voice was husky when she said, "Never again." And went on, "Coco, I'm so sorry. It was so—"

"Stop it. You apologized. I accepted. Done."

"I'm dealing with some stuff," she blurted.

Matt and I both stilled.

So he saw it too.

"When I wrap my head around it, I'll, like, talk to you. Both of you guys," she said.

"Promise," I demanded.

"Promise," she replied.

"Swear," Matt, being Matt, didn't let it go.

"I swear. God, Matt, you're *always* so *pushy*."

Her saying he was "always" so anything hit me, soft and warm.

He *was* pushy.

When it was something like this.

Important.

Sure, it could be annoying when he was that way.

But it was meant to be loving.

"If my children would quit having a highly impolite whispered conversation away from the rest of the family, their mother would very much appreciate it," Mom called.

Sash rolled her eyes.

Matt grinned.

I gave them both a squeeze and we broke apart.

When I turned, Judge's eyes were locked to me.

I gave him a smile.

His face got soft.

I moved his way.

And heard Jamie's voice saying, "Yes, please repeat the order I placed an hour ago and bring six orders of truffle fries along with it this time."

"Truffle fries, *sah-weet*," Gage praised. "I could eat a horse."

Judge claimed me.

Dad gave me a *You okay?* look.

I gave him an *Absolutely* reply.

Rix and Sully pulled in armchairs from the bedrooms, and we all found our places.

It wasn't nearly as comfortable as lying with my head on Judge's thigh.

But curled into him instead, seeing he did not hide he was touched at the dramatic gesture of my family—a family that I knew in my heart would someday officially be his—not to mention he and Jamie now had other, better things to occupy their minds, I didn't care Judge and I didn't have a full couch all to ourselves.

We had everything else.

Everything else we needed.

Family.

"I'M GLAD MATT PUT A LINE UNDER IT AND YOU THREE ARE MOVING ON," Judge said.

It was later.

The rest of our family had gone their separate ways (though, all of those were in the same hotel).

I was sitting cross legged in bed.

Judge's long body was lounged on its side across the foot, head in his hand.

And I was done with laying his worries to rest about me and my issues.

We needed to dive into his.

"What's the gulch?" I asked.

His lips quirked.

Then he asked in return, "How hard was it to hold that question in for the length of time it took after everyone said goodbye, Matt, Sul,

Gage and Rix headed down to the bar to go on the prowl, and we put on our pajamas?"

I refused to answer as to that particular difficulty being extreme and repeated, "What's the gulch?"

He let out an amused sigh and answered, "Oakbilly Gulch. Apparently, working toward a massive 'Fuck you, Dad' is an Oakley family trait. I know this because of what Dad shared at the funeral home. I also know it from knowing the family lore behind the Gulch since I could form a coherent thought."

"And this lore is?" I prompted when he didn't continue.

I got another lip quirk before he launched in.

"Well, one thing it's not is a gulch. It's a nineteen-thousand-square-foot mansion sitting on fifteen thousand acres that has cattle, horses, a swimming pool, a tennis court, and an indoor theater and bowling alley. The main structure, which began as only eight thousand square feet, another Oakley tradition is for each generation to add on in order to make it more ostentatious, was built by my great grandfather. It was his middle finger to his dad who told him, if he left West Virginia, and their *other* family tradition of letting the coal mines kill the men early, and he went off wildcatting, he could never come home again. He left. He struck black gold. And he built that mansion and called it Oakbilly Gulch as a take on the family names and his way not to be mistaken since his people lived next to a dried-up gulch in West Virginia. A gulch that regularly flooded with rain, trapping them across the water, and even on occasion washing out their home. But the men of the family were so stubborn, they rebuilt right there, living on that spot for generations and never moving."

"This is a rather troubling story, *chéri*," I noted.

"Because you're hooked up with a stubborn Oakley man?"

"Indeed."

"Just to say, I knew my great grandad. He died when he was ninety-eight. His father, and brothers, were gone long before that. So sometimes stubborn isn't bad. Like, say, when you meet a beautiful woman and she's dead set on holding you back, but you don't give up."

I rolled my eyes.

When I rolled them back, he was grinning.

"So your dad is going to wrest hold of the family home?" I inquired.

Sadly, his grin faded.

"Apparently it, everything in it, and every head of cattle, horse, and structure on the land around it, Granddad has put up as collateral for some deal that should have earned him a whole new fortune. But it fell apart, and he's scrambling to piece it back together. It's not looking good, and the people he promised a cut, people who gave him the cash to make magic happen, aren't thinking good things."

"So your dad is going to close in."

Judge nodded.

"Can I make a suggestion?" I requested.

He nodded again.

"Don't get involved."

"Chlo—"

I pushed up and over my knees so I was on my belly and closer to him. There, I reached out with my fingers and touched his mouth.

"They should have worked together to take care of you," I said. "Your grandfather should have been your father's eyes and ears here. Your dad having to fight your mom *and* his father, at the same time struggling to figure out what was best for you being caught in the crossfire would have been far easier if his father was not a point of that triangle, but instead had been at his side. He was not. Jamie made bad decisions, but it's easy to see that now considering the man you've become. He couldn't know you'd be this smart, this strong. He erred on the side of protecting you. I understand that. He still erred. And he knows it. Let him do what he must to work out those demons."

I paused and then stated my last.

"And your grandfather deserves it."

Judge wrapped his hand around my wrist and pulled it away from his mouth, starting again, "Chlo—"

"He does."

"He's an old—"

"*He does*," I hissed.

Judge fell quiet.

"He knew how bad she was, he was right here," I explained. "He made moves to keep you in that situation so he could keep you in his sights. He behaved entirely selfishly. And that isn't okay for a grandfather, it isn't okay for a father, it isn't even okay for a human being. Your dad did not push him to make bad financial decisions. He is, on all accounts, reaping what he's sown. It's simply that his own son is handing him the sickle. Let it happen."

Knowing me, Judge did not push it.

Instead, he replied, "Remind me not to get on your bad side."

"That would be impossible, Judge."

I said that, I meant it, and I very much liked the consequences of it.

Those being, Judge pushing up and reaching out to me.

He then dragged me up his chest and we collapsed so I was on my back and he'd pinned me.

He had a look on his face that was familiar, and I adored it, but we weren't done.

"Before you get busy," I started and his gaze went from my mouth to my eyes, "that scene in the house—"

It was my turn to be interrupted.

"We had it, we let it out, it's good."

He was avoiding again.

"Judge—"

"Although he threatened it, he's not going to make Granddad move there," he shared. "Mom didn't have a will. Not that we know. So the property goes to me. Dad's going to hire someone to go through it to see if there's anything that needs keeping, or if there's important paperwork we should know about. Then he's going to hire someone to come and fix it up. We're selling it. And I'll get the money. The deal, though, is that he insists on paying for all of that. I don't like it, but I agreed because I think it will help him put some closure on what we saw, and what happened when we did."

"Will that be closure for you too?"

"Sure."

That was a lie.

Judge didn't lie.

He cheated (not the bad kind, the adorable kind, or the sexy kind, but he did it).

He didn't lie.

"You threw things through a window, breaking said window," I reminded him cautiously.

"I haven't been home in a decade. I didn't know it had gotten that bad. It was a thing. It happened and I'm over that thing."

He *so* was not.

"Darling—"

"Chloe, honest to God, I'm okay."

He wasn't that either, but I wouldn't help him by pushing him to process things he wasn't ready to process.

I'd be there when that time came.

For now...

"You've not once mentioned your maternal grandparents," I remarked.

He sighed, but it wasn't an impatient-let's-stop-going-through-painful-history-and-have-sex sigh.

It was something else.

I would find out what it was when he answered.

"Hate to share this with you, baby, but there's some pretty serious stubborn on that side of the family too. Apparently, Mom's dad was not only ticked she'd fallen down the rabbit hole of drink and drugs, he was pissed way the hell off she got divorced. It's my understanding they weren't Bible thumpers, but they were religious and traditional and conservative. More, they really liked Dad. Can't say they were big fans of Granddad's, but I honestly don't know. Mom cut them out, so I didn't know them very well."

It shouldn't have been a surprise that this wasn't starting out well.

However, I was still surprised, mostly because, considering Belinda's chaotic and wasteful use of the resources at her disposal, I'd think she'd tap in to all that were available.

"Your mom cut them out?"

"I was really young when we moved down to Texas, I don't

remember a lot of it. But I do remember there was fighting. Drama. Grandma crying. Grandpa shouting. One of my friends' moms made mention about how they tried to get hold of me through the courts when it became clear Mom wasn't going to find the right path, but Granddad got in their way."

I felt my mouth tighten.

Judge didn't miss it.

"Yeah," he muttered.

"One of your friends' moms?"

"I still have friends here, babe. You'll meet them Wednesday. Granddad isn't the only one who's been blowing up my phone. They've been calling, I just haven't been picking up. They've also been texting, and that's easier for me now, so that's how we're talking. The word is getting out. But back then, Mrs. Taylor said what she said in passing, and then Mr. Taylor gave her a look and she shut up. They probably thought it'd upset me. By the time I was old enough, free of all that shit and able to contact them and ask, I didn't care."

Mm.

"Anyway," he continued, "between Mom not wanting anyone confronting her with her issues, and through love or any other reason making her face them, and Granddad not wanting anyone in the way of his direct line to me, they disappeared. I suspect from what I heard, and this was from Granddad, so take it with a grain of salt, part of the problem was Grandpa. He was standing staunch on the way he thought Mom should be, that way being clean and sober, and it wasn't just her cutting them out, they cut her out too. Or he did. And by extension, me."

I didn't trust myself to speak.

It would seem, at every turn, that Jamie was in one way very correct.

Judge was caught in the crossfire of a lot of selfishness, self-righteousness and pride.

Regrettably, he wasn't done with the story.

"Dad has made mention, though, that he reached out to them, undoubtedly to recruit them as allies. That said, he doesn't badmouth them. Reading between the lines, there has to be some truth to what Granddad said. Because if they were all in to help, he'd have had them here, helping. And it was left unsaid, but it's clear he did not."

I remained silent.

Judge carried on.

"Grandpa died of a heart attack when I was seventeen. Mom forbade me to go to his funeral. Grandma came to visit me twice when I was at ASU. She was sweet, but it was awkward because I didn't know her very well, and I sensed she was feeling frustration at that, and maybe some guilt at all that had gone down. She died about two weeks after I graduated. Mom was an only child, but they left me everything. Probably because they knew how Mom would use all they'd worked for their whole lives and left behind, and they didn't want that. Also probably because Grandma was the last one standing, and she might not have been able to do it like she'd liked to have done it, but still, I knew she loved me."

I did not break my silence, but for a different reason this time.

"Dad swooped in and did somewhat what he's going to do with Mom's house. To make it so I didn't have to come back to Texas, he paid someone to go through their stuff and send me what was worth keeping, including pictures and heirlooms. The rest was auctioned and sold. It's how I bought my house."

Well, that explained why Judge had such a great home when he hadn't taken any money from his father.

"You didn't come to Texas for her funeral?"

"Explicit instructions," he murmured, his tone odd. "She was cremated. Her ashes sent to me. In her will, it stated plainly that, not only did she not want a service, she didn't want me in Texas. She asked that I," he cleared his throat, "keep her if that was my wish, or put her somewhere I liked to be. I put her in the Dells."

"Oh Judge," I whispered.

"It's gorgeous," he explained, as if I was entitled to some opinion on how he laid his grandmother to rest, or more, that I might make some judgment about the fact he didn't "keep her." "It seems the sun shines brighter there for some reason, maybe it's the red rock. But I think she'd like it there."

"Anyone would like it there," I said quietly.

"Mm…" he hummed noncommittally.

"So in the end, she did the only thing she could to protect you."

"She kept me from Texas," he finished for me. "So…yeah."

"Have you been through the pictures and heirlooms?" I asked.

"Yes."

That was short, and he gave nothing more.

So I gave him a look, and it was up to him if he kept going.

"They were a good-looking family," he said. "Seemed close. Mom was beautiful, always beautiful. Popular in school. A cheerleader. She and Dad started dating when he was a senior and she was a junior. I have their prom pictures, or at least the ones Grandpa took in what I suspect was their yard by some rose bushes. Dad came back from college to be her date when she was voted homecoming queen. And when she was in the court at prom. She didn't go to college. She got out of high school, worked her way up to an assistant manager in a clothing store at the mall and bided her time until Dad graduated, something he worked his ass off to do early, probably for the same reason as me. To get as far away from home as possible as soon he could do that."

Even with the very little time I'd spent in AJ Oakley's presence, I still could absolutely see *that*.

"They eloped in Tennessee. Granddad was not invited. Glamma, that's Dad's mom, was there. So were Grandma and Grandpa. All of them were happy, fucking beaming. Mom and Dad did this on their way to NYC," Judge kept sharing.

Upon hearing what he called his paternal grandmother, I made the instant decision to be called that by my grandchildren.

"Do you have their wedding photos?" I asked.

He shook his head. "Dad does. He told me a long time ago if I wanted to see them, he'd pull out the album. But it wasn't a big thing, seeing as they eloped. I've just seen snapshots that Grandpa took or had someone wherever they were take of all four of them. And before you ask, she seemed happy, but looking back now, I think she also seemed a little freaked. Like she didn't know what life meant after becoming homecoming queen. She'd landed the big man on campus, achieved her loftiest goals, her life was complete, and she was only nineteen."

Good God.

"I don't know what to say about that," I noted gently.

"You wouldn't, because you aren't like that."

Now I didn't know what to say about *that* or the way he said it, the words having a sharp edge that skimmed the line of acidic.

"Let's talk about how awesome your family is," he suggested.

I got quiet.

"You and they cannot know how big that was," he continued. "What it meant to me. But also Dad, knowing I have that. And Dru too."

"I know how big it was," I said softly.

"Oh yeah, forgot, you started bawling," he teased.

I scrunched my nose.

He kissed it.

Then he kissed my mouth.

After that, he whispered, "Just you and me now, Coco. Okay? I get you want to know, you need to know, and you're concerned for me. But I just want it to be us for a while. I want to be all about you and not about any of that. Until we have to face it again tomorrow. Can you give me that?"

He knew the answer, but I verbalized it anyway.

"Of course, honey."

That was when he kissed me.

Our first time together sexually, or at least the making love part of it, had not been repeated since. Both of our tastes were of a different bent.

On my part, there was the thrill that Judge in everyday life was sweet and laidback, thoughtful and affectionate, and in bed he was assertive, aggressive, powerful and domineering.

There was also the fact that in everyday life, I felt most everything

—including the happiness and well-being of everyone I loved—was my responsibility, and that meant I could be hyper-sensitive and controlling. So it was not only a turn-on, but a relief to give over to Judge when we were having sex.

But that night, I knew from the beginning it was going to be different just with the way he kissed me.

He moved on to touch me the same way: reverent, lingering, lazy.

I reciprocated.

I knew what this was about.

It was about the feelings we had for each other.

It was about the time we had before us that stretched long with possibility and promise.

It was about touch and sound and staring into each other's eyes and sharing without speaking.

It ended with us wound together on our sides, my leg over Judge's hip, our arms around each other, his cock stroking inside me as we kissed softly, spoke no words, and held gazes.

So it came as a surprise when my orgasm built and exploded without any warning.

And it felt beautiful as Judge took my mouth as I was gasping through it and absorbed my climax.

Then he rolled me to my back, and I held him with everything I had as he rode me to his.

We were in love, I knew this. The words hadn't been spoken because they didn't need to be.

It was not just me, or more him.

We loved each other.

I knew that the night he carried me to my bathroom.

And what we just shared was delayed, but it was about that.

It was about looking after each other now.

And looking forward to doing it forever.

Judge carried me to the bathroom again that night. We took care of each other there. But the difference was, I didn't dress myself. When he carried me back to set me on my feet at the side of the bed, he slipped my nightie over my head and knelt before me so I could step into my panties.

I did that, studying his broad shoulders, the muscles across his lats, the depth of the indent of his spine, and I was not a crier, I detested doing it, it was only that recent circumstances had warranted my emotional displays.

But the tears again welled in me.

I held them back as he looked up at me and then righted his head, kissed my belly and rose, reaching for his pajama pants.

All right, so...

Maybe it was more me in the love department.

"Good?" he asked when I didn't move after he'd pulled on his pajamas.

"Good, honey," I answered.

A soft smile from my Judge.

A soft kiss.

Then we slid into bed together, wound ourselves around each other, and we put another day behind us, knowing we would face what was ahead of us the same way.

That way was our way, and always would be.

Together.

CHAPTER 28

THE MAGIC AND THE MIRACLE

Chloe

*T**he next afternoon...*

BEFORE EVERYONE MOVED OFF THE EVENING BEFORE, WE'D MADE OUR plans as a family for the next day.

It was Mom and Dad who did it, with Bowie encouraging it, Jamie leaning into it, and the rest championing it.

And the plan was genius.

We'd breakfast together in Judge, Rix and my room, however and whenever people drifted in, no pressure for a time for all to meet (Jamie had called one of his assistants to contact the hotel to set up a buffet in the bar area).

One of Jamie's assistants had also secured two tennis courts at a local club.

Therefore, mid-morning, Dad, Bowie, Matt, Judge, Jamie, Gage and Sully were going to go play tennis (Rix had opted out, he was going to work out instead, however, he ended up in someone else's room last night for a pre-workout workout and texted Judge that he'd meet up with the rest of us as agreed, later in the afternoon).

In the meantime, Dru had gotten on the phone and arranged spa appointments for her, Mom, Sasha and me. Facials. Body wraps. Massages. Several hours of bliss and pampering.

After the tennis tournament was over, we'd reconnect for a late light lunch and then we had time to visit and get ready because, even later, we had a private room in a fancy restaurant Jamie favored for dinner.

The plan offered opportunities to do what we enjoyed, with plenty of together time before what was to happen tomorrow.

See?

Genius.

It was also private.

Various patrons couldn't miss Mom, Bowie, Dad or Jamie walking through the lobby or halls. But we weren't out there and visible.

Mom had taken me aside the night before and shared what I hadn't thought to investigate.

Belinda's death had been picked up by the media.

"It isn't a big story," she said. "But it's a story."

Her point was made.

The candle was burning, and as ever, we needed to do what we could not to throw gasoline on that flame.

As I checked my phone between my massage and body wrap, I realized the Family Plan was even more perfect than I expected.

Judge followed sports, though he wasn't that huge of a fan, except of tennis. So his texts reporting the goings-on at the club shared that, even if the match he'd played with Dad in their tourney was a match he'd also lost to Dad, he'd loved playing him.

And I loved that.

As well as the fact that Gage had started a full-family text string, with Dru, Jamie and Rix included. This was where he shared pictures and short video clips of Dad and Judge's match, hilariously declaring it the "Rematch of the Century."

My baby brother was amusing in the way I almost hoped he wouldn't finish growing up.

Though I knew, when he did, he'd just be even more fantastic.

But mostly, when the boys' short, forty-five-minute-or-to-ten-points matches brought the final two competitors together, and it was Dad and Matt, it had, according to Judge been *So cool, you wouldn't believe it. They're both so good, everyone stopped to watch. It was fucking amazing.*

The "everyone stopped to watch" thing concerned me.

But Matt and Dad battling it out on a court concerned me more.

Fortunately, the very next text shared *I think they got something out, baby. At first, it was weird. Not ugly, just weird. Then they started messing around and joking and you could tell it was their gig. Duncan was hyped up but he started to relax and Tom and Matt hugged when it was over. By the way, your dad won. He's still totally got it.*

I could feel his happiness through the text. Maybe it was for Dad and Matt, but also it was for me, because that was the best family news I'd had in a very long time, and Judge knew it would be.

Even though that was big (*huge*), what was bigger was that Judge sounded excited and happy. He'd enjoyed his day (as he would, not everyone got to play against Tom Pierce, and Judge had in his life now *twice*, and so far, they'd both taken a match).

And I was beside myself and would be forever grateful to Mom that, after all that had happened in the last few days, she had arranged things so Judge had some relief from it.

At the spa, I had opted out of a facial, because I didn't like to wear makeup after I had one delivered by a professional, and instead had a blowout and a cosmetics application after my services.

I was in the middle of the last when, out of the corner of my eye, I saw Dru hurrying to me.

She'd had a facial, her skin was dewy and gorgeous, and her look was something that never needed makeup, no matter how fancy our dinner was going to be tonight.

Yes, she was that striking.

"Excuse me," she said to the lady swiping mascara at the base as a final touch to my fake eyelashes. Then to me, she got close and whispered urgently, "We have to go."

"We do?"

"Yes. The press knows your mom and dad are here, and Duncan, and my dad, and Judge and what happened to his mom. They're swarming the front of the hotel. I guess it's so bad, the police had to come and put up barriers."

I nodded to my stylist, she backed away, and I got out of the chair, murmuring my apologies to her, my thanks, and then moving with Dru toward the dressing rooms.

"I suppose we should have known we couldn't escape this," I noted irritably as we pushed through the doors to the dressing room.

"I don't know," Dru replied.

I stopped and looked down at her. "Why don't you know?"

"They're all back from the club. Dad and the guys. They had to run the gamut out there to get into the hotel. And, Chloe..." She got closer to me. "The reporters were shouting questions so Dad knows that Granddad pulled his usual antics."

I stood completely still as I whispered, "His usual antics?"

"Well, I mean, you know, sorry...but everyone knows about Genny and Duncan and your dad. They didn't care about that. Sully told me they were shouting at *my* dad. And Judge."

My blood ran cold.

"What were they shouting at Judge?" I asked through stiff lips.

"Stuff about how he turned his back on his mom and—"

She didn't finish.

I was a flurry of motion, pulling off my robe and getting dressed.

Then she and I dashed out of the dressing rooms to the checkout desk.

"I'm sorry, can I possibly deal with gratuities and—?" I began.

"Ms. Swan has explained things, Ms. Pierce, and taken care of everything," the lady behind the desk said. "She asked me to ask you when you were done to go directly to your suite, if you would. Thank you for being our guest. We hope to see you again."

I nodded, relief flowing through me, and more gratitude for Mom, and Dru and I rushed out.

I wanted to kick the elevator, it took so long to get to our floor.

And then we both ran down the hall to my room.

It was fair to say we burst in, but I couldn't help it.

However, we were only spared glances upon our dramatic arrival.

All attention was centered on someone else.

My eyes moved through my loved ones, and it didn't make me feel better that each and every one looked pissed.

And then I found Judge.

He looked much like he did yesterday in his mother's home.

Enraged.

I started to rush to him but didn't get all the way there.

An arm around my belly stopped me.

I looked up to see who'd detained me, my mouth opening to protest, but Dad gave me a firm head shake.

But he said nothing.

"This is fucking *unbelievable*," Judge bit out.

I turned back to him and saw he was staring down at a laptop on the table in the living room.

Sully was seated there, by the laptop, and his face was carved in granite.

He'd found something on the Internet.

Shades of Samantha Wheeler laying out Mom, Bowie, Dad and Uncle Corey on a gossip show blanketed my sunny day in dark.

"It's what he does, ignore it," Jamie, standing close, advised.

"I don't think you get it, Dad," Judge retorted.

"I do. I've been dealing with his shit for decades, Judge," Jamie shot back.

"Okay, but did you ever have to do that when you were falling in love with a woman whose famous parents have taken pains to publicly sort their shit that's no one's business and they don't need to be dragged into Granddad's utter, complete *bullshit*?" Judge returned. "The press turns an eye to us, they turn an eye to them and that can't happen."

The room had gone still with the "falling in love with a woman" comment so no one said anything when Judge paused to take a breath.

"So I'm going out to the goddamn Gulch and shutting his mouth myself," he went on to threaten.

"Judge, darling, we live our lives like this. It doesn't affect us," Mom said earnestly. "Please, do not think of us and listen to your dad."

Judge glanced at her then returned his attention to his father. "It's you he's dragging through the mud. It's just me that's getting splattered with it."

Oh God, I needed to see whatever was on that laptop.

"So much truth and lies have been reported about me, buddy, *I* can barely tell it apart anymore," Jamie replied. "I don't pay attention to it. It doesn't matter. It's out there now. It gets them clicks. And tomorrow, they'll be attempting to suck the blood from someone else."

"*I don't give a fuck about the reporters!*" Judge suddenly shouted.

Dad pulled me closer.

The room went wired.

"*He* is doing this to *us*. To *her*. They're gonna look into her. And they've gone to that house..." he carried on.

The house?

Oh *God*.

"And they're gonna know the kind of life she lived and they're gonna tell everyone about it, and he's spinning it to blame *you* for *her* being a fucking *junkie*."

"Judge, buddy—" Jamie started softly.

"I don't need the whole goddamn world talking *shit* about my mom. I grew up with that. I put it behind me. I do not need that *shit* again. And I won't have Chloe wading through it," Judge declared.

And with that, he turned on his boot and marched toward the door.

I started to pull from Dad, but he gently set me aside before he took long, ground-eating strides in order to step in front of the door.

Bowie came in on the other side, and they stood shoulder to shoulder, barring Judge's way.

Jamie followed him, Rix closed in at Jamie's side, and Matt, Gage and Sully positioned to flank.

"Respect. Get out of the way," Judge growled to the men barring the door.

"Look at me, Judge," Dad ordered.

Judge turned his gaze to Dad.

"Listen to me, yes? Can you cut through your anger, that is justified, but I need you to get through it for just five minutes and really listen to me?" Dad asked.

"Tom—" Judge started.

"Can you do that, Judge?"

Judge jerked up his chin.

"Good," Dad said quietly. And then, "If what you said a minute ago is true, there are two people in this room that matter. Listen to me, Judge," he said quickly when Judge's head started to turn, probably to find me since clearly he'd missed my entrance, regardless of how dramatic it was.

Judge refocused on him.

"Chloe. And you," Dad went on. "Now, you can go see that man and confront him and piss off someone who is notoriously unpredictable, nasty and vengeful, or you can do the only thing that will beat him at his game. You can act like his shit is the baseless nonsense that it actually is. The only one who doesn't know AJ Oakley is a joke is AJ Oakley. If you give time and attention to his bullshit, you negate that. You give him power. Don't give him power over you. And absolutely do not give him power over the woman you love."

Judge took a moment with that, I saw a muscle in his jaw bulge, and then he asked, "What about the memory of my mom? Do I give him power over that?"

That was when Bowie spoke. "I'm sorry, man, but your mom is gone. There is nothing that can have power over her now. It's hateful she's gone, and we all hurt for you, but that's the bottom-line truth."

Judge stared at Bowie after this honesty came from his mouth, and then I tensed, Dad tensed, Bowie tensed.

And Jamie had a view to his back, but he felt it and moved in as Judge turned and asked his father, "Why couldn't she love us?"

"Let's go," Dad whispered, and everyone moved.

Everyone but Jamie, Judge, Rix, Dru and me.

It was my turn to position at Judge's back.

And I didn't mess around getting there.

"Come here, buddy," Jamie encouraged.

Judge didn't take the last step to his dad.

He dropped his head.

The door closed on Gage.

I put my hand on my man's back but otherwise didn't move.

It hurt to stay away from him, but he had to get this out.

He had to process it.

He had to face it.

So he could truly let it go.

"I..." Judge stopped, that word so clogged, he had to clear his throat, and I felt pain in mine. He lifted his head and focused again on his dad. "I lied at the funeral home. She didn't want us together. She didn't love you. She didn't love me. She—"

Jamie cut him off. "Judge, she loved you."

"She didn't love me. Love is not that."

"No," Jamie said softly, coming closer, but not too close. "Love is not that. But when she found out she was pregnant with you—"

At these words, Judge stepped back and almost ran over me.

I scooted out of the way.

He didn't even glance at me.

"You've told me this story so many times, Dad, it isn't fucking funny," he stated bitterly. "She might have been excited she was pregnant. She might have been thrilled to have a healthy baby boy. I'm sure she nurtured me and took care of me when I was little. And then... that stopped. And it didn't stop because New York made her feel small. It didn't stop because you fucked up by taking her from Texas. It didn't stop because she did what countless other people have done, except for her it would have terrible consequences, she snorted her first line of coke. It stopped because she was just *not a good person.*"

Oh God.

My eyes darted to Rix, and I saw he was still mid-flinch.

He felt my gaze and looked at me, the uneasy in his eyes warming, but he said nothing and didn't move.

I didn't either.

"Addiction is not that simple to characterize," Jamie said carefully.

"You know," Judge said matter-of-factly, "when you told me she was dead, I blanked out. I couldn't speak. I couldn't move." He tossed a hand my way. "It freaked Chloe out. And I thought about that. I thought, 'I not only don't give a shit my mother's dead, I'm not surprised she is. I'm just surprised it took this long.' So I had to think on that, Dad. I had to think about why I blanked when I don't give… that first…*fuck* that she's gone."

No one said anything.

So Judge kept going.

"I figured it out. And you know why that is, Dad?"

"No, Judge, why is that, buddy?" Jamie asked.

"Because that was *it*."

Oh God.

Oh God.

Oh God.

I closed in him after the way his voice broke on the last word.

"Do you know what it's like to live for twenty-nine years *hoping your mother will give a shit about you?*"

At these rough words grating up his throat, I was done.

I moved into his back, put my cheek to it, pressed my body to it, and wrapped my arms around his middle.

It was like I wasn't there.

"Do you know what it's like to lie in bed with your woman pressed to you, your dog, both of them, even my *fucking dog*, Dad, showing me more love in the time I've had them than she has *my entire life?*"

I closed my eyes tight and held on tighter.

"You can't possibly know what it's like to have that moment where everything stops because any last hope you had that your mother would someday give that *first shit about you* is *gone*," he declared.

Then, he wrapped his fingers around my forearms so strong, it hinted at pain.

"Look at this," Judge demanded. "She can't even stand listening to this *fucking garbage* without doing everything she can to show me love. How hard is it, Dad? Just a movement and I'm surrounded with it."

I swallowed.

Judge kept speaking.

"You'd call and she'd shout at you for an hour and wouldn't let me talk to you and it was like she *got off* on the fact she could hang up on you and you'd call again and again and again, and she'd scream at me not to answer. And I'd sit there and listen to you calling and that's what I thought love was, the sound of a phone ringing, because in that house *that's the only love I felt.*"

I heard Jamie make a low, pained, ugly noise that hurt me almost more than what Judge was saying.

But I just held on.

"She was so fucking beautiful, and I'd look at her and I'd swear to myself never, *never* to be with a beautiful, weak, empty shell of woman. And that's what it was. It wasn't addiction. It was that she was empty."

He was right.

His mother was empty.

My mother had known him mere months, and she flew our entire family to Dallas, the boys leaving school, planning things that would take Judge's mind off his loss.

And *his* mother had given him nothing.

But this pain.

Judge kept going.

"You told me she was something in high school. But she lived her glory days then, being pretty and dating the local rich man's tall, handsome, ambitious son and that was all there was to her. And she knew it. She never reached for more, worked for more, hoped for more, dreamed about more, wanted more. And because she knew it, because she knew there was nothing to her, she couldn't hack it. She had to bury it, live in an alternate reality where she couldn't think or feel. Or make up devils she had to fight who did her wrong. She knew you were destined for greatness, and she couldn't just know this about herself, and simply stand at your side, love you, support you, make a family with you and take care of that family, all of which is something beautiful. Something real. But in the end, it's *something*. Instead, she hated you for being what she fell in love with in the first place. And she hated you because you reminded her that her peak was senior year and then her life was over."

He took a huge breath and finished it.

"And I didn't factor at all."

It took Jamie a second, but he finally said, "I wish I could argue, say you're wrong, but my greatest fear has always been that you're right. Everything you just said is right."

"You know what her greatest fear was, Dad?"

"What was it, Judge?"

"That I'd spend time with you, and I'd know it too. The same with Granddad. They worked in tandem to keep me from you because they knew, if I spent time with you, I'd know *exactly* what those two wastes of flesh were. And my reason for being would be getting to you. She tried to turn me against you. She'd lie about you. And Granddad is not dumb. He saw early what I was like, and what I liked. He'd come and get me and take me out on a horse and tell me it all was going to be mine, and how I should thank my lucky stars I wasn't growing up choked by concrete and steel."

Jamie made no reply, but the room was seething with emotion, heavy and dark, and Judge sharing that didn't alleviate any of it.

"So Tom is right. And Duncan is right," Judge continued. "He's a piece of shit, a joke, playing games, striking out when he has to know on some level we are both dealing with some serious fucked-up shit. Talking trash, when anyone who'd listen to him isn't worth knowing, and everyone else gets that he's an old man desperate to stay relevant."

He paused, and I was behind him, but I could still hear the ragged breath he pulled in.

And then he finished.

"As for Mom, she's dead, and she didn't care about much when she was alive, including me, so why should I give a fuck anyone knows that?"

When he was done, no one said anything, and no one moved.

It was Dru who broke the tense, heartbreaking silence.

"I don't know if it's the right thing to say, if it'll help. But you should know that my mom thought the world of you, Judge. She loved you. She loved you loads."

I turned my head and pressed my forehead in Judge's back as I felt the tremor go through his body at hearing those words.

"It means everything, doll," he said hoarsely.

And then I was sharing a Hug Judge Moment as I felt Dru's hands clasping my waist because she was hugging him from the front.

Yes, it was official.

I loved that girl.

"See, Dad? A movement and I'm surrounded by love," Judge groaned.

And that was when I was forced to shift around his body, gently press Dru away and go down to the floor with my man as he folded.

He ended on his ass, cross legged. I ended in his lap with his face pressed into the side of my neck, holding him around his head and shoulders and rocking him as his anger and sadness wet my skin.

"It's fucked up to cry for her," he grumbled against my flesh.

"No, it isn't, honey. It's perfectly natural," I cooed.

"She didn't earn this."

"What's coming out right now is not for what you lost, but what you never had."

"Fuck," he grunted, and I took this to mean he was overwhelmed by my wisdom.

Therefore, it was a moral imperative to remind him, "As you know, I'm always right."

This time, Judge did a laugh-cry, pulling away from my neck and looking at me.

He then blinked.

"Jesus, what happened to your face?" he asked.

Oh no!

Did one of my eyelashes come askew, holding on to him?

I lifted a hand to check, but before I could assess, he asked, "How the fuck do you find new ways to be even more gorgeous?"

God, I so very, very, *very* much *loved this man.*

I dropped my hand to his shoulder and whispered, "Magic."

"Then I love a witch," he whispered back.

Yes.

Yes.

He loved me.

"And I love a miracle," I returned.

"Babe—"

I knew my magnificent, humble boyfriend was going to refute that.

So I didn't let him even start.

"You became you. In your circumstances, that's almost impossible. But you did. You're my miracle, Judge. And I'm so glad you are, because you hold my heart in your hands, and there's no man on this planet who has what I need to take care of it, except you."

His beautiful brown eyes framed by their now spiky-with-wet lashes heated and then we were kissing.

"Right, brother, that was all super awesome, but a surprise porn ending is not the way to go when your sister is in the room," Rix called.

And Judge and I broke the kiss with neither of us laugh-crying.

We were both just laughing.

Keeping hold on me so I went with him, Judge took his feet.

We were barely up when Jamie requested quietly, "Just very quickly, Chloe."

I took in the expression on his face and stepped aside.

Father and son hugged.

It wasn't very quickly.

It lasted a long, long time.

And at the start of it, I heard Jamie say low to his son.

"That phone ringing *was* love, Judge."

And then I saw my man's shoulders heave.

Within seconds, Rix's arm landed along my shoulders, and he used it to tuck me to his side. I tore my gaze away long enough to see he had his other one slung around Dru.

And three people who loved Judge Morgan Oakley watched as the original one held him close to his heart.

Magic.

And miracles.

CHAPTER 29

THE GOSSIP

Elsa Cohen

The Elsa Exchange
Celebrity News and Interviews
YouTube Channel

hursday...

"TO END MY SHOW, ALL MY WONDERFUL WATCHERS, WE *MUST* SPEND some time chatting about all that's happening in Texas. Woefully, we have to start with what a truly impossible endeavor it is to wrap my head around the sad fact that the woman who was once the talk of New York, in good ways, then *very bad*, died too soon from a reported lethal cocktail of drugs and booze."

Photo on screen of a young, vibrant, stunning Belinda Oakley wearing a vintage Halston swathe-front, sleeveless, satin gown walking on the arm of the young, dark, dashing Jameson Oakley. He's in profile, looking to the side, smiling a dazzling white smile that crinkles the corners of his extraordinary blue eyes. She's face front, ice-blue eyes and carved cheekbones aimed to the camera, looking cool and chic and butter-would-not-melt.

Cut back to Elsa.

"The glorious Belinda Oakley lost her way long ago, she also lost her man, but one thing you could say for the woman, she kept hold of her son. But now, my wonderful watchers, many are asking, was that a good thing?"

Photo on screen of Jameson Oakley and his ridiculously handsome son, Judge, walking shoulder-to-shoulder into a posh Dallas eatery the night before Belinda Oakley's memorial service. They look subdued, but tanned and healthy, with Jameson's head again turned, this time to speak in his son's ear. Judge's head is tilted toward his father and slightly downcast as he walks and listens with visible intent to whatever his father is saying.

Cut back to Elsa.

"Much is being said about the former Mrs. Oakley after her former father-in-law let a few things slip, as he has an alarming tendency to do. At first, even I was shocked at news that Jameson allowed his first wife to wallow in such dire circumstances. This from a man who became known for his utter devotion to his second wife, Rosalind, a woman he heartbreakingly lost not too long ago after she succumbed to her battle with breast cancer. I'll refrain from sharing the photos that have been circulating that depict where Belinda was found by a dear friend, dead on her couch. Photos we have reason to believe agents of the senior Mr. Oakley took themselves, and then in a shady move that's signature to said senior Oakley, they released."

Photo on screen of AJ Oakley, cowboy hat on his head, mouth wide open, buxom, blonde woman five inches taller and sixty-plus years younger standing, looking bored, at his side.

Cut back to Elsa.

"However, barely an hour after AJ planted this morsel in our ever-hungry ears, news started spreading about the senior Oakley's dastardly deeds. And we're not talking about the most recent ones, my watchers. We're talking about how he contrived with Belinda to cut Jameson's visitation of their son to cruelly meagre levels, financing her never-ending battles against her ex-husband, keeping a boy from his father. About how he bribed officers of the court to look away from Belinda's troubling downward spiral into drug, alcohol and even sex addiction, and how this detrimentally affected his grandson. Friends of Judge Oakley's are coming forward and telling it like it was, my wonderful watchers. And it was grim. Tales of a mother who lost her way and a grandfather who enabled it, barring a young man from the functional upbringing every child should be entitled to."

Photo on screen of Jameson Oakley, his striking, flame-haired wife, her cute-as-a-button adolescent daughter somewhat hidden from view, and a tall, straight, teenage Judge emerging from the Lincoln Center after a performance of the New York Philharmonic.

Cut to photo of a haggard Belinda Oakley emerging from a liquor store with a very full brown paper bag cradled lovingly in her too-thin arm.

Cut back to Elsa.

"I'm afraid to say, it's not surprising the devious senior Oakley connived in such a fashion. Though the fresh horror of him putting on one of his, let's face it, what's becoming tired and boring shows for reporters, is just..." delicate sniff, "*not on.* Doing this while his grandson grieves, and his son comes to terms with the mother of his only blood child no longer being of this world? Bad form, Mr. Oakley. Bad form. And just a note, sir, from one who watches, it's not good when it gets boring. But this? Well, this is just desperate and sad, and no one is interested in that."

Photo on screen of Tom Pierce in an attractive blue and black tennis outfit and Duncan Holloway in navy performance joggers and white short-sleeved compression shirt, sitting together on a bench, courtside at an elite Dallas athletics club. Both men have their dark heads thrown back and the camera has caught them laughing.

Cut back to Elsa.

"But what have we here? With the things I see and the tidbits that pass my way, I will admit to some...*doubt* as to the assertions that all is well in the Pierce-Swan-Holloway world. Really, *no one* is *that* adjusted. But could it be? Is it indeed all friends and family?"

Photo on screen of Imogen Swan in a form-fitting Alice+Olivia bateau-neck, black midi-dress standing with Tom Pierce wearing Tom Ford and

Duncan Holloway wearing Emporio Armani outside a funeral home in Lucas, Texas. The three are huddled close, talking, with Duncan having his hand on the small of Imogen's back, and both Imogen and Duncan seeming riveted at whatever Tom is saying.

Cut back to Elsa.

"It would appear it is. We should have never doubted America's Sweetheart. Lesson learned, my wonderful watchers. But let us talk about the next generation."

Photo on screen of Sasha Pierce, Matthew Pierce, Sullivan Holloway, Gage Holloway and Drusilla Lynch, all in funeral black, walking, heads bent, faces grave, into that same funeral parlor. Sasha Pierce is between her brother, Matthew, and Gage Holloway, a hand on both their arms. Sullivan Holloway has Drusilla Lynch's hand in his, and his body is positioned as such, it looks as if he's attempting to protect her from the camera's lens.

Cut back to Elsa.

"Is this not a collection of the best and brightest *and most beautiful?* Don't answer that. It is. I, for one, wonderful watchers, would *just love* to see Tom Pierce settled and happy with a new love in his life. But my breath is absolutely *bated* with what might come for this confoundingly exquisite quintet. And no, I haven't forgotten."

Photo on screen of Judge Oakley and Chloe Pierce, Judge wearing a black suit, gray shirt, black tie. Chloe wearing a black knit Alexander McQueen with a plunging twisted neckline, sleeves that hug her arms down to her knuckles, hem below the knees. This accompanied by a slender, black leather, double-wrap belt with silver rivets and McQueen's punk spike stud pumps. They're holding hands, walking closely into the aforementioned funeral parlor. Judge is facing straight ahead. Chloe's eyes are cast down.

"This gorgeous pair. What? Rumor has it love is in the air and the powerhouse Pierce-Swan-Holloways are looking at a merger with the power magnate Oakleys. It is, reportedly, a match made in heaven, and not only because these...two...are...*glorious.* But also, Judge Oakley has a heart of gold and spends his days getting urban kids out into nature, overseeing Duncan Holloway's Kids and Trails program. But Chloe herself runs a lowkey program out of her *delicious* boutique in Phoenix, Velvet. FFF, or Fabulous Foot Forward, where Chloe

Pierce, who had every leg up imaginable in her life, gives the same to other women who were not as lucky. Whoops! Let's hope Chloe doesn't mind that this program of hers will be lowkey no more. But *someone* needs to shout it from the rooftops, and that, my wonderful watchers, as you know, is always me. Please, see below for your link on how to donate to this fantastic cause."

Cut to Fabulous Foot Forward graphic of a file of five line-drawn women wearing varying stylish business attire, striding forward with linked arms. Features and coloration depict women that are Black, Brown, Asian, Native American and white.

Cut back to Elsa.

"It really is all no surprise, Tom and Imogen are both known for their charitable endeavors, Duncan far from shies away from the same. Not to mention, this is shades of Chloe's *de facto* brother, Hale Wheeler, whose blood runs half Szabo."

Photo on screen of Hale Wheeler in aviators and slim fit Prada suit folding into a limousine.

Cut back to Elsa.

"He's got more money than God, since his father laid his empire on his shoulders, but the Extraordinary Mr. Wheeler still spends most of his time and efforts with wayward kids out in the wilderness. And word is being whispered that Hale is preparing to take a very good deal of that money his father made and do something most interesting with it. I mean, could this entire family be *more perfect?*"

Close in on Elsa.

"Well, my wonderful watchers, *no one* is that perfect. So we'll just wait and see. And as ever, be watching *very, very closely.* Until our next exchange, keep it positive. And for now, Elsa is signing off."

The branded Elsa wink and blowing of kiss.

Sign off.

Chloe

Saturday afternoon...back in Phoenix...

"What's this?"

I was all about rubbing down Zeke, who had greetings and love to give after I arrived home from spending the day at Velvet, and he spent the day with his daddy and without me.

But at Judge's question, I turned to him.

And I saw him at the island, holding an envelope.

My brows drew together, I straightened and moved to him. "I don't know. What is it?"

"It was sitting here." He gestured to the island. "And it wasn't there when I left to pick you up."

I made it to him and saw on the front of the envelope, handwritten in black, it only said, "C."

Oh my.

I held out a hand. "Can I see?"

Judge gave it to me.

Upon touching it, I noted the cardstock was thick and expensive.

I turned it over, slid a nail under the flap and slit it open.

I pulled out the notecard inside.

A familiar one.

An embossed edge, the paper creamy, like the envelope.

But that was it.

Except the words scrawled on it.

I have more. Say the word. -R

"Jesus Christ," Judge bit out, looking over my shoulder at the card.

I was confused and turned my gaze up to him. "What?"

"It's from that Rhys guy. He broke into your house and left it."

Of course he did.

Though, I doubt he "broke in." He probably just activated a special mechanism some mad genius made him so he could apparate and walked through one of the walls.

"I know. But what does he mean—?"

I stopped myself and then made an entirely unattractive noise as I swallowed a delighted giggle.

"Yeah, that mystery is solved," Judge groused. "*He's* the one who laid Granddad out."

Back in Texas, that fateful afternoon, once things started turning in the media, this being before we even left the hotel to go out to dinner that Tuesday night, we'd all wondered.

I thought it might be Jameson's spin doctors, but he assured us it wasn't him.

I then thought Mom's PR people might have stepped in, because she'd be launching a new series money was being poured into this fall and they'd want to nip any bad press that might cling to her in the bud.

But that couldn't be possible, because what was leaked was too intimate, too deep. Given a few weeks (or even a few days), maybe.

Within hours of AJ's nefarious deeds?

Impossible.

(She'd called to check regardless, and they'd shared it was not them.)

It was a mystery we'd all chewed over since.

I should have thought of Rhys Vaughan from the start.

And now I was curious as to what "more" he had on AJ.

I stared up at Judge, then asked an unnecessary question, "Are you angry?"

I watched, again fighting a giggle, as Judge's eyes went wide.

Then he spoke.

"First, he broke into your house. Second, he investigated my grandfather. Which means, third, he *is* keeping tabs on you, and as an extension of you, me."

"Because I love you."

Judge shut his mouth.

I tossed the card on the island, turned to him, and scooped him in my arms.

He dropped one of his own around my shoulders, the hand at the end of the other one, he sifted into my hair.

"As good as this feels, this does not make me any happier about this dude out there doing random shit for you," Judge remarked. "I can't believe I have to say this to you, but it's creepy as fuck."

"Let me explain the love of Corey Szabo," I said quietly.

Judge had looked annoyed, not at me.

He now looked intent, definitely at me.

"AJ was hurting you. I was hurting for you. Enter Uncle Corey," I said softly.

"Babe—"

I shook him with my arms. "That's the way he works. That's the way he always worked. In the background, seeing to things. And frankly, I am not sorry that happened. Furthermore, I will admit right now that I'm not only happy it did, I'm gleeful it did. I'll even go so far as to share I feel strongly it needed to happen. Your grandfather was a bastion of the old days, who some looked at with nostalgia, others just found him amusing. Now, he seems like a mean old man who had a hand in abusing his grandson, doing this for no reason but to take pieces out of the son he was pathologically jealous of. Now, most everyone thinks he is what he is. A complete asshole, one of the last of a dying breed we'll all be glad to see gone. And I think that's the perfect comeuppance for someone as arrogant and destructive as your granddad. Or at least it's half of it. Deservedly, your dad will deliver the other half."

"And maybe you'll also admit to it meaning something to you, that even though your uncle is gone, he's also not. He's still looking out for you."

"I will freely admit that," I replied blithely.

Judge's eyes warmed.

And I knew with the way they did that he was giving in on the topic of Rhys Vaughan.

At least on this.

He then murmured, "You're ruthless," but it wasn't an admonition.

Not at all.

"I am a beast made by the hands of Corey Szabo. So when it comes to the ones I love…absolutely."

Judge gave me a look.

Then he gave me a kiss.

It was much later when I would find my phone and the business card Rhys Vaughan left me.

First, I programmed him into my phone.

And then I sent a text.

Thank you. I think that did it. But we may talk later. Best, C

I was not expecting him to, but even so…

Rhys did not reply.

CHAPTER 30

THE UNDERSTANDING

Corey

*T*wenty-four years ago...

His ass covered in linen trousers, the hems rolled up, the loose-fitting linen shirt billowing against his chest, Corey sat in the sand, his head turned to look down the beach.

Marilyn was wearing a black, one-piece swimsuit with a plunging neckline. It showed cleavage. It was cut high on her thighs.

She was in her fifties and her figure was fabulous.

She was also dancing with the sea, racing the waves up the sand as they arrived, chasing after them in their retreat.

And in her arms was a baby.

Head covered in a little, white, baby sun hat with a wide brim and laces at the sides that tied under her chin. Her body was covered in a tiny red bathing suit with white polka dots and a tufted white skirt made of tulle.

Coming in with the breeze, Corey could hear Marilyn's peals of laughter accompanied by abandoned squeals from the child.

Grandmother and grandbaby were consumed with the sun and the sand and their dance with the waves.

And each other.

Eventually, as was always Marilyn's way, her dance brought her to Corey.

She blocked out the bright rays as she stood above him, half her body coated with droplets of water.

Baby Chloe clung to her neck, but like her grandmother, she gazed down at Corey.

Although she often smiled and giggled, she could be a solemn child. Watchful. Assessing.

Corey didn't know many babies, but he knew ones like that were few and far between.

He didn't want to, but he found her utterly fascinating.

"We don't need a bodyguard, honey lumpkin," Marilyn said to him.

"You are holding Imogen Swan and Tom Pierce's firstborn in your arms and there is not a man out here with you, strapped with a gun and trained to protect," he retorted.

Marilyn threw her head back and sang with laughter.

This time, Chloe did not do it with her.

She watched her grandmother for a spell, then she cast her gaze down to her Uncle Corey.

She reached both her chubby arms his way.

Corey grew tense.

Marilyn stopped laughing.

"We're fine," she assured.

"You are, because I'm out here making sure you stay that way," he returned.

She clicked her teeth and shook her head.

And then she whispered, "You were always such a good boy."

He was not.

He didn't inform her of that, and regardless, he'd lost her attention.

She'd looked to her granddaughter, who was now straining Corey's way.

Don't, don't, don't.

Don't do it.

"Do you want your Uncle Corey, my gorgeous girl?" Marilyn asked Chloe.

Chloe didn't even look at her.

She emitted a little baby grunt and pushed further Corey's way.

"As long as I have breath in my body, you will have what you want," Marilyn decreed.

And then she dumped Chloe into Corey's lap.

"And I suspect your uncle feels the same way," she finished.

With nothing further, Marilyn turned in the sand and ran gracefully into the surf, eventually diving over a wave and disappearing under it, to emerge much further out with hair flat to her head and face pointed to the sky.

It was the first time Corey had been left alone with Genny's baby girl.

Chloe banged on his chest.

He looked to the little girl whose blue eyes were shading brown.

She studied him, and it was uncanny, the girl couldn't even speak her first words, but he felt...

Seen.

She then wobbled and fell forward against his chest, her sun hat brushing his throat, her arms splayed to his sides.

And Corey did not know how he knew, but he knew.

His little girl was tired.

It was fun being with Grandma.

But it could wipe you out.

"I know, honey," he murmured, sliding an arm around her, holding her diapered bottom secure with his other hand.

Since he'd stationed himself out there, that moment was the first he felt the sun penetrating the linen of his shirt and pants, the warmth of the rays welcome as the sea threw its breeze.

He also felt her weight against him.

It was very heavy, even if she was light.

She fit there, tucked to him, having reached to him because she watched, she assessed, and even in her little baby brain she knew, above all, he would give her what she needed.

Corey remained in a Z shape, back up, knees up, cocooning her and holding her close, checking her skin for that first hint of pink that would declare the sunscreen her grandmother slathered on her before they came out wasn't doing its job.

And then he felt her little baby sigh as she settled in to knowing it was the sun and the sea and the breeze and her Uncle Corey, she was safe, and all was right in the world.

As he knew it would happen if she was tossed in his lap, with that sigh, Corey's worst fears came true.

He had known love and some of it was harmful, some of it he'd used to cause harm, some of it he'd thrown away before he realized how precious it was, some of it he'd thrown away even knowing that.

This was something else.

The realization of his love for this small being.

And as Marilyn frolicked in the surf, Corey Szabo bent his head so his lips were to a white baby sun hat on a little baby girl who, based on sheer instinct, loved her Uncle Corey, trusted him, and in his arms, she fell asleep.

And there, his voice raw with feeling, he whispered his vow.

"You will want for nothing. No one will harm you. You will find great love. I will see to it, my beautiful Chloe. I will see to all of that. You will be happy. And you will be safe. I will see to that too. When there is breath in my body, but even when I'm no longer here, I'll look after you. I'll do it forever, Chloe. Forever and ever. Don't you worry about a thing. Your Uncle Corey's got you."

Chloe Marilyn Pierce slept against her uncle's chest, not a care in the world.

And Corey sat in the sand and waited for Marilyn to come in. When she did, with great care he took his feet. He then stood and waited for Marilyn to towel off and put on her coverup.

And with one of his hands in the hand of the only woman in his life who would ever love him purely and completely, and his arm wrapped around the only girl in his life who would love him for who he truly was, Corey walked his girls up to Genny and Tom's house.

Experiencing the only moment he would have in his life when he felt completely at ease.

Completely content.

And wholly loved.

EPILOGUE

THE PICTURE

Judge

ine weeks after the funeral...a Tuesday...

ALEX'S HEAD POPPED IN THE DOOR TO HIS OFFICE JUST AS HIS PHONE rang.

He glanced at the cell first, seeing it was Chloe calling.

That was weird, because his woman texted, it was rare she called.

He turned his attention to Alex to tell her to hang on a second, but he saw she was practically coming out of her skin with excitement.

That was not Alex. She had reactions. She had emotions. She showed them. But it was never too overt.

"Judge—" she started.

For him, the decision was a no brainer.

"Two seconds," he told her. "Chloe is calling."

She was almost hopping foot to foot.

But she nodded and moved away from the door.

He picked up the call.

"Hey, baby, everything okay?"

"Okay, well, I did something," she announced.

Shit, fuck.

With Chloe, that could mean anything.

From her presenting him with three suits and accompanying shirts (and fucking ties, not to mention shoes) that he'd find out later she'd spent twelve thousand dollars on (and that was just the suits) because, "You *are* an Oakley and you're hanging with the Pierce-Swans and it's not like you don't already have several pairs of trousers and sports jackets. And if I can't spend my trust fund on you, who am I going to spend it on? And youhavetheperfectbody so pleaseletmedressyou."

It was that last bit that he gave in on.

Though, it had to be said, he'd eventually give in anyway, it was just that he would have given her far more shit about it first.

And then there was Judge coming home on a Thursday evening and finding his deck having two low planters filled with flowers in the outer corners and two potted evergreens by the backdoor with two more flower-filled planters flanking his front door. Plants *he* had to water because he was there more than she was.

This because, "You have three highly attractive women that live in your development. They check you out when you're on your deck, and nothing says, 'A woman lives here!' like planters filled with flowers. And I know, a woman doesn't live here. But these flowers stand in my stead to tell those women to back off when I'm not around."

He'd explained that if the unlikely happened, and one of those women made their move, *he* could tell them he was taken.

To which she'd replied, "Let's let the planters do your talking for you, shall we?"

He didn't argue further. It was cute, her staking her claim. And she took Thursday duty with watering and deadheading the flowers.

And then there was the time she floated the idea of, "What do you think about me contacting Rhys and asking him to look into a few lovely ladies the mom of a friend of mine in New York says are attractive, nice and unattached."

To that he'd said a firm, "*No.*"

And to his surprise, even if she gave him a squinty look, she hadn't pushed it.

Though he had no doubt she was biding her time.

As far as he knew, she had yet to unleash "Rhys."

But that was only as far as he knew.

And he was afraid to ask.

So with Chloe being Chloe, and this mysterious Rhys guy in the mix, "doing something" could mean just about anything.

"I don't need another suit," he told her. "Seeing as I haven't worn any of the ones you've already given me."

"I got a dog," she blurted.

He was silent.

"Okay, listen, I know this is probably something we should discuss," she said quickly.

She was right, they should.

But—

"And I want you to know, I get that. But Montana is, well, Judge, honey, *she has a mohawk.*"

"What?"

"She's part pittie and part Rhodesian ridgeback and she is *so* sweet. There's a terrible situation with her current family where they've learned the baby they're about to have is going to be significantly special needs. They're understandably freaked out about that, they need to focus on it and how that will change their lives, and sadly, they're worried Montana will suffer along the way. Now, they're being picky because they want to be certain their girl has a good home. Mi told them about me, and I went to go see her today and they liked me, and I left with her and, Judge...you're just going to fall in love with her. I promise. I *swear.*"

"Chlo—"

"And it was awful, everyone was crying, even me."

She insisted she wasn't a crier, but it was his experience his woman cried all the time.

"Hon—"

"And she misses her mommy and daddy already, I can tell. We had the difficult discussion, but we think it needs to be a surgical cut. As awful as it is, and as much as they want to visit her, we all agreed that it would be confusing for her. So we're going to have to be extra sweet to her for a while."

He had visions of her talking on the phone while cooking a skillet of bacon at the same time.

And maybe frying up a filet mignon.

"So she'll know who her new mummy and daddy are and that we're going to take the best of care of her," she continued. "Do you think Zeke will be okay with her?"

"Zeke loves everything."

"Well then! See!" she cried.

God, she sounded like a little girl, all scared and excited.

It was fucking adorable.

"Chlo—"

"I promise to do research about introducing new dogs to a family and—"

"Coco, baby, shut up so I can talk."

Silence.

"I don't care," he said.

And he stopped talking.

"That's it, you don't care?"

"That's it. You want her, we'll figure it out. We'll give her love. It's all good." It was then her story about adopting a dog and three cats hit him, and he added, "Just, now, promise me, no more unless we discuss it. Two is one thing, if Montana will be good with Zeke, Zeke'll be good with her. We got enough love to go around. But we both do a lot of traveling back and forth and we need to consider who's staying with who, if they eventually should be separated at all, and what it's doing to them, all the moving around."

"In other words, don't get a cat...yet."

He grinned at the "yet."

"Babe," was all he said.

"We need to talk about moving in together."

Judge went still.

"Zeke loves the car. Dogs love cars. But humans, all this moving around, it's not fun," she declared.

Leave it to Chloe to throw it right out there.

He was outrageously thrilled.

Even so.

"Let's talk about that when you come up tomorrow."

"I'm moving up there."

Judge went rock solid.

"I can come down for the day once or twice a week, but Mi doesn't need me. And with recent events, we've needed to hire another full-timer anyway."

She had.

The double whammy of Elsa Cohen, with her seventeen million followers (not to mention the public's sudden highly increased fascination with all things Pierce-Swan-Holloway-Oakley) sent people in droves to Velvet and Fabulous Foot Forward's donations to stratospheric levels. And unbeknownst to Chloe, she'd impressed a patron who had significant social standing and a shit ton of friends, all of whom, after Chloe plied them with champagne and helped style them, were now regulars.

This meant, in the last two months, Velvet moved from solid, sustained, but moderate growth to being the It Store in Phoenix, quadrupling her gross, and doing triple that in online sales.

And with that, including Chloe launching a new marketing scheme where she styled actual clients, promoting that on social media, she'd formed an alliance with big-time stylist to the stars, Wyn Gastineau, who was also stationed in Phoenix.

Specifically, she was working with Wyn for clients who were beyond the celebrity sizes of -0 to 4. And this came with she and Wyn talking about curating an offshoot of Wyn's popular subscription boxes for people over size 14.

Judge was experiencing much the same with Kids and Trails, because the Elsa Cohen mention was followed up with the social media rollout of Duncan and Tom's outreach and fundraising appeal. The success of that campaign far exceeded their expectations. It was massively popular. And this included several other tennis stars, golfers, football and basketball players who got in touch and wanted to get involved.

Shit was real for his small staff that included him doing everything but volunteer coordination.

Which meant it was time for them to grow, one way or another, and Judge knew exactly which way he wanted to take that. It was just finding the time in all the extra work to write a proposal and present it to Duncan.

"And it's time to expand," she continued, speaking his thoughts out loud, but on another subject. "My market research would not scream that there needs to be a Velvet in Prescott, but there's a lot of money up there. There are art dealerships and jewelry stores on the square that sell pieces of quality at a certain price point. So I think a small shop with perhaps a slightly more casual bent to the stock would fly and it doesn't have to be another Velvet. It can be something all new. But as I ponder that, and look for space, I need to concentrate on how to expand Triple F. I have so many stores and brands offering in-kind gifts, makeup artists and hair stylists wanting to sign up, I need to buckle down and organize that, or I'll lose the momentum. And I can do all of that from your living room."

When Judge remained speechless, he was so damned happy this was where her mind was going, she kept talking.

"And I rent, you own. My lease isn't up for another couple of months, so we have time to plan the move. Obviously, it'll be difficult to leave Dad, but he seems to be handling things okay, and he won't be too far away. He's up there a lot, anyway. And, well, we talked about this, and it's unusual that it seems his new best friend is Bowie, but that's just how it's shaking out. I mean, it's really no surprise they like each other. They're both exceptionally likeable. I still want to talk about maybe discussing things with Rhys—"

"Baby, you do not have to talk me into you moving in with me. I'd go down there tonight with a Mack truck to load up all your clothes and shoes. But let's take a few weeks to discuss furniture and logistics and let the new member of our family get used to us, make a plan and then get you up here."

"Really?" she whispered.

Shit.

"All right, I need to throw this out there," he began. "But even if things are off the hook with Trails, I was going to offer to move down there. I don't have to do this work here. I don't need to be at corporate. I can do it anywhere. So we have to have that discussion too. I love you'd consider coming up here, but it makes far more sense for me to come down there."

Now, Chloe was speechless.

But he'd been thinking about it. He was ready. He was prepared. His program could now afford to rent a small space and add additional staff. And it made sense. When the hikes were on, they traveled a lot, and the airport was in Phoenix.

He just wouldn't like it.

That said, it wasn't an urban jungle. Phoenix sprawled, but there was Papago, Camelback Mountain, Piestewa Peak—

"I can't allow that."

"Sorry?"

"I love that you'd offer, I love you, but Judge, you'd hate it here."

"I'd cope. It's not like—"

"Judge, no. I won't have it."

Judge bent and rested his weight in his hand on his desk, such was the emotion burning through him.

He'd forgotten.

Forgotten who he was talking to.

Forgotten how she was with the people she loved.

He wasn't used to it.

Not yet.

Maybe he never would be.

Maybe that was why Chloe was thrown in his path.

To give him an overabundance of all that he'd lacked all his life.

To give him someone he could give his love to.

Someone who gave that in return.

"Do you think I can abide it if you're just *coping?*" she asked.

"It makes more sense, baby."

"It makes no sense at all, darling."

"You're a city girl, Chloe."

"I'm *your* girl, Judge."

Christ.

Christ.

"We could move to a deserted island, and on the condition I'd be able to have new bikinis air dropped to me on a frequent basis, I'd be fine, as long as you were with me," she declared.

"There might be snakes on deserted islands, Coco," he teased.

"Well, you'll have a machete...or something."

He started chuckling.

Through it, he warned her, "You're taking care of those damned planters."

"Whatever. Zeke and Montana can frolic in the water from the hose as I do that. And Burberry makes wellies. I'll need an entirely new mountain girl section of my wardrobe. It'll be *fabulous.*"

"I love you so fucking much," he whispered.

"And I you," she whispered back.

They sat with that a second.

Then he quipped, "At least, one way or another, I'll finally get my coat back."

And her soft laugh struck him, straight through the heart.

She didn't comment on that, instead, she said, "Now, I need to go spend time with Montana. She's getting antsy. I can't wait for you to meet her, but remember, she did not come from a bad place. So we're going to need extra loving care to give her."

Then it was good Chloe Pierce came into her life.

She was going to be just fine.

"I'm warned. I'll talk to Zeke tonight. We'll make her welcome."

"All right, letting you go. Love you, Judge Oakley."

"Love you too, Cocoroco."

He heard her soft chuckle before she disconnected.

He took a minute with all that just went down before he looked to his door.

Alex was still gone.

He'd go find her in a second.

For now, he engaged his texts, typed one in, and sent it to his dad.

Chloe is moving to Prescott. Moving in with me.

That went off and he sent another one.

And our family is growing, she adopted a dog today.

Since Texas, he'd made a concerted effort. At first it felt strange, but he did it.

His father was so receptive to it, it felt strange for about a week.

Now it was just the way it was.

Judge started around his desk to go find out what had made Alex so excited, when an indication of why that concerted effort didn't feel strange for long chimed on his phone.

Jameson Oakley was a busy guy.

But Judge wasn't sure he'd ever had to wait but a few minutes for his father to respond.

He looked down and read from his dad, *Excellent news. I'm happy for you both. Make plans in a few months to fly out and take you both to a celebratory dinner?*

With zero hesitation, Judge replied, *Absolutely.*

He then resumed on his way to find Alex but ran into Rix at the door.

He was in his chair.

When he'd talked to her about it, Chloe had an explanation for this.

"Maybe there's a difference between being on his legs for a bit and being on them for nine hours."

That made sense.

She'd added, "But I think you should ask him, *chéri*. Maybe it's personal. Though, maybe he needs someone to be interested. Someone to talk to about it. You can broach it in a way he has an out if he doesn't want to discuss it. But I imagine he has times where he feels very alone, without anyone around who's been through what he's been through. You can't understand what he's experienced. But it's never a bad thing to care."

She'd been right, and he'd been procrastinating about bringing it up with his friend.

Judge was interested. He did care. He wanted Rix to know he was there to talk if he needed it.

But he didn't want to inadvertently cause pain, say the wrong thing, or trip something in Rix when it seemed Rix had it going on.

He needed to find that time.

And as he greeted his friend, he resolved to do that.

"Yo," he said.

"Yo," Rix replied. "You're not in on this thing?"

"What thing?" Judge asked.

"I don't know what thing. I just got a call from Duncan to get my ass up here to talk about the program."

Rix managed the store. He volunteered for the program, and he pitched in when things got overwhelming for Judge and Alex, and recently, he'd been doing a lot of volunteer overtime work because things were overwhelming.

But it was weird he'd be called by Duncan to talk about Kids and Trails.

He nodded to his friend and said, "Alex came in earlier and she seemed hyped up about something. Maybe she knows."

Rix's face shut down when Judge mentioned Alex, and since Chloe put that sitch in his face, he'd noticed that Rix didn't say anything, or do anything, and often ignored it, but if you were watching, it was not hard to read that the man actively disliked her.

As they moved to Alex's cubicle, the reason why was apparent.

This being that she was headed out of her cubbie, to come back to Judge's office no doubt, but she skidded to a halt almost comically when she saw Rix, and her face filled with panic.

Judge instantly looked down at Rix and saw a muscle dance up his jaw.

Rix thought she was uncomfortable around him because he didn't have full legs.

How a man who scored the way he did with the ladies didn't see a woman who had a massive crush on him, Judge didn't know.

He resolved to talk to Rix about that later too.

"Hey, Alex, what's going on?" Judge called.

Her face had gone the shade of red of one of Judge's favorite pairs of Chloe's shoes.

Now, seriously.

How could Rix not see this?

She dragged her gaze with visible effort from Rix, and when she saw Judge, she was reminded of her earlier excitement.

It was then her eyes lit and the pink in her cheeks became about something else and Judge, after working with her for a year and a half, suddenly saw a woman he'd never met before.

He'd never looked at her in that way. She was his co-worker, and he was her superior.

But damn, she was pretty.

"Tom Pierce is here," she declared.

Okay, he knew she was a fan, she'd told him, but they'd both been working closely with Tom now for months. He thought she was over that.

"And Hale Wheeler is with him," she breathed.

Judge smiled.

Well, *cool*.

He'd talked briefly on the phone with Hale once, the day of Judge's mother's memorial.

Hale had called from Singapore. Chloe had put him on speaker-phone and done an introduction. Wheeler had conveyed he was sorry for Judge's loss and then Chloe didn't push that any further. But she did talk to Wheeler for fifteen minutes, and Judge could tell how she did that they were close, and she got something out of her call with her "adopted" brother.

He settled her, like Matt and Sasha did not (but he'd also noted that, in somewhat the same way, Sully did).

Therefore, Judge liked the guy because he was, for all intents and purposes, Chloe's big brother, and he gave her what Chloe gave to her younger siblings.

Even all the way from Singapore.

"They're in the conference room," Alex shared.

Judge looked that way, and sure enough, through the glass, he could see movie-star handsome Hale Wheeler, one of the world's richest men, and thus most eligible bachelor, sitting with Tom, Duncan and Harvey, smiling and chatting.

He'd seen pictures of the guy often since his dad died. With his money and looks, it was impossible to escape him. The media latched onto him like a parasite.

But in the flesh, he was different. Not even being in the same room with him, Judge could see he had natural charisma.

A lot of it.

No wonder Alex was buzzing with excitement.

They all moved that way. Duncan noticed them coming so they were all up out of their chairs by the time he, Rix and Alex were through the door.

"Great, you're here. Judge, Rix, Alex, this is Hale Wheeler, Chloe's brother," Duncan introduced.

Judge walked up to the guy, hand out, smile on his face.

"Really good to meet you in person, man," he said when they clasped hands and shook, the hold not too strong it said he was trying to prove anything, but it wasn't wimpy either.

"You, too, Judge. Finally. Everyone says good things."

"That means a lot, Hale. Seriously."

When he was about to release their hold, Wheeler kept it with a subtle jerk.

Judge focused on him.

"Really sorry about your mom," he said low.

Judge stared into his eyes, knowing he'd just met a kindred spirit who knew something about losing a parent too soon.

A parent that left you with anger and confusion and a legacy you didn't know what to do with, but you did know it would forever haunt you.

"Thanks, brother," Judge replied quietly.

Wheeler dipped his chin, let him go, and the rest of the introductions were made before they all sat down, and Duncan immediately punted.

"Hale has something to propose, and since it's his deal, I'm not gonna speak for him." He nodded his head across the table. "Go, Hale."

Everyone looked to Wheeler.

"Right, I'll start by apologizing. I'm not gonna get real flowery with this. I wish I had more time, but I've been attempting to impose changes in Dad's company that will put our carbon footprint at a zero within ten years and the board is losing their shit," he said as an opener.

Judge and Rix exchanged glances, and he knew in his, and saw in Rix's gaze some of the excitement Alex had shown earlier.

"So I'm probably gonna be forcibly removed in about a month," Wheeler continued, saying this like he gave zero fucks about it. "But until then, I got unions to set up and as many inroads to make as I can with our environmental impact, so I don't have a lot of time. I need to be in California tomorrow. But I had a window, and I took advantage of it, so here goes."

He was setting up unions...

In his own shop?

Wheeler took a deep breath.

Then he said, "I've earmarked five hundred million dollars for a program that integrates Kids and Trails with Camp Trail Blazer. Integrates and expands. I've got a lot of ideas that'll take so long to go over, I've gotta fly you to LA to discuss them. But right now, I also got my mind on other shit. So I need your ideas. I think with that kind of money, I don't have to tell you that you should get creative. But I'll give you the foundation. I want a focus on respect for each other and community, respect for nature, and respect for animals. I want things taught like how changing a natural ecosystem, like giving Phoenician homes green lawns when it's a desert, affects the whole of the planet. What suburban sprawl means to wildlife, the end of natural predators, and the resultant proliferation of disease-spreading vermin. I want them to understand what they're eating and how it gets to them, grass-fed and free-range versus farm factory and feedlots. I want an emphasis not only on executing, but also learning and education. I want a diversified staff, and I want a diversified experience. And that kind of money will easily endow, but I want a look to expansion even before we've started. Aggressive fundraising, awareness and outreach."

He paused.

No one said dick.

Then he looked Judge right in the eye and said, "We all know, to make any kind of impact, we gotta take care of our kids. We'll start here, in Arizona. But I want you to think global, Judge. And when we roll out, I'll need you at the helm. Are you up for that?"

"Hell yes," Judge replied immediately.

Wheeler grinned.

Judge returned it and didn't miss Duncan, Harvey and Tom sharing their own.

Wheeler turned to Rix. "It's my understanding you have an excruciatingly personal experience of the effects of climate change."

"You could say that," Rix drawled.

Wheeler's lips twitched, and this time, Judge shared a glance with Duncan, who looked just as amused as Judge was.

Amused and appreciative.

Rix couldn't hide, and he valued it when other people didn't hide either.

"This is gonna be big, so it's gonna need a team, but at the start, I want that team to be small, close-knit, with an already proven track record. Duncan says you kill it at what you do, but you're wasted in this store. You need bigger challenges. Could you work for Judge, with him steering the ship?"

Judge would have preferred not to be sitting there when that question was aimed at Rix, but it seemed Wheeler took the no-bullshit, let's-get-on-with-this approach to extremes.

"I'd need him to because I don't know half the shit he does, but I can learn," Rix replied.

Wheeler nodded and then to Alex, "Duncan says you're exceptional and you being a member of this team invaluable. Are you interested?"

"Yes!" It was nearly an exclamation.

Wheeler smiled at her.

And Judge saw Rix had competition, because when he did, it looked like Alex would faint.

Then to the table, Wheeler said, "Tom's considering a role as spokesperson. Depending on what we come up with, he might also lead the charge to get more celebrities involved and maybe add an athletic or activity element. I'll speak for Tom to tell you that Sam Cooper saw Tom and Duncan's piece and reached out. Tom shared with Sam that we're looking at merging the two programs. And Sam made the approach to discuss the possibility of offering teamwork, athletic training and even some military aspects as an alternative program to grounding troubled kids who lean more to that than hikes, camping and riding the range. That's further down the line."

Judge said nothing, but even though some years ago Sampson Cooper's football career was cut short by him retiring and joining the Army after his brother died in the service, he was not forgotten. Not even close.

Specifically because he cut short a promising and lucrative football career to serve in the United States military.

"What you need to know right now is that this will still be intimately attached to River Rain and Duncan will be buying in," Wheeler continued. "As such, when that time comes, we'll be negotiating titles and increased salaries through HR here at River Rain."

Well, damn.

Judge again looked to Duncan.

Duncan had his eyes on Wheeler.

So he looked to Harvey.

Harvey was smiling so huge at him, his cheeks had to hurt.

Which was exactly how Judge felt inside.

"That's it," Wheeler continued. "Do we have a team?"

Judge shifted his gaze to Alex and Rix in turn.

He got nods from them both.

So to Wheeler, he said, "We've got a team."

His eventual brother-in-law shot him another grin, then he gave Judge his first directive.

"I'm blinded by the white in here, man. First order of business, bring me some color."

That was when Judge grinned at him and replied, "You got it."

And that was it.

He turned to Tom and asked, "Walk me out?"

Judge appreciated the personal touch. It was obvious he had zero time, but still, they didn't take a Zoom call. He sat there with them just in order to pitch this.

A dream job.

Just a fucking dream come true.

Judge dealt with saying goodbye and see-you-soon-with-Chloe as Wheeler took off.

Then he dealt with Alex's lowkey but still flowing excitement, Rix's shock, and also excitement, Harvey's joking, as well as excitement, and then he was alone in the conference room with Duncan.

"Was that Chloe or you?" he asked his boss, his friend, and his eventual stepfather-in-law.

"Neither, Judge," Duncan replied. "It was all you."

Duncan was also a no-bullshit type of guy.

And Christ, that felt good.

Duncan clapped him on the shoulder as he walked out,

Judge tipped his head immediately to the phone.

His first text was to Chloe, *Just met Hale.*

His second was to his dad, *Met Hale Wheeler. He's endowing what will be a massive, global, kids, nature, activity program, and I'm heading it.*

Chloe's return text proved Duncan's assertion true. *You did? In Prescott?!?! Without me there?!?!!!!!!* (this was followed by a wide-eyed face, three red angry faces with about seven red angry faces with characters over their mouths and *that* was followed by a gif of Marie from *Aristocats* blowing a raspberry).

Which made him smile.

His dad's response was, *Where do I send a check?*

Which made him feel something else entirely.

Six weeks later...

"You don't have to stop, you can walk right in," Genny was saying over his speakerphone.

Not Chloe's phone.

His.

Judge was trailing Chloe into Corey Szabo's epic beachfront property in LA to which Judge had just driven them from the airport.

The last ten minutes of that drive he did it talking to Genny over the phone as she went over—again—what he'd be facing tomorrow as he walked Chloe up the red carpet to the premiere of Genny's new TV show, *The Next Life*.

He'd been warned there were sex scenes.

He'd been warned that interest had remained at a fever pitch because of all things Pierce-Swan-Holloway-Oakley.

And the fact that his dad and Dru were right then flying to LA to be with "the family" during this celebratory event wasn't going to help matters.

He'd also been warned how disorienting the shouting and flashbulbs could be.

He'd even been warned not to wear green (whatever that meant, but whatever it meant, it wasn't like Chloe, who had dressed him (fortunately in one of the getups she'd already given him), would allow that to happen, especially if it was a bad thing).

But he'd learned over the last months, as he'd learned well before with her daughter, just to let Genny do her thing.

For Chloe, it was a love thing.

For Genny, it was also a love thing.

That love being mom love.

She was one hundred percent running to catch up in giving him the care and attention he should have had growing up, with the handicaps of him being a grown man and both of them having demanding careers.

But it was happening anyway.

He just let it roll.

He couldn't stop her anyway.

And it felt great.

"Got it, Gen," he muttered as Chloe shot a sunny smile over her shoulder at him (suffice it to say, his woman, too, loved the love he was getting from her mom), and they entered the house.

Duncan and Genny were staying in their new small, but reportedly amazing Craftsman bungalow in the Hollywood Hills.

They'd made that decision because she had to be in Cali on more than the rare occasion, and they'd happened onto a place they both really loved.

Not to mention, Genny had a predilection for interior design (something else she shared with her daughter, as Chloe's touch was now all over their home in Prescott—she hadn't overwhelmed his vibe, she'd just added hers—and Judge loved it, it was perfect), and for Gen, this was a fun project.

Lastly, they'd decided on owning because the show had already been picked up for two more seasons. And this renewed interest in Genny included her signing on to do a weepy romantic dramedy where her character dies too soon, but she comes back a matchmaking ghost and sees to it that her four children find love even as she, herself, finds ghostly love as she reunites and rekindles the love she shared with their father, who died even sooner.

Genny had asked Judge if he wanted to read the script, and since he'd never done that, he'd taken her up on it.

It was really good, equal parts funny, sad, with love stories that weren't sappy, they were just heartwarming and cool.

And her role was perfect for her.

Since she and Duncan had their own space, and this massive house was sitting here, Hale had invited all of "the kids" to stay.

Including Gage and Sully, Gage taking a break from studies he'd finally found interest in at U of A, Sully flying in from the new job with an alternative energy operation he got in Texas after graduating from Purdue.

Sul was taking a year for experience then making the decision to go after his master's and concentrate on that alone, or do it while still employed.

But now, they were all converging, including Matt, Sash and Hale, it was just that he and Chloe got there first.

"So walk, smile, nod, and if you don't want to step and repeat, just keep walking. They've got people there who can handle getting you through without disruption," Genny kept on.

"We're in for the full thing, Genny. I'll be all right. I have a six thousand dollar suit I need to show off anyway," he said, setting their bags by the door and moving into a massive, open, bright space with an insane view of the ocean and the coolest furniture he'd ever seen.

But the burn from his woman's eyes took his attention off it as she shot him a scorching look.

He jutted his chin at her teasingly.

He knew his suit "only" cost five thousand.

But the other shit he'd be wearing put it well over six.

"I'm afraid that's something we'll never break her from, darling," Genny replied on a sigh.

He was grinning when he stopped looking around, taking in the space.

He also stopped dead.

"This will be good," Genny went on to mumble. "Practice for the wedding."

Vaguely, he thought of that and how Chloe described Genny and Duncan's wedding as an event that was going to be "subdued, but still sensational." That meant it was going to be small (ish). It was also going to be happening soon.

Not in LA.

In Prescott.

"See you tonight. Give my love to Chloe," Genny bid.

"I can hear you, Mom," Chloe called.

"Right, darling. Bowie and I'll be there around six. So will your dad. Jamie and Dru are staying closer to you so they might be there earlier. Do not cook! We'll order when we get there."

Judge tore his gaze from what he was looking at to catch his woman's scowl.

What was left unsaid was that Paloma would be here too.

Her father was dating someone.

Chloe detested her.

Tom was coming to the premiere.

And bringing her.

Judge had to admit, he was with Chloe. He couldn't put his finger on what exactly bugged him about Paloma, but she wasn't right for Tom.

Or maybe it was that definitely Chloe, but also Judge felt no one would be good enough for him.

Except, sadly, Genny.

"Okay, Mom. See you soon," Chloe said.

"Yeah, Gen, see you soon," Judge added.

"Love you both."

In unison, they replied, "Love you more."

He hung up and now Chloe was smirking at him, because he'd fallen into that Pierce-Swan-Holloway habit of the "love you more" thing (mostly doing this with Chloe). It wasn't the first they'd chatted together with her mom on speakerphone, so it wasn't the first time it happened, and he knew his woman really dug that unison gig.

She opened her mouth, probably to say something smug, but he got there before her.

"What's this?" he asked, gesturing to a framed picture with his phone.

She walked up to where he stood at the mantel over the fireplace and peered at the photo.

"I think that's me. And Grandma. With Uncle Corey."

He knew it was her.

Chloe, as a baby.

The polka-dot bathing suit with a skirt. The curl of dark hair you could just barely see coming out from under her sun hat.

Sasha was blonde.

The photo was black and white, but you could still see.

Judge studied a picture of Szabo and Chloe's grandma standing out on a beach, her grandma in a dark bathing suit, Szabo in linen pants and shirt, and then he stared at Chloe standing beside him.

And carefully, he asked, "Do you see this picture, baby?"

"Yeah, I think Gramps took it. He had a thing for photography. He was always taking candids of people when they didn't know he was doing it."

He turned again to the photo.

Corey Szabo, who was unmistakable, was holding her to his chest like she was his own child.

Treasured.

Precious.

Beloved.

And her grandmother, who was a looker, was smiling at them, smiling at them both, with all three of those things in her face.

He then glanced around.

And after that, he urged, "Chloe, honey, look around."

She finally gathered his tone, grew attentive, then she gazed around.

She ended on him.

"What do you see?" she asked quietly.

"There are pictures everywhere," he told her. "A lot of them. All in groupings. But there is only one right here. Only one, pride of place. There's nothing else on this mantel, not your mother. Not Hale. Nothing. Except you, and your grandmother, and your uncle."

He saw her body still, but her gaze drifted back to the photo.

"He adored her," she whispered.

"He adored you," he whispered back.

Her eyes came to him, and they were bright with wet.

"I hope Hale never sells this house," Judge said. "I totally get why your uncle took his last breath here. It's filled with love."

He barely finished his last word before she walked into his arms.

Judge held her, gaze on that photo.

Thanks, man, he said to the universe.

There was no reply.

Even so, deep down in his soul, Judge knew…

He was heard.

After all, he was granted this moment and this woman in his arms, all she had given him, and all she would.

And he knew one thing for certain about Corey Szabo.

If Judge wasn't worthy of her, he wouldn't be there.

Seven hours later, there were thirteen people in that house.

And it was true.

Corey Szabo's home was as he'd always wanted it.

Filled with love.

The End

The River Rain Series will continue...
With the story of Rix and Alex.

POST-SCRIPT

The Assessment

Rhys

The Next Life *Premiere Night...Two Thousand and Seventy-Three Miles away from Los Angeles...in Brownsburg, Indiana...*

Rhys sat at the bar.

It was bordering on seedy.

Worn in.

Welcoming to locals.

Not intimidating to out-of-towners.

The sign over the door called it J&J's Saloon.

Rhys thought it was trouble.

This had a lot to do with the two men that sat at the end of the bar. Both dark-headed, both good-looking, one built like a linebacker, the other just plain built.

They had eyes on Rhys. They did not share that they were happy with his vibe.

And they reeked of cop.

They did this even though Rhys knew who they were.

And that they were both cops.

He sat with his vodka rocks and gave all appearances of ignoring them, but he tracked every move they made.

This didn't stop him from looking to the door when it opened.

He already knew the man entering was the man he came to see.

Like he knew one of the men at the end of the bar was Alec Colton, one of serial killer Denny Lowe's first two victims.

Lowe obviously hadn't killed Colton, but he'd taken something else from him that, from Rhys's research, was more precious to him than his life.

Fortunately for Colton, he'd gotten it back.

Now, the man walking his way was another story.

Rhys didn't like it, but he'd come into this bar without his guns or his knife.

They'd know he was armed just looking at him.

He didn't need that headache.

And the man who walked right up to him and gave him a once-over would know it too.

Anthony Joseph Callahan.

"You Vaughan?" he asked when he stopped at Rhys's side.

"Yes, and you're Joe Callahan."

Callahan jerked up his chin.

He was a big man too.

Big.

Built.

And more dangerous than the two at the end of the bar put together.

And the man with Colton, a man called Tanner Layne, had been government trained, even if that was by proxy, and Rhys didn't mean military.

Layne knew entirely different kinds of ops.

Specialized.

How this crew converged on this small town in Indiana, Rhys had no clue.

He also didn't care.

That was not his directive.

He focused on the man in front of him.

"Got your message, I'm here," Joe Callahan grunted. "What's this about?"

"I'd like to talk to you about Susan Shepherd."

Callahan's eyes narrowed under menacingly knit brows.

They then flicked across the bar, to Colton.

They came back to Rhys.

And then, assessment concluded, he took the stool next to Rhys's.

DISCUSSION & REFLECTION QUESTIONS

1. Divorce is now commonly accepted in many societies. As such, was it a surprise to you the differing nuances of the fallout for the children of divorced parents, even if those children are adults, and the split was for the most part amicable and functional when it came to the Pierce-Swans? Or the prolonged fallout when the divorce was not amicable, and the child was young, when it came to the Oakleys?

Further, what were your thoughts around the fact that the parents understood on some level there was fallout but did not actively press assisting their offspring to directly deal with these issues? Do you think they should be treating them as adults and letting them find their own way, as Genny and Tom are doing? Or interceding so they didn't have to deal at all, like Jamie did? Or should they be more forcefully intervening?

2. What were your thoughts about Chloe's reaction to Genny's inability to forgive Tom's betrayal and preserve their marriage? Did you feel Chloe was being too hard on her mother?

And as Chloe ruminated about some of her parents' marital history, did you feel there might have been things Genny missed that led to the disintegration of her closeness to her husband—not in the sense she held any responsibility for the ultimate betrayal—but perhaps bore some shared responsibility for the failure of their marriage?

3. Hounded by the media throughout his divorce, Jameson Oakley sought to shield his son from that and eventually made a judgment call on how best to protect him. What did you think about this decision? What were your thoughts as it came back to haunt him? How did you feel about Judge's acceptance of it?

4. At first glance, Belinda Oakley appears to be an almost villain in this novel. But addiction is an illness, and for Belinda, it not only went untreated, after Jameson felt the need to give up on her once she'd betrayed their marriage to that compulsion, no one in her life, including her parents, made much effort to press her to seek help.

Do you think Belinda would have eventually benefitted from some love and intervention? Do you feel she was lost to the machinations of powerful men and the recriminations of a disapproving father? Do you feel her father's attitudes, and perhaps Jamie's ambitions, may have had some effect on how quickly she became unanchored after high school? And do you think it's a child's responsibility, when they reach adulthood, to press a parent to recovery?

Or is there a point of no return for a person struggling with addiction who shows no willingness to seek help where those around them must break ties for their own emotional health? Or even, do you feel it is not anyone's responsibility, but this is solely owned by the person who is struggling?

5. It is distinctly the author's opinion that we all should be socially responsible, but in this book, she makes clear those of privilege should understand that and consciously work at leveling the playing field. What did you think about Chloe's Fabulous Foot Forward program? Judge's determination to make a career in mutual aid? Hale's crusade to use the wealth and power his father left him for good? Was this believable? Are they doing enough? Is it your opinion they're focusing

on the right things? If not, what should they be focusing on or do you think this is their responsibility at all?

6. Sizeism and ageism are issues. It can be argued that ridiculing and discriminating on the basis of weight and age are still socially accept-able to many. In fact, a large number of people feel it is not objection-able in the slightest to openly share their derogation of people, especially women, who are considered overweight.

How did you feel when you read the description of the clientele Chloe caters to in Velvet and her opinions about why she does? When shopping, have you experienced some of the things that Chloe's patron mentioned? Or have you never thought of this? No matter your age or size, would you welcome and patronize a store like Velvet?

7. In this novel, the reader learns even more about the complex character of Corey Szabo. Introduced in *After the Climb* as terminally selfish and deceitful, he also has significant demons.

However, in this book, we discover even more about what makes him tick. What were your thoughts as his relationship with Chloe unfolded? What are your thoughts about his bequeathal of Rhys Vaughan and his clear initiative, even after his death, to continue interfering in the lives of people he cared about, but deceived? Does this make you consider the fact that one act, no matter how dramatic, or the ripples it creates in many lives, does not define a person? Does it give you pause to reflect how those who were supposed to love him also missed how long and how deeply he was struggling?

8. Chloe and Judge are an example of opposites attract. But this is only surface. Were you surprised how they found so much common ground, even if, at first glance, they would not seem to suit?

9. AJ Oakley is the villain in this book, however, he is also an example of a character who was, and sometimes still is, admired and even revered as a traditional model of the esteemed masculine traits of

being straight-speaking, aggressive, wealthy, philandering and unapologetic. What are your thoughts on that?

10. Did you think Chloe should so easily forgive Sasha?

11. Did you think it reasonable that Chloe moved to Prescott, rather than Judge moving to Phoenix?

12. What was your favorite outfit of Chloe's?

13. Do you think, even though they end the novel living together, that Chloe has relinquished custody of Judge's coat?

14. Both Rix and Tom are set to have their stories story told next. But whose story would you like to see after those?

SNEAK PEEK

Taking the Leap
River Rain, Book 3
By Kristen Ashley
Coming February 15, 2022

PROLOGUE

SOMEONE LIKE ME

Alex

It was happening.

He was flirting with me.

John "Rix" Hendrix, the coolest guy I'd ever met, the most interesting person I'd ever known, the most handsome man I'd ever seen, was flirting...

With...

Me.

And I was somehow managing to flirt back (kind of).

Okay, I might be relying on something from Moscow to do so (that something being their mules), but it was happening.

And I knew I wasn't making more of it than I should.

I knew that because Chloe and Judge were with us. We were out having drinks, celebrating the official beginning of our new Trail Blazer program (that day, Judge, Rix and me had signed on to new job titles with new responsibilities and new salaries with the expanded program—I got a promotion and a fifteen percent raise!—definitely worth sitting down to drinks with the man who terrified me most on this earth).

Chloe was giving Rix and me smug looks, but mostly me, and once, she'd even winked at me.

As an aside: Chloe Pierce, my boss Judge's girlfriend, was the coolest, most interesting, most gorgeous woman I'd ever met.

And even though (fortunately, so far, though maybe not now?) Rix had missed it, but although she hadn't said anything, I knew Chloe knew I was crushing on Rix...*big time.*

And I had been.

Crushing on Rix.

Big time.

She was happy for me.

I was happy for me!

Because Rix was *flirting with me.*

Me!

And the reason why this was crazy was not only because he was cool and interesting and handsome, and as yet, such a man had never shown any interest in me.

It was because I was, well...

Me.

First off, I was shy around cute guys (okay, I was just plain shy, but it got a lot worse around guys, and off-the-charts worse around cute ones).

Not to mention, I knew how to put on mascara, I just wasn't a big fan of wearing it (so, unless it was a super special occasion, or I was with my family, I didn't).

I had a little house up in mountains (TBH, it was more like a big shack), but I was rarely in it because there were a lot better places to be (and my house was awesome, I just had a ton of interests and not a lot of them happened in my house).

I knew how to cook in a kitchen, but I cooked way better over a campfire (and in a hot coal pit).

There were Star Trek nerds, I was just a star nerd (that being, lying under them at night in the middle of nowhere and staring at them until I fell asleep).

I would rather snowshoe into a forest in the dead of winter, set up a tent and spend a couple of days in nature, reading by a headlamp at night cozied up in a one-woman sleeping bag in a one-person tent than sit by a fireside during a snowstorm with a mug of hot cocoa (though, that was nice too).

Women didn't get me.

Men didn't either, and it was actually more men who didn't get me than it was women because I wasn't stereotypically womanly. Most woman got there were lots of different kinds of women. Most men (in my experience) weren't that broad minded.

No, actually, it was more my family who didn't get me than anyone else.

My family didn't get me at all.

"Sexy as fuck," Rix was saying.

I came out of my musings to focus on his words.

Words he was aiming at me (me!).

Words of which one of them was "sexy."

A flutter assaulted my belly at hearing his gravelly voice utter that word (at me).

"What?" I whispered, like talking louder might break the spell of how close he was sitting, leaned in even closer, talking to me, but doing it with his attention centered right...on...*me*.

Yowza.

"That glass dome glamp sitch in Joshua Tree," he answered, reminding me what we'd been talking about. "Never thought I'd say those words, glamping is better than not camping at all, but it isn't my gig. But it was just that fuckin' awesome. Bedding down under the stars at night..."

Oh my God!

He was into sleeping under the stars just like me!

"Waking up with the sun..."

That wasn't as great as stars, but it was cool.

Something happened to his eyes which saw results in specific parts of my body before he finished.

"The shower that was top and sides all glass. Getting wet and clean with a near-on three-hundred-and-sixty-degree view of the Joshua trees and the desert. Only thing missing was I didn't take a woman with me."

He stopped speaking.

Shoot!

That meant it was my turn.

"You'll have to..." My voice was clogged due to the fact my mind was on Rix in a shower that was all glass. Rix...*wet* and *slick* and *slippery*...in a shower that was all glass. So I cleared my throat, and when I did, his lips hitched in a way that those specific parts of my body, already perked, became veritably *primed*. "Text me the deets for that. I, uh...don't usually glamp but..."

I let that trail off, not because I didn't have more to say, but because I'd lost the ability to speak.

This was because his eyes were watching my mouth while I was doing it.

"Text you," he murmured to my mouth, like that wasn't where his mind was going.

I also had a sense of where his mind was going.

As in, he didn't want to text me the info.

He wanted to personally show me the site.

With the glass shower.

That he would be using.

With me there.

Or, perhaps, in it with him.

Lordy!

"Yeah," I forced out, and it did, indeed, sound forced.

No, that wasn't right.

It sounded breathy and strangled.

As you could probably deduce, I was generally no good at flirting (or chitchat, or mingling, or social situations on the whole, but definitely top of that heap was flirting).

However, with Rix, I was a mess and not only now. All the time.

I didn't think in the time I'd known him we'd ever had a single one-on-one conversation.

This was the first of those too.

His attention returned to my eyes. "Yours?"

"Uh...sorry?"

"Coolest place you ever spent the night," he reminded me of the subject we'd been discussing.

It had been my question, and it might have been the ballsiest question I'd ever asked any man, not just Rix.

"I go off route," I told him.

"You mean off trail?" he asked.

I nodded, but then shook my head, which meant I ended up making a circle, which made Rix's lips hitch again, this time just with amusement. And making him smile like that, I felt like throwing my arms out and arching my back, like I was breaking through the tape at the finish line, coming in first, winning the prize.

"That too," I made myself say. "But I meant off route. I'm a byway person, not a highway person. And I was on a byway, outside Ouray—"

"Colorado."

I nodded.

"One of the prettiest places on the planet," he stated my personal opinion.

"Yeah," I said softly.

He let that soft sound float between us for a second.

I felt weird about it, weird in a wonderful way, like the sound I'd made was pretty and the word was meaningful, and he was getting off on riding it and the feeling behind it, before he prompted, "You were on a byway..."

Good God.

He was.

He was paying complete attention to me.

Listening to every word I said.

So *this* was how it felt to be the center or Rix's attention.

I'd wondered for a very long time.

I'd been a lot of beautiful places (a lot, a lot), but none was as heavenly as that right there.

"I was on a byway," I repeated, "and I pulled into this diner. Cool place. Had a counter with a pie under glass at the end of it and every-thing. Sat next to an old-timer, we got to talking, and he told me about some hot springs not many people know about. I remembered the conversation, what he said. So, on a long weekend, I drove back up in the winter, snowshoed in where he said to go, and he was right on the money. It was exactly as he described. Trees and snow and this tuft of steam coming up from the spring. Pristine, not a footprint, no one around. Pitched my tent close to the rocks around the spring, barely had to use my sleeping bag they were so warm. Sat in the spring until my fingers wrinkled. Slept with my head out of the tent, gaiter pulled up over my nose, listening to the burbling of the water, staring through the evergreens up at the stars."

I stopped talking, and Rix didn't start. He didn't move. And some-where in sharing this memory with him, I'd missed his eyes had slid back down to my lips.

When he continued not to move or say anything for a long time, I finished, "So that's the coolest place I've ever spent the night."

"Heaven," he murmured, not shifting his gaze.

A shiver trailed down my spine.

"Yeah," I whispered. "Heaven."

He still didn't move.

I started freaking out, my lips with his attention on them begin-ning to feel tingly, and not thinking, I caught the bottom one with my teeth.

When I did that, his gaze came up to my eyes, and he had such a cocky look in his own, knowing just how hot he was, knowing just what reaction he was causing in me, it was not only mesmerizing, it was akin to about twenty minutes of foreplay.

Great foreplay.

So great, I almost moaned.

I did whimper (slightly and horrifyingly, because he heard it, and I got another hitch of his lips, and not the amused hitch this time, the *other* one).

Holy crap.

I might orgasm…

From flirting!

I instantly stood.

He sat back as I did, his brows snapping together as he looked up at me.

"I'll be back!" I cried.

I was unnecessarily loud. Thus, I felt Judge and Chloe's startled attention come to me too.

But I raced away.

Straight to the bathroom.

I didn't have to use the bathroom.

I had to give myself a pep talk.

Because this was Rix, *finally*, Rix and me talking, *flirting*, and I couldn't muck this up like I did practically every interaction I'd had with him (and we worked together at River Rain Outdoor stores, before Hale Wheeler swept in and offered Trail Blazer, new titles and pay raises, Rix and me were not in the same department, but now we were on the exact same team, so not only would I see him every day, I'd be working side by side with him...every day).

I was in luck, when, upon a panicked check, I saw the bathroom was empty. Therefore, as I tried to instill myself with some courage, I wouldn't have an audience of some pretty, mountain-fresh, tanned, boho goddess washing her hands or using the facilities (which would, as every shy girl knew, have the opposite result when it came to courage).

It was just me in the restroom.

Me and my insecurities.

I stared at my hazel eyes in the mirror (a tortoiseshell brown around the pupil, leading to a marbled green that filled out the rest of the iris, not the violet of my sister and mother, not the green of my father, plain-Jane hazel (as my sister described it)).

Then I took in the big, fat, dark pigtails that contained my curly hair and fell either side of my neck, down my chest.

Prescott, Arizona, where we all lived, was not a bustling metropolis.

I'd been here a while.

So had Rix.

This meant I not only worked with him, but I saw him out and about.

He was who he was, *how* he was. Those wide shoulders. That dark hair, short at the sides, sweeping high at the top, most of the time messy and sexy, but sometimes sleek (and sexy). The square jaw. Those thick eyebrows that traveled to the corners of his eyes.

And the brown eyes that said he had a thousand stories to tell, some you wouldn't like, others that would leave you breathless.

Being all he was, he was never out alone.

What I meant was, unless he was with his buds, he was always with a woman.

He had a type.

Tall. Slender. Leggy. Athletic.

I was not tall.

I hiked. I paddleboarded. I kayaked.

I also ate.

So I did not have a svelte bod.

And those women I saw him with, they might all be mountain-fresh, tanned, boho goddesses who could keep up with him on a trail run (something he still did, on his running blades, even after he tragically lost both legs below the knees while fighting a wildfire in his previous occupation as a firefighter—see? totally the coolest guy I knew). But they also wore flowy dresses or Daisy Dukes and billowy blouses with flat sandals with tons of straps and mascara and maybe a winged eyeliner if they were feeling feisty, accompanying all of this with funky-chic wide-brimmed felt fedoras.

I'd look like a moron in a fedora.

I could just imagine what my sister would say if she saw me in a boho fedora.

As I was wont to do, the instant a thought that included my sister hit my brain, I shoved it aside.

But when I did, I was stuck with me.

Staring at my round face with its rounder cheekbones which was, indeed, tan, I tried to see myself with broad, tanner, muscled Rix, and I couldn't even conjure the image.

"What am I thinking? I work with this guy," I mumbled to my reflection.

I had no business flirting with a co-worker.

That was stupid. Crazy.

Embarrassing.

Maybe I was wrong.

Maybe it wasn't even flirting.

(Though I didn't have a ton of experience, it *felt* like flirting, not to mention, Chloe knew I was crushing on him, and she'd winked at me.)

"But this is Rix," I kept mumbling.

And it was.

Rix.

My perfect man.

He camped. He hiked. He kayaked. He came to work in the morning after a trail run or a ride on his handcycle. He headed out to parts unknown on his days off with his tent in his truck, coming back to work practically shimmering with the rapture of spending time in nature.

I did not trail run or ride, but I definitely came in from the outdoors shimmering after spending time in nature (at least, I felt like I did).

I'd never asked, I'd been too shy, but I'd bet actual, real money Rix had often fallen asleep under the stars, and not just in a glass glamping dome among the Joshua trees.

I bet he knew how to cook an entire meal under the earth.

I bet he knew what an impending thunderstorm smelled like, that certain snakes were threats (if you're caught by surprise…or being stupid), but bats and coyotes and bears were usually not (unless you caught them by surprise, or you're being stupid), and that you never, ever drank water from nature unless you went through the process of treating it.

Was all that not worth the risk?

Worth the risk of being embarrassed should I not be reading the current situation right?

Worth the risk of feeling the thrill?

The thrill of finding someone, and being with them…

Someone who got me.

Someone like me.

It was.

It was totally worth it.

To have Rix's big hand (I'd noticed his hands—his *big, rough* hands —and I'd noticed them about seven hundred thousand times in the exactly two and one-eighth years we'd been working together) wrapped around mine as we picked our way across a natural stone bridge over a creek.

To zip our sleeping bags together and whisper (and do other things) to each other under the cover of night.

Yes, even someone to cozy up with by a fire with cocoa and read on snowy days when we weren't under a ceiling of sky.

But to have those moments, say, to look into his eyes over coffee in the morning, and know he felt like me.

He was like me.

Because he was the one soul on this planet who *got me*.

"It's *so* worth it," I whispered.

A toilet flushed.

I jumped.

Someone was in there?

Yes, someone was.

A pretty, mountain-fresh, tanned, boho goddess wearing a felt, wide-brimmed panama hat and a big smile came out of a stall and headed with that smile aimed at me to the sink next to mine.

"Just to say, sister, it *is*," she declared. "If you're talking about that hunk of tall, dark and handsome who was up in your space out there, it is *so worth it*," she declared. "Especially if he looks like that, is as into you as that and has a kickass name like Rix."

"I'm a nature nerd," I blurted, why, I did not know.

She shrugged even as she rubbed soap into her hands. "I've read

The Shell Seekers thirteen times, and if a dude is not down to read it, even if he might not like it, he's out. We all got our thang. And by the by, that guy didn't look like a banker to me." She turned off the tap, shook water off her hands and turned to the dryer, exclaiming, "Killer! They have an Airblade!"

She then stuck her hands into the Airblade.

I stood staring at her attractive, sinewy back and shoulder muscles exposed by her spaghetti-strapped, oversized, muted-but-dizzily-printed dress, and I did this so long, the Airblade had worked its magic, and she'd turned.

"What are you still doing in here?" she demanded. "Go get 'im, tigress."

"I work with him."

She tipped her head to the side the same time she hitched a hip and put a hand on it. "So?"

"That could get messy."

"A non-messy life *totally* sucks."

This might sound crazy, but I knew she was right.

I got into a Zen state when I cleaned my house, and I dug it.

Nevertheless, when it was done, a part of me I always missed the boots thrown by the door, the coffeepot upended in the drainer, the Oxo pouring canister filled with homemade granola left on the counter, the throw tossed wide over the couch, the book spread open and lying on its pages, the jacket thrown over the back of a chair. All the signs that said, "Someone lives here, and they're not here tidying, they're out, busy *living*."

Did that translate to relationships?

To romance?

"I'll tell you what, a guy was that into me, I'd be *all the way* down with getting messy," my new bathroom friend announced.

Had Rix been *that* into me?

"I'm shy," I whispered.

"No shit?" she asked. "Girl, I noticed you two a while ago. At first, I wanted to walk by and high-five you for the way you were playing that player. Then I realized, well, hell. This is no play. This bitch is scared out of her brain about this dude, and it's so cute, *I could just die.*"

I was back to staring, this time at her mountain-fresh face.

"He thought it was cute too," she proclaimed. "But he thought it was so cute, he was itching *to pounce.*"

Rix.

Pouncing.

Oh Lord.

Now I was in danger of a standing-up, Rix-nowhere-near-me, bathroom orgasm.

"*Really?*" I breathed.

"Hi, I'm Dani." She stuck her hand out.

I took it. "I'm Alex."

To that, she for some reason shared, "Your hair is *goals.* I'm about to go and do what no woman under seventy has done in twenty years. Schedule a perm. Only so I can plait thick, fat braids like yours. You could play tug of war with those bitches. They're glorious."

I couldn't stop my smile.

She let my hand go. "Now we know each other, I can tell you, I've had my fair share of experience with players."

She was seriously pretty (and sinewy and tan and could pull off a panama hat, even in a ladies washroom), so I bet she did.

She kept talking.

"And as such, being a self-proclaimed expert, I could regale you with many tales of my field experience, so I know that man is seriously into you."

"I know him, and I've seen him with other women. He'd be more into someone like, to be honest...*you.*"

She shook her head, came to me, hooked arms, and guided us to and through the door.

"This is what shy chicks don't get," she started. "Guys like that have had me, over and over again. If they wanted girls like me, they wouldn't throw us back."

She seemed very sage, however, it should be noted that was a sad thing to say, but she didn't seem sad at all in saying it.

Maybe she'd found one who didn't "throw her back."

"Are you with someone?" I asked.

She made a scoffing noise, complementing it with, "Hell no. Hark back to aforementioned field experience. But also, I'm not settling down. I don't have a hold on even half my own shit. I don't need to take on some guy's shit too."

I pulled on our arms before we exited the back hall that led back into the bar so we'd come to a stop, and considering what she heard in the bathroom before she came out, I shared, "I don't think I have to tell you that I'm leagues away from owning anywhere close to half my shit."

Dani grinned. "Okay, what I didn't say was, even if that's the case, if a big, broad, hot, seriously-into-me guy got up in my space, and we clicked, like, bones and hearts and souls and stars aligning *clicked*, and he wanted to be along for the ride as I figured it out, I would *not* say no."

Stars aligning.

"I'm twenty-six," I told her. "And I've never had a long-term boyfriend."

She swayed back. "You a virgin?"

At this question, I started to pull away because it was in that moment it hit me how much I was baring to a complete stranger.

She held on tight.

Even so, I said, "We're getting kind of deep. I think you're cool, Dani, and I appreciate you cheering me on, but I just met you."

"That's fair," she replied. "We won't go there. And you're right, we don't know one another, so I may be wrong, but maybe you haven't had a long-term situation because you never took the risk. I mean, I got experience, and some of it tore me up." Her grin returned. "But that doesn't mean I haven't also had loads of fun."

I had no reply because I knew she was right, and it wasn't like I didn't want to admit it, it was just that I didn't know where to find the courage to go for it.

She got closer. "Nothing is permanent, Alex. Not peace. Not happiness. Not joy. People don't understand that. They want those feelings all the time. But they're just not to be had. Also not permanent?"

Her last sentence was a question, an indication she wanted to be sure I wanted her to continue imparting her wisdom on me.

Obviously, I nodded.

She continued, "Heartbreak. Or pain. Or fear."

Holy crap.

She was right again!

"Once you understand that," she started to sum up. "Once you get that everything comes and then it goes, you learn to take the leap."

When I had no reply, she kept going.

"You even learn how important it is to take it." Dani turned her head toward the bar, looked back to me, and gave me a big, encouraging smile. "Leap, sister."

She then gave me an arm hug, let me go, and she and her panama hat floated into the bar.

I stared after her.

Then I remembered the way Rix looked when he stopped staring at my mouth, he gazed into my eyes, knew he had me, and he wanted that.

He wanted *me*.

"Leap," I said under my breath.

Still totally scared to death, I nevertheless lifted my chin, headed into the bar and straight to our table.

Chloe, Judge, no Rix.

Did he take the opportunity of me leaving the table to hit the loo as well?

I was almost to my vacated chair when I noticed Chloe and Judge were not sitting close, murmuring to each other, like they had been when Rix and I were doing the same.

They were staring across the bar.

And they looked ticked.

Even Judge, who was the single most easy-going guy I'd ever met. His jaw was all tense and a muscle was flashing up his cheek.

Curious as to what was pissing even Judge off, I turned in the direction they were staring and stopped dead.

Rix was at the bar with a blonde, mountain-fresh, tanned goddess. He was also in her space, listening to her with rapt attention.

I could almost hear the propellers lifting up my heart, making it soar, splutter and give out and then it was in a nose dive.

Free falling.

I'd been gone...what?

Ten minutes?

"I gotta go," I said, again loudly, and both Chloe and Judge's heads swung my way.

If I wasn't entirely engrossed in the fact my heart had crashed at my feet, I would have stepped back because Chloe looked like she was about to spit fire.

Instead, I grabbed my army-green hobo bag and tossed the long strap over my shoulder.

Judge started to rise from his seat. "Are you okay to drive?"

Damn it.

I probably wasn't.

"I—" I began.

But Chloe was now up too. "We'll take you home, Alex."

"No, you guys stay...um..." I didn't know what else to say because I couldn't drive, and I didn't want to make them end their night, and I couldn't catch a thought in order to decide which of my friends to call to ask for a ride home.

It was then, my eyes, without my permission, strayed back to Rix.

My throat tightened.

But my attention was caught by something else.

And I saw Dani was now sitting behind Rix, eyes to me, and when she caught mine, she mouthed, *Asshole*, then she magnificently frowned.

I wanted to find that funny. I wanted to feel the bolster of female camaraderie.

I didn't do either.

"We're taking you home," Judge decreed. "I just had one beer, Alex, so I'm good to drive. And Chloe and me are ready to roll."

I bet they were, in their loved-up bliss, perfect for each other, all moved in together, building their family (of dogs, for now).

They were *the best couple ever.*

If you asked me a year ago, that a gal like Chloe would be it for Judge, I'd have said no.

But she was.

Top to toe, inside and out, she was sophisticated and a city girl and had traveled the world and was super rich, and she worshiped him and didn't hide it.

She was lucky, she got that back. But that was Judge. When he found the one for him, that would always have been what he'd give.

And he did.

But me?

I was going home alone.

Again.

Having a great day, getting a promotion and a raise, heading into a future working on an amazing program doing good things for kids endowed by one of the richest men in the world, downing some drinks with good people, flirting with a gorgeous guy...and ending all of that crawling into bed alone.

Again.

Way to go Alex.

Awesome celebration.

Yay me.

Ulk.

"You sure?" I asked Judge.

"Absolutely," Judge answered, his tone flinty.

I nodded.

We headed out, me ducking my head as I trailed behind them.

"I'll talk to him later," I heard Judge mutter.

I then heard Chloe reply, "You are not saying a word to him."

"What?" Judge.

"We'll talk. Not now." Chloe.

We hit the door and then the cool air hit my face.

But for the first time in my life, heading outside didn't make me feel free.

No.

Instead, it cost me a lot...

But when I stepped outside, I just stopped myself from dissolving into tears.

DISCOVER MORE KRISTEN ASHLEY

Wild Wind: A Chaos Novella
By Kristen Ashley

When he was sixteen years old, Jagger Black laid eyes on the girl who was his. At a cemetery. During her mother's funeral.

For years, their lives cross, they feel the pull of their connection, but then they go their separate ways.

But when Jagger sees that girl chasing someone down the street, he doesn't think twice before he wades right in. And when he gets a full-on dose of the woman she's become, he knows he finally has to decide if he's all in or if it's time to cut her loose.

She's ready to be cut loose.

But Jagger is all in.

Wild Fire: A Chaos Novella
By Kristen Ashley

"You know you can't keep a good brother down."

The Chaos Motorcycle Club has won its war. But not every brother rode into the sunset with his woman on the back of his bike.

Chaos returns with the story of Dutch Black, a man whose father was the moral compass of the Club, until he was murdered. And the man who raised Dutch protected the Club at all costs. That combination is the man Dutch is intent on becoming.

It's also the man that Dutch is going to go all out to give to his woman.

Every 1001 Dark Nights novella is a standalone story. For new readers, it's an introduction to an author's world. And for fans, it's a bonus book in the author's series. We hope you'll enjoy each one as much as we do.

Quiet Man: A Dream Man Novella
By Kristen Ashley

Charlotte "Lottie" McAlister is in the zone. She's ready to take on the next chapter of her life, and since she doesn't have a man, she'll do what she's done all along. She'll take care of business on her own. Even if that business means starting a family.

The problem is, Lottie has a stalker. The really bad kind. The kind that means she needs a bodyguard.

Enter Mo Morrison.

Enormous. Scary.

Quiet.

Mo doesn't say much, and Lottie's used to getting attention. And she wants Mo's attention. Badly.

But Mo has a strict rule. If he's guarding your body, that's all he's doing with it.

However, the longer Mo has to keep Lottie safe, the faster he falls for the beautiful blonde who has it so together, she might even be able to tackle the demons he's got in his head that just won't die.

But in the end, Lottie and Mo don't only have to find some way to keep hands off until the threat is over, they have to negotiate the overprotective Hot Bunch, Lottie's crazy stepdad, Tex, Mo's crew of fratboy commandos, not to mention his nutty sisters.

All before Lottie finally gets her Dream Man.

And Mo can lay claim to his Dream Girl.

Rough Ride: A Chaos Novella
By Kristen Ashley

Rosalie Holloway put it all on the line for the Chaos Motorcycle Club.

Informing to Chaos on their rival club—her man's club, Bounty—Rosalie knows the stakes. And she pays them when her man, who she was hoping to scare straight, finds out she's betrayed him and he delivers her to his brothers to mete out their form of justice.

But really, Rosie has long been denying that, as she drifted away from her Bounty, she's been falling in love with Everett "Snapper" Kavanagh, a Chaos brother. Snap is the biker-boy-next door with the snowy blue eyes, quiet confidence and sweet disposition who was supposed to keep her safe…and fell down on that job.

For Snapper, it's always been Rosalie, from the first time he saw her at the Chaos Compound. He's just been waiting for a clear shot. But he didn't want to get it after his Rosie was left bleeding, beat down and broken by Bounty on a cement warehouse floor.

With Rosalie a casualty of an ongoing war, Snapper has to guide her to trust him, take a shot with him, build a them…

And fold his woman firmly in the family that is Chaos.

Rock Chick Reawakening: A Rock Chick Novella
By Kristen Ashley

From *New York Times* bestselling author, Kristen Ashley, comes the long-awaited story of Daisy and Marcus, *Rock Chick Reawakening*. A prequel to Kristen's *Rock Chick* series, *Rock Chick Reawakening* shares the tale of the devastating event that nearly broke Daisy, an event that set Marcus Sloane—one of Denver's most respected businessmen and one of the Denver underground's most feared crime bosses—into finally making his move to win the heart of the woman who stole his.

Sign up for the Blue Box Press/1001 Dark Nights Newsletter
and be entered to win a Tiffany Lock necklace.

There's a contest every quarter!

Go to www.TheBlueBoxPress.com to subscribe!

As a bonus, all subscribers can download FIVE FREE
exclusive books!

DISCOVER 1001 DARK NIGHTS COLLECTION EIGHT

DRAGON REVEALED by Donna Grant
A Dragon Kings Novella

CAPTURED IN INK by Carrie Ann Ryan
A Montgomery Ink: Boulder Novella

SECURING JANE by Susan Stoker
A SEAL of Protection: Legacy Series Novella

WILD WIND by Kristen Ashley
A Chaos Novella

DARE TO TEASE by Carly Phillips
A Dare Nation Novella

VAMPIRE by Rebecca Zanetti
A Dark Protectors/Rebels Novella

MAFIA KING by Rachel Van Dyken
A Mafia Royals Novella

THE GRAVEDIGGER'S SON by Darynda Jones
A Charley Davidson Novella

FINALE by Skye Warren
A North Security Novella

MEMORIES OF YOU by J. Kenner
A Stark Securities Novella

SLAYED BY DARKNESS by Alexandra Ivy
A Guardians of Eternity Novella

TREASURED by Lexi Blake
A Masters and Mercenaries Novella

THE DAREDEVIL by Dylan Allen
A Rivers Wilde Novella

BOND OF DESTINY by Larissa Ione
A Demonica Novella

THE CLOSE-UP by Kennedy Ryan
A Hollywood Renaissance Novella

MORE THAN POSSESS YOU by Shayla Black
A More Than Words Novella

HAUNTED HOUSE by Heather Graham
A Krewe of Hunters Novella

MAN FOR ME by Laurelin Paige
A Man In Charge Novella

THE RHYTHM METHOD by Kylie Scott
A Stage Dive Novella

JONAH BENNETT by Tijan
A Bennett Mafia Novella

CHANGE WITH ME by Kristen Proby
A With Me In Seattle Novella

THE DARKEST DESTINY by Gena Showalter
A Lords of the Underworld Novella

Also from Blue Box Press

THE LAST TIARA by M.J. Rose

THE CROWN OF GILDED BONES by Jennifer L. Armentrout
A Blood and Ash Novel

THE MISSING SISTER by Lucinda Riley

THE END OF FOREVER by Steve Berry and M.J. Rose
A Cassiopeia Vitt Adventure

THE STEAL by C. W. Gortner and M.J. Rose

CHASING SERENITY by Kristen Ashley
A River Rain Novel

A SHADOW IN THE EMBER by Jennifer L. Armentrout
A Flesh and Fire Novel

DISCOVER THE WORLD OF BLUE BOX PRESS AND 1001 DARK NIGHTS

Collection One
Collection Two
Collection Three
Collection Four
Collection Five
Collection Six
Collection Seven
Bundles
Discovery Authors
Blue Box Press
Rising Storm
Liliana Hart's MacKenzie Family
Lexi Blake's Crossover Collection
Kristen Proby's Crossover Collection

ON BEHALF OF BLUE BOX PRESS,

LIZ BERRY, M.J. ROSE, AND JILLIAN STEIN
WOULD LIKE TO THANK ~

Steve Berry
Doug Scofield
Benjamin Stein
Kim Guidroz
Social Butterfly PR
Ashley Wells
Kasi Alexander
Asha Hossain
Chris Graham
Jessica Johns
Dylan Stockton
Dina Williams
Kate Boggs
Donna Perry
Richard Blake
and Simon Lipskar